Tom Bradby is Asia correspondent for ITN. He is the acclaimed author of one previous novel, *Shadow Dancer*. He lives in Hong Kong.

www.**booksattransworld**.co.uk

Also by Tom Bradby
SHADOW DANCER

THE SLEEP OF THE DEAD

Tom Bradby

BANTAM PRESS

LONDON · NEW YORK · TORONTO · SYDNEY · AUCKLAND

TRANSWORLD PUBLISHERS
61–63 Uxbridge Road, London W5 5SA
a division of the Random House Group Ltd

RANDOM HOUSE AUSTRALIA (PTY) LTD
20 Alfred Street, Milsons Point, Sydney,
New South Wales 2061, Australia

RANDOM HOUSE NEW ZEALAND
18 Poland Road, Glenfield, Auckland 10, New Zealand

RANDOM HOUSE SOUTH AFRICA (PTY) LTD
Endulini, 5a Jubilee Road, Parktown 2193, South Africa

Published 2001 by Bantam Press
a division of Transworld Publishers

A catalogue record for this book is available
from the British Library
ISBNs 0593 042344 (cased) 0593 044193 (tpb)

Typeset in 11/13pt Palatino by Falcon Oast Graphic Art

Printed in Great Britain
by Clays Ltd, St Ives plc

1 3 5 7 9 10 8 6 4 2

'Suspicion always haunts the guilty mind.'

Henry VI, Part 3

For Claudia, Jack, Louisa and Sam

ACKNOWLEDGEMENTS

Still training under the world's greatest agent and editor, Mark Lucas and Bill Scott-Kerr.

Would be going nowhere in any field of life without Claudia.

PROLOGUE

THE AIR WAS STILL. A LIGHT WIND BRUSHED THE LEAVES OF THE TREES, but it was not strong enough to reach Julia on the path. She walked slowly, glancing at the mud on the toes of her black church shoes and thinking she ought to have changed them. The entrance to the common had been muddy, but here the ground was firm. The branches overhead thickened and the path darkened. It was like a tunnel. The river murmured beside her. Julia watched her feet, one placed in front of the other.

Rounding the corner, she saw the body, Sarah's head resting on the ground next to the stream, her long black hair trailing into the water. With an effort of will, Julia moved closer.

Sarah's face was pale, her lips pursed as if offering a kiss. There was no grimace of agony, no sign of distress, but her body was twisted awkwardly, the way she'd fallen. There was nothing to suggest life, no connection with the infuriating, arrogant, vivacious beauty Julia had seen leaving church only a few minutes ago.

Sarah's hands clasped her stomach and Julia saw the blood there. It was flowing. She thought it was *still* flowing and the movement jolted her. She turned, but did not run. She listened and looked, trying to catch focus, but there was no sound or movement, the common unnaturally still and silent.

1

And then Julia ran and the blood in her head and the thump of her heart and the sound of her lungs blocked out everything but her fear.

CHAPTER ONE

THE VOICE WAS CONFIDENT, SLOW AND VERY ENGLISH. 'HELLO, THIS IS Captain Benson once again. We're about to begin our descent into London and we've made up some time *en route*, so we should have you on the ground a few minutes ahead of schedule. It's ten in the morning local time, cloudy, with better weather on the way tonight and tomorrow.'

As she listened, Julia leant forward and picked up Sergeant Balfour's book, which had fallen from his lap while he slept. He didn't thank her.

'To our regular customers and to anyone flying with us for the first time, thank you for choosing British Airways. We do value your custom and hope you'll fly with us again ... Cabin crew prepare for landing, please.'

Julia stretched her back, pulled the seat up straight and fastened her seat-belt.

Sergeant Balfour was holding the book in his right hand. It was a Frederick Forsyth thriller about Russia and she could see from his marker that he'd almost finished it. It had been a long flight.

'Sergeant Balfour?'

He turned his head, without making eye-contact or speaking.

'You know, I wish you wouldn't talk so much,' she said.

He turned away. His expression, in so far as she could discern it, suggested that he believed humour was not a luxury she could afford.

Julia looked straight ahead. The family to her right contained two sleepy children. They had been heavily drugged throughout the flight and sat with dazed expressions and weary eyes. The younger moaned quietly, the elder was still wearing earphones for an in-flight entertainment system that had now been switched off. Julia tried to imagine what life for a western family was like in Beijing, but it only served to remind her of how narrow her own experience had been.

There had been dead-letter drops, covert meetings and the shaking hand of a pale, frightened agent, one walk on the Great Wall, the condescending detachment of the military brigadier who had first received the approach and did not want his role as attaché compromised, and the vague hostility of most of the embassy staff.

And the video of the execution, delivered two days ago in a brown paper parcel to the man at the front gate and addressed to her, Captain Julia Havilland, Army Intelligence Corps.

Cover blown, mission ended.

To her left, London appeared through the clouds, but Julia did not want to lean across Balfour to get a better view. It was eight months since she had left the base in England for Beijing, but almost three years since she'd had time to go home and visit her mother. Ashford had plucked her from Ireland before her time was up and dispatched her straight to Beijing.

Total success had led to total failure.

And now, disgrace.

Julia tried to find a way back to the body of thought that had been forming in her mind during the long flight – an alternative to the dead ends that awaited her – but could not. The impact of the wheels on the tarmac and the Boeing's brief bounce inter-rupted her and she felt a momentary thrill at the thought of real television, Sunday newspapers, afternoon tea, Marmite, book-shops, green fields, civility and a warm log fire.

Before the plane had come to a halt Julia stood up. 'Come on, Balfour. We're home.'

The plane was half empty and the wait short. Two men in rain-coats were standing by the aircraft as she stepped out.

'You shouldn't have,' she said, half to them, half to Balfour.

4

'Cut the crap, Havilland,' Balfour said.

'*Sir*, to you, Sergeant Balfour.' He glowered at her. 'Anyway, thanks again for the chat,' she went on. 'The journey really flew by.'

Julia led the way and, with a hint of awkwardness, they followed, unable to impose the authority they possessed and reluctant to try. Her bag was the first off the carousel – she'd been checked in first – and they marched her straight down to the VIP exit.

'I'm a VIP,' she said, with a smile, to the man who examined her passport, but he did not respond, and tired of sarcasm – tired in general – she walked without further comment to the black Ford Escort that sat with its engine running in the car-park beyond.

'Remember,' Balfour said, as she was about to get into the back, 'you must stay within reach of your home at all times.'

'I'm not a child, Balfour.'

'You're lucky not to be confined to base.'

'Or a criminal.'

'That's to be seen. Thanks for the trip.'

Julia could not tell if this last comment was his own black humour or a misplaced attempt at genuine communication. She did not look back, ducking her head slightly to stare up at the clearing sky and the signs of a country that seemed more comforting and familiar than at any point she could remember. They passed a Shell garage and a row of billboards, advertising Peugeot at one end and BMW at the other.

The driver did not ask her where to go and she did not attempt to talk to him. As the M4 gave way to the M25 and then the M3, she found her way back to the train of thought on the plane and could not tell whether its direction disconcerted her.

She was returning home and, though she had had no choice in the matter, it felt a deliberate act.

The journey passed quickly, the outside world rarely penetrating her thoughts, so that her arrival was sudden, finding her unprepared. The driver had stopped at the neck of the valley, awaiting instructions. Julia watched the smoke rising from the houses bunched around the church spire as scattered clouds drifted across the sky, shielding the sun. She felt the flutter of nerves in her stomach.

A black Mercedes was parked outside the post office next to the green, but otherwise the village seemed deserted, a model replica without visitors. What struck her was its scale; smaller than in her mind's eye, as if lives here were being lived in miniature. The houses, the breadth of the valley and the gradient of the surrounding hills seemed diminished, but after the concrete jungle that was modern Beijing, it was impossibly green. It was how she liked to remember home: in summer bloom, a mature riot of nature.

As they came level with the Rose and Crown Julia was pulled from her reflections. 'Sorry, you need to go right here,' she said. The driver reversed up and turned down Woodpecker Lane.

Alan Ford's drive was empty behind the newly painted white gate and so was her own. As Julia got out, the soles of her boots sank into the thick gravel, and the sun burst through a patch of cloud, its warmth immediate. She took off her jacket and slung it over the bonnet of her old blue VW Golf parked close to the garage.

Julia raised her hands in thanks to the driver as he reversed out of the drive on to the road then disappeared without acknowledgement. She glanced at the Golf. There was more rust around the wheel rims than she remembered.

Her footsteps were noisy and regular as she approached, then climbed up on to the edge of the brick surround of the flower-bed that separated the drive from the garden. The house was called Rose Cottage and had been fashioned several centuries ago from mellow red brick. It had a slate roof and a single chimney with a weather-vane. The kitchen had been extended at the back and the entire length of the house was covered with vines and laburnum. From where Julia was standing, she could look down over the expanse of lawn in front to the field, which dipped then rose again to the edge of the wood that formed the boundary of Welham Common.

Julia circuited the brick wall and stepped down on to the lawn. It was springy and a deep, verdant green. She took off her suede boots and socks and felt the dampness beneath her feet, the grass newly mown, the clippings piled in the corner by the garden shed.

Inside her parents' house, Aristotle was parked on the floor of the dining room. He didn't stir himself, his mournful eyes fixed on her, his tail beating the floor in a lethargic tattoo. Eventually, he rolled half on to his back and she knelt and scratched his stomach,

6

before bending down and kissing the side of his head. In the past, the house had always been noisy, but now it seemed unnaturally quiet.

Upstairs, her room was crowded with the accumulated detritus of a frozen childhood: teddy bears, dolls, books, photograph albums, gymkhana rosettes, gymnastic medals, swimming certificates. It was warm in here, so she leant across to push open the window, looking out over the de la Rues' garden next door and the colourful flower-bed that ran along the length of the house. Stiff from the journey, Julia crossed her legs and brought the palms of her hands down to her toes, stretching.

She sat down on the cane chair at her desk and looked at the bulging bookshelves ahead. Her mother had tidied them so that each shelf roughly reflected a level of maturity, with the big picture books at the top. She reached up and took down Richard Scarry's *Great Big Air Book*. It was dog-eared and some of the pages were loose so she turned them carefully, recalling her father sitting on the bed beside her here, with his back to the radiator. Julia read the words aloud, smiling: ' "Aaaah-chooo!" sneezed Huckle. Huckle sneezed so hard he blew Little Sister out of bed. Oh, it must be windy today!'

She put her feet on the bed, clearing a path among the teddy bears, then bent down and pulled open the bottom drawer of her desk, taking out an embossed leather box. It contained her father's Victoria Cross, the highest award for gallantry the British army can bestow; it was cold to the touch, the braid above it smooth. Julia turned it over; running her fingers over the name: 'Lieutenant Colonel Mitchell Havilland.' She asked herself, as she had so many times, whether she could have performed the same act of heroism.

She reached forward and took down a scrapbook from the shelves in front of her. It had a dark blue cover. Inside, she had posted newspaper articles and photographs. There was a picture of her father standing outside a sheep shed in Teal Inlet on the Falklands with members of his regimental support staff. On the opposite page, she had pasted a letter that one of his corporals, Wilkes, had written to her after the war:

> Your father was the best officer I ever served under. When he gave us the first briefing about going down south to

fight, he assembled us on the paradeground and said, 'Right, lads, this it. This is what it's all about. There's millions of buggers that'd give their eye teeth to be in with a shout at this.' He said there would be buckets of s*** and that he'd see us all right. You knew it was true.

It's a tragedy he didn't make it.

I've a load of memories. I remember in Germany we used to have to go and clean the OC's office and one time I go in and there's a bloke crawling on the floor, with kit all over the place. I say, 'Are you taking the piss or something? You can't do that in here,' and he turns round and it's the OC sorting his kit. 'Sorry, sir,' I say. 'Don't worry, Wilkes,' he says. 'Carry on.' So I went on cleaning and there's this wig on the floor. 'What's that?' I ask. And he looks at me, all confused. 'Wilkes,' he says, 'you never know when you may need a disguise.'

Julia turned the pages, a smile lingering at the corner of her lips until she reached the photographs she had taken in 1984 on the trip to the site of his death with her mother. There was a picture of the craggy rocky outcrop beneath which he'd sheltered before that last charge and another of the machine-gun nest further up from where the fatal shots had been fired. The last picture was of his grave – a lonely white cross on a desolate hillside, bright as it reflected a few isolated rays of sunshine breaking through the clouds above.

What would he think of her now?

Julia reached down to the drawer that had contained the Victoria Cross and removed a small, dark, well-thumbed leather notebook – a war diary, given to her by Adrian Rouse. She leafed through the pages:

Wed. 7 April. It could be war. Hard to believe it. After all that's happened in Welham, it seems like God's idea of a bad joke, but then maybe it's what everyone needs.

Word we're going tomorrow. Southampton, then leave on Friday. Cops came to base today to talk to Alan again. Frustration all round with their efforts. Still not found man in leather jacket the old lady saw who seems obvious culprit. Asking everyone offensive questions. Especially fat psychologist. Alan generally silent. Still not certain if he goes tomorrow, or stays. Mike H says Alan doesn't see point of staying, because Alice is dead and everyone knows it. He's being given a wide berth. None of the usual piss-taking, obviously. Mike H says good for him to get away.

Alice is on everyone's mind. Even the lads remember her and Sarah from events on the base. Sports day, etc. There's gossip in the ranks, but dries up when an officer enters. Most gossip centres around S. Air of unreality all round. War or not? Nobody knows.

Julia looked up at the shelves, tapping her fingers against the table-top, then returned to the page.

More fired up in the afternoon. CO briefing on parade-ground. Mitch says def off tomorrow unless w****** change their mind again. Not nec war, but should be prepared for any eventuality. Says not many soldiers get a chance like this. Quite inspiring. Made it sound like the world was going to be jealous not to be in on the action. Everyone more aggressive afterwards. At last, action, not speculation. Busy, now, much to do. Windproof smocks finally arrived. Can't believe they've had this stuff sitting around at HQ UKLF. Probably trying to hold on to it for their skiing holidays. Mitch got on and said if they didn't f****** release it, he'd go up and take it himself. As usual, emphasis on getting things done and no time for time-serving w******. He'll never make General. Or maybe he will.

Julia flicked forward, then paused again.

19 May. It really is war. Helicopter containing members of D squadron SAS got an albatross stuck in its engine and crashed into sea: 22 dead.

Sense of nervous readiness. Only problem is Alan and Danes again. Mitch too busy and preoccupied to notice any more – 'time for them to b***** get on with it,' but hope it will not be a problem. Actually, have noticed, Alan and Mitch hardly ever communicate directly. Mike H spoke to Danes and was told that Alan was an uptight w***** who knows nothing about tactics and couldn't lead his men out of a paper bag. Trouble is, Mike H and Danes and Mitch are all of a type – gung-ho, no bullshit, break the door down, etc. Alan is competitive enough, just a bit more reserved. Less in-your-face. The men say he's taciturn, but not surprising, given the circumstances. Think Danes may feel Alan should have stayed at home.

Sense of relief we're behind Mitch. Was talking to Wilkes today who said he'd not thought about it before but was f****** grateful he had a commander he could respect and not some w***** out to make his career. The men feel Mitch is looking out for them.

However, feel there is danger of falling victim to a 'cult of personality'. Mitch doesn't stand bullshitters or arse-lickers, but equally doesn't really listen to a word anyone says. Any criticism is 'negativity'. Sucks people in like a vortex. Personality so strong it can be overpowering. It's 'Mad' Mitch all right. That's leadership, but sometimes a little less force might produce more considered results. Still, rather him at this point than anyone else. He doesn't leave you much room for doubt.

Julia breathed in, exhaled forcefully, and shut the book, turning towards the window. She stood up. 'Aristotle,' she shouted, as she went downstairs. 'Aristotle.' He hauled himself up as she approached. 'Come on,' she said. 'Walk.'

She took her socks from the dresser, fished out wellington boots from the cupboard in the corner and let herself out into the lane. Aristotle loped ahead, sniffing the banks, pissing already.

She turned right at the end of Woodpecker Lane and passed the darkened windows of the pub. As she reached the village green, Henrietta de la Rue emerged from the shop and climbed into a new Volvo estate. Julia stood on the edge of the grass and waited for her to come level. The window was lowered and Henrietta was leaning across, her alice band pushed to the back of her head, thin hair pulled taut over a narrow face. 'Hello. Your mother said you might be coming home. How long are you here for?'

Julia smiled. 'I'm not sure yet.'

'She'll be so pleased to see you. Will you be there tonight?'

Julia frowned.

'We'll be in the Rose and Crown. Alan didn't want her . . . either of you to be alone tonight.'

'Oh. Yes.' Julia nodded. 'Of course.'

'We'll catch up then.'

Julia watched the car disappear up the hill then turn left into Woodpecker Lane. Aristotle was sniffing around the edge of the war memorial and she shouted at him.

It was like Alan Ford to be solicitous of her mother's feelings.

Julia walked over the green and stood in front of the small cross at the entrance to the common. The words read, 'In loving memory of Sarah and Alice Ford, taken from us', a simple inscription that reflected the sorrowful anger of a community robbed of its innocence.

Aristotle had ducked under the stile and proceeded down the path, and Julia took a step forward, then hesitated. She had thought of coming here on the long journey home from Beijing. It was a simple act, but not easy to achieve.

She climbed over the stile and followed the dog down the path, watching the clouds drifting along the crest of the ridge opposite, making slow progress across the sky. For a hundred yards, the track descended through two of the de la Rues' fields and, as she reached the entrance to the wood, the sun broke free again, fractured through the branches of the trees above.

Julia stopped to listen. The path was dotted with puddles – it must have been raining these past few days – the mud soft, wet and glutinous, the air hazy with insects. As she walked, the wind picked up, whistling through the trees above and down the hedgerows, tugging at her hair.

There was an overwhelming sense of timelessness about this place. She glimpsed one of the de la Rue maize fields on the other side of the valley, just as the trees began to thicken, beech and maple leaves obscuring the blue sky. The de la Rues owned so much of the land around here, enveloping the village in their wealth. The ivy was thick along the edges of the path, vying with bramble and fern, even holly here and there, as the ground turned from mud to grass. The sunlight provided dappled pools of light, which even the nettles, growing thick beside her, seemed to crane towards.

11

The path twisted gently until the point where she had found Sarah's body. Julia walked slower as she approached, then stopped in roughly the same place as she had that day.

Nothing had changed. Her return, after so long, was as ordinary as she had determined it would be.

Julia walked to the edge of the river and looked down into the dark pools of swirling water. She moved forward, so that the stream began to wash away some of the mud and grass from the toes of her boots. She looked about for Aristotle, but could see no sign of him. He was not a companionable dog.

She waited. No ghosts assailed her and she felt her tension ease a little.

She walked to the opposite bank, climbed it and continued on up through the trees. The wood here was silent, the only sound that of her own breathing.

As she emerged into the much larger clearing at the top of the slope and walked through the long grass, the sun fell gently on her face. The tree stump ahead of her was white, with a giant hole in the middle and long, bare, scarecrow branches. It was from here that they had begun the search on the night after Sarah's murder and Alice's disappearance. Julia listened to the crickets and watched the branches dancing vigorously in the circling wind. 'Aristotle,' she shouted. '*Aristotle.*'

He was gone and would hide now if she went looking for him; let him find his way home in his own time. She retraced her steps, noticing a badger sett as she descended towards the main path and thinking she had been foolish to shy away for so long from returning here.

And then a picture was emblazoned on her mind: of Alice's red and blue check dress – the one she had worn to church that day – her white skin, with the scar at the base of her neck, where she had caught herself on a barbed-wire fence, her small hands, her pretty white socks and her dainty blue shoes, her muddy knees, her shy smile, her ragged breathing as she ran, and the fear . . . her looking back, the world closing in, her colliding with trees, too scared to cry, trying to think, looking for a place to hide, her capture . . .

And then the last, silent moments.

Did he stab her?

After killing Sarah, where did the man reach little Alice? Did he hold her still, look into her eyes, as he slid the knife in? What did he see as she died?

What did he do with her . . . dress?

Did she fight? Scream? Cry?

Did he drag her body to a car? Did he wrap it in plastic sheeting? Did he seek a place here where no one would find it?

Was it still here, the small bones, infused with that terror, resting beneath her?

Julia was back to the point where she had found Sarah's body. 'Come on,' she muttered, under her breath.

She turned for home and walked away, moving purposefully, the blood thumping in her head.

When she reached the village green, there was still no one about. It was an ordinary, quiet afternoon. She waited for a while, but no one came past.

A car approached slowly, but she did not recognize the middle-aged woman behind the wheel.

Julia crossed the road and walked through the lychgate at the entrance to the churchyard, intending to visit her father's memorial stone, then thinking better of it. She turned back, emerged on to the road and carried on up the hill, stopping briefly beside the Rose and Crown and looking down the narrow road beside it towards the former council house that had belonged to Pascoe's mother. Now that she was dead, was it technically his? If they ever released him, was this where he would come back to? He shouldn't be released. How could someone like that be allowed into any community?

At home, Aristotle was waiting beside the front door. 'Deserter,' Julia told him.

She gave him some water and watched as he slopped half of it on to the floor. 'Pleasure before loyalty, that's your motto,' she said, before retreating to the living room and the giant CD holder she had given her mother on her last birthday. Ahead, the CD player stood next to their old stereo system, of its time, the family's great luxury. Her father's records were still stacked neatly in the corner beside it. She leafed through, wondering whether her mother ever listened to them, before picking one out, switching on the machine, pulling the needle across to the right track.

The speakers crackled into life and her eyes were drawn to the big picture of her father on the mahogany card table. He was smiling, the turn of his mouth tilting his broken nose to the right. It was a good smile, the way he had been when he was about to make people laugh.

Duke Ellington began. The tune was 'In A Sentimental Mood' and Julia turned up the volume so loud that the music echoed around the empty house. She faced the empty fireplace, closed her eyes and imagined it booming across the valley. The sweet sadness of the piano keys was mixed with the melancholy, languid drawl of the saxophone.

Julia remembered the music drifting out of his study upstairs: Ellington, Stan Getz, Charlie Parker – Louis Armstrong, above all.

Suddenly the volume was turned down, reducing the saxophone to a whisper. Her mother, Caroline, was standing beside her, smiling. Julia flung her arms around her.

'I got your message,' her mother said. 'What a lovely surprise.'

Caroline put down her bag on the chair behind her, took out a hair clip then replaced a strand of hair and refastened it. Her appearance was as neat as ever, a beautiful woman growing old with grace, age barely diminishing her.

'Sorry,' Julia said. 'I wasn't sure exactly when I'd get here.'

'Don't worry. How long will you be home?'

Julia shrugged, then followed her through to the kitchen. 'I'm not sure,' she said. She'd not considered what she was going to tell her mother about Beijing. 'How was the gallery?' she asked, stalling and wondering if the army had already said something.

'It's very quiet at the moment.' Her mother put on the kettle and took down a teapot. 'We've got an exhibition by a local painter, but he only does oil and that's never as popular.'

'I'm sorry I missed your exhibition.'

'You didn't miss much.'

'Alan said they all sold.' Julia thought of the letters from her mother and Alan, to which she had not replied.

'I know,' Caroline said. 'There are a lot of fools around.'

'I should have bought one.'

'You hate still life,' Caroline said.

'I know, but it's an investment.'

Her mother laughed, almost inaudibly. Then she said, her expression serious, 'Alan offered to take me to the pub tonight, just so that I'm not alone.' She hated being alone on the anniversary of her husband's death. 'I think the de la Rues will be there . . . They'd all love to see you.'

'Yes, of course. I saw Henrietta in the village earlier. She mentioned it.'

'Unless you'd rather we were alone?'

Julia shook her head vigorously. 'No.'

Caroline disappeared into the dining room and returned a few moments later with a piece of paper. 'Professor Malcolm rang. He said you'd called and left a message saying you would be on this number. He can see you at ten tomorrow morning, if that's all right.' She passed the note to Julia and busied herself with the tea. 'The de la Rues asked me to lunch on Saturday too,' she went on, 'but I'm sure you'll be welcome if you're going to be here that long. I didn't really know when to expect you.'

'I'm sorry,' Julia said. 'I should have given you some warning, but you know . . . it's hard to say whether you're *actually* going to be able to get away until the last minute.' She felt as if she was cheating.

'Are you going back to Beijing?'

'No.'

'How did you find China?'

'Cold in winter. Grubby, polluted. Rude. Interesting. Sometimes beautiful. Foreign. A very long way away.' Julia was drumming her fingers on the table. 'Lonely,' she added.

'I suppose it's fortunate, in that way, that you're not married yet.'

'I suppose it is.'

'It feels odd not being able to talk more about what you've been doing all this time.'

'Yes, but at least you're used to it.'

Julia looked at her mother's impassive face and wondered what she thought. Did she resent the lack of contact and the restriction on information imposed by the nature of the work? It was impossible to tell.

'Did you manage to make any Chinese friends?'

Julia smiled bitterly.

'I'm sorry,' Caroline said. 'Was that naïve?'

'No, ironic.'

'It wasn't that kind of assignment?'

'Not really.'

15

'What did you do when you weren't working?'

'We were always working.'

'Always?' Caroline was frowning. 'You must have had some time to relax.'

'Not really. I walked the Great Wall once, but was so convinced I was being tailed I thought it wise not to try again.'

'What was it like?'

'Being tailed?'

'No.' Caroline smiled. 'The Great Wall.'

'Long.'

'You don't say. Long! That's a useful observation – taxpayers' money well spent.'

'All right, it was long, *beautiful* but crumbling. It's falling down apart from the areas they're restoring for the tourists. And the taxpayer, sadly, wasn't paying me to go sightseeing.'

'Don't be such a bore.' Caroline looked at Julia. 'You must have got to know some of the embassy people.'

'We didn't socialize much.'

Caroline frowned again. Julia could tell she did not think this much of a life for her only daughter, for all that Caroline was familiar with the sacrifices demanded by a Service career.

'Well, I hope it was worth it,' she said.

'No, not really.' Julia tried to smile, but an image of the agent's pale, frightened face intervened. She could vividly see his thin, hairless hands, with their slender fingers and long nails, which always shook, sometimes violently.

'I suppose it's fascinating work,' Caroline said.

'How is everyone?' Julia asked, changing the subject abruptly.

'Mostly well.'

Caroline stood up, filled the teapot and put it on the table. 'Alan is off on another tour to Ireland,' she went on.

'When?'

'Next weekend. Not this one, the one after.'

'I might nip over and see him in a minute.'

There was the warmth of combined affection and approval in Caroline's smile. 'He'll be pleased if you do. I mentioned you might be home and he was hoping you'd be back before he went away.'

'What's happening in Ireland? I've not looked at a paper in eight months.'

16

'Goodness.' Caroline brought a tin of biscuits to the table and began to pour the tea. She had forgotten the milk – distracted, Julia could tell, by having her home – and went to get it from the fridge. Julia thought again how slim she was. She was as attractive as a woman of her age could be, even if she did her best to hide it in worn green jeans and an ill-fitting jumper. Only her face, and the lipstick she always wore, betrayed vanity.

'Jessica de la Rue is getting divorced,' Caroline said, apparently forgetting the previous drift of the conversation.

'That's awful. How are the family taking it? I mean . . .'

'Jasper is very upset. Henrietta is . . . phlegmatic. I think she always thought the marriage had the potential to run into difficulties.'

'They've children?'

'Three.'

Julia sipped her tea and thought of Jessica, with her long auburn hair. She was older and had always been wild. 'It's funny,' she said, 'I would have thought their reactions would have been the other way around.'

Her mother didn't respond.

'After all that Jasper has done. I mean . . .'

'I think Jasper believes very strongly in marriage.'

'But not in monogamy.'

For a moment, there was silence. This was not destined to be an easy topic of conversation. Julia recalled Jasper's slightly too affectionate dances with Jessica's friends at teenage parties and weddings, and the casual way in which he stroked their buttocks.

'You haven't talked about Paul for a long time.'

Julia shifted lower in her seat. 'Yes, I probably should have said. But it's not been edifying.'

'Why not?'

Julia shrugged. 'He hung on for me and I didn't see him for about a year after I went to Ireland because I said I was too busy. Then I came back to England for a weekend and dumped him.'

Caroline did not respond to this, and Julia could see that her mother was upset that she had come back to England but not visited. She got up and turned up the volume on Duke Ellington. 'Is it okay if I have a bath?' she asked.

'Of course.' For a moment they looked at each other, then

17

Caroline added, 'I'm glad you're home. If I may be permitted to say so, you look like you need a rest.'

Upstairs, the water tank thumped loudly as Julia turned on the taps. She undressed and sank into the bath. Listening to the music from below, she thought again of Ellington and Armstrong drifting out from behind the closed door of her father's study and wondered what he had been thinking in all those hours on his own.

Eventually Ellington came to an end. Julia got out, dried herself and walked down the narrow corridor to her room. She could hear her mother moving the kitchen table and realized that she was sitting down at the piano. She waited, the towel resting lightly on her shoulders. Her mother began 'Song For Guy', by Elton John, which Julia, as a child, had often asked her to play.

She went into her room, sat at the table in the corner and looked at the photograph albums stacked on the shelves ahead. The music was beautiful, haunting – comforting in its familiarity yet melancholic in the memories it evoked. Had her mother chosen it deliberately?

She pulled down one of the albums. The first page contained a sequence of shots of Julia on her pony, Alfie, performing at the local Pony Club gymkhana, and the last picture was of her father in a scruffy green country jacket smiling into the camera at the same event. In almost every picture she had ever seen of him, the smile was the same: broad, genuine, as if he was seeking to share his amusement at the vagaries and uncertainties of life.

Caroline played on. Julia doubted that anyone else could infuse this song with such feeling.

She put away the album, feeling guilty now that she had not visited her father's memorial stone – it reflected her inadequacies, not his. She dressed, picked up her suede jacket from the back of the chair and walked down to the kitchen.

Caroline did not hear her approach and, for a moment, Julia watched her. Her head was bent slightly, her concentration intense.

After a few seconds, Caroline took her hands from the keys. They looked at each other.

'Don't stop.'

'Sorry, was it disturbing you?'

'It's beautiful, as always. I wish I could play.'

'Perhaps I could teach you.'

'Perhaps. One day.'

Julia had been leaning against the doorframe, but she straightened now. 'I'm going to wander out and say hello to Alan.'

'All right. He might not be home yet, but . . .' Caroline looked at her watch '. . . give it a try.'

Julia stepped over Aristotle, slumped across the entrance to the hall, and walked out into the drive. It was still light, the air warm. Alan's car was not in his drive, but Julia had intended anyway to go to the churchyard first, so she walked down Woodpecker Lane and turned right again at the Rose and Crown. The pub was an old red-brick building, its lights on, the door open. The de la Rues' Volvo rounded the corner and Julia stepped aside. It was Henrietta again. This time she waved but did not stop.

Julia hesitated at the lychgate and read a notice about the appeal for the new roof. The church ahead of her had a square Norman tower and was built of clear grey stone; its white clock told her it was almost six thirty. The path from the lychgate to the door ran up a steep incline and the gravestones beside it were at an angle, as if tilting towards the evening sun. The grass around them had been newly mown and was springy beneath her feet.

There were fresh yellow roses by her father's stone and Julia squatted in front of it, looking at the name then closing her eyes, thinking again of that desolate hillside.

An image came to her of her father in combat fatigues, in the darkness and cold of that last battle. She saw vividly the set determination in his face, the grit and bravery and power, watched him lift himself, turning and raising his head in slow motion. He was a big man, big hands, big shoulders, a face that seemed outsized, overpowering and invincible.

She opened her eyes again. No one was invincible.

Was bravery about strength of character or life circumstances? Those who seemed least hidebound by fear were, in her experience, those with the least to lose.

Julia stood up. She had expected to find here clarity of thought and emotion, but instead had experienced neither.

It was impossible to pass the small stone in the next row without stopping. The inscription here also began with the words 'In Memory' and the plot was small, befitting Alice, who had just

19

turned five when she died. There were fresh flowers here too, also yellow roses. Next to Alice, Julia saw that the vase on Sarah's grave was empty. She paused, her eyes narrowed. There was a gust of wind and the full vase in front of Alice's memorial stone creaked and tilted.

As she walked down towards the lychgate, Julia tried to throw off the melancholy that this place always induced in her, but as she turned on to the road and looked across to the other side of the green, she saw a man in a dark blue duffel coat carrying his small daughter over the stile and stopped. For a moment, she thought it was Michael Haydoch and that somewhere in the intervening years he had married, had a child, but it couldn't be him. She watched as the man placed the child on the ground then held her hand as they walked towards the war memorial. The little girl had dark hair that curled over the collar of her long blue coat, and bright red wellington boots.

The man, who had thick, curly dark hair and whom she did not recognize, smiled as they walked past the post office, down towards the cricket pitch and the new homes that had been built beyond it. They moved slowly.

It was a few seconds before Julia realized she was following them.

She turned and walked back up the road.

Alan's car was in the drive now. His house was called Gardener's Cottage, and it was of a different architectural style from her mother's home next door. It was bigger, probably even older, and made of yellowish brick. It had mullioned windows and a steep grey slate roof, with two attic windows and a chimney at either end. Julia knocked and stepped back to wait.

She tried the bell, but it was broken, so she knocked again.

Perhaps he was in the garden.

She opened the door and stepped into the gloomy hallway. 'Alan?'

Julia could not avoid looking at the poster-sized picture of Alice that dominated the hall: it was the photograph that had been used for the Missing posters and the child's dark eyes had stared directly into the camera.

The photograph had been taken on the lawn outside during the summer before the murders, when Alice's hair had been long and scruffy. Julia could remember the exact moment – they had been playing in the tree house when Alan came out with his camera. Alice had not wanted to have her picture taken.

The interior of the house was dark and did not have the decorative neatness of her mother's home, but Sarah had not been interested in domestic affairs and Alan had done little to make the place homely since her death, although he was an essentially practical man. From the outside, you could tell that it was well maintained, but inside it felt neglected. It had not been re-decorated, Julia guessed, for twenty years or more.

She passed through to the living room at the back. The french windows were open to the terrace, the sun streaming in. An arm-chair had been turned in that direction and a pile of newspapers lay on the floor next to it. On the bookshelf above there was another picture of Alice, this time in a thick winter coat, standing in the snow – alongside a photograph of Alan, Julia and Caroline in ski-wear, with their arms around each other. It had been taken on holiday in Val d'Isère when Julia was about fifteen. She noticed how like her mother she was: they had exactly the same nose and eyes.

There was no sign of him on the terrace. 'Alan?' she called.

She retraced her steps to the hallway, wondering whether to stay and wait for him or go home.

It was possible he was up in the attic room and hadn't heard her, so she walked slowly up the stairs, the floorboards creaking beneath her feet.

'Alan?'

The corridor upstairs was dark.

Julia looked down towards Alice's bedroom at the end, took a pace towards it, then hesitated.

She walked forward slowly, telling herself she'd be able to see down to the far corners of the garden from there.

The room had been stripped. Not just of pictures, or belong-ings, but everything. Even the Winnie the Pooh wallpaper had been removed, though traces of it stuck to the corners. The curtains had gone, too, which made the room seem doubly bleak. Julia moved to the right, touching the wall and picking at the bits of wallpaper that remained.

She turned slowly around.

She felt uncomfortable, shivering involuntarily before walking away, stopping briefly in the corridor and looking into Alan's bedroom, which was neat, the large bed covered in a white bedspread.

The floorboards creaked again as she came down the stairs.

'Julia!' Alan's broad smile dispelled her sense of awkwardness as he strode forward, gripping her hard for some seconds then pushing her back, holding her shoulders, still grinning. 'It's been too long.'

He wore faded cords and a baggy green sweater big enough to share. His greying hair was too long and curly for an officer. He had a bulbous, squashed-up broken nose, and a generous, round, lived-in face that had not aged since she had known him. She thought he was like a hobbit, in Tolkien's *Lord of the Rings*.

'Yes,' she said.

'Bloody army.'

He led the way through to the back. 'We're due at the Rose and Crown in half an hour, but come and have a drink.'

Alan came in with a bottle of white wine and poured two glasses. He gave her one and they stepped out on to the terrace. She looked down at his feet. His trousers were too short, his suede brogues battered and scruffy, and she realized that he, almost more than anything else now, was England to her. England and decency, survival and regeneration. Home. She found herself smiling.

'What is it?' he asked.

'Nothing.'

She sipped her wine, then took the bottle from him to look at the label. It was a semillon sauvignon from the Margaret River in Western Australia.

'Moved on from Coca-Cola,' he said.

'Oh, shut up.'

'Your mother bought it for me.'

'Yes. She seems to have got into her wine. It's your influence.'

He smiled, shrugging. 'Have you left China for good?' She didn't answer immediately and his expression became apologetic. 'Was your mother wrong to tell me that was—'

'No, of course not.'

'I thought you were in Ireland, the next thing I know you're in China.'

'A life of excitement and glamour.'

'An emergency?'

'In a way.'

'Did you see much of the country?'

She recognized that, for both her mother and Alan, this was a sufficiently neutral question. 'No, I think I can safely say that I didn't.'

He frowned. It was a gesture of care, like a school chaplain. Or like a father. 'Are you okay?'

'Fine.' Julia took a sip of her wine and then turned to face the common.

They both looked down across the fields to the barbed-wire fence and the wooded bank that rose beyond it. Julia wondered suddenly why Alan had never chosen to move away.

'It must have been quite an experience,' he went on.

Julia tried consciously to relax. 'Depends on what you call an experience.'

His expression altered. 'I'm sorry, I should know better than to start prying.'

'Oh, come on.' She smiled at him. 'Don't be stupid. Our defence of the realm, or its interests, was a battle lost, that's all.' She tried to sound, and feel, casual.

'Well, I'm sorry to hear that. Ireland went so well,' he said. 'Or that's the impression I got from your letters.'

'I'm sorry I wasn't very good at replying in Beijing.'

'Don't worry about me.'

'But Mum . . .'

'She worries about you, gets herself wound up, but she doesn't want to make you feel under pressure.'

Julia looked at him. 'She thinks I don't confide in her enough.'

'Perhaps.'

'I don't confide in anyone.'

He did not answer.

'So, are you preparing to go measure for measure with the local RUC commander in Northern Ireland?' she asked.

'Do you know, I hate whiskey and *especially* Bushmill's?'

'I used to insist on Jack Daniel's,' Julia said, 'which was almost as bad, in their eyes, as demanding water.'

He smiled. 'I suppose we should all hope for a new IRA cease-fire, but I can't help wondering if boredom for six months in a barracks in Londonderry is going to be harder to manage than the usual crap out on the streets.'

'I thought the IRA had done with their ceasefiring.'

'Apparently not.'

Alan sat on the table next to her, pulled up a chair and propped his feet over the back. He massaged his neck. 'Can you imagine six months confined to barracks? The men will be killing each other. I spoke to a friend in the Grenadiers who was in Belfast during the last ceasefire and he said it was absolute hell.

'Anyhow,' he said, standing up again and pulling his trousers around his waist, 'I'd better get changed. I've persuaded your mother that she needs another skiing holiday, probably next February, in Val d'Isère again – or maybe even in the States, for a change. Vail or Beaver Creek. The de la Rues are coming, possibly with one or two of their offspring, plus or minus families . . .'

'I heard about Jessica.'

'Yes.' He shook his head. 'Not good. Anyway, if you're interested, and if you want to bring anyone . . .'

Julia was embarrassed and flushed. Alan responded in kind. Neither of them acknowledged it.

'Great to have you back,' he said.

'It's good to be home.'

Julia put the glass on the table and, rather than going through the house, walked down the steps to the garden. As she did so she looked out again towards the common, and relished the novelty of looking out over green fields and well-ordered countryside. This was not just a response to Beijing, but to the last three years of stress and confinement. It was a rejection of neon lights and polystyrene coffee cups, of difficult, emotionally charged decisions and the aggression that sometimes accompanied the debates surrounding them.

She ducked through the gap in the hedge and walked across the newly mown lawn to the back of her own house.

With its red carpet, open fire in the corner, the line of spirit bottles above the bar, the horseshoes, the hunting pictures, the riding boots and the stuffed foxes, the Rose and Crown was just the same, its air of faded comfort not yet having tumbled into the seediness for which it had long seemed destined. There were three men leaning against the bar, one still dressed in boots and an outdoor jacket. Julia did not recognize any of them, but she wanted to say hello to Doberman, the pub's owner. He was a big man with unkempt hair, a scruffy moustache and a face to match the curve of his belly. Today, as always, he had a tea-towel over his shoulder. He boomed her name and leant over the bar to give her a sloppy kiss on the cheek.

Doberman had moved to the village just as Julia had turned seventeen and she had spent a couple of university vacations working for him, either behind the bar here or at outside functions, mostly weddings. He had always been known by his surname.

She extricated herself and followed her mother to the corner, where Alan Ford was the first to his feet. Julia kissed Adrian Rouse, then his wife Leslie. Before they'd had time to sit, the de la Rues arrived. Alan bought the drinks and Adrian brought up the chairs, Leslie leaning across to ask Julia how long she was going to be home. Alan drew up a stool next to her.

'You probably wanted to be alone with your mum tonight,' he said, picking up on their earlier conversation.

She looked at him. 'No. Rather like this,' she said. Seeing the concern in his eyes once again made her aware of her disgrace, which had not seemed real until now, when she was finally in context. He sighed, noted down everyone's food order, and disappeared to the bar again.

Henrietta de la Rue leant across. 'Lovely to see you,' she said. Jasper sat next to her, his oversized face fixed in a paternal smile. More than ever, he looked a caricature of the man he was, like a seal that had ballooned into a walrus but remained unaware of the transition. Leslie and Adrian Rouse were at either side of Caroline and the three were in deep conversation about hunting – or, rather, Adrian was listening to the two women. A nearby meet had been attacked by saboteurs the week before – it was becoming a regular occurrence.

Julia studied Adrian's face. He was, she thought, one of life's natural listeners. An observer, the kind of man who, however sporadically, would have kept a war diary. He seemed to have aged more than anyone in the village and was squarer, his hair thinning and receding fast. He had a thin nose with black hairs poking out of the edge of it. When she had been a child he was a sleek, good-looking man, but he was neither now.

'It's absurd,' Adrian said.

Julia looked at him. So did Leslie and Caroline.

'What is?' Leslie asked.

'This new lot. The Government – being opposed to hunting and encouraging the antis. I bet they eat meat, every last one of them.'

'What's the relevance of eating meat?' Julia asked.

'Well, have you ever been into an abattoir? It's ghastly. Hundreds of thousands of animals are slaughtered every week and the antis come out after a few bloody foxes, which are horrible creatures anyway.'

Julia was reminded of the moment of naked terror that must be the precursor to any execution.

Alan had returned from the bar. He picked up his glass and raised it. The moment was upon them and Julia felt a twist of dread. Everyone stopped talking. 'Before the food arrives,' he said, 'a brief toast. I know we always propose one on this occasion, but since Julia is here tonight for the first time in a few years, home from doing her duty . . .' Julia felt her face reddening at the attention and the inappropriate nature of the tribute. '. . . I wanted to say a few more words than usual about Mitchell Havilland. We know, each of us, how much he would have enlivened this gathering. That was his skill. And *I* think, as the years go by, we perhaps miss him more, not less.' He cleared his throat. 'Looking back now, he seems to me to have had enough life for several people, a big man in every sense. Funny, *full* of life. But also honest, decent. *Fair*. Which mattered if you happened to be serving under him as both Adrian and I had the privilege of doing.' Adrian's face remained impassive. 'A man of unusual integrity. A *rock*. We all experienced the benefits of his belief that you had to work to help people in your community.'

He looked around meaningfully.

'I don't want to eulogize – we all knew his faults. Energetic to an intolerable degree. Driven. Too much so for some tastes, though not mine. Now, fifteen years after his death, I occupy the position he once did as commander of the battalion, but if I am half the man he was then I'm doing damned well. And I don't believe I am.'

He paused once more.

'And finally, hard as it is, let us ponder the manner of his death. A terrible night that Adrian and I here remember too well. At the end of it, when our small section hung in the balance, Mitch put his own life on the line. Would I have done what he did?' Alan shook his head. 'Was what he did sane in the normal military sense? No. Does knowledge of the true nature of the individual he chose to save bring bleak and bitter irony? Yes. But it *symbolizes* the man Mitchell Havilland was. The decision to save Pascoe was a simple act. A wounded man cried for help and Mitch gave it. That was who he was. He knew no compromise. To live like him would be exhausting, but he was an inspiration. He is one still.'

Alan raised his glass. 'So that's enough. To Mitchell, still sadly missed, whose contribution to the lives of all who surrounded him demands to be remembered.'

'Well said,' Jasper de la Rue muttered.

Caroline's head was bent.

That night, Julia knelt by the side of her bed, where she had always prayed as a child. She had been moved by Alan's speech in the pub. She unhooked the latch at the front of the dolls' house and opened the doors. It was a Georgian building that her father had made up from a design in a book. It had been intended as a Christmas surprise, but she had found the doors in the shed months before and had sneaked in periodically to monitor its progress.

It looked shabbier now than on the day she had opened it, but it was still a work of art. On the ground floor, the dining room had tiny wooden floorboards and wood panels. Her father had bought the chandelier, but the miniature paintings had been done by her mother. He had made the long dining-room table and chairs. Most of the kitchen had been bought from the shop, but he had built the wooden cupboards. Upstairs, almost everything had been fashioned by hand. Her mother had made the curtains, her father the bed and the Austrian wardrobe. The dolls had been lost, but the house was intact, a poignant reminder of a distant past.

Julia took out the grand piano from the living room, blew off the dust and held it up to the light. Some of the furniture needed repainting. She remembered the way Alice used to quietly lie on the floor here while Julia directed their games. Sometimes her father would come in and lie on the bed and Julia would tell him what all the dolls in the house were doing. She cherished these memories.

She lay down, put her hand under the bed and pulled out a red box. On top was a battered leather photograph frame, inside which was a smaller version of the picture downstairs, with her father smiling, and another of her mother and father sitting on the lawn with Socrates, the dog that had preceded Aristotle.

Julia looked at the photographs, then placed the frame carefully on the bed. The box was a mish-mash of memories, superstitiously kept. There was a card she had made for him, with silver glitter stuck to the words 'Happy Birthday Daddy'. Most of it had fallen off. Inside, she'd written, 'Daddy, I love you, Happy Birthday!' and next to the words had drawn a picture of a girl smiling with her hands in the air in celebration.

She took out and turned over the letters she had written to him while he was heading south towards the Falklands and the war that followed. The letters looked well thumbed, as if he had read and reread her banal reflections on school and home life. She ended each one with, 'Daddy, I love you, please come home safe.'

There were his letters back, full of cool, calm reassurance. The war was important, preparations were going well, he missed her and Mummy but this had to be done. He would be fine. Each letter ended 'your loving Daddy'.

Julia looked at the frame and the letters set out on the bed and suddenly her shoulders began to shake. Then, her face creased and her eyes stung. She could not control it. She sobbed and shook, and felt a pain in her stomach as she climbed on to the bed and curled around the collection, hating herself for this display of weakness.

It was a long time before her face was dry.

Eventually, she pulled herself upright, put away the contents of the box and closed the doors of the dolls' house.

She did not hear her mother come in.

Caroline sat down beside her. She placed a hand on her shoulder then an arm around her back and pulled Julia's head on to her chest, holding it there, stroking her hair. 'What is it?' she asked.

'Nothing.'

'Come on, my girl. What's wrong?'

Julia shook her head. It was many years since they had sat like this and she enjoyed her mother's warmth, but she could not shake off the pervasive feeling of discomfort. 'I don't know,' she said. 'I don't know.'

CHAPTER TWO

MAC'S DESK WAS AT THE BACK. HE LOOKED UP AS RIGBY CAME OUT, holding up a file.

'A cautionary tale, gentlemen. An officer with everything going for her – father a war hero, first woman to win the Sword of Honour at Sandhurst, top flight Intelligence Corps recruit, glittering career, all gone . . .'

Mac stared at Rigby, until he saw him lowering the file in Sanderson's direction. 'I'll take that one, sir,' he said.

Rigby looked at him. 'It's not a public auction, Macintosh.'

'Sanderson's stacked.'

Rigby looked at Sanderson, whose narrow face betrayed no interest in the case.

'What about the Wren file?' Rigby asked, moving to Mac's side of the office.

'Done. Just typing it up.' Mac flicked the file shut. It wasn't anywhere near ready.

'And were the breasts fondled?'

Sanderson snorted. Mac tried to smile. 'I believe they were.'

Rigby frowned. Mac knew his own attempts to join in with the bar-room culture were half-hearted and unconvincing.

'Hang the culprit,' Rigby said.

He placed the file on Mac's desk, his intense eyes resting on his face. 'You don't *know* Julia Havilland, do you, Macintosh? She must be about your age.'

Mac frowned and looked at Rigby. 'No, but the case sounds interesting. A change from bloody sexual harassment.'

Rigby's face lost its suspicion. He put down the file and ran his fat hand over the bald patch on the dome of his head. 'All right,' he said, 'but don't go easy on her just 'cos she's pretty. Registry prepared the file, so they'll want hard copies of everything when you're done. She's at home with her mother, so you need to monitor her, make sure she doesn't go anywhere.'

'Her CO doesn't want it dealt with in-house?'

'He might do, but he's not going to get his way. She went on the rampage inside a bloody embassy, so it's tough shit if he does.'

Rigby turned away, then changed his mind. 'By the way, you'll need to liaise with Jones. Know him?' Mac shook his head. 'Our man at the Ministry of Defence. He keeps the top brass up to date on sensitive cases and they'll be taking an interest in this one, so keep me informed of your progress.' Rigby hesitated, the bluster gone. 'Be careful with this one, Macintosh. There will be a lot of interest.'

He retreated to his office and shut the door, the blind banging against the glass panel. Sanderson glanced back at Mac with a look that might have been anything from gratitude to hostility. No one else was present.

Mac stood up and walked through the swing doors and across the stairwell to the toilets. As he urinated, he looked down on the empty square outside. Sheila, the office secretary, was walking up from the gate with a cup of coffee and a chocolate brownie in her hand. Mac found himself trying to remember if Julia had ever phoned him at the office and, if so, who had taken the call.

He got some coffee from the machine and returned to his desk, flicking open the buff-coloured file as he sat down. He glanced around the room. Rigby was bent over his desk, Sanderson was on the telephone, Wellar had disappeared. Sheila would still be having a cigarette at the bottom of the stairs.

Mac stared at the passport-style picture stapled to the front sheet. It was an old photograph, because her lustrous, wavy dark hair was longer now than depicted here, but the image displayed the exact perfection of her face, the neatness of her nose and the elegant curve of her cheeks. One corner of her mouth was pulled upwards in a sardonic smile.

Mac remembered her body, its litheness, and he wished he had not experienced it.

The code on top of the file was E4111468.SIB.W. SIB stood for Special Investigations Branch, and W for Woolwich – or head-quarters. He typed the numbers on his keyboard to pull up the matching computer files, but continued to read from the printouts inside the folder. The photograph had been attached to a CV, which he turned over, confident it could tell him nothing he didn't already know. Beneath it was a closely typed sheet from Julia's commanding officer. It was headed 'Background: Captain Julia Havilland'. It said:

Julia Havilland came to the Intelligence Corps after becoming the first woman to win the Sword of Honour at Sandhurst six years ago. She scored very highly in psychological and intellectual tests and interviews and was given glowing references, including one by a serving officer who knew her family well, Lieutenant Colonel Alan Ford.

In my own opinion, she has been one of the most exceptional young officers I have ever encountered. She has a strong and transparent desire to prove worthy of her father's name, but this has only translated into a devotion to work, a determination to get results, and a commitment to integrity and honesty in everything that she does.

After a period of initial training, she was sent to serve in Londonderry and Belfast in a junior capacity for two years. She then returned to headquarters in Ashford to work in an analytical role on Irish affairs. During this time, she had partial responsibility for liaising with the domestic intelligence service, MI5, and the Special Branch units of the Metropolitan Police and other police forces around the country. She briefed the Joint Intelligence Committee on two occasions and they made a point of noting that they were impressed by her performance.

After a brief posting to Russia and an even briefer one in the Balkans, she was retrieved and sent, by me, to be head of the JSG cell based in Bessbrooke barracks, in South

Armagh, Northern Ireland. JSG stands for Joint Support Group, a unit that was formally the FRU – Forward Research Unit. This is one of our most sensitive and difficult posts for an officer of Captain Havilland's level. She was responsible for finding, approaching and recruiting agents to provide information on the Irish Republican Army, the IRA. South Armagh is the heartland of that organization, where each member has close family links with the next. It is clannish and notoriously hard to penetrate. I am not at liberty to divulge specifics of our operations there, save to say that Captain Havilland achieved a quite extraordinary measure of success. She was brave, often venturing into IRA-controlled areas in plain clothes to research potential recruits, and seems to possess a particularly acute understanding of the psychology and motivation of a wide range of individuals.

For this reason, I chose to move her on suddenly almost exactly eight months ago. The military attaché in Beijing, Brigadier David Wright, had received what he believed to be an approach from a colonel in Chinese Military Intelligence. He had no idea whether the approach was genuine and anyway did not wish to compromise his position as attaché. Nor was he qualified to take the matter further. I could think of no one more capable of handling such a potentially complex and dangerous situation than Captain Havilland. Although I was reluctant to remove her from Ireland, I took the decision to dispatch her to Beijing along with one of the sergeants she was working with in South Armagh, Sergeant Blackstone, an experienced man with a faultless record, and another, Sergeant Jarrow, with whom she had previously worked in Russia and who had had considerable experience with 14 Intelligence Company, our street surveillance unit. Although both men were older, I had reason to believe, and still do, that they had the greatest respect for her.

I have not yet received a full debrief of what happened in China and am inclined to let the dust settle and tempers calm for a week or two before attempting to do so. In retrospect, I can see it was a mistake to send Captain Havilland directly from Ireland to China, without any sort of break, since I believe she has not had a holiday for almost three years. In my defence, I would only say that she was one of the most ambitious young officers I have ever encountered and she repeatedly indicated her willingness, indeed desire, to take on new challenges. I never saw or heard anything to suggest she was under pressure with which she was unable to cope. She always struck me as a young woman of exceptional tenacity and toughness.

I make no secret of the fact that, if this incident had not occurred in an embassy, I would, despite its severity, be trying to deal with it in-house. We are an unusual unit, with unusual work, and, quite simply, we cannot afford to lose officers of Captain Havilland's calibre.

It was signed and dated. Mac turned it over. That was the Julia he knew.

Next was an incident report, typed on headed embassy paper. It had been written by the security officer and was full of barely suppressed outrage. Mac glanced over it. He would read it in detail later. He took in 'video of agent's execution . . . argument ensued . . . threatened subordinates with gun . . . barrel of pistol placed in Jarrow's mouth'.

Mac was startled by the image of a Julia he could not imagine. He wondered where she had managed to get a pistol from.

Both the sergeants had given written depositions describing the train of events leading from the arrival of the video of their agent's execution through to when they watched it together. The specifics of the argument that followed were not spelt out, though Sergeant Jarrow admitted that the pistol belonged to him and had been bought illegally from a Chinese street market.

Julia's statement was the shortest: 'I have read the statements of both Sergeant Jarrow and Sergeant Blackstone. I do not disagree with their description of the aforementioned events and see no reason to dispute it. I do not wish to state anything else at this time.'

Mac did not know if this statement reflected a brittle or defiant state of mind. As so often, she had given little away.

The last item in the file was a series of newspaper cuttings held together with a paperclip. The first was from *The Times* and its headline was 'War Hero's Daughter Wins Sword of Honour'.

There was a similar article from the *Daily Mail*, with the catch-line: 'I'll make him proud, says war hero's girl.' There was a picture of Julia in uniform, holding the sword. She looked sombre, and Mac remembered her determination to resist the photographers' attempts to make her smile.

He sat back in his chair, with his hands behind his head. He thought about the day of their graduation from Sandhurst and the interest Julia had attracted, but was soon recalling instead the night in the log cabin in Norway's frozen north when he had gone briefly beyond the protective shield she had so carefully erected. He could still remember Julia's arrival on the plane as they departed for that trip and the lull in conversation that had accompanied it.

Until the Arctic warfare training course, they had had nothing to do with the girls at Sandhurst, who shared separate facilities and formed their own companies and platoons, so Julia's impact had perhaps been unsurprising. She was taller than the other women and carried her femininity easily.

Discipline during those two weeks had been more relaxed. Not a holiday, but the closest they ever came to it in training. Even Mac's public-school-dominated platoon had managed to stop looking down their noses at him.

He had talked to Julia during the training, mostly in the evenings, over dinner, card games and whisky in front of the log fire in the communal hut, but she had never seemed to take much notice of him. She always seemed to be laughing at him. And then, when they had all got smashed on vodka, he had found himself being invited to go and have a cigarette outside – they were allowed to smoke in the hut but she had said, smiling, that she preferred it in the cold air. Mac had tramped through the snowdrifts, laughed and fought with her in the new powder, then gone back to her log cabin and made love to her in the moonlight.

He thought now of her small hard nipples, the curve of her spine when she threw her head back, and tried to suppress a physical ache.

He drummed his fingers irritably against the table-top. Even though he flattered himself that he had built a friendship with Julia, he had never understood why, from that day to this, she had made no mention of the incident in the Norwegian hut. She had not been embarrassed by it. The next day, she had just smiled at him and, after a period of studied formality in which he had grown increasingly desperate, the sardonic smile had come again, accompanied by a frown, which indicated that the night they'd shared had been a gift and not a reason for further demands.

Mac thought of the file on his desk and the explosively violent incident it detailed. Not for the first time with Julia, he did not understand, but he wanted to.

Rigby burst out of the office and marched towards Wellar, holding up a buff-coloured file. 'What the fuck is this?' he demanded.

Wellar sat up straight. 'I don't understand, sir.'

Mac tried not to look at them. Wellar was the youngest and newest in the office and Rigby enjoyed humiliating him. Paying attention made it worse, because Rigby, with the mindset of a bully and the charm of a Rottweiler, liked to have an audience.

'This piece of shit. Where's the interview with the girl?' Rigby demanded.

'I thought I attached it, sir.'

'Well, it isn't here, is it?' Rigby threw the file on the desk so that the contents spilled out on to Wellar's lap. 'Sort yourself out,' he said, dismissively.

Before Rigby had got to his office, Mac stood up and patted Wellar's shoulder. Rigby turned and saw him do it and Mac was glad that he had.

As he turned into Woodpecker Lane that night, Mac tried hard to suppress a sense of nervous excitement.

He had called Julia three times, but there had been no answer.

However, turning in at the gate, he wondered if he'd miscalculated and coming in person was, in fact, a mistake. Both cars were in the drive, but the house was in darkness, save for a sidelight in the living room. If they were in, Julia and her mother showed every sign of having gone up to bed.

Beside the front door, he hesitated, then knocked.

There was a long wait.

He heard someone descending the stairs, then looking through the spy-hole at him for a moment, before the door was pulled open. 'Mac!'

Caroline Havilland was wearing a dark green silk dressing-gown, her hair tumbling over her shoulders.

'Mrs Havilland . . .'

35

'Caroline, as I've told you so many times. Come in.' She took a step back, flicking on the light in the hall beside her. 'It didn't take you long to locate her.'

'I'm so sorry, I know it's . . .'

'Don't be silly.' Caroline was smiling, intimating that she understood his feelings more clearly even than he did himself. 'I'll get her for you,' she said, turning and disappearing, as if his arrival at this time of night was perfectly natural and before he could offer any qualifying explanation for his presence.

Mac ducked under the doorway as he stepped in, then ran his hand through his hair, trying not to look at himself in the mirror opposite as he heard the thump, thump of Julia's footsteps on the stairs. A second later, she was rounding the corner, dressed in faded blue and yellow pyjamas, her long hair, like her mother's, falling down over the front of her shoulders. 'Mac!' she said, before he could say anything, moving swiftly to close the last few paces and hugging him, her hair in his eyes, the intoxicating smell of her skin filling his nostrils, so that he gripped her harder than he meant to.

She let go, taking a pace back, still smiling. Perhaps it was his imagination, but her eyes seemed red and puffy, as if she'd been crying.

'I'm so sorry,' he said, looking at his watch. 'I know . . .'

'Come in.' She tugged at his arm, leading him around the corner to the kitchen, flicking on the light, almost tripping over the dog before moving to the Aga and pulling across the kettle.

'Coffee, or something stronger?'

'Coffee.'

'I'm sorry . . .' She looked at him. 'You'll have to excuse the pyjamas . . .'

Mac smiled, taking off his jacket, putting it over one chair and pulling back another. As he sat down, looking at her bare feet and hands, he wished suddenly that he did not have to explain why he was here and wondered if he could get away without doing so.

'I heard you were back,' he said.

'And somehow you've found yourself on my case.' She was looking at him. 'Okay, that's a good guess. There's no point in looking crestfallen, Mac, I'm sure it's not your fault. It's the inevitable sod's law – I knew it as soon as they told me your unit was going to be handling the investigation.'

He wondered if he should tell her he had chosen to be involved.

'You've come to arrest me.'

'No, of course . . .'

'I only accept golden handcuffs.'

She was smiling at him. He relaxed a little. 'You've hung on to your sense of humour.'

'Just about.'

Julia moved slowly over to the table, reaching across and taking hold of his wrist. 'You don't have to look so worried, Mac, it's all right.'

'I want to help you,' he said simply.

'Don't worry . . .'

'I'm not, but . . .'

'I don't want any help.'

'I know, Julia, but . . .'

'I won't accept any. It won't do any good, so just do what you have to and forget that you're my friend.'

He looked at her, but she was staring at her feet.

'Julia, of course I'm not going . . .'

'Mac.' She looked up, her face more severe. 'Please, I don't want any help or special favours. It won't do you any good either. If you have been forced to be involved, then just do what you would normally do.'

'Well . . . At some point, I am going to have to talk to you about it.'

'No you're not, because I have nothing to say. I don't dispute the statements and I've nothing further to add.'

Mac waited. 'Julia, you're my friend. Of course I'm going to help you in any way that I can, but . . . it doesn't have to be a confrontational thing.'

As he'd been speaking, Mac had watched the aggression and anger draining out of Julia to reveal the brittle, vulnerable girl he'd seen in the log cabin in Norway.

He leant forward, but she didn't move.

'You know,' she said. 'Once you let emotion get in the way then . . . you know, then it's over. That's the point.'

Mac looked at her for a long time, trying to resist the temptation to reach over and give her the affection that he thought she wanted but seemed determined not to accept. 'No human being can shut out emotion for ever and remain human,' he said. 'And, although you will feel it is not my position to say, I think you are too hard on yourself.'

Julia shrugged. 'Perhaps.'

The kettle was boiling and she stood, taking down a coffee pot and two mugs from the cupboard. Neither of them spoke as she brought the coffee to the table and went to the larder to get milk, sugar and a packet of digestive biscuits.

She sat opposite him and filled the two mugs, pushing one towards him. 'Do you ever think of your father, Mac?'

'No.'

'Why not?'

'Why not?' He breathed out heavily, staring at his coffee. 'When I realized, aged about fourteen, or fifteen, that I was going to be . . . you know, tall, I remember being pleased because it meant that, in the unlikely event that I ever met my father again, I would be able to beat him into very tiny pieces.'

Julia's face was thoughtful. 'You hate him because he abandoned you?'

'Abandoned all of us.' He paused. 'For someone he met on a train.' Despite the fact that he was used to this history, Mac felt his face colouring with anger again. 'That was more than twenty years ago and I've not heard one word from him and neither has my sister.'

Mac filled his coffee to the brim with milk and put in two tea-spoons of sugar. 'Why do you ask?' he said.

'It just seems . . . odd, that's all, him being alive and . . . it would feel odd to me.'

Mac thought that another woman might have pursued this with more tact, but Julia had a relentless, almost naïve honesty in the way she approached everything.

'Do you think of your father?' he asked.

'Yes.' She nodded. 'Every day.' Julia sat up straight, leaning on the table. 'I can still . . .' She smiled at him. 'You'll think I'm a nutter.'

'No I won't.'

'You already think I'm a nutter.'

Mac smiled. 'You are.'

Julia's face grew more serious. 'I can still feel his arms around me sometimes . . . the strength of him . . . the feel of his scratchy face and jumper. And . . . almost as if he were here, I can hear him say, "Hello, champ." Do you think that's odd?'

'No.'

'Why not? It's been such a long time and sometimes I can feel it – his presence, I mean – more strongly than I could ten or fifteen years ago. That's odd . . . don't you think that's odd?'

Mac did not know what to say. Julia was looking out of the window above the Aga, her face solemn, and he had to restrain himself now from reaching out and putting a hand on her shoulder, or touching her cheek.

'I guess,' he said quietly. 'There's no loss without love. And with love, loss doesn't necessarily fade.' She turned to face him. 'It's harder for you,' he said.

'No . . .'

'Yes. I have hatred to sustain me, but you still feel the loss.'

She hesitated, as if about to say something else. 'Yes,' she said. 'You know, even after all this time, I still often think, why me? Why me, what did I do wrong?'

Mac had never heard Julia be so intimate or open about the past and he didn't want to do anything to break the spell.

'I mean,' she went on, 'as I grow older and time and events pass by I think about all the conversations that I could have had with him – probably wouldn't have done, but . . . why has that been denied me? I just wanted to be an ordinary teenager and instead . . .'

Mac nodded.

'I hate it that I can't be with him, adult to adult, and that . . . he can't see how I turned out, you know . . .'

Mac reached forward to touch her arm. 'It's okay.'

Julia stared at the table. 'I suppose I should be glad he can't see me now.'

'That's a stupid thing to say.'

'I wish he hadn't been so perfect.'

'I'm sure he wasn't.'

Julia cleared her throat, straightening, recovering herself and apparently suddenly embarrassed by the display of emotion. 'You're right. Of course, you're right.'

'The difference between us,' Mac said, 'is that I can always resolve these issues if I want to and you can't. For you, it's just unfair, there is no other way of looking at it. Your father . . . he sounds a good man, and dying in such a tragic, heroic way . . . it

39

places an impossible burden . . . just remember that. So . . . don't punish yourself.'

'I'm not.'

Mac waited until it became clear that Julia didn't want to talk any more about this, then looked at his watch and stood. 'I should go.' He rounded the table slowly, until he was close to her, but she did not move, so he passed beyond her.

She stood. 'Thanks, Mac.'

He stopped and turned around.

'Thanks for coming.'

'Julia, I . . .'

'No, don't. Please. You probably think you can help me, but you can't.'

CHAPTER THREE

JULIA WOKE EARLY AND LEFT THE HOUSE BEFORE HER MOTHER WAS UP, driving across the border from Hampshire to Sussex, through undulating fields of wheat and over the rolling hills of the South Downs to the seaside beyond Chichester. It was warm again, so she kept the windows of the Golf open, one forearm sometimes hanging down, fingers drumming on the side of the door.

She reached Professor Malcolm's house with her hair a tangled mess and her stomach protesting, wishing she had eaten something before leaving home.

Professor Malcolm swung the door open and looked her up and down reprovingly. 'The prodigal returns.' He stepped back to allow her to enter.

Walking in, she pointed to the sofa, which was covered by a white dust sheet, and asked if she should sit there. He nodded, and she noticed a suitcase standing by the door. It looked out of place.

He sat opposite her. The route between his seat and the french windows was mapped by eight or nine pieces of carpet tile, placed in a row. Another line went towards the door in the opposite direction. They matched the new carpet beneath, roughly, and she assumed they were there to protect it.

To say he lived alone really didn't do justice to the sense of it. This room was unloved and felt unlived-in. The television dated

41

from the seventies, or before, a large square box with big push-button controls. The curtains were old and made from a thick, faded green fabric. Only the morning sun streaming through the window on to a glass coffee-table prevented the atmosphere from being gloomy. There was a picture on the wall above the fireplace – a watercolour view of a beach seen from a cliff-top with a silhouetted figure walking down the middle of it, but there were no photographs on the mantelpiece. A bookcase ran the length of one wall with bundles of the *Journal of Clinical Psychology* stacked unevenly; some had fallen on to the floor and Julia began picking them up and rearranging them.

'How long are you home for?' he asked.

She cleared her throat. 'I don't know.'

There was a side-table next to the bookshelf, and she took a small white paper bag from the middle of the blue pot on top of it and examined the contents. It was half full. 'Still at the jelly babies?'

'Every man must have a weakness.'

'Like Ron Reagan.'

'He ate jelly beans. Not the same thing at all.'

Julia looked at the curve of his stomach and the slack line of his jaw and remembered him telling their tutorial, in a discussion about the psychological impact of bullying, that his nickname at school had been 'Bunter'. This information had been offered without explanation or embellishment and was the only personal thing she could ever recall him sharing.

He stood. 'This may seem eccentric,' he said, 'but I was about to go for my morning swim.'

'That is eccentric,' she said.

While he got changed Julia went outside to stand at the end of the lawn in front of the knee-high palisade that separated it from a dirt path and the beach beyond. The garden had been transformed since her last visit. Once unkempt and neglected, it was now almost too ordered. It was no bigger than a badminton court, but the grass was neatly clipped and bordered on three sides by flower-beds, mostly filled with roses.

He emerged from the house in a florid dressing-gown, thinning hair scraped back across his head, highlighting the Roman curve that ran from his forehead to the tip of his nose. He was wearing white plastic sandals good for swimming off pebbly beaches such as this.

It was windy, the gate in the palisade swinging on its hinges. Professor Malcolm walked through it, she followed, and they crossed the path in tandem.

At low tide, it was possible that this was a sandy beach, but now there was no sand in evidence, the shingle held in place by the breakwaters that stretched almost to the end of the bay.

He removed his dressing-gown and strode forward into the sea, a great white whale in blue and green check shorts and plastic shoes.

Professor Malcolm didn't hesitate, or shout, but advanced into the water as though it were the Caribbean. Julia took ten or twenty paces to her right and picked up a handful of stones, discarded all but the flattest then skimmed them out across the top of the waves.

He was swimming. Not flapping or splashing or kicking, just making stately progress towards the line of the nearest breakwater and she wondered what the tides were like because he seemed to be drifting further out than she had expected. She asked herself at what point she should worry, but just as she was growing alarmed, he turned back towards her.

Looking at him face on, his head rising and falling with the incoming swell, Julia wondered if he was engaged in the uncomfortable process of mentally cleansing himself of all the darkness that, as one of the country's foremost psychologists, he had witnessed, investigated and studied. She did not see how anyone with his experience of the dark side of humanity could live comfortably with it.

Professor Malcolm waded out of the sea. Beside her, he picked up a towel, shook his head and cleared the water out of his ears. She wondered if anyone else came here and was part of this ritual, but concluded not. He dried his face carefully, before putting on his glasses.

'You'll catch a chill,' she said.

He dried the rest of himself and put on his dressing-gown, without removing his wet shorts. His dressing-gown looked new and she wondered where he had bought it. The idea of him shopping was vaguely disconcerting.

Julia slipped back through the french windows ahead of him and was careful to follow the tiles across the carpet to the galley kitchen at the back. 'I'll make a cup of tea,' she said. 'Do you want me to cook you something?'

He disappeared without answering.

The kitchen was the antithesis of the rest of the house. To the left of the door, there was a bookcase that ran from floor to ceiling, full of cookery books. There was a wooden block with ten or more new-looking knives in it, and the first cupboard she looked in was full. On the top shelf, there were bags and bags of Barilla pasta of different shapes and sizes; below, there was a jar of porcini cèpes, three of Hellmann's mayonnaise, alongside cans of pitted olives and smoked mussels. There were two pots of rock salt and three different types of olive oil. In the middle, there was a white bag with a handful of congealed jelly babies inside it.

Julia located the tea-bags and flicked on the kettle. In the fridge, she found sweet mango chutney, sun-dried tomatoes, butter, eggs, cheese and Japanese horseradish, but no milk.

She moved to the side and glanced over the cookery books, thinking how effectively his forensic, clinical manner obscured his passion for fine food.

Fine food and jelly babies.

She made him a cup of tea and brought it into the living room, placing it beside his chair. The room seemed unnaturally bare and she recalled that this had been her overwhelming impression of it on her first visit many years ago. There was not a sign in this house of any form of private life: no pictures of relatives, or friends, no holiday snaps left casually on the side (did he take holidays? She could not imagine how, when, or to where). This room told of a life lived lean, but she did not believe this could be the case, because that wasn't possible, surely, even for him. She wondered if he had deliberately stripped his surroundings of his past.

When he emerged, he wore a rusty brown sweater and green corduroys. 'You're still busy?' she asked, as he sat down heavily in his chair in front of the television, which she knew he rarely watched.

'None of my other visitors,' he said, as she handed him the cup, 'make me tea.'

Julia pondered the notion that he had other visitors. 'It's all police work, no teaching?'

'I don't miss university departmental politics.'

She sipped her tea, grateful for something to take the edge off her hunger. 'There's no milk, by the way.' He looked down at the

44

mug in his hand, without comment. His face was more lined than she remembered. 'You should slow down,' she said, 'relax more.'

'I'm touched by your concern, but it's difficult to say no.'

'Isn't it arrogant to assume you're the only one who can help?'

'Possibly. But while they ask, while a crime remains unsolved and a diseased criminal mind out there, and while there is even the smallest chance I might make a difference, it is hard to turn them away.'

Julia recalled how he had once told her that he had never forgotten a face – not of the dead, for a corpse is lifeless, but of those who stared out from pictures stuck to the walls of investigation rooms. Photographs of victims.

'What are you working on now?' she asked.

Professor Malcolm was staring into the television. She waited a long time. 'Robert Pascoe will be released tomorrow,' he said.

Julia felt the shock in her spine and in the base of her stomach.

He turned to her. 'You'll remember he appealed before so there has not been much publicity this time but, of course, that will change when he is released.'

Julia found that she was staring at her hands. 'Tomorrow?'

'So I'm told.'

'Why?'

'They have proved that his confession was altered and embellished to make it more convincing. The other evidence was circumstantial.'

'Does that mean . . . So he has been let off on a technicality?'

'No. It means he is probably innocent – and certainly of committing the crime in the way that is commonly supposed.'

Julia thought of the day she had missed games and slunk down to the town to stand in the back of the court-house, watching Pascoe's shaven head as he stared resolutely at the floor.

'What do you think?' he asked.

Julia tried to think of something to say. She saw that he was frowning deeply, his forehead furrowed. He appeared to be wrestling with himself.

'I feel,' he said, 'like a priest who's waited a long time for someone to come to confession, to God.'

'I don't view you as God.'

'No, that's not what I meant.'

45

He had not taken his eyes from her face and Julia could feel her heart beating. 'I don't understand.'

'I interviewed you because you were the person who found Sarah's body. We ... formed ... a bond. Then, eight years later you turn up in my tutorial at Sussex University, an eager young student. Is that a coincidence? I ask myself why you of all people, with so many choices of course and university and tutor, should find your way to *my* door. Once or twice I thought we might broach the subject of our first meeting, but we never *quite* do so. We become friends, sure, but never do we talk about this.'

The unusual sentence structure was a rare indication of his East European origins. That his mother was Polish was one of the few personal facts she knew about him.

'I am honoured,' he went on, 'to be invited to your graduation from Sandhurst, to the day you emulate your father – go better than him – and receive the Sword of Honour, but still this is never mentioned. You come here sometimes. Just call up and come over. We talk about your work. We talk about the army. We talk about your father sometimes and the legend you feel the need to live up to. But we never talk about the case in West Welham and the inter-view I conducted on the day after you had found Sarah's body.' He shook his head. 'And yet all the time I feel that is why you have stayed close to me.'

Julia was looking at the blank television again. She was uncom-fortable and wanted to stand up, but didn't. Conversations with Professor Malcolm so often developed an immediate, savage and unstoppable momentum, no matter what the subject matter. 'How come,' she said, 'the police have told you they think Pascoe will be released?'

'They need help. They know they will be under pressure to reopen the case. They will claim they believe they convicted the right man and that there is no need for a new investigation, but in the meantime they are, of course, panicking and want me to review the evidence to see if there *are* any grounds for reopening the case. I think it is called "covering your arse".' He looked at her, his face softening as he took in her unease. 'I haven't said yes, yet. They only called me last night.'

'But you will. You said yourself, you cannot say no.' Julia sat back and watched the steam rise from the untouched tea on the glass-topped table beside his chair. The room seemed to have darkened since they came in, but he had made no move to turn on any lights. 'Why do you say Pascoe is not guilty in the way commonly supposed?'

'It was the way the investigation went. I cannot say who was innocent and guilty, only that the methodology that produced Pascoe as a culprit was wrong.'

'How?'

Julia recognized the tightness in her voice. She found herself imagining Robert Pascoe walking casually back into the village as if nothing had transpired, and was confused that she did not understand clearly what her own reaction to this would be.

What would everyone else think? They would be angry. And frightened. Wouldn't they?

Professor Malcolm looked at her. '*I* said to the police that, whichever way you looked at it, this crime had to be about the woman, *not* the child. No paedophile is going to tackle a healthy young woman in broad daylight to get at a child – too many easier targets. They don't need the fear of adult involvement interfering with their thrills.'

Julia swallowed, wishing he could sometimes be less direct in his language. His eyelids had sunk and his eyes were hooded, like a hawk's. It was how he looked when he was concentrating. She recalled how intimidating so many had found it.

'This was about anger. With the woman. I said either someone who knew her, most likely, or if not, then a local, or a stranger – but one way or another it was about the control of this young *woman*.'

He sighed again. 'The evidence was right there. And I said, I *said*, "It's *not* about the child," but, you know, the media police-men didn't want to see that. It was a big case, they were out to make their careers and the press were portraying it as the act of a dangerous predatory paedophile because, of course, the story ran better that way. A man who murdered the mother to get at the daughter. That was enough to keep everyone watching, listening and reading in terrified, uncomfortable awe. It was a drama. When would he strike next? Where would he go? Was any child safe? Would the police stop him? As I said, a diseased criminal mind was still *out there*.'

There was bitterness in Professor Malcolm's voice. Julia considered the way in which it had been a drama for the nation.

Had she feared when and where the killer would strike next? She could not remember being frightened for herself.

'The careerists said we were ambling, Barnaby and I, we were slow, we didn't know what we were doing. The in-fighting dragged on. Then, eventually, there was a coup. Barnaby was pushed aside and I went with him. The media policemen took their time, but they got to the end they wanted. One of the detectives unearthed allegations by a jilted former girlfriend, who said that Corporal Robert Pascoe, who lived with his mother next to the pub, had abused her young daughter, and after that the investigation never looked back. Pascoe came back slightly injured from the war, his life saved by your father, and the media policemen pounced. Out came the confession. Better late than never, the investigation a big success at last, promotions all round.'

'It doesn't sound like you made a mistake. They just didn't listen.'

He didn't respond. She hadn't meant to imply he'd made a mistake. She'd never known him admit to being wrong about anything.

'If it was a crime of passion,' she asked, moving on quickly, 'I mean, if that was the original direction of the investigation . . . if you thought it was anger at the woman and, therefore, perhaps a crime of passion, what would one be looking for in the murderer?'

'Well . . .'

'But the little girl?' Julia asked, before he had a chance to answer. 'I mean, to kill out of passion . . . If Sarah had been making a man jealous, it's not so hard to understand her death, but the man, whoever he was, must have gone further. He must have murdered a little girl.'

Professor Malcolm looked at her searchingly and she found it impossible to hold his gaze, dropping her head again. 'But it's still about control,' he said quietly. 'We're talking here about someone who has a tendency to bury his feelings deep within himself, who distances himself from his actions and his feelings, who disowns them, blaming others, seeing himself as a victim, perhaps. You are understanding, almost accepting, the murder as a natural result of adult passions. It is the murder of the little girl you are setting apart and considering an aberration, but in fact they come from that same sudden catastrophic loss of control, that aggressive, frustrated desire to dominate. The anger stimulated knows no boundaries.'

Julia looked up at him. His eyes were still upon her. He stood up and walked to the windows, sliding them open a fraction, letting in a blast of cold air. He had his back to her, his eyes to the sea.

'You know,' he said, 'it's very therapeutic watching the elemental forces of nature.'

She stood up too, and followed his gaze down to the waves crashing on the shore and wondered at the sudden change of direction. With Malcolm, there was usually a reason. An old man crossed in front of them, walking his dog on the path, but her eyes strayed to the foreground and she noticed again how a garden that had once been overgrown – a reflection of a man with more important things on his mind – was now immaculate. 'Your garden's neat,' she said.

'Yes. You see, I have relaxed a little. A great retreat from the world.' They stepped out into it and advanced to the centre of the lawn. 'I need a bigger one, really, but I'm too old to think about moving.'

She was standing just behind him, her heart still thumping. He turned. 'So what happened?' he asked.

'What do you mean?'

'Something has happened. Something bad. Something to make you think long and hard . . .'

'No . . .'

'It's all right, Julia.' He looked at her. 'It's what you came here for.'

Julia stared out to sea. She tried to think clearly, but it was hard here – she felt like a compass that had strayed too close to an electrical force and has lost its bearings. 'The agent I ran in China was lost,' she said. 'We lost him. He was executed.'

He waited.

'I felt . . . *feel* that, considering the risks he was taking, he deserved a hundred per cent professionalism. A clean sheet. Complete focus. But I believe I may have brought psychological baggage to the equation. At any rate, I threatened a subordinate. With a gun.'

'That can't be very good for your career.'

'No.'

'So you came home, which is a sanctuary and refuge, but also a prison.'

She frowned. 'No . . .'

'Drawn home and then drawn here.'

Julia shook her head.

'You cannot be comfortable in the present, in a place where you do not trust the past. Imagine.' He stopped. His voice was gentle. 'Imagine,' he went on, holding up his hand, 'that a person is like a building. The older you get, the taller it gets. Doubt about the past, suspicion, uncertainty, a lack of confidence in who you are and where you came from, a level of uncertainty about the veracity and trustworthiness of positive memories . . . Imagine *that* is like a worm that eats through concrete. If you leave it long enough, it'll eat through the foundations and then the whole building topples.'

'A laboured analogy,' she said.

'Yes.'

'I . . .' She stopped. He waited. 'I don't . . .'

'Finish your sentences?'

She didn't smile. 'I didn't find it *surprising*.'

'What?'

'Nothing about that year. Even as I walked down that path and saw Sarah's body lying there, I was conscious of not being surprised.'

'Go on.'

'Then with Alice. I knew . . . I watched the appeals for help on the television and I saw from the attic the search of the common and people coming and going and gathered in groups talking quietly, and I knew that they were never going to find her. I *knew* she was dead. It was *complete* certainty.'

He waited.

'And then the investigation. I didn't know what to think of that, but I knew they would never find who did it. Then the war, my father goes with all the others. Alan has given up hope, so he goes – everyone does. And then the news that Dad had been killed and . . .'

'You weren't surprised by that?'

'No, of course I was, but at the same time I was conscious that I had been dreading and . . . somehow expecting it. Each night I'd gone to bed clutching the photograph album with his picture in it. I would pray then go through an elaborate ritual of superstition, and on the night he died, well, I couldn't find the album and . . . I think someone stole it. I think they moved it because they thought that was funny.'

She drew breath. He did not interrupt her.

'I was surprised, but I knew it was coming. *Absolute* certainty.'

The man who had crossed in front of the house with his dog came back in the opposite direction. They both looked disconsolate and old, the dog ambling on a lead behind its master.

'If it is the fact that the events were not surprising that is disturbing,' he said, 'it is because it makes you doubt all your memories. You cannot say for sure any more what was real and what not, what you should value and attach importance to and what was a mirage. It is . . . confusing. You have lost your past, and everyone needs a version of the past they can rely on.'

He turned to look at her. 'You have maintained our relationship because you think I can explain you to yourself. But I can't. Not really. Only you can do that.'

Julia didn't respond.

He put his hands in his pockets.

'Most of the memories have receded . . . faded with age, but lately . . . I don't know . . .'

'Some images come back vividly?'

'Yes.'

'Which ones . . . is there a theme?'

'In my dreams . . . yes.'

'Only in your dreams?'

'Mostly.'

'What do you see?'

'My father . . . most commonly, I'm in my room, lying in front of the dolls' house that he made me and he comes in and says, "Hello, champ."' She smiled. 'I mean, who on earth would ever say that to a girl? He's got back from work and he's wearing his uniform still, and it's the summer, so he just has a khaki woollen shirt on and fatigues.'

'And then what?'

'No . . . well, then he comes to lie alongside me and . . . he asks me what I'm doing, so I tell him . . . and that's it.'

'A happy memory, then.'

'Yes, of course.'

'A moment of easy intimacy.'

'Yes . . . yes, definitely. Then, recently, I mean in the last few weeks particularly, we are walking in the wood, but . . . again, it's just me and him. We used to do that a lot together. Then, sometimes, we meet up with Alice and . . . sometimes Sarah and then I'm hiding . . .'

'Hiding?'

'Yes. We used to play games in the wood and I liked to play hide and seek. So, in my dreams, I'm hiding, watching the clearing, waiting for him, but I fear something has happened and he's not going to come and then I discover I'm trapped so that I can't move and it gets worse and worse and I feel more trapped and I wake up covered in sweat, suddenly awake and sitting bolt upright, as if . . .'

Julia let her voice trail off, not sure how to finish.

'As if what?'

'As if he is dying out there somewhere and I can't help him. I want to, but I can't. I'm trapped, I can't move and that's what is making me sweat. And there's another image that has always recurred. I went out . . . a few years after his death, I went out to the Falklands and saw the hill where he died and we looked at where he'd been sheltering, roughly, and where the machine-gun nest had been and ever since then I've been able to see him breaking cover and charging out to help Pascoe so vividly that it's as if I'd been there. I can see the furious courage in his face and the determination and it's almost as if these two images are tied together. Do you see? It's as if that is going on and I'm trapped under this bush, watching the clearing, knowing what is happening to him, unable to do anything about it. The two scenes are totally dislocated in terms of geography, but they're not in my mind. Do you see? But it's also more than that, it's as though it is in some way my fault that I'm trapped. It's because of my inadequacies or doubts or . . .'

'Suspicions.'

She frowned. 'No. No, it's not that.'

He nodded.

'It's just that I feel it is somehow my fault that my father . . .'

Julia stopped.

'A sense of loss does not always fade with the passage

of time. In certain circumstances it can even grow.'

'What do you mean, in certain circumstances?'

Professor Malcolm shrugged, staring out towards the sea. 'I'm going to work on this case. On this review. Partly because if I don't someone else will. Perhaps you should help me.'

She looked up to see if he was serious. 'You must be out of your mind.'

'The professional Captain Julia Havilland has the resourcefulness and ability to work through this if the personal Julia Havilland does not stand in her way.' He came closer and placed his hand lightly on the top of her head, as if blessing her. 'Let me get you another cup of tea.'

Moving next to her, he leant down and closed his right hand around her own. It was only then that she realized she had been tugging at her jeans. 'Do you remember?' he said. 'That was what you did in the interview room.'

Julia went for a long walk on the Downs. She was no longer hungry or bothered about lunch. It was only after she had left him that she came to feel Professor Malcolm had been carefully manipulating the conversation all along and that he had probably set out to enlist her help in the review.

Why did he want it?

On the way home, she took a detour via Cranbrooke, intending to do some shopping. She parked at the top of the high street, half blocking the road, put her hazard lights on and dashed into Boots, which was situated in one of the old buildings. She bought what she needed, hurried by the horn of a lorry that was stuck behind her, then got back into the car and drove on down the high street, which widened as it descended, the pavements getting broader on both sides. She passed the Cross Keys pub on the right, a tall grey stone building that looked less forbidding in the sunshine.

On the corner, Julia saw a group of girls wearing a modern version of the uniform she had been forced to put up with less than ten years ago. She indicated, then filtered off left and parked on the pavement, underneath a sign that said 'Rubin Gallery' in big, gold letters.

A bell sounded as Julia stepped inside, but no one was immediately visible. She looked at the paintings, which were mostly landscapes in oil. In the middle of one wall, there was a photograph of the artist and Julia moved closer to read what was written beneath it.

'Can we help you, madam?'

Julia turned to see her mother smiling. 'I wondered,' she said, 'if you had any Havilland paintings left?'

Caroline frowned. 'Havilland,' she said. 'Havilland ... Havilland. Hmm. Don't think I've heard of her. What are you doing here?'

'Passing.'

'Well, that's fortuitous, because I've dropped the car in the garage and need a lift home.'

Gazing at her mother, Julia remembered what Professor Malcolm had said about Pascoe and wondered if Caroline and Alan knew about it. 'Now?' she asked.

'There's no need to look so down in the mouth about it.' Caroline went back through the rear door. She was in a good mood.

A few seconds later Felicity Rubin emerged with her. Then Caroline got her coat and bag and they climbed into the Golf. As they drove up the hill out of the town Caroline explained that she had the village fête committee coming to tea for a final meeting and Julia had better make herself scarce if she wanted to avoid it. Then she was laughing at a private joke.

'What's so funny?'

'A man came into the gallery today and said, "I want to buy a painting." "Right," I said, "what kind of painting?" "A painting," he said. "Yes, but what kind of painting? Oil? Watercolour? Landscape?"' Caroline was dissolving into fits of giggles, like a schoolgirl. '"A painting," he said. "An investment. Just a painting."'

They both looked at the road ahead. Julia didn't feel like smiling. 'Do you remember that skiing holiday in Scotland?' she asked.

Caroline turned to face her. 'Yes, of course.'

Julia was stuck behind a lorry on the hill coming out of Cranbrooke. 'What time of year was it?'

'Easter. April.'

Julia pulled out to overtake the lorry and put her foot down on the floor until she was past it. Then she slowed again. They were coming up to the crest of the hill now, a wood on either side of them.

'What about it?' Caroline asked.

'I was just thinking about it, that's all. Remembering Dad learning to ski.'

Caroline smiled again. 'Yes.' She wiped her eyes. 'God, he hated not being the expert.'

'It was so cold and I was wearing all those thick sweaters and that thin anorak and I was freezing and then the next day I went up with all those layers on and it was absolutely boiling!'

Caroline was still smiling.

'How come you never skied?'

'It was more fun laughing at your father.'

'He wasn't very good, was he?'

'Well, no. But it's hard learning late in life.'

They were on the long hill down now, the afternoon sun directly in Julia's eyes. She pulled down the visor. 'It was good fun, wasn't it?'

Caroline frowned. 'It was lovely. Yes, it was.'

'When did the Fords move in? It was after that.'

Caroline hesitated. 'Yes. I don't remember exactly.'

'And then I went to Cranbrooke in the autumn?'

'Yes, but you wanted to go,' Caroline reminded her. 'Why?'

'I was just trying to remember when I left East Welham Primary and went to Cranbrooke.'

They were already coming over the hill into the village and Julia had to pull over to allow a Land Rover to pass. Caroline was looking out of the side window and they drove the last few hundred yards in silence.

When they got home, Leslie Rouse was waiting by the front door. She was dressed in unfashionable blue trousers with an elastic waist, which exaggerated her plumpness. She gave both of them a wry smile as they approached the front door. 'Cynthia Walker phoned me this morning,' she told Caroline, 'to say that *you* had promised her she would be running the fête next year and taking over the cake stall. I told her you'd promised me the same.'

Leslie and her mother grinned at the shared joke, and Julia found herself thinking how much happier and more fun Leslie was when she was not with her husband. 'Who is Cynthia Walker?' she asked.

They walked into the kitchen. Aristotle lay on his back on the floor, inviting someone to scratch his belly.

'Cynthia Walker is a former banker,' Leslie responded. 'She has given up work to look after her young daughter, but is suffering acute management withdrawal symptoms.'

'She has made feeling slighted into an art form,' Caroline added.

'They live in Devreux cottage, between the cricket pitch and Travers the builder.'

Caroline had begun to make tea while Leslie sat opposite Julia. She had put on a pair of square, clear plastic glasses to glance over some papers she had brought with her.

There was a knock at the door. Henrietta de la Rue came in, looking harassed and apologizing for being late. She was followed a few seconds later by a tall, thin, beautiful woman with long, wavy dark hair. Julia was introduced to Cynthia Walker.

Julia thought she looked like Sarah Ford. Then, on closer inspection, she realized the resemblance was fleeting: Cynthia's hair was almost identical, but she was taller and her face, while well formed, was narrower, with a mean set to the mouth. She had none of Sarah Ford's vivacity or voluptuousness. Alongside her was the little girl with curly dark hair and red wellington boots – though it was hardly the weather for these – whom Julia had seen yesterday, emerging from the common with her father.

'Say hello, Sarah,' Cynthia Walker said.

'Hello,' the little girl said shyly, hiding behind her mother's leg.

Hattie Travers, the builder's wife, came into the kitchen wearing a dirty white T-shirt over ample breasts. She was with another large woman whom Julia did not recognize and both were greeted warmly by Cynthia, who suggested they all went out to the terrace.

Julia picked up the tin of biscuits and followed them out. As she emerged, Cynthia, who had her back to the door, was saying, 'I don't how he could ever have stayed . . .' As she saw Julia her voice trailed off.

Julia put down the biscuits in front of Hattie Travers. 'The tea will be a minute,' she said, and went back inside.

Just as she had with Doberman, Julia had spent one university holiday working for Travers, doing his books, and for some reason Hattie had viewed her with suspicion from the start, perhaps suspecting her husband of having designs on his young employee. Julia did not like either of them: they were aggressive, money-conscious and bordering on dishonest.

Julia brought out the sugar, milk and plates.

Hattie's friend had short dark hair and wore a tatty blue outdoor jacket, despite the warmth of the day. The pair were less well dressed than Cynthia Walker, but Julia could see that the three instinctively felt comfortable together. It was probably, she thought, a question of class, and she could see that, for all her smart clothes and neat face, Cynthia Walker had not been educated at a private school and this was at the heart of her resentment of the village establishment. It was something indefinable in the way she had held herself and responded to Caroline, Leslie and Julia.

Or was she reading too much into this? Julia wondered. Her job sometimes gave her a tendency to over-analysis.

'What would you like to drink, Sarah?' Cynthia asked, as if Julia were a waitress.

The little girl did not reply. Julia moved closer. 'Would you like some apple juice?' she asked softly.

The child – Julia could not use her name, Sarah – looked at her. She had big green eyes. Her face was narrow, like her mother's, her hair neatly cut and her clothes clean and creaseless. She had a white notebook in front of her and a pencil in her hand. 'Yes, please,' she said.

Cynthia gave a satisfied nod, and Julia went inside to get the juice. When she brought it out, the little girl looked up, smiled and said, 'Thank you.'

Julia meant to turn away, but found herself hesitating. 'What are you drawing?' she asked. The three other women were watching her.

'Shapes.'

'They're very neat.'

'Thank you,' the little girl said again. She had a shy, singsong voice.

'Are you at school?'

'She goes to East Welham Primary in September,' Cynthia said.

The child did not respond. She was sitting on the edge of the chair, swinging her feet, but still managing to draw the shapes. She was doing triangles and circles alternately over and over again, overlapping them.

'Is Mrs Simpson still in charge?' Julia asked, deliberately directing the enquiry to the little girl and not to her mother.

'Yes,' Cynthia said. She turned to her friends. 'Bit laid-back for my taste.'

'You'll like her,' Julia said, thinking of how little the kind, gentle, observant Mrs Simpson and the brash, pushy, *nouveau riche* Cynthia Walker would have in common. She went back into the house and upstairs to her room.

Alice had only begun at East Welham Primary shortly before she died. It was hard not to think of the future that she had been denied. Alice, like Julia before her, had liked Mrs Simpson.

For a time, Julia sat at her desk, but then she was drawn to the spare room at the front, with its view of the terrace. The window was open – her mother was airing the house – and she could hear the conversation drifting up from below. Cynthia Walker was talking about the need to 'modernize' the village fête, bring in new attractions and leave aside all the old 'rubbish' that people had got too used to. She said she accepted it was not going to happen this year, but next year had to be different. Julia could see why the village old guard found the woman vexatious.

She moved closer to the window. The little girl had her chair pulled up close to the table and her head was bent. The apple juice stood untouched beside her and she was still drawing methodically. Julia saw that her own mother and Leslie Rouse were staring at the child, apparently ignoring what the village newcomer was proposing. Henrietta de la Rue was looking out towards the common.

Of course, Julia thought, Cynthia Walker, Hattie Travers and the other woman had all moved here since 1982 so . . . they were of the village, but could never really be part of it.

She found that she had been tugging so hard at her jeans that her fingertips were sore. She forced herself to take a step back.

Julia was drying her hair when she heard her mother shout, 'Supper!' She wound the lead around the hair-dryer and returned it to Caroline's room at the far end of the corridor, placing it in the middle of the new white bedspread. She paused by the chest of drawers, stooping to look at the photograph of her parents on their wedding day. They were undeniably a handsome pair,

Mitchell resplendent in his uniform and Caroline in a beautiful, understated, long white dress.

There was a folder in front of the picture with 'Havilland Memorial Trust' written on the front and, on top, a letter with the names of the trustees printed in red ink in the right-hand corner – Caroline Havilland, Jasper de la Rue and Lieutenant Colonel Alan Ford: 'Dear Mr Marks, Thank you for your letter dated 12 April. We have since agreed to raise our annual target to twenty-five thousand pounds. If, as you have indicated, you agree to the same twenty per cent subsidy, we believe this should provide sufficient funds for another two scholarships at Cranbrooke.'

Julia walked into the kitchen just as her mother was taking something from the oven.

'I hope you're in the mood for fish pie.'

'I'm in the mood for any home cooking.'

Caroline put the dish in the middle of the table. 'There's some wine in the fridge if you want to get it.'

There were two bottles on the shelf and Julia selected then opened a New Zealand sauvignon blanc. 'You're a great one for new-world wines, aren't you?' she asked.

'There are times,' Caroline said, 'when any wine will do.'

Julia filled the glasses already out on the table, then sat down and watched while her mother put a large helping of the pie and some peas on her plate. Suddenly she felt hungry.

'I saw the thing about the trust.'

'Yes. I meant to say to you. We've decided to try and bring in new money, rather than just relying on Jasper's donation, so we should be able to provide two more scholarships.'

'How are you going to get the cash?'

Caroline examined her plate. 'Well, various ways. Jasper has generously offered another donation, which we've resisted so far. We're opening our gardens to the public in July for a day, which will bring a little. I donated the money from my paintings. We have some other small projects, but otherwise we'll look for donations from local firms.'

Julia tried to think of something she could offer to do. She picked up one of the wooden grinders and began to twist it.

'Don't they have salt in Beijing?'

'It's delicious,' Julia said, 'but it needs salt.'

She leant back in her chair. The kitchen window was open and there was a light breeze, the sun sinking over the common, a fading blue sky shot through with orange and a hint of red. 'I was thinking again,' she said, 'of Dad skiing.'

This time, Caroline didn't smile.

'Do you remember we used to meet up at that round-domed restaurant at the top of the run – the White Lady? You used to walk up and Dad and I would fight on the T-bar and then we'd have hot chocolate out in the sun.'

'Yes. I do. But what has prompted this sudden trip down Memory Lane?'

Julia looked down at her food. 'Dad was so relaxed. It was a good time. He'd just been promoted to head the battalion, hadn't he?'

'Yes.'

'Were you happy then?'

Caroline frowned. 'Of course. Weren't you?'

'Yes, I was.'

'Then what's made you think of it?'

'Of what?'

Caroline was studying her. 'Well, why are you asking if your father and I were happy then?'

Julia shrugged. 'Just . . . It's just that sometimes he was a bit moody and withdrawn.'

'He was a man, Julia, not an angel.'

'But you were always happy?'

'No, not from noon until night every day. Your father wasn't always an easy man to live with, but that didn't stop me loving him.'

Julia pushed the remainder of the food around the plate with her fork. 'Why was he so unrelaxed sometimes?'

'Why is anyone? Stresses. External or self-imposed. He carried his own demons – your grandfather and his alcoholism. He wanted everything to be right so much that sometimes he didn't find it easy to cope when it wasn't. But he was a good man.' Caroline smiled at her. 'And he loved you.' She got up, picked up the plates and stacked them in the dishwasher, then went into the larder.

'Wasn't it odd for Alan when he moved in next door?' Julia asked, as Caroline came back with a pear tart. 'I mean, I'd hate to live so close to my CO.'

Caroline was frowning again. 'I think there was a mutual agreement to steer clear of each other to begin with, but it settled into its natural rhythm. It helped that you and Alice were friends.'

'And Sarah and Dad.'

'Yes.'

'Did you like her?'

Caroline looked at her. 'This really is the third degree.'

'It's just coming home after all this time.'

'It's not been *that* long.'

Julia watched as her mother cut two pieces of the tart then pushed the cream towards her. 'Feels like it,' she said.

Caroline refilled their glasses.

'I sometimes felt nobody liked Sarah,' Julia said.

'Well, she wasn't my type,' Caroline said, thoughtfully, 'but only, I think, because she chose not to be. A part of her wanted to be involved and a part thought we were all beneath her in some way.'

'I didn't think you liked her.'

'No, that's not true. She could be very charming when she chose. Your father was one for trying to set people on the right track.' Caroline smiled again, this time with less conviction. 'He should have been a priest, really. And Sarah was certainly a lost sheep.'

Julia ate the last mouthful of her dessert. 'I still miss Alice sometimes,' she said quietly.

'Poor Alice. I think everyone does.'

'Dad really loved her, didn't he?'

Caroline didn't answer, and this time when they'd finished it was Julia's turn to stack the plates. The last of the sun had been almost chased from the sky now and the common was shrouded in darkness.

Julia watched the headlines on *News at Ten*, but there was no reference to an appeal by the Welham Common murderer. She watched until the break, but most of the news was political and she wasn't concentrating.

Caroline came in just as she was leaning forward to switch it off. 'What's been happening?'

'Nothing.' She leant forward to give her mother a kiss and a brief hug. 'Good night, Mum.'

Julia was lying on the floor of her bedroom, trying to fit all the family of dolls into the wooden car her father had made.

She heard him coming down the corridor and turned her head as he came in.

'Evening, champ.' He smiled at her. 'Hard day at the coal-face?'

'I've been dressing the dolls.'

'Of course you have. Do you want a walk?'

Julia got to her feet.

'Give me a second and I'll take the fatigues off – get Socrates' lead.' He stepped away, then came back, his head around the door. 'Mum's stuck into the garden, so it's just us.'

Julia went down the stairs and took the lead from the hook behind the front door, calling for Socrates, who ran out of the kitchen at the sound of his name, scurrying around her feet until she opened the door and let him out.

And then they were on the common, the grass firm and springy beneath their feet as they moved from sunshine to dappled pools of shade and back again, the sound of birdsong in their ears, rabbits on the path ahead scattering into the undergrowth at their approach.

He was wearing his brown leather ankle boots and an old pair of brown corduroy trousers, his woollen army shirt replaced by a thin T-shirt that had also once been military issue, the hairs of his chest poking out of the top.

'Your school report came this morning, did Mum tell you that?'

'Yes.'

'It was very good – I'll show you when we get back. I was in a rush and, selfishly, took it to work.'

He moved closer to her, a thick forearm around her shoulder as he hugged her. 'You're a very clever girl.' He ruffled her hair, then smoothed it down with the flat of his palm. 'Chemistry's the only blind spot.'

'I know, I'm sorry.'

'I don't want you to be sorry, or in any way influenced by the fact that I'm spending my retirement fund . . .'

'You talk rubbish. Mrs Beak is really crabby and . . . you know everyone laughs so much teasing her and she sets up these experiments and then disappears into the back and somebody sabotages them . . . you know, putting in a tiny bit of sulphuric acid or something and she comes out and looks bemused and can't understand what went wrong.'

Mitchell put his arm around her again.

'I suppose I should try harder.'

'Well, don't beat yourself up about it. It's only chemistry.'

Julia had not noticed the figures ahead, perhaps because Alice was small and Sarah was standing in the shadow of a tree, watching her daughter as she played with a long stick, pretending to fish in the river that ran alongside them.

'It's the neighbours,' Mitchell said easily.

'We're fishing,' Sarah said, with a tired look on her face. 'And we've been fishing for quite some time . . .'

'All right then,' Mitchell said, clapping his hands together. 'We'll play hide and seek . . . Alice?'

Alice looked up. Her face was solemn and she did not catch Julia's eye.

'A week's pocket money says we find you both inside ten minutes, with a minute's head start.'

And then they were running, up the hill, along a narrower path, Julia holding Alice's hand and occasionally looking into her eyes. Alice rarely smiled, but did so now, as a gesture of trust in the older girl.

They hid, close to the wizened tree stump, under a thick bush, looking out towards the centre of the clearing.

Julia could feel her heart beating fast, Alice's small hand still in her own.

They waited, Julia's eyes fixed on the centre of the clearing. Daddy and Sarah would break cover any minute. They must know that the two of them had run in this direction.

They waited and watched.

Julia's heart thumped.

They waited.

The clearing was silent but for the sound of the birds, the grass ahead still.

Julia watched a rabbit jump out from the cover of the wizened tree stump, sniffing the air. Another followed, until a whole family had emerged from hiding.

She scanned the clearing again.

Where had they got to?

Thinking they might be coming from a different direction, Julia craned her neck, but behind her she could only see a low branch of the beech tree swaying in an isolated gust of wind.

Julia turned back, catching Alice's eye and seeing the nervousness there. She tried to smile, reassuringly, before turning her eyes back to the clearing.

They waited. Her heart seemed to be thumping harder in her chest.

Julia sat bolt upright, then got out of bed, the light of the moon spilling through her bedroom curtains and across the wall opposite.

Her pyjamas were damp, her whole body covered in a thin film of sweat. She wiped her forehead and sat down, with her back to the window, head bent.

CHAPTER FOUR

MAC HAD BEEN STANDING OUTSIDE THE CLASSROOM FOR TEN MINUTES when the door opened and the men came pouring out. He nodded to the last and slipped in behind them through the springloaded door. Lieutenant Colonel Callum Bland was shuffling papers together on the lectern at the front. Behind him, there was a blackboard with LOCATIONS written in white chalk at the top, then a list, which included 'car-parks, city centre street (car pick-up), train stations, sports centre, remote location (but agent must have cover story to explain presence), wood, etc.'. As he followed Mac's eyes to the words, Bland pulled the last sheet off the overhead projector and closed the file.

Bland was Julia's commanding officer and Mac towered over him, but at six foot six, he towered over most people. 'I'm sorry to bother you. I'm Captain Macintosh. I left a message . . .'

'I got it.'

Mac tried to smile. 'New arrivals?'

Bland nodded. 'You want tea?' he asked. 'Or would you prefer to get on with it here?'

Mac sat in front of one of the tables. Bland took a chair and pulled it round so that he could sit opposite.

Mac looked briefly out of the window at the well-kept corner of lawn and the line of men crossing it. This had once been home to Julia the professional woman, but would she ever come back here? The potential consequences of the incident in Beijing were coming to seem very real.

He turned back. Callum Bland had thick, wavy blond hair and a lived-in face, like a drunk. He was in uniform, but wore black ankle boots. He was not as warm or attractive a man as Mac had expected from the brief he had written about Julia.

Bland looked at Mac reprovingly. 'We could have done this on the phone.'

Mac forced another smile. 'I'm sure it can be brief.' He thought of the completed application for a transfer to the Intelligence Corps that still lay in the drawer of his desk at home and wondered if that was why he had bothered to come in person, but knew it was more than that.

'Let's make it so,' Bland said.

Mac cleared his throat. 'Your background report was comprehensive.'

Bland waited. 'And?'

'You said that you would prefer to have dealt with this in-regiment rather than getting into the business of having a charge laid.'

'Yes, I would.'

'I just wondered if you can think of anything that would mitigate the circumstances, so to speak.'

'You're seeking to mitigate? That's an unusual position for a military policeman conducting an investigation.'

'She's a bright young officer of my generation. I'm reluctant to see her cast aside.' Mac looked down at the table in front of him. 'I think we both know she's in a lot of trouble, but it's a high-profile case.' He looked up at Bland again. 'You know, first woman to win the Sword of Honour. If I can put together a com-prehensive enough argument that the circumstances were exceptional then I'm sure they would be interested in the possibility of letting her off with a warning.'

'Who is they?'

'The Ministry of Defence. There is a high level of concern because of the potential public interest, especially if she were to be discharged. The MoD, I'm sure, will want to avoid a scandal if they can.' Mac leant back in his chair, feeling suddenly more hopeful. Perhaps the way forward was to skirt Rigby and appeal to the powers above him. 'I suppose,' he went on, 'quite a lot depends on the attitude of the man she assaulted and I've yet to talk to him. I believe he's on his way back from Beijing.'

Bland sighed and his face softened. 'I admire your optimism and compassion, Captain. Perhaps if it hadn't been in an embassy it would be easier, but I'm told that the ambassador in Beijing and the FO are absolutely livid and they want her head. They're terrified the Chinese will find out that they had a gun in the embassy.'

'No shot was fired.'

'True, but there's a guard on the gate. In the scuffle Havilland pushed Jarrow into one of the windows in the lobby, breaking it. It directly overlooks the courtyard at the front. If nothing else, it's damned embarrassing.'

'I suppose I have two questions,' Mac said. 'One, what actually happened? And two, can you think of any reason why someone you held in such high regard would behave in such a . . . surprising manner?'

'The first is easy. Julia . . . Captain Havilland and her team went out to see if there was anything in an approach made to our attaché there, as I said in my note. The Chinese colonel's name was Li Queng. With the help of an asset the Americans possess, Julia was able to ascertain to her and our satisfaction that he was genuine. All he was asking was that we bear the costs of educating his son at Cambridge – he was very specific about the university – when the time came. The boy was twelve. We agreed that the British Council would ensure he was offered one of their scholarships and that we would find additional funding, if required.'

'So, what happened?'

'Well, I can't go into specifics, but you know the points of tension . . . Taiwan, new technology. It was helpful to us and to the Americans to have some accurate information on certain aspects of Chinese military deployment. The British embassy in Beijing is only a short walk from the American one and Captain Havilland was responsible for liaising with her equivalent officers there.'

Mac was taking notes and Bland waited for him to finish. 'This must remain completely confidential.'

Mac nodded.

'There are various points of tension with an agent – whether he is telling the truth, whether what he is telling you has value, and

67

whether he's going to get caught. The first our team knew of anything amiss was when the video-tape of the execution was dropped into the letterbox at the British embassy.'

'What was the argument about?'

'I don't know exactly, but I believe Jarrow and Blackstone thought Captain Havilland had pushed Li Queng too hard. In the argument, they accused her of trying to impress her superiors and, in particular, the Americans.'

'Could that be true?'

Bland sighed again, leaning back on his chair and resting one foot on his knee, the leg at a right angle. He stretched his arms above his head, clasping his hands together. 'That's a judgement I don't yet intend to make. She was ambitious, of that there is no doubt, but she was also absolutely loyal. She ran an agent in Ireland and on several occasions went right to the wire to protect his position when she felt she was being pushed too hard for information.'

'In what way?'

Bland tilted his head to one side, as if trying to find the best way to explain this. 'The intelligence community always has major flaps on. Vague "int" on an assassination threat, perhaps. Then the word comes down the line – "See what your agent can find out about the target." Suppose it's a potential threat to the Prime Minister or the Queen. Big target, big flap, *big* pressure. Fuck the agent – he can, in theory, be replaced – this is the Prime Minister we're talking about. But push too hard and the *agent* may push too hard and then he gets rumbled. That leads to a termination. A careerist is always inclined to do what his superiors want. Julia was nothing like that. She'd given *her* word to *her* man. If she didn't feel it was safe, she wouldn't even brief her agent on it. That's why I sent her to Beijing.'

'So what went wrong?'

'I wish I knew.'

'Ideas? Thoughts?'

Bland's face was pensive. Mac thought he was trying to decide whether or not to confide in him.

'I knew her father a bit. I worked with him in Ireland once in the seventies for a few months. He was a big man. Too . . . bullish for my taste, but – and don't bloody quote me on this – I'd say there was a lot of pressure to excel when he was alive and I would *imagine* she felt that even more strongly once he had been killed, especially given the circumstances of his death, war hero and so on. I don't know, in retrospect, if she is a . . . *settled* personality. If everyone is a mixture of sometimes contradictory forces, most have achieved a balance. That's what allows them to know who they are and what they want. I don't think she has achieved that balance. That is all I think I can say.' Bland looked at his watch. 'I really must go, I've so much to do. Do you need more?'

Mac looked down at his notebook and shook his head, but before he could thank him, Bland was marching away, the class-room door emitting a hiss as an electronic lever pushed it shut behind him.

An hour and twenty minutes later Mac's old Ford Fiesta wheezed into the car-park at Woolwich.

Thoughts in the car had not led anywhere. Julia had never talked about her ambition in Norway but, then, she had never needed to. It was there. It was obvious. Everyone had known she would be the first woman to win the Sword of Honour yet he had never discerned any sign of resentment or heard accusations of political correctness from those around her.

The door of the Fiesta didn't lock. The driving seat was bent and broken, which was why it was uncomfortable, but having paid his mother five thousand pounds for it – about five thousand times what it was worth – Mac was not going to be able to afford anything else for a while. It had been the only way he could persuade his mother to accept any money from him.

Inside, Rigby's office was dark, but Corporal Wellar was there. Unlike Sanderson, Wellar had no family so was always hanging around. Rigby didn't trust him with any responsibility.

'How's it going?' Wellar asked.

'Fine.' Mac never meant to be terse with Wellar.

'Did you finish with the Carpenter file?'

Mac frowned.

'The tit-rubbing.'

'That's not very politically correct, Wellar.'

'What did you do with the file, sir?'

'It's on Rigby's desk.'

Mac sat down and took Julia's file out of his satchel. He flicked open the front cover and once again Julia stared out at him. He picked up the phone and dialled her mother's number, which he knew by heart. It was engaged. He pulled the keyboard off the top of the screen and logged on. Wellar offered to get him a coffee, but he said no.

Mac had not yet placed a check search in 'Investigations and Charges', which was a procedural oversight. He called up the search engine and typed in 'Havilland, Captain, Julia', before hitting the return button.

The screen went from white to blue, the word SEARCHING flashing in the middle of it.

The system was slow. He put the end of a pencil in his mouth.

The screen read: 'Entry found (1).' It turned white again as the listing came up. 'No exact match. Havilland, Colonel Mitchell (1).'

Mac hit the return key again to pull up this entry: 'File 66743/B,' it read, 'Havilland, Lieutenant Colonel, Mitchell. Investigation into death. No discrepancies found, save for informant. No further action due to informant's psychiatric condition. Current battalion CO informed official complaint made and investigated. No action to be taken.'

This was a summary. The bottom line asked him whether he wished to call up the full file, so he moved the cursor to cover 'Y' for yes and hit the return key once more.

The screen turned back to blue while the computer searched for the full file. After a few seconds, the instruction bar in the middle said: 'Enter access code E1A.' Mac frowned. He'd never before needed an access code. He stared at the screen and the words ACCESS DENIED flashed at him. He sat back, putting his arms above his head, stretching again and thinking. Julia's father's death had been the result of one of the few genuine, undisputed acts of heroism that the modern army had produced.

He tried to think of a way to gain access to the file. Asking Rigby seemed the obvious step, but he wasn't here, so he returned to the screen containing the brief summary and pressed the print key.

Rigby came in. Mac realized he was staring into space. 'Time on your hands?' Rigby asked, as he passed.

Mac didn't bother to smile. He followed Rigby into his office, glancing at the page in his hand and at the words 'discrepancies' and 'informant'. He wondered what discrepancies and which informant.

Rigby sat down heavily. He had a picture of his wife and two sons on the desk beside him – a portly woman with curly blond hair and two equally rotund dark-haired children. Mac wondered if Rigby's wife knew about the occasional games of 'badminton' with Sheila in the Stakis Hotel in Woolwich, or about his devotion to the bottle of whisky in the bottom of the desk.

Mac handed him the sheet. 'I've never heard of access codes,' he said.

'You've never needed to.'

'Can I have a look at that file? Can I get the access code?'

'What's the relevance?' Rigby looked suddenly shifty.

'You said it earlier. Sensitive case. Sword of Honour. Father died a hero, danger of negative press. Just want to look at anything that might be relevant.'

'Give me ten.'

Mac turned to go. Rigby was stalling.

'Oh, and, Macintosh,' Mac stopped in the doorway, 'it's a simple case. She doesn't dispute anything, so check with her that she hasn't changed her tune, then talk to the CO to see if there's anything else to take into account, then straight in here for a proper briefing. I'll get Jones down from the MoD.'

'Yes, sir.'

'Anything to tell me so far?'

'Not yet.'

Mac walked to the end, passing Sheila's desk, before pushing through the swing doors. Sheila was a thirty-seven-year-old divorcee who dieted religiously and made herself available. Mac wondered if Rigby knew she occasionally made herself available to Sanderson as well.

He washed his hands, looking into the fractured mirror. He thought he was beginning to look older than his years, his face lined and leathery, as his father's had been.

He walked slowly back into the office.

Rigby's office door was flung open. He marched over. 'Forget about that file,' he said. 'Not relevant.'

'Not relevant, sir?'

Rigby nodded. 'Yes, that's right. The file on Havilland senior, not relevant. Forget about it.'

'With respect, Major Rigby, isn't it for us to decide what is relevant?'

'Not in this case.'

'But, Major Rigby, sir . . .'

'Captain Macintosh.' Rigby's face was flushed. 'I say it's not relevant so it's not relevant. Is that clear?'

'Yes, sir. Very.'

Rigby turned, then thought better of it. He was constrained by Wellar's presence. 'Come into my office,' he ordered Mac quietly.

Mac shut the door behind him as he entered. He had never seen Rigby so agitated.

'Think you're better than me, is that it, Macintosh?'

'No, sir.'

'Don't you fucking "no, sir" me, you insolent bastard.' Rigby gestured at the rest of the room with his open palm. 'Lording it over the rest of us just because your mother was stupid enough to get you a university degree.'

'I don't think my mother has ever been to a university, sir.'

Rigby's face was cold. 'If you're not careful, Captain Macintosh, I am going to shit on you and your precious career from a very great height. I'm told you want to transfer to the Intelligence Corps. Well, you can bloody forget that for a start. Military Police not good enough for you?'

'No, sir.'

Rigby moved behind his desk. 'I can see that's why you wanted this case, so that you can go ingratiating yourself with all those limp-wristed faggots down at Ashford—'

'I don't think homosexuality is a prerequisite of intelligence work, sir.'

'I wouldn't be so sure.'

'Well, I'm certainly willing to give it a try.'

'I warn you, Macintosh,' Rigby told him.

'Warn me of what, sir?'

Rigby glowered at him. 'This is a simple case.'

'And what if it's not?'

'It's a simple case and you will complete it quickly and pass it to your superiors for a decision to be taken.'

'I understand, sir.' Mac turned to go, but stopped in the doorway. 'You seem vexed, sir. Perhaps a game of badminton would be in order?'

Rigby flushed. Mac walked out.

*

72

Mac waited until Rigby had stormed out of the office before going down the staircase to the square outside. Most of the cars had gone, except those on the far side parked in front of the lecture hall, and to his right the evening sun gave the red-brick administration building a mellow warmth, its white-domed clock-tower starkly beautiful against a clear blue sky. It was a balmy evening and Mac slipped off his jacket as he walked into Registry at the far end of the block.

There was no one at the counter, but a sign above the desk warned, 'Do not remove any file without authorization.' Another added, 'Bring files back!' A large poster listed names and files under the heading 'Sin Bin'. Mac's name appeared twice and he knew that both files were still in the drawer of his desk.

There was a cool breeze coming from a window open above the computer at the back, which made the room smell less fusty than usual. To Mac's right, tall metal storage shelves on rollers ran the length of the room. He heard the hiss of the door behind him and turned. 'Hello, Maurice.'

'Working late again.'

Mac looked at his watch. 'Not too bad.'

Maurice retreated behind the counter. He had greasy dark hair, thick black spectacles and long thin white fingers. He reminded Mac of a chemistry teacher from school, so much so that he would almost have sworn the two men were twins. He did everything behind this counter with exaggerated precision.

'File six, six, seven, forty-three slash B, please,' Mac said.

Maurice picked up a Biro and wrote this down, then walked to the far end of the room without the piece of paper. He bent to turn the wheel on one of the shelves, rolling it back to allow himself access. As he watched, Mac thought that Maurice was older than he looked. Past retirement age, probably, but indispensable due to the arcane nature of the system he and his colleagues had invented.

Maurice shuffled back towards him, looking down at an open folder. 'Not here,' he said.

'Who has it?'

Maurice was back behind the counter. 'Classification Red.'

'I thought all files in here were blue.'

'Almost all.'

'That's why it asks for an access code on the computer.'

'Correct.'

'So who has it?'

Maurice shook his head dolefully. 'Classification Red,' he said.

Mac smiled. 'All right, Maurice, you old bugger, who's got it?'

'You've not got clearance.'

'Well, who has?'

'I can't tell you that either.'

Mac raised his hands, attempting to be genial in defeat. Maurice pushed his glasses to the bridge of his nose. 'The hard copy of the file was lodged here for the first time by Rigby on 11 February 1996. It was taken out by Rigby on 12 February 1996 and has not been returned.' Maurice pointed a long finger at him. 'And it's only 'cos it's you. Don't tell a soul.'

'Thank you, Maurice.'

That night, when Mac walked into his flat on Battersea Rise in south-west London, there was a message on the answering-machine from Rigby, tersely informing him that the two sergeants from Beijing would be arriving at nine o'clock the following morning on flight BA 771.

Mac's flat was small and cold in winter but, being on the top floor, it was bright at this time of the year. He liked sitting by the window and taking in the last of the light. If you leant out, you could just see the edge of Clapham Common.

It was nine o'clock and Mac had stopped at Domino's on the way for a pizza, which he now put on a plate. He took a Budweiser from the fridge and sat in the armchair by the window. The flat had only one bedroom and he lived alone. He liked it that way. He had ordered pepperoni, which was cold now but he couldn't be bothered to reheat it. He had meant to go to the gym on his way home, but it had got too late and he didn't need to exercise to stay in shape.

He poured the beer into a glass and drank, putting his feet up on the coffee-table and pulling the plate to his lap. He ate mechanically, his mind not on the food, then got up and chucked the rest of the pizza into the bin, before taking the address book from his satchel, locating and dialling Professor Malcolm's number.

'Professor Malcolm.'

'Yes.'

'It's Mac . . . Julia's friend. We met at the Sandhurst passing-out parade.'

'Mac. Yes, of course. How are you?'

'I'm pretty good. How's retirement? Julia said you were going to retire.'

'Well, yes, but . . . She was here today, as a matter of fact. Did you know she was back from China?'

Mac felt unaccountably irritated. Julia's relationship with Professor Malcolm was another part of her that was inexplicable.

'Yes,' Mac said. 'There has been an . . . incident, a bad one, and I find myself as the investigating officer.'

'Investigating Julia?'

'Yes. It's quite serious. She's a high-profile individual so they'll be lenient if they can be, I think, but I need to find some mitigating circumstances.'

There was silence.

'I'm not sure how I could help, if that is what you're seeking,' Professor Malcolm said.

'It would be easier to discuss it face to face.'

Professor Malcolm hesitated. 'All right. I suppose so. From tomorrow night I will be staying in West Welham, at the Rose and Crown. If you want me, you can find me there.'

Mac wanted to ask what Professor Malcolm was doing in West Welham, but didn't get the chance. There was only a buzz in his ear. He replaced the receiver and returned to the window and his beer. The sky outside was losing the last of the light, silver clouds shredded by the encroaching night.

Mac liked to live alone yet he was lonely. It was a contradiction he had yet to unravel.

He walked over and took out of his satchel the video from Beijing. It had come through this evening from the Chinese capital in a diplomatic bag. He put it into the player and sat on the leather sofa opposite the television with the remote control in his hand. The film was grainy, as if shot on an amateur video camera, and depicted a dusty yard with a high breeze-block wall. The light was bright and two guards slouched against it in ill-fitting dirty uniforms. There was a shout in Chinese, a barked order, and the camera panned suddenly to a scruffy-looking doorway, where another guard was looking agitated. This was the one, Mac saw, who had issued the command.

There was a low scuffing sound and two more guards appeared, dragging a man between them. At first Mac thought he was dead, because he appeared lifeless, but then the camera jumped back and swung away, its operator moving to a different position. The lens lost focus and, when it recovered, the man was kneeling on the ground. He was wearing blue trousers and a white T-shirt, already covered in dust from the floor of the yard. He had no shoes. The two guards were beside him and, as he looked towards the camera, he was crying silently and shaking violently, hands tied behind his back. The camera closed in and Mac saw the terror of a man who knows he is about to die.

There was another barked order then one of the guards produced a pistol. The man was sobbing audibly now, attempting to bend his head in a gesture of supplication. Then there was a dark explosion from the front of the man's head and the crack of the pistol. His body slumped forward, trussed hands pointing into the air. The camera closed in on the dark patch in the dust, already apparently drying in the sun. It tried to find his face, but Mac pressed the stop button. 'Shit,' he said, under his breath.

Julia's legs hurt and she could feel the cramp in her calves, but she dared not move, scanning the clearing, believing they must find them soon. Alice's hand was still in her own, the little girl's eyes resting upon her face, looking for a lead.

Julia did not know what to do. It had been at least forty minutes since they'd run to hide and it had never taken her father this long to find her.

Her head hurt.

She scanned the clearing from right to left. She tried to move, but could not. She was trapped again and began to panic, her heart beating faster, the sweat gathering on her forehead.

What were they doing to him?

Why was she not free to help him?

'Hah!'

Feeling his hand on her leg, Julia turned. He released her and offered her and Alice a hand each as they ducked out from under the bush. 'To find someone, you look for the points of natural cover,' he said, smiling at them. He did not seem to notice that she was soaked in sweat and she dared not draw attention to it by wiping her forehead.

'Mum's gone home,' Mitch said to Alice, ruffling her hair. 'It's all right, we'll go back now, you just hid so well, she got bored of looking.'

Julia noticed that he had mud on the knees of his trousers. Was that from kneeling down to grab her leg just here? She could not see any mud – the bush was surrounded by long grass.

He walked away, whistling softly, putting an arm around both their shoulders and squeezing gently.

It was all right.

Everything was okay now.

CHAPTER FIVE

THE FOLLOWING MORNING JULIA WOKE UP WITH WHAT FELT LIKE A hangover, but was not alcohol-induced. Her watch told her she had been asleep for ten hours, but she did not feel rested and she got out of bed quickly, uneasy from unwelcome dreams. It was a clear day again, the sky above the de la Rues' house a vivid blue.

She listened for her mother, but there was no sound from downstairs so she assumed she must already be at the gallery. Julia tried to remember what day of the week it was. Friday, she thought.

She had a shower, then looked out of the window at the de la Rues' garden while she brushed her teeth. As from her bedroom, she could see the corner of the patio and most of the garden from here. In the middle of the lawn, there was a child's bike, with stabilizers attached to its rear. It had fallen or been pushed over and one wheel was bent backwards.

Woodpecker Lane was a good place to learn to ride because it was a cul-de-sac with only three houses – the Fords', the Havillands', then the de la Rues' at the end. Julia had been taught there, her father behind, her mother ahead. She had learnt quickly. Julia learnt everything quickly.

Perhaps Jessica was at home, with her children, as she was getting divorced, and the bike belonged to one of them, she thought.

Jessica was an only child. She was two years older than Julia and, as a teenager, had considered her neighbour painfully unfashionable and square. Jessica had smoked marijuana, dated art-school students and lost her virginity under the willow tree at the end of the garden on her fifteenth birthday.

Julia had left most of her own clothes at home while she was in Ireland and China, so she took out a clean, pressed pair of jeans – and discovered they were baggy around the waist – then found a T-shirt. She emptied the dirty clothes out of her case, carried them downstairs and dumped them in front of the washing machine. Its instructions were in German and she couldn't see how to turn it on so gave up.

She made some coffee and ate her breakfast in silence. The *Daily Telegraph* lay folded on the side and she opened it and began to turn the pages, but was unable to find any reference to Robert Pascoe's appeal. She wondered whether he would now bear any resemblance to the shy, ungainly, peculiar youth – the son of her mother's cleaner – who used to run around the village with a pack on his back and intensity in his face.

She reached up to the shelf and turned on the radio, but it was twenty past nine and she had missed the news.

Her father had always said he had got Pascoe into the regiment, and Julia wondered if he had regretted it.

After she had cleared away her bowl and cup, she went upstairs to the corridor outside her room and looked up at the entrance to the attic. The hook, as usual, was in the spare-room cupboard. It was the end of a curtain rail that her father had attached to a broomstick. Julia used it to open the hatch, then pull down the ladder.

She climbed up it and emerged into the light, the window to her left making it less gloomy than the corridor below. It was tidier than she remembered, with fewer boxes. Her footsteps sounded loud as she crossed the floor to the Velux window ahead.

This was the best view in the house: straight ahead, one of the de la Rues' fields sloped gently to the edge of the common with its dense wood. She could see the Ford house, too, with its garden and tennis court, and on this side of the hedge, the edge of her mother's lawn and the garden shed pushed up against the fence at the back. The shed looked old now and one or two of its planks had fallen out of place, leaving a small hole.

Julia opened the Velux. There was a cool breeze, but she was still warm enough in a T-shirt. The sound of a power-saw drifted up from the bottom of the valley. The attic was her father's place and its transformation had been his project. Ahead was a red-brick wall and, between two vertical wooden beams, a wooden workbench. At both ends he had erected a large vertical wooden board on which all the tools were hung from nails or pegs. On top of the workbench there was a vice, and by her feet, two wooden boxes with Perspex drawers containing nails and screws, neatly arranged by size.

Julia remembered listening from her room below to her father's footsteps. This way, then a long pause, then back to the window – to and fro, to and fro. Pace, pace, pace, stop. Pace, pace, pace, stop. She returned to the Velux with the same staccato tread and looked out again. What had he looked at from up here? Just the common, perhaps, a tranquil, soothing sight, as beautiful a view as southern England offered and timeless, too, since the common belonged to the National Trust, and building regulations in the village were tightly controlled to preserve its rural charm.

The other half of the attic, to her right, was storage space. A pair of her father's skis, with bindings that betrayed their age, stood against the wall at the end and next to them, pushed into the corner, was his desk, with its round-backed captain's chair. A blotter still lay on it, although the photographs that had once stood there were gone.

Julia thought of his energy and the way Alan was easier to have around. Ten years ago, that might have made her feel guilty, as if favouring one father over another, but she had grown out of the need to avoid comparison. They were both admirable, but different.

There were a lot of boxes around the desk and, closest to the Velux, her bicycle – the one she'd been taught to ride in Wood-pecker Lane – was propped up against the sloping roof. Julia knelt down and picked it up. Its handlebars were rusty and only one brake worked, with a high-pitched squeak. Caroline had probably kept it for the grandchildren.

Julia massaged the back of her neck and glanced over towards Alan's garden, to see him standing on the terrace, looking out towards the common, with his hands in his pockets. Julia wondered why he was at home and not on the base. She remembered that she had not told him about Beijing and decided that she must do so, before the army – perhaps even Mac – called to see if he could offer an explanation for her behaviour.

Julia went back down the ladder and outside the house. The back door slammed shut after her and she didn't bother to lock it. There was wind now and it brought a chill to the air. She crossed her arms, nursing a few goose-pimples with her palms.

As she came through the gap in the hedge, he did not see her at first. 'Alan?'

There was anxiety in his face, and tension. 'Julia.'

She climbed the steps slowly. 'Are you all right?'

He looked at her. He was not all right. His face was startling. It was a straight throwback to the days after the murders. His eyes stared, but she did not think he really saw her. 'You'll know soon enough,' he said. 'Pascoe has just been released. They said on the radio he was expected to return home.'

Alan turned back to look out over the common, his left hand gripping his right, its thumb rubbing the joints at the base of his fingers.

'I'll leave you alone,' she said.

'No. It's okay you being here.'

'Is there anything I can do?'

He shook his head.

Julia stood about a yard from him. All the strength and optimism, the ease of manner that defined him, had gone. She edged closer. Tentatively, she put an arm on his shoulder, wanting to show her comprehension and love, but he did not respond and she did not know what to do. She massaged his neck gently, in the way he did to himself, then withdrew her hand.

'He can't come back and live here,' she said, eventually.

'No.' He nodded. 'No, of course not.'

'Everyone will feel that, I'm sure.'

He nodded again, pursing his lips.

'Perhaps he's just coming back to collect what's left of his belongings,' she suggested.

Alan's face was white.

She began to step back. 'I'll be at home. Just – just call if you need anything.'

He looked at her, confused. 'Did you want something?'

'No. It was nothing.'

*

81

At home, Caroline sat with both palms resting flat on the table. In the few minutes Julia had been out, she had arrived home and, as Julia came in, she looked up and slowly pulled her hands towards her.

'I've heard,' Julia said.

Caroline was staring at the table. 'They say on the radio his confession was altered to make it appear more conclusive. Since it was altered, his conviction is unsound, so he has been released.'

'Have you spoken to Alan?' Julia asked.

'Yes, the police called him this morning and he telephoned me at the gallery. He said he was coming home.'

'What will he do?'

'I don't know. He has only a week to go until Ireland. He could lodge on the base until then, but he won't want to be driven away by . . .' Caroline's face was ravaged by anger at this new injustice.

They heard a commotion. It sounded like chanting. Caroline stood up and they walked out. The noise was coming from the direction of the pub and Julia looked back to see if her mother was following as she crossed the lawn, but Caroline remained on the terrace.

There were perhaps twenty people gathered at the entrance to Pascoe's lane, shouting. Some held placards with big posters of Alice – the same ones that had been used at the time of her disappearance – and Julia realized they must have had some warning. She recognized a few faces – Travers and his wife were there – but most were strangers. There were cars parked alongside the pub and two television cameras filmed the protest.

Pascoe was encircled, trapped with his back to the wall of the pub, and Julia couldn't tell if he had been caught leaving his house or trying to get back into it. He had a bicycle behind him, which he was still holding with one hand.

'Where's the body?' Travers shouted. He was a big man with curly light brown hair. There were three other men around him, who looked like some of his workers. One had a shaved head and a bullet face, another a black woollen hat and a small earring. The last was smaller, with a narrow face and a black moustache. All were unshaven and dressed in workmen's clothes.

'What did you do with her, you bloody pervert?' Travers shouted. He stepped forward and spat.

Pascoe had close-cropped hair and sunken eyes, and looked

much worse than Julia remembered. He appeared bewildered and lost. He wiped the spittle from his face.

This was a monster, set loose and cornered, but he did not look like one. Julia thought of the shy, almost childlike way in which Pascoe had smiled at her as she wandered around this village. And then again, she saw in her mind's eye little Alice running, legs flailing as her shoes slipped in the mud, her face stricken with terror, her lungs constricting . . .

'Get out of here,' Travers shouted at him. 'Go on, get out.' He edged closer, but, as he did so, with his men behind him, Julia launched herself forward, shoving through the bodies until she, too, was in the middle of the little crowd.

'For Christ's sake!' She was standing next to him. She could feel her heart thumping hard from the sudden rush of adrenalin. The skinhead and the man in the black woollen hat behind Travers had moved closer. 'For Christ's sake, back off,' she said.

There was a stunned silence.

'What are you doing?' Travers asked. He looked both confused and furious.

'You didn't live here at the time. You came afterwards. You know nothing.'

Anger gave way to confusion. He had never seen her like this. She saw the incomprehension in other faces too – all those who had been friendly before as smiles were exchanged by the green or on the common or in church or in the post office. Julia could feel herself becoming an outcast so vividly it seemed almost to be happening in slow motion.

No one knew what to say.

She watched the skinhead, his face still a mask of aggression.

'What are you doing?' Travers asked again.

'He's been proven innocent.'

'But that doesn't mean he is.'

'Pascoe has been freed by the Court of Appeal.'

'The law is an ass,' Travers said. 'And we don't want him here.'

'It's not your right—'

'Where's the body?' someone shouted. 'What did you do with her?'

'For Christ's sake,' Travers said, stepping further forward.

Julia took Pascoe's arm. He wouldn't let go of the bike. He was in shock, so she gently released his fingers from the handlebars and tried to pull him towards the door of his house, but he wouldn't move and the crowd wouldn't part.

'He didn't do it, Travers,' she said quietly.

'And what makes you so bloody sure?'

'Everyone knows he didn't do it.'

Julia pushed forward, still holding Pascoe's arm, but Travers resisted, physically backed by his men. She tried to go on, but Pascoe was holding her back and Travers refusing to budge. Julia felt her temper flare, pushed again, was repulsed, then stamped hard on Travers's foot. He let out a yelp and snapped forward, his head next to hers. 'Get out of the way,' she hissed.

The skinhead lunged for her.

Julia let go of Pascoe, dropped back, took the man's arm and went with his momentum, taking him over her leg and putting him flat on his back close to the wall of the pub, so that he groaned with pain.

The other two men around Travers had moved forward, but hesitated. There was another shocked, confused, hostile silence. Julia pushed through, dragging Pascoe. He wasn't able to look for his keys, so she had to rifle his pockets. It was impossible to avoid the smell of him, which caught in her nostrils. Eventually, she found them and opened the door, without looking back.

Behind her a voice shouted, 'We'll get you. We'll fucking get you.'

She slammed the door.

'You can't hide in there for ever,' someone yelled.

Inside, it was dark, the curtains still drawn, and it smelt of decay. Julia stepped through to the kitchen and switched on the light.

The kitchen opened on to the living area, where she took Pascoe. There was little furniture in here, the room stark. Julia could not believe this was how it had been when Pascoe's mother was alive and she wondered where the rest of their possessions had gone. There was an ugly coffee-table next to the tattered arm-chair into which Pascoe slumped. She pushed it to one side and sat down opposite him, reaching for the phone. 'Did the police bring you back here?'

He nodded.

'But they went again?'

He didn't respond.

'I'm going to call them.'

He looked up with an expression of frightened resignation. Julia saw that Pascoe was still the backward young man who had shared his sweets with her sitting on a grassy bank at the de la Rues' house, overlooking the village fête. She had not changed her perspective at all, had never begun, despite his conviction, to connect him to the crimes.

He was a child, looking to her for help.

Or perhaps he was just defeated and unable any longer to ask for it.

Julia felt angry again. His destruction was also a crime.

She picked up the receiver, but there was no dialling tone, so she replaced it and took her mobile from her pocket, beginning with Directory Enquiries because she did not wish to dial 999. Then she called Cranbrooke police station and asked for the duty officer.

All the time she was talking, Julia was watching Pascoe's face. He kept his eyes down, a thirty-five-year-old man who looked closer to fifty, and she found herself recalling the day they had lost Socrates on the common and her father had gone to ask Pascoe to help in the search. The three of them had been out there until nightfall and it had been Pascoe who had found him, carrying the puppy towards her, delight in his face. He was unnaturally thin now and his skin was in terrible condition, riven with acne.

She thought about what prison must have been like for a child-murderer and felt an overwhelming sense of guilt and responsibility. The young man jogging around the village with a pack on his back had been her father's protégé.

'Are you all right, Pascoe?'

He looked up, nodded with a half-smile, then returned his eyes to his lap. He had seemed younger than her, more vulnerable even when she had been a child.

The questions she wanted to ask did not seem appropriate. He reminded her of a source – pale and frightened – and she thought of the colonel in China and of the Polaroid picture of the son he wanted to educate at Cambridge. She realized how effectively she had blocked him from her mind.

'Is there anything I can do?' she asked, forcing herself back to the present. 'Anything I can get you?'

Pascoe didn't respond, so Julia rolled up her sleeves and moved to the sink in the kitchen. There was no cleaning equipment visible, so she went out into the hall and found some in the downstairs lavatory. She began trying to scrub off some of the dust and ingrained dirt. Pascoe didn't move.

She tried to ignore the crowd, still visible through the net curtains. Occasionally there was a burst of shouting, which would peter out.

When she had finished, Julia walked back into the room, drying her hands. 'Are you sure there's nothing else I can do for you?' He looked up and smiled. Julia thought again of the two of them sitting on the bank at the village fête, then found herself recalling how she had seen him later hanging around Sarah, watching her.

She leant against the doorframe. 'If it wasn't you, Pascoe, why did you say it was?'

There was no response.

'I think you're innocent,' she said, 'and I don't understand why you haven't helped yourself.'

'It could have been me,' Pascoe said, staring at his shoes.

'But it wasn't?'

'Everyone wanted the woman.'

'Did you . . .'

'Everyone could have her, but *no one could possess her.*' He looked up, shaking his head, his eyes burning with anger, his personality metamorphosing in an instant, so that she could see that the previous meekness was nothing more than a carefully polished act.

Involuntarily, she took a step back, looking at his ugly, cropped skull. 'You've spent a long time in jail.'

He stood, eyes fixed upon her, taking a step forward. 'Yes.' He took another step. 'Yes.' Julia edged away. 'You look like her,' he said. 'Do you fuck as well, is that what you do?'

'I've never harmed you, Pascoe.'

'Your father was with her. Always around her.'

Julia did not answer.

'Do you fuck as well, is that it? Long hair and body, I bet if you lie on your back . . .' He was staring at her. 'Spunk on your face.'

'Be careful, Pascoe.'

'Be careful, is that it?'

He lunged forward, his face rigid with aggression as he stopped

86

directly in front of her. 'Do you know what they do to child-murderers in prison? Do you *know* that?'

'Don't take it out on me . . .'

'There will be *payment* . . .'

He had raised one finger towards her, his body tensed, but as he did so, they both caught sight of the movement of figures in the garden.

Julia walked to the window, then flung open the back door. The skinhead had jumped down into the long grass and the man in the black woollen hat was on top of the wall.

'You fucking prats,' she said, stepping on to the cracked paving-stones at the back. The skinhead stopped and stared at her. The man in the hat did not jump.

There was the sound of a police siren, so Julia turned her back on them, went in and slammed the door shut. Pascoe was sitting back in the chair, head down again. For a moment, she looked at him, then forced both her hands into her pockets to prevent them shaking.

CHAPTER SIX

SHE WAITED UNTIL THE POLICE HAD CLEARED AWAY THE CROWD, THEN went home, got into the Golf and drove down to Professor Malcolm's house near Chichester, trying to calm her nerves as she went.

Professor Malcolm did not seem surprised to see her.

'If you've said yes,' she said, looking beyond him to the pieces of carpet tile stretching across the floor and the lonely, eccentric life they spoke of, 'then I'd like to help.'

'Come in.'

By the time she was inside, he was heading down the corridor to the stairs at the end. 'Follow me,' he added.

On the landing above, a ladder led up to the attic. She hesitated.

'Come on, it won't kill you.'

Julia followed him up and was surprised by how much space there was. It had been half converted, with wooden floorboards and a Velux window, which made it seem like her father's den, except that it was the polar reverse. There was a desk at one end, but everything else spoke of a man whose life had known no serious attempt to impose bureaucratic order. Boxes and files were piled five deep, in places spilling over each other. In one area, the contents of several had fallen on to the floor. This was the corner in which he was inauspiciously fumbling.

'Got it.' He straightened, clutching a long, bulky green box, which he placed on another pile and opened. 'Bugger, wrong one.'

He resumed his search, moving the boxes ahead of him and restacking them. Julia glanced through the window at the sea stretching out to the horizon. The sunlight was reflected off its surface towards them.

'What are you looking for?' she asked.

'I keep,' he said, grunting as he moved a particularly heavy box, 'records of all the cases I have worked on.'

'What sort of records?'

'Witness statements . . . everything. The police copy it all for me after the case is concluded. It is part of our *quid pro quo*. I also keep my own notes, which may be useful. Anything we're missing we can get the police to chase up.'

He turned away and bent again. 'Ah. Here,' he said, lifting a long, thin green box with what looked like a drawer in it. He pulled it open and dusted off the edges. Julia could see the words 'Welham Common' written on the top.

'It will be difficult,' he said. 'There's a construct and they will resist any attempt to dismantle it.'

'Which means?'

'It means that your friends and neighbours, even your family, have spent fifteen years learning to live with this version of events and rebuilding their lives. Pascoe being released is one thing. They'll hope he will leave, or be driven away. Pascoe being innocent is quite another. If he is innocent . . . well, you can imagine. Then, someone else is guilty.'

'You said it was a review.'

He stopped and looked at her. 'Yes, but I can't rule out a certain robustness at times.'

'I suppose I would expect nothing less.'

'Unfortunately, yes.'

'Why unfortunately?'

He shrugged. 'For your sake, we shall be circumspect,' he continued.

Julia looked at him. His face was fleshy, his skin rough, as if weathered by the sea, his eyes beady. He did not invite affection.

Professor Malcolm was still stacking the other boxes, so she stepped over and closed the drawer. She dusted off the top until the words 'Welham Common' were as clear as the day they had been written.

They drove to West Welham in Julia's Golf, Professor Malcolm asking her about China and she trying to give him the details in a manner that did not spare her own reputation. Then, after a long period of silence, Julia asked, 'Can you be sure Pascoe was innocent?'

'No.'

'But . . .'

'I said the methodology was wrong, so we don't know that he was guilty. That leaves the investigation roughly where it was on the first day.' He turned so that his back was to the door. 'Why?'

Julia shrugged.

'Why do you ask?'

'He came back to the village . . . this morning.'

'And there was a mob.'

'Yes.'

'And you helped.'

Julia hesitated. 'After a fashion . . . yes.'

'Then what?'

'Then . . . well, then we were sitting inside and he seemed . . . he reminded me of the boy I remembered, shy, defeated, but when I asked him about the murders – I said he was innocent, so why did he confess, then he transformed and the shyness dropped away – I realized it was an act – and he became very aggressive, talking in abusive, sexual language, saying I reminded him of Sarah and how everyone could have her, but no one could possess her.'

'He must have known you could protect yourself.'

'I don't know. He certainly didn't . . .'

'That kind of confidence is clear, even to someone with an unbalanced mind.'

'We were interrupted.'

Professor Malcolm frowned at her.

'One of the men from the village had some of his workers with him and they were getting a bit out of hand, so I had to deal with them and that was when the police arrived.'

Professor Malcolm turned, looking out of the window at the passing hedgerows and the fields beyond.

90

'He asked me if I knew what it was like being a convicted child-murderer,' Julia said quietly, 'and said "There will be payment".'

'Payment of what or whom?'

'I don't know. That's when we were interrupted.'

As Julia pulled into the car-park at the Rose and Crown, she remembered dimly that it was possible to rent rooms at the pub: some people had stayed there for Jessica de la Rue's wedding seven or eight years ago.

A police car was parked in the entrance to Pascoe's lane. The crowd had dispersed.

'Wait here a minute,' Professor Malcolm said.

'Why?'

'I'm trying to spare your reputation. I don't want us to look as if we're checking in together.'

'We could tell Doberman what you're doing.'

'Who's Doberman?'

'The landlord.'

Professor Malcolm shook his head. 'There's no need to alert people. I don't want to be stoned on my first day.'

As he got out, Julia looked at her watch. It was twelve o'clock. She wound down the window and closed her eyes against the bright sun.

After about five minutes, Professor Malcolm appeared at the top of the fire exit above where Julia had parked. He had put on a khaki jacket earlier and his forehead gleamed with sweat. 'Not exactly the Ritz,' he said.

Julia got out of the car, picked up the box carefully and followed him. The room was at the end of the corridor at the top and it was bigger than she had imagined, with a sloping roof, a narrow single bed and a table with a leather chair beside it. Ahead, a large desk was pushed into the alcove beneath a small window. She put down the box and looked out. From here, she could see up to the top of the ridge behind and down over the rear of the former council houses in the lane beside the pub. There were three in all: two neatly kept and then Pascoe's at the end, with knee-high grass in the back garden. There were no lights on inside his house and Julia could see no sign of the protesters.

'Just give me a moment,' he said. 'If Pascoe is still here, then we should talk to him now.'

Julia stayed where she was, assuming Professor Malcolm had

gone to speak to the police. She eyed the box, but made no move to examine its contents.

Professor Malcolm returned within a few minutes, his expression troubled, as if suddenly less confident of something. 'Pascoe demanded they take him out of the village and drop him in the centre of Cranbrooke. The police . . . they can't hold him. I should think he will be back soon.'

Julia found the idea of Pascoe returning uncomfortable, recalling how he'd said she looked like Sarah. What did he mean by that?

Professor Malcolm slipped off his shoes and placed them on the floor beside the bed, with the socks tucked neatly into them. Julia caught a faint whiff.

'Did you have to do that?' she asked.

'What?'

She shook her head dismissively.

He came over and took the box to the bed, pulling up the chair next to it. 'You'll need the desk, because you'll be doing the phoning,' he said.

Julia frowned at him, but he ignored her. She had given no serious thought to what helping him would entail.

Professor Malcolm removed the drawer from the box and Julia noticed that he was still sweating, so she went to open the window.

'This is our incident room,' he said, and from the end of the drawer he took a pile of what looked like photographs. For a moment, she braced herself for pictures of the crime scene, but as he turned them over, she saw that some, at least, were of a type much more familiar – surveillance prints.

He took a ball of Blu-tack from his jacket pocket. First, in the centre of the wall, he put up the picture of Alice. Julia experienced no emotional response and understood that it was because of the professional context in which Professor Malcolm had placed it. This was like her work: surveillance prints and the psychological study of people she had not yet met.

For now, Alice was a stranger.

It occurred to her that in fact this was what she had been seeking all along: the placement of everything that was personally important in a professional situation with which she felt at ease and over which she could exert control.

Above the little girl, he put a photograph of Sarah. Julia

recognized it as one that had been used on posters printed at the time, calling for anyone who had seen this woman walking with her daughter in the minutes before the murders to come forward.

'First, these two,' he said. He looked at them for a few moments. 'Sarah is very attractive. Provocative.'

Julia studied the knowing smile, the casual turn at the corner of the mouth and the way it emphasized the curve of her cheeks. With her long, jet-black hair, Sarah reminded her in this picture of Ali McGraw in *Love Story*.

'I never met Sarah,' he said, 'but I can see she is sexy. Her smile is knowing, ironic, *amused*.' He turned to her. 'Was she fully aware of her beauty and the effect she had on men, or was there a naïvety and innocence that does not come across in this photograph?'

Julia shook her head. 'No, your first analysis was correct. She knew exactly what effect she had on men and enjoyed it.'

He looked at the picture some more. 'She has here, to me,' he went on, 'the kind of quality that Marilyn Monroe exudes in photographs. A you-can-*fuck*-me aura, except that with Sarah it seems more calculated and amused, less unconscious and innocent.'

'I doubt Marilyn was as innocent as she appeared, but I never met her. With Sarah, you certainly did feel it was calculated.'

'At least *you* did.'

He was looking at her. She did not comprehend the point he was trying to make.

Professor Malcolm lifted up a crudely drawn map of the common and the village and placed it next to the pictures of Sarah and Alice. Then he put the rest of the photographs in a circle. 'People who knew Sarah well, or had the most to do with her,' he explained.

Julia looked at the images, but said nothing.

Professor Malcolm took a pencil from his pocket and pointed to where a cross had been marked on the map of the common. 'Scene of crime,' he said. He traced his finger back. 'At the time the crime was being committed, we know that three people were on the common. You . . .' he marked another cross '. . . walking down from the village green. An old woman here . . .' he marked a third cross at the far end, near where the disused well was located '. . . who said that, at about the time or shortly after the murder

93

was committed, she saw a man in a black leather jacket with long hair hurrying past her. She claimed he looked agitated.'

Professor Malcolm turned to face her. 'Locating this man took up most of the investigating team's energy. We never did find him.'

'I remember the photo-fit picture.'

'You read the newspapers, of course.'

She hesitated. 'Yes. Some of the time.'

'We can rule him out. This was not,' he said, 'a crime committed by a violent stranger.' He turned back to face the map, the pencil still in his hand. 'Of course, the common *could*, in *theory*, be the kind of fantasy theatre a violent stranger might find attractive. Sarah *could* have been, in *theory*, the type of woman such a man would have chosen – beautiful, provocative, the kind he could never hope to snare for a consensual sexual act. However, too many things do not add up.

'One, if this is the theatre you have chosen for the enaction of a violent fantasy, you do not pick this spot here.' He pointed to the first cross. 'It is too close to the entrance to the common. It is on the major path and it is a Sunday, which, he will know, is the most popular day for walking here. There are always people passing and this spot is too risky.'

'Part of the appeal.'

'He doesn't want those sort of risks. Also, he stabs her only once. Once only.'

Professor Malcolm looked at her. The faint trace of his East European accent had come through again, but she knew exactly what he meant. 'No sign at all of any kind of frenzy,' he said. 'No violent, *sexually* charged frenzy.'

'Aren't you relying too much on established patterns of crime? It could be that there is something unusual here we haven't considered.'

'No.' He was ignoring her. 'I don't believe so. And third, if his fantasy is the woman and he *is* a stranger, then why bother about the little girl? She has run, but she's too young to identify him convincingly. Chasing her magnifies the risks enormously.'

Julia thought about this. 'So, someone who knew them both well?' she asked. 'That's your point. That the murderer was not a stranger at all.'

94

'Yes.' He pointed again to the cross by the well. 'Whatever the man in the leather jacket leaving the common was doing, it had nothing to do with the murders.' He shrugged. 'Perhaps the old woman felt threatened by his appearance and her description of his face merely reflected her own agitation. I've no idea. It certainly messed up the investigation.'

Julia looked at the other photographs. She knew enough about surveillance to see clearly that they had been taken from a distance, probably from the ridge above the Rose and Crown, on a long lens. Almost all the people pictured had been caught entering or leaving their homes.

'Why these photographs?' she asked, pointing to them.

'Solely for my purposes,' he said. 'I asked for them. Wanted to keep them in the sight line.'

He had put up the pictures roughly in the shape of a clock. Alan Ford was at the top. He wore a raincoat and had been photographed getting into the blue Mercedes that had been his car at the time of the murders. Or mostly Sarah's car. Julia noticed how little he had changed, though the angle of the lens here made his round face look fat and mean, which in her experience it never had been.

'Surveillance pictures,' she said, 'make everyone look like a criminal.'

'Not if you concentrate on their minds. The pictures are just to help me get my bearings.'

Professor Malcolm pointed to Alan's photograph, then leant towards the map. 'Alan is at home at the time the crime is committed. He did not accompany Sarah and Alice to church that morning and, once the service is finished, they go straight to the common, rather than coming home. We'll come to the inexplicable aspects of *that* in a second. Your mother provides Alan's alibi. She was the last to leave church and she saw him at home as she passed.'

He marked a cross over the Ford house to indicate Alan's whereabouts, then pointed to the next picture in the circle, which was of her father, her mother and herself, all, again, leaving the house in long coats. Julia thought that these pictures had probably been taken on the day of Sarah's funeral and Alice's memorial service. 'Your father leaves the church first with you,' Professor Malcolm went on. 'Your mother stays behind to talk to the vicar.

You arrive home. You go upstairs to your room. You see your father go out into the garden. A few minutes later, you come down and cannot find him. Where is he? You walk down across the field to the entrance to the common, cutting around the back of the Ford property and emerging through a gap in the hedge just by the stile at the entrance to the common. You're looking for your father and you say later you think he's just taken Socrates for a walk.' Professor Malcolm looked at her. 'Why did you choose that moment to go looking for your father?'

Julia looked at her feet. 'I don't think it's fair if this becomes about me,' she said.

Professor Malcolm looked at the photographs on the wall. 'All right. You think your father has taken Socrates for a walk and . . . you're just trying to catch him up, perhaps, but you're mistaken. In the meantime – and this is all in the matter of a few minutes – your mother has walked home from church down Woodpecker Lane, has seen Alan through the window and come into the drive of your house, where, *she* says, your father was working on the flower-bed by the hedge.' He marked a cross over her home. 'So your mother, your father are at home. You've gone to the common.' He looked at her again to see if she wished to amend any of the details. 'That's all in the statements we have. Next, the de la Rues, the village landowners. She, uptight but generous. He, patrician, gentlemanly and frayed around the edges. Too fond of whisky and young girls. *They* go home after your parents and remain there. They are each other's alibi. No corroboration.' He turned to her. 'No corroboration for any of you.'

'You've a good memory,' she said, but he ignored her.

'Pascoe. At home all the time, never goes to church, has no alibi at all. His mother is away visiting his sister.'

Julia looked at the picture of Pascoe. He was wearing a dirty grey anorak and had been caught rapidly turning his head, as if aware he was being photographed. He was tall, but he slouched, his shoulders hunched and his hands in his pockets. He looked every inch a child-molester.

'At the top of the hill, close to the neck of the valley, the Rouses. They come home from church with their two children. Adrian Rouse turns round inside the house and comes out again to walk his dog. He says that as he passes the pub he sees Pascoe entering his house in an agitated state. That is the crucial evidence, alongside the confession. And lastly Michael Haydoch, included because he was a known friend of Sarah. Lives in East Welham. No alibi.'

Julia looked at the picture of the thin, dark man with wavy hair and thick eyebrows. His picture was more tightly framed than the others and he walked with an arrogant swagger, his hands in his pockets. He was wearing a raincoat, jeans and a white T-shirt. This picture was of a better quality than the others and the image, but for the scruffiness of his clothes, would not have seemed out of place in a magazine.

He turned to her. 'Anyone else you can think of?'

'All the people you've chosen are from the regiment. Except de la Rue.'

'Yes. But their density is no surprise, given the proximity of the base. And de la Rue was also once a soldier, as you know, albeit in a different regiment. The Grenadier Guards, I think.'

This was true and seemed a remarkable fact to recall. She would have thought him guilty of prior research if she had not seen him digging out this box in the attic.

Professor Malcolm pulled over the box. 'All right, you begin at this end. We'll pass in the middle, then we'll talk when we've finished.'

She hesitated.

He made no move to coax her.

The first item at her end of the box was a brown envelope. She opened it and pulled out a bundle of A4-size black and white photographs.

They were all of the crime scene. One or two looked as if they might have been taken from a great height, but this was probably illusory. Some were from a distance, some close, so as to give, when taken together, the exact detail on the ground and a sense of context. The ones shot from above showed the victim at her most exposed, her right leg twisted awkwardly backwards and her hair trailing into the edge of the stream. The close-ups showed that Sarah's mouth was open, her face pale. They were almost porno-graphic, as if a moment of intimacy had been captured without her approval.

Julia put them all down on the desk. Professor Malcolm was studying her face. 'You must have seen the dead often,' he said.

Julia shook her head. 'I try not to make a habit of seeing

97

it. Anyway, that's not the point. That's a different kind of crime.'

'It's remarkable you can look at them.'

Julia pulled out the next envelope. This was the pathologist's report and was neatly typed. She began on the first page, but kept on reaching the end without any sense of what it was that she was reading.

'It's funny,' he said. 'A few paragraphs and everything comes back.' He stood and she noticed how his shoulders hunched when he was thinking.

He leant back against the radiator next to the alcove. 'Detectives I most respect work on what I would loosely call the concentric-circle model.'

She nodded for him to continue. He was clearly being careful not to patronize her; indeed, she could see that he was leading her, though to what end, she was less able to discern.

'As you know, it means that in a crime such as this we start with the victim – victims in this case, except that I think we've established it is the woman not the child we need to focus on. We go back to the woman's life and find out as much as we possibly can about it. Whom did she like? Whom did she hate? Whom did she see? Was she in financial trouble, having an affair? More than one affair? This research is an area of work with which I should have thought you will be familiar and comfortable.' He paused again. 'What did you think when Pascoe confessed to the murders? After all, your father died saving his life.'

Julia failed again to discern what he was driving at. 'My mother said real bravery was being able to concentrate on the fact that you were saving a life.'

He was still looking at her, as if expecting more. 'Did you ever go to the trial?' he asked. 'Did you see anyone you knew there?'

She nodded again, slowly, sticking out her bottom lip in a gesture of concentration. 'I saw Adrian Rouse. He was sitting close to the back. I saw Pascoe in the dock as well, but when I thought about it later, I mean *now*, recently, when I saw him this morning, I could see that I had never made the mental leap to regarding him as a criminal.'

All this time, Professor Malcolm had been holding a sheet of paper with the front page turned over and he now rearranged it and handed it to her. She lifted the top sheet and saw Robert

Pascoe's name and signature at the bottom. 'This is the statement they altered?' she asked.

'It's his confession,' Professor Malcolm said. 'Bullied out of him after his return from the war.'

He waited while she read. 'Notice anything?'

Julia was trying to concentrate on Pascoe's account of his 'obsession' with Sarah.

'It's hardly convincing, is it?' he went on. 'In fact, it's pathetic when you bother to think about it. The detectives' theory, once they'd shoved myself and Barnaby aside, was that he was after the little girl, but that is mentioned as an afterthought in the confession. The first part, to me, has the ring of truth. Perhaps Pascoe did have an obsession with Sarah, as he says, perhaps he had been following her, but when we get down to his admission that he killed them both and that he can no longer remember where he buried Alice's body . . . I mean, if the police were able to get a confession out of him, then they were surely able to "persuade" him to reveal what he'd done with the little girl's body.'

Julia put her hands in her pockets. She thought this had all been festering in him for a long time.

'But there is one thing about the statement,' he continued. 'It is the *only* admission I have ever heard from anyone that they had feelings for Sarah, apart from her husband.' He leant forward and tapped Sarah's picture with his pencil, the lead point touching the sardonic smile at the corner of her mouth. 'And yet this was a woman who inspired strong feelings in men.'

Julia remembered Sarah at the village fête in the summer after the Fords had moved to the village, in a see-through chiffon summer dress that gave everyone a clear view of sexy lingerie, throwing her head back and laughing as Julia's father tried to teach her how to 'toss the caber'.

'Sarah provoked,' Professor Malcolm went on, 'she *liked* to provoke, she enjoyed the power she had, and once she was gone, there must have been much to hide . . . If she had a relationship, we still can't be certain with whom, and it may indeed be more complex than that. Perhaps the pleasure for her was in the teasing, in the power . . .' He looked at her. 'What do you think?'

Julia felt overwhelmed again by hatred for Sarah. Professor Malcolm seemed about to ask her something else, thought better of it, reached for the other statement he had been examining earlier and handed it to her. She glanced over it.

'Adrian Rouse's,' she said.

'Yes. Note the date. After the war. The war breaks out three weeks into the investigation, just as Barnaby and I are removed. Alan Ford is convinced his daughter is dead and wants to get away to forget. The others have no reason not to go. None is yet a suspect. But Rouse has something crucially important to say, which, at this point, he *has still not said*. After the war, he remembers, he took the dogs for a walk, and saw Robert Pascoe standing, covered in sweat and apparently highly agitated, by his front door. Pascoe appears to be in a hurry to remove his clothes and get into the house. Rouse says later that, *before* the war, he was only ever asked about his own movements and about Sarah . . .' Professor Malcolm was looking at Julia. 'Don't you think that it might have occurred to him to tell the police what he'd seen?'

Julia was thinking of the war diary that Adrian had given her and recalling that there were few hints within it of any suspicion of Pascoe's guilt. She looked at her watch, wanting time to think. 'I'll have to go to lunch.' She saw the disappointment on his face. 'Why don't you come?'

He frowned. 'I don't think your mother will be very pleased to see me.'

'She was civil to you at the passing-out parade.'

'Yes, though bemused at my presence.'

'She'll be fine. She loves having guests. We don't need to tell her what you're doing.'

Julia's mother was polite, but no more. They stood around in the kitchen as Caroline was placing cutlery on a tray. Julia opened a bottle of white wine and poured each of them a glass.

Professor Malcolm had brought with him a brown envelope that was frayed and worn close to the top. As Julia put down the glass, she knocked it off the end of the table. It fell in such a manner that one or two of the photographs within half slid out.

Realizing that these were the scene-of-crime photographs, Julia hurried to pick them up, but it was too late. She watched her mother's face move from shock to embarrassment. 'I thought we'd eat on the patio, if that's all right,' Caroline said.

Julia followed her mother out through the dining room to the terrace, where a large Indonesian umbrella gave the table just enough shade. Her mother put down yellow cloth table mats; Julia grabbed the cutlery and began to help.

'Mum, I'm in some trouble. You've guessed as much.'

Her mother was folding napkins.

'Something went badly wrong in Beijing.'

Julia rearranged the dessert fork and spoon on the placing she had just laid.

'I have to stay at home for a while. They may have called you.' She was disconcerted that Caroline was avoiding eye-contact. 'Professor Malcolm has to conduct a review of the case here and . . . It's an academic review. Just a formality. I needed to have something to take my mind off things so I said I would help.'

Caroline's shoulders sagged.

Professor Malcolm emerged, sooner than Julia had hoped. Caroline looked up, smiled at him then walked back into the kitchen to begin bringing out the food.

She had made a cold pasta salad, a plain green salad and garlic bread. Julia brought out the wine, then went to the hall to fish her sunglasses from her bag.

They did not speak as they filled their plates. Julia had forgotten how hungry she was and began to shovel the food in. The pasta salad had sun-dried tomatoes with it, basil, bacon and olive oil, with Parmesan grated thickly on top.

'I'm sorry if I have in any way offended you, Mrs Havilland,' Professor Malcolm said. 'I have . . . tricked Julia into helping me. The review is an unavoidable consequence of Pascoe's release.' He shrugged. 'It's only a formality.'

He used the neatly folded napkin to wipe the corner of his mouth. He had finished his wine already, so Caroline leant forward to replenish it.

Julia wondered if someone had told her mother about what had happened with Pascoe this morning and whether her hostility was therefore directed more against her daughter than their guest.

'What's the point?' Caroline asked.

'Going through the motions,' the Professor replied. 'Perhaps I can ask you. What's *your* view of Pascoe's release?'

'I don't have one.'

Professor Malcolm tilted his head, a gesture Julia recognized as the closest he was able to get to charm. 'Oh, but you must.'

101

Caroline stared out towards the common. 'I think a child was murdered and a child-molester was convicted. I hope he moves away.'

'And what if he's innocent?'

'He's not.'

'Can you be sure?'

'You can never be sure, Professor.'

They continued to eat in silence, the only sound that of cutlery gently striking and scraping over china. Professor Malcolm put his knife and fork down and pushed his plate gently forward, leaning on his elbows. 'What if I told you my view was that this crime was about anger – an act of rage directed against a beautiful woman and her unfortunate daughter that Pascoe could not have committed?'

'I'd say you were not as confident of your conclusions as you pretend. And I'd say this village had been through enough.'

'On Pascoe, I am confident.'

'So this is an investigation?'

'No. Not yet.'

They had finished, so Caroline stood, without offering them any more, and took their plates. 'I remember you well, Professor, with your insinuations and innuendoes. The people of this village are good people.'

Julia looked at her mother, who had reached a level of hostility that shocked her.

'One of them wasn't,' Professor Malcolm responded.

'And they *caught* him. He confessed and was convicted in a court of law.'

'The weakest member of the community. In the end, the least able to defend himself.'

'You make it sound like the Middle Ages.'

'It always is when a child dies.'

Caroline hesitated for a moment, then took the plates inside. Julia went with her. There was a bowl of strawberries on the sideboard and her mother picked it up with some side plates and returned to the terrace, leaving Julia no time to intervene.

Caroline served them without comment and they ate in silence, all looking across to the common. Caroline turned towards the hedge and the shed in the corner. 'Are you a gardener, Professor?'

He nodded. Eagerly, Julia thought, as if wanting to make amends with this offer of neutral territory.

Caroline asked him what he would recommend putting in a new flower-bed she intended to create beside the shed.

Julia stood up and went inside to stack the dishwasher. From the kitchen, she watched as her mother began to show Professor Malcolm around the garden. They stood in front of the flower-bed by the shed for a few minutes, then moved out of sight.

Professor Malcolm came in as she switched on the machine. He apologized for not helping.

'You can't be that blunt,' Julia said. 'It's rude, not clever. This is my home.'

'Of course. Of course. Would you like me to stop? Perhaps I shouldn't have started, I mean, I can easily hand it back and they can get somebody else.' His penitence was not convincing.

'No. I don't want you to stop.'

'But less blunt?'

'Considerably less blunt. And why did you bring these?' She was pointing at the brown envelope on the table with the photographs.

'I'd like to go on to have a look at the crime scene when we're done. I'm sorry if I was offensive. I did not mean to . . . hurt your mother.' He gestured through to the living room. 'Do you have . . . do you have any photographs?'

'Of what?'

'Sarah. Alice. Anything from the months before their deaths.'

'Of course.'

He noticed the hesitation in her voice. 'Your mother is the other side of the garden. I left her with a trowel in her hand.'

Stepping over Aristotle, who lay across the doorway, fast asleep, Julia led Professor Malcolm through to the sitting room, with its low roof and wooden beams. They never spent much time here in summer, but in winter it was warm and comfortable. Her mother had acquired, or probably made, new covers for the large sofa that ran along the wall, and the curtains flapped gently in the breeze. Professor Malcolm sat in what had once been her father's chair, then changed his mind and moved to the end of the sofa, next to a large wooden box with a bouquet of flowers on top in a tall white vase.

The photograph albums were on the top shelf and Julia had to pull over a chair from her mother's desk to reach them. They were marked with gold lettering, by year. Julia took down the one marked 1981–3.

She sank into the sofa next to him and opened the cover.

'Family holiday in Scotland. Easter. My mother's parents had an estate there. My father loved walking.'

The first pages showed them all standing outside a squat, ugly Victorian building in a magnificent Highland glen. There was snow on the heather and they were wrapped up warm against the cold. Most of the pictures were of Julia and her mother, though there was a sequence of them rowing out into the lake with her grandfather.

In the next section, Caroline had clearly been behind the camera, because there were several pictures of Julia's father. They were on the beach, still wrapped up against the weather, but building sandcastles and playing hopscotch, barefoot. Her father's sandy hair was longer and thicker than she remembered it and was tugged about by the wind. In one picture, he was trying to smooth it down.

'He was a good-looking man,' Professor Malcolm said, 'and that looked like a fun holiday.'

Julia wondered if he was regretting the absence of family life. 'Yes. My father always found it hard to relax. Consequently, holidays weren't restful, but they were exciting. He was exciting to be around.' She looked up at him. 'He was a brilliant officer. A leader.'

Professor Malcolm smiled at her reassuringly.

Julia had now reached their skiing holiday in the Cairngorms, which had followed the week at her grandparents' house. There was a photograph of her father lying in a deckchair in a white turtle-neck sweater, Julia next to him, with one leg crossed over his. They were both holding mugs, squinting into the camera and laughing. She could remember her mother taking this picture.

'Good memories.' Professor Malcolm was smiling at her.

Julia nodded.

'It's good to reaffirm them.'

There were some photographs of her father in uniform, on the base, then a page of him playing rugby and one of him presenting awards at the regimental sports day. 'Dad was promoted just before the skiing trip.'

Julia handed the album to him and he squinted at it. 'Hold on a second,' he said, heaved himself from the sofa and went back out to the patio, before re-emerging through the doorway half a minute later clutching his reading glasses and twisting them in his hand, the way she remembered him doing in tutorials. He sat again and pulled the album across.

'When did the Fords move in next door?'

'Just after the skiing holiday. The removals lorry was in the drive when we arrived home.' Julia turned the pages.

'Slow down,' he said. 'There's no rush.'

'They're all very samey.'

'Well, not to me. What's this?'

'This is the summer. The village fête. My father manning "Toss the Caber". That's Sarah.'

In the picture, Sarah had thrown back her head and was laughing at something Julia's father had said. As Julia had recalled earlier, she could see the woman's underwear through her dress. The feelings to which she had been prey at the time immediately returned: she felt uncomfortable when confronted with any image of herself looking overweight and gawky.

'You've certainly changed a lot,' he said. There was a moment's silence while Professor Malcolm studied the pictures intently. 'Sarah was very beautiful,' he went on. 'I suppose any young girl would wish she was like her, that she could attract similar attention.'

Julia looked at the photograph on the opposite page of her mother and herself manning the cake stall, the pennants above them fluttering in the wind.

'I can't see Alice,' he said.

Julia flicked forward two or three pages and settled on a sequence of her father, herself and her mother in the garden with Alice. She and Alice were pictured jumping into the leaves. They were both smiling, their heads poking up out of a pile.

'Alice came through the hedge quite a lot, especially towards the end. We could hear her parents, Alan and Sarah, arguing from our garden and she would just come through and sit quietly. My father was kind to her. He seemed very . . . fond of her.'

Julia cleared her throat. 'Alice asked him that day not to move the piles of leaves he was sweeping up so that we could jump in them and he agreed. He went to get the camera.'

Julia turned the page and looked at a sequence covering Alice's fifth birthday. She was wearing a pink dress and, in most of the photographs, Sarah was standing beside her. There were no pictures of Alan, or of anyone else, as though Alice and Sarah had been the only guests. In one photograph, the two of them were bending down to blow out the candles on the cake, which was shaped like a horse. Julia recognized her own shoulder and arm in the corner of the picture.

There was a prolonged silence.

Professor Malcolm lowered his head to look closer. 'You know, I think . . .' he turned back to the pictures of Alice looking out of the leaves '. . . there is something different.' He pointed at the photograph of Alice and Sarah blowing out the candles on the cake. 'The pictures of Alice and Sarah released to the media at the time, the ones we put on the wall earlier, they predate both these sequences, don't they? Do you see that?'

Julia did not understand what he was getting at.

'Well, look. The daughter is like a mini version of the mother. They *look* alike anyway, but it's more than that. They've both had their hair cut into short bobs. Alice's clothes are more adult than you would expect in a girl of this age. The dress is pretty, but if it was on an adult, one would say it was . . . sexy. And . . .' There was another long pause. 'I think she's wearing makeup.'

Julia looked closer. 'It was her birthday.'

'Yes, but that's not applied as a joke, is it? That's *neatly* applied. And look . . .' he turned back to the sequence with the leaves '. . . here. She's wearing makeup here.'

Julia felt the nerves in her stomach. She cleared her throat and nodded.

'Did she often wear makeup?'

'Quite often, yes.'

'A five-year-old?' Professor Malcolm continued to stare at the picture. 'You know, this picture reminds me of that case in America – recent one – with that little girl beauty queen who was murdered. Do you remember it?'

'Vaguely.'

He went on studying the photograph in silence. Then, 'It's . . . it's almost as if the little girl is being consciously fashioned in her mother's image.'

Julia hadn't seen this before. Alice had always been pretty, a well-presented little girl. She had not noticed anything unusual about it at the time, or at least nothing significant. Or perhaps she had. She looked at Alice smiling into the camera and suddenly the smile and the makeup and the pink dress were making her uncomfortable.

'What kind of mother was Sarah?' he asked.

'Hopeless. Totally disinterested and utterly self-absorbed.' Julia thought about it some more. 'I remember my mother telling me once that she had tried to send a taxi to pick up Alice from her new school.'

'What sort of father was Alan?'

Julia shrugged. 'The opposite of Sarah. Attentive. Not around much. None of the fathers were. But affectionate when he was there.'

'Did he play with her . . . with you, when he was around?'

She frowned.

'I mean,' he explained, 'was he the sort of father who got down on his knees and helped dress Barbie or . . .'

She was shaking her head. 'No, I guess not. He's always been quite serious in a way. Incredibly kind, decent and thoughtful . . . but my father was more like what you're getting at. He was serious, too, but sometimes he would switch into a different mode and he would come and play with me. In public, when anyone was around, my father behaved in a certain way – quite formal, but from time to time, in private, when it was just me and him, or Alice and me and him, then he would be really on our level.' Julia tapped the page with her hand, emphasizing this point. 'For instance, the dolls' house I have upstairs, he built all the furniture for that in his workshop. In the shed – the original shed behind the garage. Alan would have gone and bought that kind of thing. Very thoughtful in that way, but it would never have occurred to him to build it.'

Professor Malcolm leant forward on the sofa. He took the photograph album from her, glanced through the rest of it, then closed it and rested both elbows on the cover. 'Is there any moving picture? Cine film, or something like that? From the same period.'

Julia hesitated. 'Yes.' She stood up. 'I had it transferred as a present for my mother.' She went to the television, knelt down and opened the box beside it. The tapes, like the photograph albums, were numbered by year, but they also had the subject matter written on them. This had been done by the company Julia had asked to do the transfer.

She put the tape for 1981–2 in the video and switched on the television. It began with the skiing holiday. The video had no sound and the tape flickered with the staccato motion of cine film.

The images were of Julia skiing, shot by her father or mother – probably her father. She was doing a snowplough down a gentle slope beneath a grey sky. There were several takes and, in between, Julia could remember going up the button lift visible in the background. Then, all of the class came down together, doing the snowplough and clutching each other so that they formed a long snake. At the bottom, they fell over.

Julia could see out of the corner of her eye that Professor Malcolm was smiling.

The cine film did not mirror the photograph album, even if they covered the same epoch, because her father generally had one camera or the other with him, but not both. After the skiing holiday, there were pictures of Julia and Alice on the common. These, too, had been shot by her father, but Julia could not see now why he had chosen to film them, since they were just walking along, obviously shy of the camera. Alice was wearing long white socks, which were visible above red wellington boots. She wore a plain blue sweater and her hair was scruffy. She was a long way from pink dresses and makeup. Julia was in jeans and a blue jacket.

Alice smiled shyly into the lens, which had moved closer to her, and Julia recalled how naughty Alice had been on occasion. She remembered painting on the drawing-room wall next door and Sarah's unrestrained fury when she had caught them in the act. That had been around this time.

Julia had been clutching the remote control and now began to fast forward. 'There's no need to rush,' Professor Malcolm said. She slowed it to normal speed.

She rubbed her forehead. The film moved on to the summer and a lunch at the de la Rues' house. The shelter at the end of the pool was the same, but this was before the wall had been built so you could see the lawn beyond. Sarah was lying flat on the ground in a yellow bikini in the sunshine. Julia could see her own mother in the background in an upright chair, but the camera stayed on Sarah before moving to the other side to shoot her from a different angle. Sarah was gesticulating at the cameraman and smiling, obviously telling him to go away. The yellow bikini emphasized how brown she was, and as she sat up, shooing him away with her hand, Julia saw that, even in this position, there was little fat around her stomach.

The camera must then have been switched off and later picked up by someone else, because the next images were of Alice on Mitchell Havilland's shoulders. He swung her around and threw her off, then she climbed on him again, scrambling up, before standing and jumping with a shriek of delight.

Julia wondered if Sarah had filmed this. Alice swam after him, climbed up, jumped. Julia was in the pool, swimming on her own. She didn't join in.

Julia pressed the fast-forward button again, then leant forward, switched off the television, took out the tape and put it back in the box.

'It's hard to see her,' Professor Malcolm said.

'Yes.'

'Such a sweet girl.'

'Yes.'

'It's so much harder seeing moving images, isn't it?'

Julia nodded.

'There's quite a lot of her, though.' He coughed. 'It's nice to have. Terrible, after the event, to look back and wish you'd shot more pictures . . . somehow harder to have nothing to remember her by.'

'I suppose so.'

'You must wish . . .' He stopped.

'Wish what?'

'The new machines . . . the video cameras are so much better because they can record voices . . . they give you a much better record of personalities. That could be . . . worth a lot.'

'Yes,' Julia said, adding another 'yes' with more emphasis as she took in what he was saying.

'Would you mind if we went back to the scene now?'

Julia didn't answer. She was thinking how much she would give to be able to see her father talking on film, as if he were still alive.

CHAPTER SEVEN

MAC WAS SITTING IN THE GRANARY RESTAURANT AT HEATHROW'S terminal three, looking at the dregs of his third black coffee. It was almost twelve, he had been here for three hours and the screen above said that the delayed flight was still not due in until one o'clock.

He pressed the redial button on his mobile phone and put it to his ear, thinking he had left it long enough.

'Is that Mrs Evans?' he asked. 'Hi, it's Captain Macintosh here again. I called earlier and I'm so sorry to bother you once more. I said I was looking for the regimental personnel files for Mitchell Havilland. Did you get anywhere with Lieutenant Colonel Ford?'

'Yes,' she said. 'But we can't give them to you.'

'But, Mrs Evans, I am—'

'We don't have them.'

There was a pause while Mac tried to work out what she meant.

'The Colonel has just returned to the base,' Mrs Evans said. 'He would like a word.'

Mac waited while she put him through. He felt unaccountably nervous.

'Mac!'

'Colonel Ford . . .'

'Alan. For goodness' sake, Mac, you're practically family.'

'Well, I'm really sorry for bothering you, it's just that—'

'Mac, we had to hand over these files to the MoD and to your

110

own investigating team, led by a Major Rigby. We did it some years ago. Not only Mitch's file, but most others as well – almost everyone serving in the battalion at the time.'

'Right. Do you think it's possible I could come down and—'

'The position, Mac, is this. After the investigation was closed, I had a number of high-level visitors and was instructed that neither I nor my colleagues were to discuss this further with anyone. So, if you'd like to get these same high-level people to pick up the phone and instruct me to go ahead, I'd be delighted to help, but I would really need that kind of authority.'

Mac considered explaining the circumstances of the call and appealing to Alan's affection for Julia, but thought better of it. He was a little embarrassed.

He ended the phone call and went to get another cup of coffee.

Mac ended up bringing the two sergeants back to the Granary restaurant, seeking out a quiet corner on the far side. He had considered something more formal, but thought that would work against him. Besides, both men looked tired and clearly wanted to get on with whatever was necessary.

Sergeant Jarrow was a strikingly good-looking man, with a broad face and unkempt blond hair that curled over the back of his collar. He was short, but lean and bulky, as if he spent much of his time in the gym. Like Mac, he wore a Drizabone.

Sergeant Blackstone was older, with a narrow face and a beaky nose. He had cropped dark hair, flecked with white, and a face that, though angular, was kindly. His manner was calm and reassuring, and Mac immediately saw his value as a source-handler.

He bought them both a coffee and came to sit opposite them. 'I'm sorry,' he said. 'You're both tired, so I'll try to keep this brief.'

Sergeant Blackstone leant forward slowly. 'We don't want any part of, or involvement in, the destruction of this woman's career,' he said.

'No.'

'She's a good girl.' Sergeant Blackstone spoke with a faint hint of a Scottish accent.

'Yes,' Mac said.

'Things just got out of hand.'

Mac looked thoughtfully at the blank pad of white paper in front of him. He had not expected the two men to be so conciliatory. 'The situation,' he said, looking from one to the other, 'is quite serious, in the sense that there are a number of other agencies involved – the Foreign Office, particularly, which is sensitive to having this sort of operation housed in an embassy anyway. If you want to help Captain Havilland, then I need to have some kind of handle on what went wrong.'

There was a long silence. Eventually Blackstone looked at Jarrow, and leant forward to Mac. A young woman had come to sit at the next-door table, so he hesitated, then said quietly, 'It's very introspective. Always on call, always waiting around, worrying about the man out there. It can get to anyone.'

'Did she get on with you?'

'Yes, but, you know, we're . . .' He glanced at Jarrow. 'It's intense. She did get a bit withdrawn.'

'Why, do you think?'

'It can get to anyone. It's like that.'

'Is there any . . .' Mac stopped for a second. 'Captain Havilland has an exemplary record, can you think why it might have got to her on this occasion?'

'It's cumulative,' Blackstone said. 'Everyone knows who her father was. And the Sword of Honour stuff. I think she feels a lot of pressure to succeed.'

'She said as much?'

Blackstone shook his head. 'You learn a lot living in such close quarters.'

'But I thought she was succeeding?' Mac said.

Blackstone shrugged. 'She felt our man might have been a plant. We held his hand okay – me and Steve – but it's not our job to assess the information. That was her and the Americans. She felt he was feeding us crap and she blamed herself.'

'But he wasn't a plant?'

'Probably not.'

The Clapham district library is about a hundred yards up the hill from the junction, past Allders and opposite the bus-stop. Mac had come here often in pursuit of background information on investigations and, as before, he bought a coffee from the café opposite on the way in – his sixth or seventh of the day.

The library itself was brightly lit and he walked through the rows of tall bookshelves to the reference section at the back, where low tables were full of people already reading newspapers and periodicals. He had to hide his coffee behind his back, because there were large signs forbidding eating or drinking.

When the woman at the counter asked how she could help, Mac had to think hard to remember when the war in which Lieutenant Colonel Mitchell Havilland had died had actually been fought. It seemed to belong to a different century. 'The *Daily Telegraph*,' he said, 'from the first six months of 1982.'

It took her a few minutes, but she came back with one small plastic box, marked '*DT*. Jan–June 1982.'

Mac went over to the microfiche in the corner and switched on the light. He had been impatient while waiting for the corporals to find out more about Havilland's death and, since military records were suddenly hard to come by, he had decided to begin with those in the public domain.

There was another machine next to him, but no one was on it. Attaching the reel was a clumsy business.

It took Mac a long time to spin through the months. Occasionally he stopped and read one of the front-page articles, to familiarize himself with aspects of the war he had forgotten, but he continued swiftly until he found the report covering the death of Lieutenant Colonel Mitch Havilland, known to regimental colleagues as Mad Mitch. Most of the front page was devoted to an article describing the long and bloody battle which had claimed his life.

Havilland had been with a small group of men on the eastern end of the mountain, holed up and unable to complete the final assault on a key ridge. Under fire, he had suddenly broken cover to pull in one of his wounded soldiers only to be shot in the back while carrying him to safety.

One of the article's sub-headings was 'Decisive act spurs men on to final assault on ridge'. There was a quote underneath this, from a Corporal Richard Claverton. 'It was insanely brave,' he had said. 'We couldn't let him down.'

> After 'Mad' Mitch Havilland's death [the report con-
> tinued], the men were inspired to break the deadlock and
> push up on to the ridge, which turned out to have been
> held by a tiny group of the enemy, armed with a single
> machine-gun. The survivors were at last able to look down

to see dawn breaking over Port Stanley and to savour their bittersweet and costly victory in this, the final battle of the war.

Mac sat back in his chair and picked up his coffee, which was still warm. Then he opened his satchel, which he had placed by his feet, and pulled out the sheet he had recovered from the printer the night before. He cast his eyes over the summary again: 'Havilland, Lieutenant Colonel Mitchell. Investigation into death. No discrepancies found, save for informant. No further action due to informant's psychiatric condition. Current battalion CO informed official complaint made and investigated. No action to be taken.'

Mad Mitch or not, Mac thought, running out under enemy fire to try to save the life of a corporal did not make any sense. It was more than mad, it was utterly foolish. He wondered how the soubriquet 'Mad' had been earned. He had always assumed it to be a term of affection.

Next to him, on the table, Mac caught sight of a copy of today's *Evening Standard*. He pulled it over, then sat again, turned away from the microfiche machine. The front-page report was about the release of the Welham murderer, Robert Pascoe, and was accompanied by a picture of the man cornered against the wall of a house. Next to him stood Julia Havilland.

Mac stared at her, then at Pascoe, who looked hounded, almost messianic, as if in the final stages of deteriorating sanity. Beside him, Julia was calm and collected and . . . and as beautiful as she always damned well was. She was leaning forward, slightly off balance, one long leg behind the other. She was obviously helping Pascoe, because her arm was on his. In the corner of the photograph, a man was shouting at them both angrily.

Mac read the report, which said that she had intervened to help Pascoe away from the crowd and into his house. It detailed who she was, whose daughter, without comment. Mac returned to the article on the microfiche and glanced through it once more. Robert Pascoe was the soldier Mitch Havilland had died saving. He wondered why he had never known this.

Mac wrote down the name in his book, though he was unlikely to forget it. He thought the media frenzy, at least, would make Pascoe easy to find. Beneath, he wrote down 'Richard Claverton. Corporal.'

Mac took back the microfiche. Behind where he had been sitting was the computer used for making searches and Mac typed in 'Falklands War'. There were many titles, but he found his eyes drawn to the two most recent books, *Excursion to Hell*, and *Green-eyed Boys*. They were about the war crimes controversy of the early nineties. His department had run at least one major investigation into allegations that enemy prisoners had been shot after surrendering. Rigby had been deeply involved and it was rumoured – Sheila had told him this – that he had been instructed by the brass to make sure the investigation did not result in prosecutions.

And, in the end, there had been none.

Mac ordered up both books and skim-read them, as well as an overall account of the war by Martin Middlebrook.

He left the library four hours later, with the *Standard* tucked under his arm and a clearer than ever sense of the horrors of battle, but no more coherent thoughts about Mitchell Havilland.

He walked in the direction of home and turned on his mobile phone, which had been switched off while he was in the library. There were three messages, all from Sheila in the office, saying Rigby wanted to know how he was getting on.

CHAPTER EIGHT

PROFESSOR MALCOLM PAUSED BY THE CROSS ON THE VILLAGE GREEN
before climbing over the stile and making his way down the path.

'Do you walk here?' he asked.

'I came yesterday.'

'For the first time?' He stopped. 'I apologize. If you'd rather
not . . .'

'No. It's fine.'

They walked on in silence.

At the point by the stream where Sarah had been murdered,
Julia nodded in response to Professor Malcolm's silent question.
He opened the envelope and pulled out the photographs, looking
through them slowly and glancing at his surroundings from time
to time. He handed some to her with raised eyebrows, expecting
her to refuse, but she took them. She also looked about her.

'In the early stages of the investigation, we were very taken
with Sarah's clothes,' he said. 'She leaves church at almost eleven
on the dot, because everyone remembers the church bell striking.
She comes straight here, on a wet day, in her Sunday best,
dragging her daughter, both in inappropriate footwear.'

'A rendezvous of some kind,' she said.

'Yes, but it's not exactly subtle, is it?' He took a few paces. 'Do
you know, we asked – I asked – so many people here about that
during the original investigation and everyone gave us the

116

impression they didn't find anything strange about this. Alan, your mother, your father, de la Rue, the Rouses – none of them found it odd or inexplicable that Sarah should *suddenly* decide to go for a walk after church with her daughter.' He was looking at her now. 'It's bizarre, isn't it?'

'What is?'

'You don't just walk out of church in your Sunday best then disappear off to the woods with your five-year-old daughter. What's odd is the way in which everyone seemed to believe it was not out of the ordinary or remarkable. It's explicable if you know she was meeting a lover, but otherwise it's not – and no one ever entertained the idea that she might have been meeting a lover, despite the evidence that she was promiscuous.'

'What do you mean?'

'No one ever said a *thing*. It was almost as if they were defending her *in absentia*, defending her reputation.'

'I can see what you're saying, but—'

'Their explanation was, generally, that Sarah was inexplicable, as if they . . . as if no one could any longer be surprised by anything she did, but I don't know if that will do.' He sighed. 'I wonder what the trigger was.'

'That morning?'

'Yes. What had brought it to a pitch that day?'

Julia shook her head.

'You don't remember anything?'

'No.'

'No arguments? No banging doors in the house next door, no . . .'

She was still shaking her head.

'We know Sarah inspired strong feelings in men, so what had happened that day that made murder an imperative for our man?'

'A quarrel?'

'No. Come on. This wasn't a lovers' meeting that went wrong because he comes with a knife. Perhaps she was breaking off the relationship, perhaps he'd learnt of another lover . . .'

Professor Malcolm pulled the pathologist's report from the envelope and placed it on top of the photographs he still had in his hand. He flicked through it. 'She is stabbed. A kitchen knife is found near by, which was clearly the murder weapon, but there are no fingerprints on it. None at all. On a *kitchen* knife.'

'It was wiped clean.'

'Yes. Presumably before the murderer even left his house. Which suggests a degree of premeditation. So was she followed here, or did someone know of the rendezvous and intercept her? *Or* was it the person she was coming to meet?'

Julia stepped towards him. 'Can I have a look at that?'

'Which?'

'The pathologist's report.'

She read it through, then did so a second time. It was making sense now, but as she looked up, Julia caught sight of someone approaching, made sure the pictures were hidden behind her back and stood aside. It was Henrietta de la Rue. She was wearing a bright blue beret and walking their Jack Russell, Fido or Fifi – something that began with F.

Henrietta smiled and slowed. Then she recognized Professor Malcolm. He did not smile at her or, apparently, sense the awkwardness. Henrietta appeared to stumble, then passed between them and smiled once more. As she walked away, she did not glance back.

Julia waited until Henrietta had rounded the corner, then looked down at the report. She tried to think of herself as an outsider and not as a daughter of the village. 'Incision under left costal margin . . . perforation of the left ventricle of the heart . . . this resulted in cardiac tamponade, due to catastrophic bleeding into the pericardial sac . . .'

'And the translation is?'

'The knife went in underneath the ribcage travelling upwards.'

Professor Malcolm was still frowning. Julia put her hand to her chest. 'Most of us place the heart here, but in reality it's a little lower. If you stab someone through the ribcage, which is what most would choose to do, you run the risk of the blade being diverted by a bone. If you do it this way, you will certainly puncture the heart, which then bleeds into the space around it. This space is . . . encircled by a non-porous membrane. The space fills up with blood and the heart can't beat any more.' Julia was trying to use her hands to illustrate this. 'Basically, if you want to be sure of killing someone, this is the way to do it. Go in under the ribcage and direct the knife upwards.'

'I'm impressed with your medical knowledge.'

'It's military knowledge. I learnt it before going to Northern

Ireland, but most military people, or medics, would understand the basics.'

'So whoever did this knew something about killing people?'

She shrugged. 'It's a coincidence, that's all.'

Julia crossed the path and climbed on to the edge of the bank. 'And another thing. If he . . .'

'Or she.'

'Yes. If he or she left here to chase Alice, then why drop the knife?'

'That's a good point,' said the Professor, slowly. 'Perhaps he or she did not actually intend to kill the child.' He came to join her on the bank. 'The answer is that I don't know.' He turned. 'Where did he hide the body?' He returned to the path. 'The whole common was searched yet there was no sign of anything. Where did he take her?'

She shook her head, momentarily distracted.

'Julia?'

'What?'

'What is it?'

'Nothing.'

He hesitated. 'All right,' he said. 'This man does not have time on his side. He stabs the woman he has come here to kill . . .'

Professor Malcolm's re-enaction of the scene was obscene.

'Then he remembers the little girl. She has not featured in his calculations and he has ignored her, but now that the moment of bloodlust has gone and Sarah lies helpless and bleeding to death beneath him, some kind of rational thought returns. What is Julia doing at this point?'

'Alice.'

He looked perplexed. 'What?'

'You said Julia.'

'Alice. Yes, what is she doing?'

'She's running.'

'Is she? Are you sure about that?' He turned full circle. 'When does Alice run? As soon as he pulls the knife from inside his jacket, or when he is stabbing Sarah, or when he has finished?'

'Does it matter?'

'To him it does. I think she must have gone by the time he has bent over Sarah to enjoy his revenge and establish that she is dead or dying. He turns. He remembers the child and sees that she has

119

gone. He begins to move after her. He must have seen her leave in one direction or another.'

'He drops the knife,' Julia said.

Professor Malcolm put his hand to his lip. 'Yes. Why does he, or she, do that?'

'Why do you always say she?'

He looked up. 'Hell hath no fury like a woman scorned. You know that. Anyway, I don't like the way criminals are always assumed to be men.' His forehead creased again. 'Maybe he didn't intend to kill the little girl. His thought process hasn't gone that far. He gives chase thinking only that he must *find* her.'

'Maybe.'

'Does he enjoy her fear when he finds her?' He looked at Julia. 'Sorry.'

'Sorry for what?'

'Sorry if it's uncomfortable.'

'Why should it be uncomfortable?'

'Okay, so he must have buried the body on the common, but how come it was never found?'

'It's possible he found a good hiding place.'

'Yes, but this was a man in a *hurry*. There are people about here, walking. It's a Sunday. He hasn't the luxury of time.'

'If he was cool, he did.'

'What do you mean?'

'If he was able to keep very calm, time may not have been a problem.'

'All right. That's possible. Unlikely, but not impossible. It still doesn't explain *where* he could have taken the body.'

He was looking at her.

'I don't know the answer to that,' she said. 'I'm sorry.'

'Let's go back a step again. You're Alice, where do you run to?'

Julia was growing tired of this game. 'I don't know.'

'Come on, try. It's important. Is there anywhere here you would think of as a hiding place?'

'Nothing immediately springs to mind.'

'Which way would you run?'

'How can you be sure Alice was capable of any rational thought at this point?'

'If your mother was being stabbed, wouldn't you run in the

direction of home – towards the village where you know you will find people who will help you?'

'We don't know the circumstances,' Julia said. 'Perhaps she was on the other side of him and therefore it was natural for her to turn and run into the forest.'

'I still don't understand why he dropped the knife. And I wish I knew how he'd killed Alice,' Professor Malcolm said, lowering his head in thought.

After a few seconds, he looked up again. 'Earlier,' he said, 'in that picture, Alice was wearing a large cross around her neck – looked like silver. Did she always wear that?'

'I don't know. Pretty much.'

'Have you got a mobile phone?'

Julia pulled it out of her pocket and handed it to him. 'What are you going to do?'

'Arrange a new search.'

'Why?'

He looked up again, frowning. 'Why not?'

Julia could feel the blood in her face. 'We did all that. There were hundreds of people searching.'

'Yes, but . . .'

'Christ, it's hopeless, you'll never find—'

'They have metal detectors that can sense the shape of an object. Is the idea of it uncomfortable?'

'No. Stop saying that.'

'What, then?'

'Well . . .' She looked at him. 'Don't be so tactless.'

'I don't understand what the problem is.'

'You don't live here,' she said.

'Neither do you.'

'It's a ghoulish reminder.'

'What is?'

'The whole thing. A search, with policemen crawling over this place. It'll take everyone right back.'

'But they never left.'

'I thought this was supposed to be a review.'

'Yes, but we've established the murderer probably wasn't Pascoe. If we wish, ultimately, to point the finger at someone else, we must have evidence. In a court of law, one must have that.' He examined the phone for a few moments. He took a step closer.

121

'I'm not going to keep apologizing. It's no way to proceed. You're going to have to decide whether your approach to this is professional or personal.'

'Surely, even *you* can see it is not quite that simple,' she said.

As she was speaking, Julia caught sight of movement out of the corner of her eye. Cynthia Walker was approaching, her little girl still wearing the same red wellington boots and Cynthia frowned as she passed – a gesture of curiosity. Professor Malcolm was looking at the phone.

Cynthia did not stop, continuing with Sarah's hand in hers. The child turned round briefly and lost her footing. Julia watched them both until they disappeared from view, then she reached into her jacket pocket for her cigarettes. She took one out and lit it. Professor Malcolm declined her offer.

She sucked the smoke deep into her lungs. This was her first cigarette since she had left Beijing and it was satisfying. 'Who are you going to call?' she asked.

'The police.'

He stared at the phone until she realized he didn't know how to use it. She took it from him. 'Give me the number.' She dialled and gave it back to him.

'DCI Weston,' he said. 'Tell him it's Malcolm . . . Weston, it's me . . . no. No, I didn't know that. What's the reason? All right . . . All right. We need something doing. The little girl was wearing a silver cross and I think we should search the common again. We need the body. It will answer a lot of questions.' He was frowning. 'I know I said . . . No, you don't have to say the case is being reopened, I'm not suggesting that . . . Well, so . . . Well, tell the media . . . All right. I'm on the common . . . How long? . . . We'll be here. By the scene. I'm sure you remember. Shout. Your voice is loud enough.'

Professor Malcolm gave her back the phone and she ended the call. 'You would have taken this case without me,' she observed.

'Not necessarily.'

'You're using me as a justification, but it's not about me, it's about you. It's your past as much as mine. You can't stand that you made a mistake.'

He didn't respond. After a few minutes, she regretted having said it. She tried a different tack. 'You decided as soon as I arrived at your house yesterday that you were going to lead me through to involvement in this.'

122

He didn't respond.

'Why?' she asked. 'It has nothing to do with helping me.'

'Most people's motives are complex, Julia.'

'Well, explain to me your own.'

He ignored her. She finished the cigarette and threw the butt into the river.

Professor Malcolm wanted to get his bearings. He led her across the stream and up the bank opposite. They stood there for a few moments, before he began clambering down the other side, beneath the forest canopy, until they were at the fence bordering the de la Rue field. They could see across to the back of her home and to those of Alan Ford and the de la Rues, which were not more than a hundred yards away. She and Alice had often climbed over their fences and run across the field. He saw something in this that she could not discern.

It was clear that they were waiting for Weston, and Julia was both impressed by the power Professor Malcolm wielded and annoyed that they were apparently going to have to hang about until the policeman appeared.

Professor Malcolm retraced his steps to the stream then walked further down the path, before once again entering the undergrowth and climbing up slowly to the big clearing in the middle of the common. Obviously he had memories of his own. The wind stirred the leaves on the tops of the trees, but the long grass was still, and Julia remembered lying on the ground here, with Alice, for hours on this kind of afternoon. She left him to it and went to rest against the wizened tree stump. The grass was dry, the ground firm. She picked up a few small stones and ground them in her hands, using them as primitive worry-beads.

Suddenly he was standing over her. 'Do you think this is about vanity on my part?'

Julia's legs were stretched out, almost touching the end of his shoes. 'No,' she said. She watched a stronger gust of wind swaying the long grass.

'The best interpretation is that it is about integrity,' she said. 'And that I respect. Mistakes hurt, but more than that, it offends your intellect to not know the answer. In that sense, it is about intellectual vanity.'

He looked at her. 'I want you to be all right.'

'I am all right.'

He ignored her hostility. 'There are so many things about this that don't make any sense,' he said.

'Like what?'

'Like what did he bury her with?'

'What do you mean?'

He turned to her again. 'Well, he didn't come down armed with a kitchen knife *and* a shovel, did he?'

Julia was finding it hard to think clearly, so she got up, said she would be back and marched away from the clearing, down the hill, rejoining the path beyond the murder scene. She walked for about ten minutes, her mind blurred by endless cross-currents of sometimes contradictory thoughts. Although her working life had been all about intense focus, she had never experienced anything like this. Of course, it was going to be impossible to separate the personal from the professional here.

On instinct, she found herself turning on to another small track that wove through what she had once called the bluebell clearings to the old well at the bottom. This was close to the far end of the common and you could just glimpse the fields beyond, though the well itself was shielded by thick gorse. Julia had to force her way through to reach it, because it was even more overgrown since her last visit. She came up to it, took a coin from her pocket and dropped it, listening to gauge how far it fell. The wooden beams were still across the middle.

The well had once belonged to a farmhouse that had since been demolished. It dated from the days before the common became National Trust property.

Julia leant against the brick surround. The sun was still high and she closed her eyes, enjoying the warmth on her face.

She could feel herself running down the path and ducking under the gorse. She could see herself tugging at Alice's hand and helping her climb down into the well, resting on the beams, while her father hunted them. Julia could feel herself squeezing Alice's hand and telling her the game was brilliant, even if she no longer believed it.

Julia opened her eyes.

Could Alice have run here?

Professor Malcolm was right. It seemed likely that she would have run in the direction of home, towards people who could offer help.

Julia wondered if Professor Malcolm knew the answers, if he was aware of where he was leading her and where they would end up. She could see how much trust she was placing in him and suddenly doubted that it was wise.

She ducked under the gorse and moved away.

Julia walked back slowly. She arrived at about the same time as Weston, a small man with a beard who had his hands pushed firmly into the pockets of a blue raincoat.

'Lionel Weston,' Professor Malcolm said. 'Julia Havilland.'

They shook hands. Professor Malcolm stood with his legs slightly apart, but towered over Weston.

'I thought about it on the way here, David,' Weston said, 'and it's an insane idea.'

'Then you need to think harder.'

'The common was thoroughly searched at the time. Looking for a small silver cross now will be like looking for a needle in a bloody haystack.'

'It's still worth doing.'

'You may think so, but I'm telling you it's a waste of my resources.' He glanced around. 'I mean look at this place. It's huge. She could be anywhere. Maybe he even stole the cross. We could search from now until Christmas, have the whole place dug up and find nothing. We don't even know that she was buried here.'

'Lionel.' Professor Malcolm had raised his hand. Julia could see that he was irritated, although she thought that the policeman, in practical terms, was correct. 'I'm going to explain some things. The two murders are quick, horribly so. Our man kills the woman. Stabs her once, *clinically*. So, the little girl had a head start of just a few seconds. I would say it's overwhelmingly likely that she was murdered within two hundred yards of her mother and buried right there. Our man was in a hurry, a big hurry. He wasn't going to go carrying a little girl's body around on his shoulder on a Sunday with hundreds of people walking on this common. But he had no spade on him – nothing to bury her with. So *what happened to the body?*'

Weston shook his head. 'You're the theorist.'

'It's not a matter of theory. We need to know how the little girl died and what he did with her body. It may tell us everything.'

'Even so,' Weston said, 'the problem is the same. We did this all before. There is nothing more we can do.'

'Well, you have more sophisticated metal detectors. Can't they tell the shape of an object?'

'No. They're more sophisticated, but not in that way.'

'Use thermal imaging or radar or whatever you normally do.'

'Thermal imaging is done from a plane, but you have to have some heat still in the body and I don't think . . .'

'Yes, all right.'

'Radar is ground-probing radar. It could tell us if there is a cavity down there that might be a primitive grave, but, you know . . .' He looked around again in exasperation. 'I mean, the area is vast.'

'Draw a three-hundred-metre circumference from the point of the murder and search it.'

'It's still a huge—'

'It's what we *need* done.'

Weston looked shifty. Julia had some sympathy. He looked as if he didn't believe he really had the power to refuse Professor Malcolm.

'We've said we're not reopening the investigation,' Weston said. Julia could see that he was gradually conceding defeat. She remembered that Pascoe had only been released this morning. Of course, Weston would have plenty on his plate. Perhaps he had given interviews to the media already.

She wondered what had happened to the cameras in the village. What were the media saying?

'Then don't tell anyone,' Professor Malcolm said.

'They'll find out.'

Professor Malcolm sighed. 'That's really your problem, Lionel.'

'This was supposed to be low-key. That's what you said – to see if there were any grounds before the media get interested.'

'They already are interested.'

Julia realized she had got the balance of power wrong. This review, or whatever it was, had been Professor Malcolm's idea. He had seen that he had a nervous and compliant police force.

Weston looked exasperated. 'Maybe it was Pascoe. He knew the common. Perhaps he came back to move the body.'

126

'Lionel, don't confuse me with the media. What have you done with Pascoe?'

Weston looked tired and sheepish. 'We took him out of the village, but he insisted we leave him in the centre of Cranbrooke this afternoon.'

'You've got a problem. The world thinks he's a threat, but you know he isn't.'

'You said it was not impossible that he'd committed the murders.'

'Yes, but not on the basis of the original investigation and trial. He is not a threat to children, *per se*.'

Weston sighed in frustration.

Weston walked back with them and, after agreeing to a new search, said goodbye at his car, which was parked by the green. After he had gone, Professor Malcolm looked at the cross by the stile for a few moments, before wandering over to the war memorial. 'It's sobering, isn't it?' he said. 'You go to any village or hamlet anywhere in England or France – or even Germany – and you see the names.'

'At the risk of being rude, you must remember the Second World War.'

'My father died in it.'

'I'm sorry. Where?'

'Burma.'

'How old were you?'

'Old enough to know that we were penniless. My mother died the following year. I was brought up by an aunt, my father's sister. My mother's family died in the gas chambers.'

'A kind aunt?'

'Yes. Very much so. She only beat me twice a day.' He looked at her. 'Sorry, poor joke.'

'So, she didn't beat you?'

He moved to the other side of the memorial. 'No, she did.' He looked about him, glancing back at the shop. 'You know, it's very quiet here. There never seems to be anyone about. The post office is still run by the two sisters?'

Julia nodded, looking at the front of what must once have been an ordinary cottage, now painted white with an old-fashioned advertisement next to the post office sign announcing that 'Brooke Bond tea is good tea'.

'Shall we go in?' she asked.

'Later.'

She wondered if the air of tranquillity had something to do with Pascoe's reappearance. Perhaps everyone was barricading their families inside. The crowd and the cameras seemed to be from a different world and she could only assume that the television crews had taken their pictures somewhere to be edited and broadcast and, now that Pascoe had been taken out of the village, there was nothing further to be filmed. The reporters had their story.

Professor Malcolm crossed the road and they passed underneath the lychgate at the entrance to the churchyard. Julia wasn't sure what he was looking for now, but assumed that he would be interested in the relevant section of the graveyard, so led him round the edge of the church and up to the top, by the wall.

The yellow roses in front of Alice's memorial stone were wilting.

There were still no flowers on Sarah's grave.

'I once worked,' he said, 'on the case of a fifteen-year-old boy who had been found hanging in the apple tree behind his parents' house. Not far from here – Witheram. For years afterwards and to the present day, so far as I know, the father obsessively tended the boy's grave. The grass around it was mown three or four times a week.'

'And there are no flowers on Sarah's grave?'

'It's more than that. Look at Alice's memorial stone. Sure, there are flowers, but they're a couple of days old at least. The stone itself is covered in this moss-type stuff. The grass around the edges hasn't been clipped.'

'Alan does have a job, you know. He's in charge of the whole battalion. He can't come down here every day.'

'No, well.'

Julia could not work out if this was meant to be a substantive point, or merely an idle observation. He had not asked if there was a stone for her father and she did not wish to tell him. There was moss on his memorial stone, too.

Professor Malcolm opened the black gate in the stone wall next to them and began to climb the ridge behind. This was scrubland, the grass damp enough to make him lose his footing once or twice, the incline steep and a hard climb for someone of his bulk and level of fitness. He stopped after forty yards or so and they both looked down. The clock on the face of the squat Norman church-tower told her it was half past four, the weather-vane on top of the spire above it creaking as it turned. You could see miles from here – out over the common to the hills beyond, where the fields were dotted with sheep.

To the left of them was a flintstone building with an old tiled roof, covered in moss.

'The village hall,' Julia said, following the direction of his gaze.

Beyond that was the cricket pitch and the road leading out of the village. There were twenty or thirty houses along it, in differing architectural styles, and this was where most of the villagers lived, including the Traverses, and Cynthia Walker, her husband and the little girl. The Traverses' house was the closest with its big, neatly tended garden. It had been built from new stone on a single level with two tall chimneys and was ugly outside and in. Julia remembered the living room, which was *hacienda*-style and freezing in winter, even when the central-heating was on.

Once again, Professor Malcolm led the way down, skirting the churchyard this time and climbing over a fence back on to the road. He walked slowly up to the porch of the old village hall and Julia found herself recalling the awful teenage disco her mother had thrown for her here, in the days before she was mature or gregarious enough to derive any pleasure from such an event.

There was a noticeboard on the porch, but their eyes were drawn to a sheet of paper pinned to the door.

It read, 'Meeting 8.30 p.m. tonight, Tuesday, to discuss Appeal Court decision.'

He looked at her. 'I think we should attend.'

CHAPTER NINE

THEY RETURNED TO THE ROOM IN THE ROSE AND CROWN. WHILE Professor Malcolm went to the toilet, Julia flicked through the green box. She looked for, then pulled out the statements given by herself, her mother and her father.

Professor Malcolm came back in so silently she did not hear him, or perhaps was too preoccupied to notice. He sat on the bed. 'Did your mother have a career before or after she married your father?'

Julia looked at him. 'She was a nurse when she met him. Her parents didn't think it a career for a lady, but she did it anyway.'

He nodded, as if expecting this answer, and reached for the box. His brow was furrowed in concentration. 'I think we should begin the process of trying to understand Sarah's life,' he said, as he began to take out folders and pile them on the desk.

From one, he pulled out a thick sheaf of paper, looking at it for perhaps a minute, before pushing it across to her. 'All I have are photocopies, obviously. This is Sarah's appointments diary for the year of her death.'

Julia leafed through it. It was not an account for the whole year, because neither Sarah nor her daughter had lived to see April or May or any of the months beyond. This was more poignant than the photographs of Sarah's body and, for the first time, Julia felt some sympathy for the dead woman.

She went to the desk, sat with the papers on her lap and began to work backwards. There was a page for each week and they were notably sparse. The Saturday before the murders was blank. The Friday had the letter M written in capitals and circled, followed by 'wts'. For Thursday, there was a doctor's appointment listed as 'Alice – Dr Simon' at 9.00 a.m. Wednesday was dinner at the de la Rues' at 8.00 p.m. On Tuesday, the letter M reappeared, circled in the same way, this time with 'r' next to it. There was a time, too: 7.00 p.m.

On the previous Saturday, M appeared again, once more with 'r' next to it. The time was 7.00 a.m. On the same day, Sarah had written, 'Alan – fishing, all day.'

Julia continued to work backwards. There were ballet and riding lessons for Alice, dental appointments, more for Dr Simon. The word 'London' appeared on several occasions, which Julia assumed must be a reference to a day spent shopping. She could all too easily imagine Sarah going to Harrods and returning with armfuls of bags. She had never been short of money.

Professor Malcolm had opened another envelope and was glancing through its contents.

'What do you think?' he asked.

'The constant reappearance of the letter M might suggest meetings with someone.'

'A code? Or a nickname?'

She shrugged. 'Yes. I suppose that's possible.'

'What about the letters next to the M?'

She looked down at them again. 'I'm not sure about that. Code or shorthand for the place they arranged to meet. I don't know. I notice there is no reference to a meeting on the day of the murders.'

He looked up, frowning.

'If you remember,' she went on, 'we were discussing earlier that the clothes she was wearing – the inappropriate footwear and so on – suggested Sarah was hurrying to a rendezvous. But there is no reference to one in the diary.'

Professor Malcolm nodded. 'Yes, but isn't it the point that it has the ring of a hastily arranged rendezvous, in which case it wouldn't have appeared in the diary? I assume that Sarah only wrote down those arranged some time in advance, to be sure she did not forget.'

Julia pursed her lips and looked down at the papers in her hand again. She turned something over in her mind for a time. 'Actually, there is something odd about these diary entries, or our interpretation of them. If you're having an extramarital affair in a community as small as this, it's likely to be super-highly charged, isn't it? You're unlikely to forget a rendezvous, in which case, why bother to write it down at all? Surely then you just run the risk of discovery.'

'On the subject of which . . .' He handed her the sheets he had been reading. There were about twenty, handwritten. They were stapled together, so she folded them over and began at the top. 'These were found in the back of an atlas in the bottom drawer of her desk.'

Julia began to read the first page:

> I was standing with a glass in my hand close to the Christmas tree and looked over to see him staring at me. All the snakes of the village establishment were there, cloaked in the respectability they so love to wear. He wasn't talking to anyone and I excused myself politely, saying I was called by Mother Nature and as I walked towards the stairs, he turned up them – maybe ten yards ahead – and I followed him in, locking the door behind me. It was above – right above them all!
>
> I had a split cream skirt on and he put his hand on my leg above the knee, then slowly ran it up, pushing me gently back against the wall. I thought he would kiss me, but he sank to his knees, ran his fingers up to the band of my tights and then in, pulling them, and my knickers, slowly down, kissing my legs, until he was at the base when he slipped them off, replacing my high heels once he'd done so.
>
> He worked back up.
>
> When he lifted me eventually, later – ten minutes, more? – he was strong and I can't believe we were silent, though when I groaned, he put one hand over my mouth, holding me up with the other.

Julia turned the page. She didn't look up, not wishing to catch Professor Malcolm's eye.

> On the common. Don't know why he likes this. Suppose it is the potential innocence of our togetherness, though secretly

I've decided it's the open-air thing ... I wasn't turned on today, but when the rain came and the thunder ... He's like a bull and ... there is something about the decadence of not caring that the weather is crashing down all around you.

Felt stupid afterwards, so did he. Having your trousers down in a thunderstorm looks ridiculous when the passion's gone and he knew it. I gave him a new nickname today, 'Like Thunder', because it's how he looks all the time he's with me. He's not amused when I say this, as if I've insulted his integrity! I think he adopts a persona like a cloak to suit his environment – it's like a pose, almost, but it shifts like quick-sand. I don't think there is a constant. Sometimes, in down moments, it makes me feel guilty about Alan. Big row today. He says it was about my emotional coldness, but I know it was about my unwillingness to let him fuck me. Does he know? Is it right that I refuse him his conjugal rights? Do I do it out of spite? Do I enjoy it? I can see the frustration – see it in the way he grips the pillow at night when I've refused him. I try not to take pleasure in touching the raw nerves, but it's hard not to.

Julia's mouth was dry.

Horny as hell today, couldn't wait and got what I wanted. He's cool about the dangers of discovery in the open, I'll give him that. Nothing stops him. He gets himself into a frenzy and I wonder how he'd respond if I said, 'No, thanks, not today, Squire.' I still don't know if anyone else can guess at what he's like. He's got such a reputation as a cold fish and yet there's this intensity hidden right in there ... God knows where it comes from. But that used to be intriguing and just isn't any more. Now I know all this is hidden behind the façade and the façade is just that, it's not intriguing. What makes me laugh is men, though he ought to be too typical to be funny. There is the aura and persona; Mr In-control, in charge, parading his integrity, but it's just funny when it's got bark marks on its buttocks from rubbing against a tree.

Julia looked up. Professor Malcolm was staring at her intently. She tried to keep her face impassive, but it was hard to control.

Her stomach tensed, she closed her eyes.

'Come on, Julia.'

She bit her lip so hard she could taste her own blood. She fought to control herself, but the dam burst, her body shaking, tears flooding her eyes.

'It's okay,' he said quietly.

'Of course it's not,' she whispered. '*Of course it's not.*'

She had stood. Now she sat, head in hands. 'Oh, Christ. She was such a *bitch*. Everything was okay until she came here. The way she pranced around, flaunting herself, throwing herself at him.'

Julia's shoulders shook uncontrollably.

'Have you asked your mother about this?'

'Of course not.' Julia laughed bitterly. 'She says Dad was helping Sarah because she seemed . . . lost . . .' Julia wiped her eyes with the back of her hand. 'God, it sounds crap, but that was how he was about so many things. He was just *like* that. He was *decent*, but she was so manipulative.'

'He was helping Sarah, but then there was more? It went beyond that.'

'I don't know.' Julia shook her head. 'I don't know.'

Professor Malcolm waited. The tears dried up and her shoulders stopped shaking, but her eyes were wet. She wiped them again, head bent, thinking of the diary she had just read and the Christmas drinks party her parents held every year.

'Is it possible that your fears about Sarah and your father . . . I assume you believe they were having an affair?'

Julia nodded slowly.

'Looking at it now with an adult mind, even if it is fractured through the prism of childhood memory, can you see anything that seems to you *now* to be concrete evidence rather than just febrile imagination?'

Julia sighed. She saw that he was trying to impose his own order on events and thoughts and feelings in her mind that had none. 'They were always together. It began around the time of the fête. That's where my sense of unhappiness begins. Before then, on that holiday in Scotland just before they moved in, I think . . . everything was fine. Happy. That's how I remember it. And then the Fords came here and at first I didn't notice, but at the fête . . . that was the first time I *felt* it. I saw her flirting with him that day.'

'She did flirt with people.'

'Yes, but he seemed to laugh at her too easily and vice versa.'
Julia thought again of Sarah's see-through skirt and the sexy
underwear she had worn underneath. 'The night of the fête, I was
tired,' Julia said, 'and went to sleep early. When I awoke, there
was the sound of a woman crying, coming from across the hall. I
went into my father's study very quietly – he hated to be disturbed in there, but I thought it might be Mum. The woman,
Sarah, was standing beside the desk.'

The breeze strengthened, caught the curtain next to her, and
Julia glanced out of the window at the tree-tops on the ridge
above them. 'He . . . had his arm around her. She was crying and
he had his arm around her. He told me to get out.'

'A paternal gesture, or more? To her, I mean.'

'How could I know?'

'Where else did you see them together?'

Julia tried to gather her wits. 'My father and I used to walk a lot
on the common together. I don't know why, particularly, it wasn't
that Mum didn't like walking, but it was just something we'd
always done together. They were . . . they were the best times.
Occasionally, we would play games, as I said. He . . . I thought
he'd always wanted a boy, so I always said I was keen to play the
games. Hide and seek, sometimes more advanced, like hunter
and hunted. I enjoyed . . .'

'Did you?'

She did not respond. She heard a car passing outside. 'No, but
I said I did. I liked the role I fulfilled. I liked the feeling of fulfilment that came with that.'

'Were you frightened?'

'Sometimes, but it meant something to me to . . .'

'To play that role.'

'Yes. You probably think it was odd, but it wasn't. The games
were active, that was all.'

'It made you feel close?'

'I suppose so, yes.'

'And presumably it was a pattern. Seeking to please him.'

'No, you're sounding like a shrink. There were some things that
were straightforward. The dolls' house. That was on my level.
Others that were more . . . difficult. He was a complex man.'

'So how did the games change?'

'Alice came to play. Then Sarah and Alice. We'd all go for a

135

walk together, just the four of us. Alan and my mother would be left here. When the hunted ran, the hunters . . . there was a feeling . . . I had the feeling . . .'

'The suspicion?'

'Yes, the suspicion. Sarah and my father were supposed to be looking for us in the wood. I had the suspicion that they might not have been looking *that* hard. I stopped wanting to play.'

'That upset your father?'

'He seemed increasingly preoccupied.'

'Did Alice feel the same, in terms of her suspicions about your father and her mother?'

Julia shook her head. 'It was somehow understood, but we never discussed it. She was too young.'

'A little sister to you?'

'Yes.'

Professor Malcolm was tapping his knee. He waited a long time, before asking, 'Julia, why did you go down to the wood that day?'

She looked at her feet. 'You asked me that before. You asked me that when all this began fifteen years ago. That was the reason I liked you, because you could have been cruel and you weren't.'

'Why did you come home and then go down to the common without even changing out of your best shoes? Why did you do that?'

Julia did not respond.

'Why were you worried when your father was not at home?'

Julia was looking down at her hands.

'Why did you say earlier that you were not surprised by what happened?'

'People felt sorry for Alan. They hated Sarah.'

'Who hated her? Did your mother hate her? Did your father hate her? Was your father angry with Sarah? You said you were not surprised by his death either, in the Falklands. Did you see that as divine retribution for what he'd done?'

Julia fought to control herself.

'What was it you thought he had done, Julia?'

Her head was down. She was staring at the floor. Fears, anger, flooded her.

'What—'

'All *right*. All *right*. All *right*. *All right*. Is this what you *wanted*?' She was on her feet. 'What do you *want* me to say? Do you want to know about the humiliation, the *shame* of what he was doing with that woman? Do you want to know how I *wanted* her dead? About the *fear* of what had happened, of what he'd done . . .'

Professor Malcolm was stony-faced. 'It's what *you* want,' he said, a long, bony finger stabbing in the direction of her stomach. 'You've *got* to talk about it. Who can deal silently with such fears of what their own father might have done? The attachment to the good memories before Sarah? You have to know they're real, don't you? You're clinging to them. If he could do this terrible thing, then what kind of man was he before? If he was the one who went down to the common that day with a knife in his hand, if he stabbed Sarah and then chased—'

'Please!'

'Then in your mind he's defined by it. It's your childhood you're fighting for and don't deny that this is what you have *always* wanted.'

'I think it is what *you* want.' Now it was her turn to point. 'You had to get me to admit it. That's your game. Okay, well, here it is. Yes, I thought, perhaps, that my father killed that woman. I did. Yes. I was scared. I'm still scared. I'm terrified. I've been white with terror for fifteen years.'

'And Alice?'

'Christ!' She put her head in her hands once more. 'Yes, Alice, too. He has to have killed her, but I cannot accept that.'

'I am here to help you,' he said.

'No, you're not. You're here because your wounded vanity won't tolerate the notion that you failed.'

Suddenly his expression was fierce. 'That is the second time you have said that and it is unworthy of you.'

His sincerity punched a hole in her anger. 'All right, I'm sorry.' She stared at the floor. 'I don't know,' she said, 'if I trust you.'

He frowned in confusion. 'I don't understand.'

'You have your own agenda. I don't know precisely what it is . . .'

'My agenda is to discover what really happened here.'

'Or to prove a long dormant theory.'

She could tell she had hurt him. His mouth had become very thin. 'Julia, I am a lonely old man with drawers full of dead faces,

137

no family to speak of and friends who don't call much any more. You're one of the few things in the world I do care for, so *give me some credit.'*

He stood and his exit was furious, the door hissing shut behind him.

After he had gone, Julia was immediately overcome with remorse. To avoid looking at all the pictures on the wall above the bed she turned to face the desk and the alcove.

The confession of her suspicions had brought unexpected relief. It was impossible that her father could have done such a thing. Completely impossible.

'I'm sorry,' she said, as he came back in. 'I'm really sorry.' She groped for some other explanation. He sat and stared at her, forcing her to drop her eyes. He was a ruthless inquisitor and yet she knew he was gentle with her. She had seen the way he destroyed the ill-prepared, arrogant or lazy in tutorials. 'In the last three years,' she explained, 'I've just ceased to view truth as an objective thing.'

'If your father was in any way involved, can knowledge of his guilt be worse than this suspicion?'

Julia didn't think it was likely to prove that simple, but perhaps he was making it appear so. Could he really be acting in her interests alone? She thought of her assistants in Beijing and the way they said she never trusted anyone with anything. Is that what she was like?

He pointed to the sheaf of paper on the desk. 'You've read the soft porn she wrote, now let's go back to the appointments diary. If there were meetings with "M", *perhaps* Mitchell Havilland, your father, and perhaps not, what does "wts" stand for when written next to M?'

'Wizened tree stump. A meeting-place on the common.'

'R?'

'I'm not sure. Ridge, maybe.'

'It's a curious read, the soft porn, I think. Doesn't read like fiction.'

Julia picked up the papers again. She didn't really want to touch them. It was getting darker in here now that the sun was on the other side of the valley, but neither of them had moved to turn on any lights. She tried to think. 'It's obviously some kind of *ad hoc* diary,' she said.

Professor Malcolm leant back, twiddling his reading-glasses. He got up and looked at the photograph of Sarah on the wall, resting one knee on the bed. 'Most people who write diaries,' he said, 'do so because they want to be liked. It may be an honest portrait, but there is the maximum possible justification for everything they've done. That's what makes them so dull, often. But this woman is crying out to be *dis*liked. She's shouting to be condemned.' He shook his head. 'No pleasant reference to anyone, really, not even herself. A portrait of a selfish woman.'

'Don't diaries always make us feel selfish?' Julia countered. 'Perhaps they aren't written to be read. And anyway, she probably never intended this to be a complete picture. It's just what she felt like writing down, not a cogent summary of her state of mind.'

'Were the Fords rich?'

'Sarah was – from her parents. It was her house, really.'

'Your father must have been, what, twenty years older than Sarah?'

'A bit less. He was very young for his post.'

'So your father was about forty. Your mother was about thirty-two. Alan was thirty. Sarah was about thirty-two.'

Julia nodded. She had never considered her mother and Sarah to be the same age.

'Wasn't it odd having two people of such different rank as neighbours, especially since the Ford house is bigger than your own?'

'It was Sarah's decision. She'd always had the money. She made the choices and she didn't like being an army wife. If they were going to live in this area near to the base, then I guess it must have been her call. Knowing her, she probably did it deliberately. And, anyway, my father didn't bother about that kind of thing. He was nervous about money – Mum was always telling me how worried he was and how there was never any money to do anything, but I don't think he was interested in it as such.'

Professor Malcolm turned back and stood behind his chair. 'Here's what we have to do. You need to go back and try to establish an accurate picture of Sarah's life. Go through everything that might lead us to things that have been overlooked. Her bank records, for example. Was there any issue about money? You need to see if we can get the phone bills for the month – no, let's say three months – before her death. Whom was she calling and with what frequency?' He moved to the box and pulled out yet another brown A4 envelope. 'This is her address book, or a photocopy of it. Unfortunately, but inevitably, it is alphabetical, with no hint as to who any of these people are, or the closeness of her relations with them. You'll just have to work through it. Of course, we could short-circuit much of this by talking to those closest to her, like her husband, but I think, for the time being, we should avoid that. Anyway, we're agreed that that is ... difficult for you. We need to establish a basic picture of who this woman was, from the widest possible number of sources. There are people in the village who were not in the immediate circle but who would have had a reasonable idea of what was going on – the sisters in the post office, to take one example. Who did they think she was having an affair with? Was it more than one person? Was it all just fantasies in her own mind?'

'Shouldn't we at least inform Alan Ford what we are doing?'

He was shaking his head vigorously, and she nodded, implicitly acknowledging that sentimentality could have no place.

Professor Malcolm disappeared down the corridor to the toilet yet again. Julia sat looking at the telephone on the desk. Was that what she was supposed to do, sit here and call people? She picked up, then replaced the receiver. The note on the phone indicated that 9 brought an outside line and Julia assumed the police would be paying for the calls.

She thought about what she was being asked to do and it made her feel better. This was the first time she had been tasked with piecing together the life of a dead person, but it was not dissimilar to what she had done in Ireland, Russia and China. There, she had been required to get to know living individuals without ever speaking to them or anyone who knew them, and it was surprising what you could discover by reading people's mail, checking what library books they took out, or what clothes they wore. That was how the value and psychological state of a potential agent were assessed. Mistakes could be, and sometimes were, fatal. Sarah was going to receive the same rough hand as any potential recruit, dead or not.

The statements given by Julia's parents were still on the table, so she glanced over them, then walked to her jacket, which was on the edge of the bed, and slipped them into the pocket.

When Professor Malcolm came back, he took a diary from

inside his jacket and looked up a telephone number. 'There are some phone records there, I think, and probably the bank ones, but if you need anything else, call Detective Constable Baker on this number.'

As he said it Julia wrote it down on the side of one of the brown envelopes on the desk in front of her.

'I've asked her,' he went on, 'to provide us with a catch-all letter on headed paper saying that we are conducting an official review of the case and should be given all necessary assistance. She can send it round.'

Julia was again impressed, if not surprised, by the influence he was able to exert.

'Baker does crime liaison. If there is anything else you need in terms of documentation, you may have to get a court order. She can arrange that. I'm supposed to be speaking at a symposium in Bournemouth this weekend but I'll cancel it.' He closed the diary and replaced it in his pocket. 'I hate Bournemouth,' he said, with feeling.

Julia looked through the box to see what records he had kept. She could not find any bank statements or financial details, and the only phone records were those for the Ford number in the week before Sarah's death. She pulled these out, turning the pages until the day of the murders. Four calls had been made from the Ford home that morning and she recognized two of the numbers instantly: one call had been made to her own home and one to the Rouses. The other two were not Cranbrooke numbers.

Julia began to work backwards away from that Sunday, but no discernible, meaningful pattern emerged. There were calls to her home, some to the Rouses and the de la Rues, but no number came up so frequently as to appear suspicious or out of the ordinary.

She flicked through the address book. Julia hated people listening to her telephone conversations, even those related to work, and she had no wish to have him sit and listen to her, but she needn't have worried. Professor Malcolm fell asleep sitting on the bed, his head resting on his chest, the corner of an A4 envelope gripped between thumb and forefinger.

She listened to his breathing as she called DC Baker at Cranbrooke CID, who was friendly and helpful. She said she had done the letter and would get someone to drop it round. Baker said she doubted they had kept the bank records but would look. If not, it would take time and, as a result of the Data Protection Act, would definitely need a court order. Julia asked for the phone records for the Fords stretching back further than the week prior to Sarah's death as well as those for her own home, covering a similar period. She was looking at the photographs on the wall to her right and, after a moment's hesitation, she added a request for the telephone records of the Rouses, the de la Rues, Mrs Pascoe, and Michael Haydoch.

Julia was well acquainted with the Data Protection Act and the ways of getting round it, or the incidences when it was best ignored. But this was not the time to suggest any of them.

She reached for the photocopy of the appointments diary in the hope that there would be a record she had missed of 'frequently used phone numbers', but there wasn't, so she returned to the address book, resigned to having to do this the hard way. She concluded that the real thing would have looked very different: it would have had many pieces of loose paper jammed into the front and back. As it was, it was more like a Filofax. In the Notes section at the beginning there was a design for a new kitchen, complete with cupboard measurements and colour schemes. The paint was to have been 'Mandarin Blue – Sanderson'. Julia was moved anew by Sarah's fate. There was something pathetic about studying someone's plans for the future fifteen years after they were dead. It gave Sarah a humanity Julia had never permitted her in life.

The kitchen designs went on for more than a page – there were three or four, though Julia could not see much difference between them. Beyond that, there was a page headed 'Alice', which listed numbers for a playgroup, Dr Simon in Cranbrooke, health visitor, the Cranbrooke hospital and finally East Welham Primary School and Mrs Simpson.

West Welham did not have a school, so East Welham was the nearest.

There was a page headed 'Birthdays', which listed only those of Alice and Alan – strange that Sarah had felt the need to make a note of those – and then the heading was 'Personal Expenses' but the page beneath was blank. The following section had a series of figures written down – generally small ones – but Julia couldn't work out whether they had any meaning. At the bottom, Sarah had written, 'Lloyds, Cranbrooke, Mr Tyler'.

If the page headed 'Personal Expenses' was blank, the last three in the section were full of numbers. There was a summary at the top, which listed a figure for 'Outgoings', broken down into mortgage, rates, water, electricity. There was an 'Incoming' figure, too, but it was smaller. On the next page there was a list on the left-hand side of specific expenses, with corresponding figures on the right, including 'Alan's birthday', probably a present, which had cost only ten pounds – not much even in 1982. Other sums corresponded to supermarket shopping, clothes, Cynthia's wedding, Peter's wedding, Joanna's present, B&B and a deposit for Cranbrooke prep school. There were no references to anything unusual, certainly no listing for a present for M. It occurred to her that Alan might have used this address book, too. Certainly, most of the men she knew in relationships were not good at keeping a track of even their own friends' telephone numbers and addresses.

Sarah's handwriting was not neat. In the main body of the address book, almost every entry was scrawled, except one or two that she recognized as having been written by Alan, in his precise, organized hand. None of the entries gave anything away in terms of the closeness or otherwise of those listed, and many were illegible. The only way of reducing her workload that Julia could see was to concentrate on those names that had numbers crossed out and replaced by others, which suggested prolonged contact.

There was one entry for 'M & D' and it was for this that Julia lifted the receiver first. She couldn't remember Sarah's maiden name, but it didn't matter, because the woman who answered the telephone told her that the elderly couple who had lived here had passed away seven years previously and she did not know of any surviving relatives. She and her husband had bought the house from a solicitor.

Julia wondered if, in Sarah's absence, the money had gone to Alan. After all, they had never separated.

There didn't seem any other obvious shortcuts, so Julia turned to the first page of the address book and began at the beginning.

Midway through the second call, Professor Malcolm started snoring quietly. She wondered if anyone at the other end would hear.

Julia had decided against lying, so she told the respondents that a review of the case was taking place and that she and her colleagues would be grateful for any help they might feel able to give. Julia asked them first of all to outline, in a sentence, their relationship with the deceased. The majority described themselves simply as friends.

Each successful call began with the same explanation, which was followed by a momentary silence, as the man or woman the other end of the line recalled the long dead and, perhaps, was reacquainted with old emotions. Some had heard about Pascoe's release and asked if the case was to be reopened, but none betrayed more than academic interest.

About the tenth call was to a man called Adam Forbes, whose name was listed under 'A' rather than 'F'. A woman answered the phone and, while a baby screamed in the background, explained that Adam was at work and gave Julia another number.

A receptionist answered, 'Salmon Forbes Barnaby,' and, after explaining what she wanted and while waiting to be put through, Julia tried to guess what business Adam Forbes was in. Public relations or advertising, she thought.

'Hello, Adam Forbes here. You're the police?'

Forbes's voice was deep, low and confident. He was a man used to being in command of situations, Julia thought.

'In a manner of speaking,' she said.

'How can I help?' There was a wariness in his voice, but Julia had already grown used to this. All those who picked up the phone were reluctant to be drawn, fearful of bringing trouble upon themselves.

'We're conducting a review,' Julia said. 'It's only a formality – a review of the evidence. You may have heard that the man convicted of Sarah's murder has been released . . .'

'No, I hadn't.'

There was a pause.

'Your name is in Sarah's address book.'

'Yes. We were at art school together.'

Julia was surprised by this. She'd never seen Sarah paint anything.

'Which art school?'

'The Slade.'

'So, you were friends?'

'Well . . . yes. I don't think I'd seen her for a few years by the time of her death.'

'Were you good friends? What kind of woman was Sarah when you knew her?'

There was a long pause. Julia knew this kind of conversation was difficult over the telephone, but she wasn't going to have time to seek out each of these people individually.

'Sarah is a hard woman to explain.'

'I'd be grateful if you would try.'

He sighed quietly. 'She was attractive . . . vivacious.'

'Tending to provoke strong reactions in people?'

'Yes.'

'Particularly men.'

'Perhaps. Yes.'

'Did you ever . . . Sorry, I don't mean to intrude, but did you ever have a relationship with her?'

He hesitated. 'When I first met her, I asked her out. We made a date and she just never showed up. I waited a long time in the restaurant and felt a fool, naturally. I was angry, but the next time I saw her, she was charming and deeply apologetic, but she never explained why she hadn't turned up, except to say that she forgot.'

'So you became friends, or drifted?'

'Friends, yes. Shortly after that I came to accept that she was probably not for me. Too . . . complicated. We did become friends, of a sort.'

Julia doubted that Adam Forbes had ever stopped wanting to sleep with Sarah.

'Did you stay in touch with her after art school?'

'No. I'm quite surprised my name is still in her book.'

Julia had been taking notes on the pad beside her. She put the pencil down for a moment, thinking. 'Was she popular at the college? I mean, how was she viewed by others?'

There was another pause. 'Sarah is, as I've said, hard to categorize.'

'Flighty?'

'Yes. I always got the impression that to her men were a bit of a game. That made her relations with them difficult and almost equally so with women. But there was another side to her that I think many people liked. She was well off and generous with her money. She could be kind and thoughtful at times, but rather careless and thoughtless at others.'

145

Julia had written 'generous' on the pad and circled it. 'Did she have close female friends?'

'I don't know.'

'Life revolved around boyfriends, perhaps.'

'Yes, I would say that was probably true.'

Julia thanked him and replaced the receiver, pondering the contrast between Sarah's freewheeling generosity at college and the carefully recorded figures in the Notes section of the address book. It was hard tying these together.

As she went, Julia continued to make notes – a paragraph summary for each person, just in case she ever had to come back to any of them. By six o'clock, she had almost reached the end of the Bs – she was at Dennis and Amelia Brown – and was bored of listening to Professor Malcolm snoring. She wrote him a note saying that she would come back to pick him up for the meeting at the village hall, then walked home in the afternoon sun, which was warm on her face.

She had a strong image of Sarah in her mind in that yellow bikini, with her dead straight, jet-black hair and willowy figure. The impression that Adam Forbes had given her had not been substantially altered by subsequent conversations, although the objective picture she was forming was tending to make her seem a more attractive figure. Almost everyone, it seemed, remembered her generosity and occasional thoughtfulness. Julia wondered why she could recall no such positive memories of her next-door neighbour.

Caroline was not at home, so Julia went up to her room, read her parents' statements, then folded them up again, put them in the drawer of her bedside table and sat down on the mattress, trying to dispel the image of Sarah's inert body that had found its way back into her mind.

CHAPTER TEN

MAC WAS SITTING AT HOME, BY HIS WINDOW, LOOKING OUT OVER THE roof-tops towards Clapham Common. He looked at his watch, concluded that Alan Ford would probably have left the base, stood and reached for the phone. He took out his mobile and searched through previously called numbers until he found the one for the base in Cranbrooke, which he dialled on the land-line. 'Duty officer,' he said to the operator.

'Duty officer, Lieutenant Benson.'

'Good evening, Lieutenant Benson. This is Major Rigby from the Royal Military Police Special Investigation Branch at Woolwich. We've got something of an incident and I urgently need an up-to-date address and telephone number for one of your former soldiers, a Corporal Richard Claverton.'

'I'm sorry, sir, the P files are with Admin. The block's all locked up. If you call back on Monday, they'll be able—'

'Benson, I'm not sure you understand. It's important and I wouldn't be calling you on a Friday night if it wasn't, would I?'

'No, sir.'

'I need to know the answer now – not in an hour or two or on Monday but now. You've got keys, haven't you?'

'Yes, sir.'

'And a brain?'

'Of sorts, sir.'

'Right. Go to the admin block, find the filing cabinet that lists former regimental personnel and look under C for Claverton. Corporal Richard Claverton. I will call back in forty-five minutes and I expect you to have the answer. Understood?'

'Yes, sir.'

'Telephone number and up-to-date address.'

'Yes, sir.'

Mac wondered if Benson would contact Lieutenant Colonel Ford to get clearance, but he calculated that, on a Friday night, the duty officer would be anxious not to disturb his boss.

Forty-five minutes later Mac called back. 'Benson, it's Major Rigby here.'

'Yes, sir. It says on the file that Richard Claverton is deceased. Eleventh of November last year. Eleven Albany Mews, Strathallan Road, London SW18. No telephone number. Next of kin, Mrs Sandra Claverton.'

Mac thanked Benson and hung up. He thought for a minute, then picked up his jacket and walked towards the door.

He drove down Battersea Rise, then up the hill, turning left past the railway line, navigating with the A–Z open on the seat beside him. Strathallan Road was down towards Southfields, and Albany Mews was a new development set back from the main street, full of neat grey houses, each with a parking space.

Mac looked at his watch again as he walked up the short path to the front door. It was getting late, but he knocked quietly. The wooden front door had small square panels of frosted glass, which he could not see through, but he heard someone approach and waited while whoever it was examined him through the spy-hole.

The door opened. A small Jack Russell darted out and got caught between his legs, before circling him rapidly.

'Tibbett, come here! Stop it!'

'It's all right.' Mac stooped to pick up the dog and held her at head height as she tried to lick his face.

'I'm sorry, she's only a puppy.'

Mac placed the dog in the woman's outstretched arms, but holding her still was not easy.

'Sandra Claverton,' Mac said, smiling.

She looked at him and nodded.

'Captain Macintosh, Royal Military Police.'

For a moment, Sandra Claverton paused, then her instincts overcame natural suspicion – or so it seemed to Mac – and she stepped back to allow him into her home.

The small hall led immediately to the living room. It was cramped, but not gloomy, despite the dark upholstery and carpet. All the surfaces, including the top of the large television, were covered in photographs.

'Would you like a cup of tea, Captain Macintosh?'

'Yes, please.' Mac looked at her. 'Milk, no sugar.'

'May I take your coat?'

Mac slipped it off and handed it to her. She put it on a peg by the door, then went to make his tea, taking the dog with her. Mac put his hands in his pockets and bent to look at the photographs on the mantelpiece. In the centre was a picture of a tall, handsome, blond man with a bushy moustache, wearing a sleeveless fishing jacket and holding up a large, silver fish, the blue waters of a lake behind him. There was a much shorter man standing next to him, squinting in the sunshine, his bald head glistening. Next to the photograph was a tall metal fish standing upright on a wooden base. At the bottom of it was a plaque, with an engraving: 'Nomads Annual Bullshitter of the Year Award 1995'.

Mac smiled and moved along a step to look at a formal picture of Richard Claverton and his wife – an engagement photograph, perhaps. With their blond hair and good looks, they were Nordic in appearance, Sandra seeming much younger here, but her husband exactly the same.

'Just before we got married,' Sandra said, behind him. Mac turned and took the cup of tea she offered. They faced each other awkwardly, neither comfortable enough to sit. Sandra had half-moon glasses around her neck and wore a brown cardigan, her blond hair in a bun at the back of her head. Like her husband, she was tall, but she was larger around the waist and hips and her calves were bulky and swollen.

'Did they send you?'

Mac sipped his tea. It was hot. Bitterness had crept into her voice, he noticed, a slight emphasis on the word 'they'. 'No,' he said.

Sandra Claverton sat, legs neatly together. Mac followed suit in the brown armchair next to the fireplace, which faced the television. He wondered if this had been Richard's chair.

'Mrs Claverton . . .'

'Sandra.'

'Yes. I'm . . . sorry about your husband.'

Sandra Claverton looked down. She had placed the tea on a side-table and her hands were in the middle of her lap, one clasping the other.

'Mrs . . . Sandra. I'm working on something to do with Mitchell Havilland and I've found that, though a public event in all kinds of ways, actual *details* of his death are somewhat hard to come by.'

Sandra Claverton continued to look at her hands. She was frowning, as if concentrating on holding herself in check. Mac did not want to upset her.

'I'm sorry to trouble you, Sandra. It's just that your husband's is one of the few names that I have . . . one of the few who can definitively be said to have been present.'

She looked up. Mac saw that if there was hurt in her eyes at her husband's death, there was also anger. 'They're wrong,' she said. 'They're all wrong.'

Mac waited for her to clarify this, but she was now staring at the floor. 'Wrong about what?' he asked.

She looked up again. There was confusion in her face. 'You don't know about Richard?'

Mac shook his head. 'No. As I said, all details that should be routine seem difficult to come by.'

Sandra frowned more heavily. 'I found him . . . upstairs, on the bed . . .' She placed a hand over her open mouth, then crumpled, her head in her hands.

Mac waited as she composed herself. 'They said it was suicide,' she went on.

'That was the coroner's verdict?'

'Yes, but Richard would never have done a thing like that. Why would he? He would never have done that to me.'

'I'm sorry, Sandra.'

'He'd never have let me find him like that.' She sniffed and wiped her eyes. 'I'm sorry.' She looked at him. 'I'm sorry, Captain Macintosh.'

'You referred to "they"? You said, "Did they send you?"'

'Yes.'

150

'Who is they?'

'The Military Police.' She took out her handkerchief and wiped her eyes.

'If you were willing, Sandra, I think it would be helpful to me if we could start at the beginning.'

'But who are you?'

'I'm ... Put it this way, I think I might be of more use to you than whoever it was who came to see you before.'

Sandra Claverton looked at Mac, still unsure. Then she seemed to make up her mind. 'There was a letter. That began it. It had a terrible effect on him ... I wasn't supposed to read it, but it was postmarked Winchester, it was from a prison and it was written in poor handwriting. It said, "It's time for the truth, Richard." It wasn't signed or anything, just one sentence in the middle of a page, with the name of the prison written at the top. Winchester Prison.'

'The truth about what?'

She shook her head. Mac waited for her to continue.

'Then nothing happened for a long time and I forgot about it. I asked Clive . . .' Sandra pointed towards the man in the picture with the fish. 'That's Clive Danes you were looking at earlier. He was in the same regiment. And he said ... well, he said, forget about it. Just someone they'd served with who'd lost his mind.'

The next pause was longer. 'But it didn't go away?' Mac asked.

'No. Then the men from the Military Police came and asked Richard questions. They came three or four times and, like the letter, the effect on him was terrible each time.' Sandra tilted her head to one side. 'You see, my Richard was a sunny man. He didn't get depressed often, but after each visit he was not himself at all. He would withdraw to his study upstairs for hours, and when he came out he wouldn't want to talk about it, and if I asked, he'd be angry with me. That was out of character, too.'

'This was just before he died?'

'No, there was a gap. The men from the Military Police stopped coming. They wrote him a letter saying that the investigation was complete and no further action was to be taken – he didn't want me to see that either, but I did. Things improved for a while. He seemed more back to his own self, but then, just before he died – a few weeks before – there was another letter, which he was care- ful I didn't see, but I knew it was from the prison again and then there were other visitors. A man in a smart suit came twice, with a briefcase.'

'What did he look like?'

'A square-looking man. Balding, with a thin belt of hair running from the front to the back. He was not attractive, but his manner was kindly. Each visit had the same effect on Richard, and I would try to talk about it, but . . .'

'Were there any other visitors in the same vein?'

'Only Clive. He saw a lot of Clive. They were close. Fished together.'

'Would you have an address or telephone number for him?'

Sandra looked at him oddly, as if he were stupid, and Mac wondered if he had said something inappropriate.

'Clive is dead as well. He died two days after Richard.'

Mac stared at her. 'Suicide?'

She began to cry again, shaking her head in frustration at her lack of self-control, or perhaps just in grief, Mac couldn't tell.

'You told the Military Police of your suspicions?'

She gathered herself, clearing her throat and straightening. 'Yes. They came to look at my Richard's study and they took some of his things away – the letter from the prison and some of his papers. They said they would look into it and contact me, but . . .'

'They never have.'

'I've called them. Many times.'

'Who were these men, Sandra?'

She shook her head. 'There was a Major Rigby. He was in charge. The others . . . I don't know.'

Mac looked at her, thoughtfully. 'Sandra, do you have any idea what the letters were about? Were they to do with the war?'

She shook her head. 'We met after the war, in 1984. He never talked about his experiences. Never. Not a single word. Clive Danes was the same. I sometimes talked to Jennifer about it. Clive's wife.'

'You still have a telephone number for her, presumably.'

Sandra nodded. 'I'll get it for you in a minute, if you want.'

'Did you ever hear any mention of Mitchell Havilland's death?'

She shook her head again.

'Richard never commented on it – on the articles about Mitchell's daughter a few years ago or anything like that?'

152

There was a glimmer of recognition. 'Yes, he did see those. When she won that award?'

'The Sword of Honour at Sandhurst.'

'Yes. A sword with a picture of her in uniform.'

'It was in most newspapers.'

'Yes, he was reading that.'

'And he commented on it?'

Sandra was thinking. 'He said the man would not have been a hero if he had come back from the war.'

'What did he mean by that?'

She shrugged. 'I don't know. He was . . . it was in the morning and he was never at his best, just stuck into the newspaper, and I asked him what he meant and he ignored me. I suppose I thought it was military tactics or something but I knew better by then than to ask about the war.'

'What did you think he might have meant?'

'About what?'

'When he said it, presumably you thought he meant that if Havilland had come back from the war, if he'd not been killed and therefore had returned with everyone else, then something would have come to public light which would have caused him not to be viewed as a hero, in fact the reverse.'

Sandra looked confused. 'I suppose so, yes.'

'That was the tenor of what he said. I'm sorry, but it might be important.'

She thought about it some more. 'It was a throwaway remark.'

'But memorable enough for you to recall it some . . . what – six or seven years later.'

Sandra sighed. 'I suppose I just thought it was not pleasant to speak ill of someone who had died in that way . . . Richard was normally very respectful of colleagues and it struck me as odd that he'd say such a thing, but again . . . it was the war. He just didn't talk about it. It was off-limits.'

Mac stood and put his cup of tea down on the mantelpiece. 'Sandra, you said that they took some of the things from his study. Would it be possible . . . I mean, I don't know if you have packed all his effects away but, if you haven't, it would be useful to me to look through to see if there is anything they might have left behind.'

Without saying anything further, she led him up the staircase to the landing above and a small room at the far end. As he turned to thank her, Mac saw only the door being quietly shut.

He sat in a tall, high-backed wooden chair with red decorative painting across its head, which looked Scandinavian in style. Mac wondered if the Clavertons really did have Nordic connections.

The desk had an old Apple computer in one corner, but was otherwise bare. Underneath, to the left of his legs, there was a cabinet with three drawers. Mac switched on the computer, and opened the top drawer, which was full of files.

He pulled them out and looked through the contents of each. Richard Claverton had been a neat, methodical man. There was a file for car insurance, another for the house and one with 'Army' on the cover, which Mac opened with a sense of expectation. It yielded thin pickings, containing only his discharge papers (12 November 1984, at the rank of sergeant) and details of his pension. There was another file headed 'Postal Service', which dealt with his career after the army. He had been in the human resources department and had retired in 1994.

Mac paid careful attention to the 'Bank' file, but again learnt nothing of substance. The Clavertons were not wealthy, but neither were they profligate, living comfortably within their means.

He combed through all the bank statements that had been kept – about two years' worth – but found that the Clavertons had been overdrawn only once and then only by a hundred and twenty-nine pounds for three days at the end of a month.

The other drawers held nothing of interest – some French money, details of an Air France frequent-flyer programme, paper-clips, three films and a new-looking camera.

Mac browsed through the computer, but there was not a single file on it.

He stood up and went downstairs to find Sandra, who was sitting on the sofa, with her hands in her lap.

'Sandra, did Richard have any files on the computer?'

'I'm afraid I don't know how to use it. I'm sure he did.'

'Did the men who came . . . did Rigby use the computer?'

'I left them in the study.'

Mac put his hands in his pockets, looking at her out of the corner of his eye. He thought about the way in which he'd suddenly started speaking about his own colleagues as if they were enemies and how it seemed so natural.

'There's nothing in his drawers to suggest he was in the army at all, except his discharge papers. Did he keep any mementoes, photographs or letters – anything at all from his career or from the war?'

'No. As I said, he never talked about it. Of his former colleagues he saw only Clive. I suppose they must have talked about it, after all they'd gone through together, but never in front of me or Jennifer. When Richard received any communication from the regiment or the army, if it wasn't about his pension, he threw it straight in the bin.'

'There's nothing else?'

Mac was forming the impression Sandra was holding something back, but instinct told him not to push too hard. He stood with his back to the fireplace, his hands still in his pockets, his head bent in thought. After a minute, or perhaps more, Sandra stood and left the room.

Mac listened to her climbing the stairs. When she came back, she had a small leather book in her hand. 'I don't think it will be much use, but it's the only other thing I have.'

Mac took it and sat down in the armchair. He was hoping Sandra would leave him to look at it in peace, but she returned to her position on the sofa. The room seemed to have grown darker, but there was enough light from the window to enable him to read.

The diary was leatherbound and obviously personal. It had a string wrapped around it with what looked like a Chinese coin on the end. Mac's heart sank as he opened it and began to turn the pages. It was evidently some kind of fishing journal, with headings written in ink. The first was 'River Test', the title and date underlined, 12 June 1993. It was a factual account of a day spent fishing, including the size and nature of the catch. There was nothing personal about it.

The fourth page was headed 'Nomads to Norway, Summer of '94' and, again, it provided a bald account of the fishing, written up day by day. On most occasions, the sub-heading was 'Self and Clive', though sometimes other names were added. What engaged Mac's interest were the illustrations, because Claverton had been a talented amateur, depicting landscapes and sometimes individuals with an impressionist's flair. There was a particularly attractive pencil sketch of a man in a hat fishing in a broad river with a mountain behind him. The man was short – Clive Danes, probably, Mac thought.

After the fishing trip to Norway, there was a pencil sketch of what looked like a large garden shed and it took Mac a few seconds to work out that this was a design drawing. He held up the page to Sandra and she smiled, pointing out of the window at the garden.

Mac began to turn the pages faster. There was another Nomads trip to Scotland, again with illustrations.

Then he stopped. In the corner of one page was a list of names – two lists, in fact – and they had caught his eye because they were written in very small letters in the margin and set out as if they were two opposing football teams.

On one side, Richard Claverton had written, 'Pascoe, Claverton, Danes, Wilkes'. On the other, 'Ford, Rouse, Haydoch'.

But most striking was the heading. Claverton had written above the list the letter H, which he had neatly circled and placed a cross through.

Mac got up. He handed her the book and pointed to the list, but she shrugged.

He took a step back and half turned away. 'Sandra, I'm going to have to ask you how, exactly, Richard died.'

'It was a gun.'

'Do you know what kind?'

'A Browning pistol, they said at the inquest.'

'Did he own such a gun?'

Sandra shook her head.

'And Clive Danes, how . . .'

'The same way.'

'Exactly the same?'

'No, they found Clive in a wood behind the house, but . . .'

'But he shot himself, also with a pistol?'

'I don't know the make of the gun.'

'Did you . . . Are you aware that the man who wrote those letters, Robert Pascoe, was in prison because he was convicted of the Welham Common murders? Do you remember . . .'

She was nodding her head.

'Did you ever hear Richard or Clive refer to them?'

She did not respond.

'What I'm getting at is what "truth" it was exactly that Pascoe

156

may have been referring to in those letters and why he had decided it was "time" to tell it.'

She shook her head.

Mac looked down. 'Something was important enough to trigger, if you are correct, not one but two murders.'

Mac found it hard to leave that night. Each time he stood to go, Sandra would ask if he wanted another cup of tea with a soulful loneliness in her eyes. Mac did not know if it was company she sought – any company – or whether she had already come to hope he would offer a resolution of the circumstances surrounding her husband's death.

Eventually, he stood up firmly and thanked her. She did not get up to say goodbye and, as he pulled the door shut, the last thing he saw was Sandra Claverton sitting with her head in her hands, her body shaking.

CHAPTER ELEVEN

PROFESSOR MALCOLM WAS SITTING BY THE DESK, STARING OUT OF THE window. As Julia came in, he hurriedly picked up some papers and shoved them into his pocket. He looked surprised to see her and it was a second or two before he remembered the meeting at the village hall.

They climbed down the fire exit, avoiding the pub below, and walked down the road, past the green and the churchyard to the village hall beyond.

There were about twenty people in the hall, half of whom Julia recognized. She guessed that some of the strangers were from neighbouring East Welham, the rest newcomers to this village. Most were standing, some leaning on the same trestle tables that her mother had used at the disco all those years ago. Cynthia Walker was there, without her husband and daughter, sitting next to Hattie Travers and her husband, who was not, this time, supported by his thugs.

A small group were on the stage at the front: Alan Ford sitting, head bowed, Jasper de la Rue leaning against the side, Adrian Rouse standing just in front of them. Adrian was holding the meeting.

Julia had been spotted now. Jasper, Adrian and Alan all seemed to register her presence at the same time and their frowns were uniform, though Alan's was more surprise than annoyance and was quickly replaced by a smile. Adrian, who had been addressing the gathering, stared at them, as if he had seen a ghost. One or two of the others, who faced the triumvirate on the stage, now turned towards them and an awkward silence fell, punctuated by the sound of metal chairs scraping against a wooden floor as people swung back.

The hall was run down, old and unwelcoming. Once, it had even been used for amateur dramatics, but now it was rarely occupied.

'I share your sentiments,' Adrian went on, 'but we have some responsibility to ensure that whatever we do does not teeter into illegality.'

'That's easy for you to say,' Travers told him. 'Your children are grown up.' He looked at Cynthia Walker as he said this.

'That's true, but I repeat what I said earlier.' Adrian looked straight at Julia and Professor Malcolm. 'None of us want this man here, but most of us are agreed we have a duty to respect the law.'

'We're still *not* agreed,' Travers said. He was wearing a mustard-coloured cardigan and spoke with the vowels of someone whose upbringing had been spent north of Watford Gap, which set him apart from the men on the stage and, Julia assumed, most of the rest of the room. Travers had sought to dominate the village before, swaying planning meetings with bluster and threats of legal action for discrimination, having bought out an old village couple then decided to knock down their red-brick cottage to make way for his home.

'We've a duty,' Travers said slowly, 'to the children of the village, to take any action necessary to ensure their safety is protected.' Again, he looked at Cynthia Walker meaningfully. 'Where is he?'

To Travers and Cynthia Walker and all the other relative newcomers, this must seem simple, Julia thought.

'He was taken to Cranbrooke this afternoon,' Rouse said, 'at his own request.'

'So where is he now?'

'We don't know.'

'How do we know that he won't come back?'

'We don't.'

'They should be watching him . . . filth like that . . .'

159

'But the difficulty is that he is no longer a criminal. There's a limit . . .'

'Oh, fuck the law,' Travers said. 'There are people here with young children and I don't care what the judiciary, in their wisdom, have decided. If the police believe they got their man, then that's that. There are people in this village and in this room with young children and we'll go on using every available means to show Mr Pascoe that he's not welcome.'

There were murmurs of agreement.

Adrian glanced at Alan Ford. He slipped off the stage, an athletic and youthful figure alongside Jasper and Adrian, despite his slight tummy, though he was Adrian's age. He pulled his sweater down over his belt and ran his hand through his thick, wavy dark hair, flattening it at the front. He stood with his hands in his pockets for a moment. Adrian Rouse touched his shoulder, a gesture of support befitting an old friend.

'I don't want this man back here,' Alan said. 'We'll make sure he does not remain.' He looked around the room. 'However, this is one of the moments by which a community must judge itself. We cannot be seen to be hounding him . . . however terrible he may be and however much we may . . . wish to.'

'Hold on a second.' It was Cynthia Walker. Heads turned in her direction. 'What if Pascoe is innocent?' she asked.

Silence fell once more.

Alan, Adrian and Jasper were all frowning. 'We can only go by the law,' Adrian said.

'Yes, but what if Pascoe *didn't* do it? The judiciary have freed him on the grounds that his guilt cannot be proven and we're all assuming that's a technicality, but what if he didn't do it?'

'I'm not sure I understand what you're getting at,' Adrian went on.

'If Pascoe didn't do it, then someone else *did*.'

There was another silence.

'I'm not sure what you're saying,' Jasper said, stepping forward, his voice resonant with the authority of his position in the village.

'I'm saying that if Pascoe has been proved innocent by the law, then isn't it possible that he is? Shouldn't we be asking for a new police investigation?' Cynthia said.

Jasper looked around the room. 'We're confident the police got

160

the right man.' He turned towards Professor Malcolm. 'I understand the police *are* conducting an informal review of the
evidence, but I doubt any of us would want to go through a full
investigation again. Let us concentrate on ensuring an appropriate response to the circumstances with which we are now faced.'

'You might not want to go through it, but you've not got
children at risk.'

Jasper cleared his throat. 'I don't think your daughter is at risk,
Cynthia.'

'Why not? If it wasn't Pascoe, it must have been someone else.
Perhaps he is still here.'

'But there has not been an incident for fifteen years.'

'That doesn't mean there's never going to be one.'

'We should call for an investigation,' Travers said. 'Why not,
what is there to lose?'

'Police investigations create a great deal of ill-feeling,' Alan
said, 'and attract unwanted media attention.' He took another
pace forward, putting his hands back in his pockets. 'Most of you
already know that a semi-official review is being conducted by
the Professor here.' People in the room turned their heads once
again to look at Professor Malcolm, but he ignored them. 'I think
we should do all we can to help. If there are any grounds for
further suspicion, then they should be pursued.'

'But that doesn't prevent the danger to our children,' Cynthia
said.

Julia saw that both Adrian and Jasper were beginning to look
exasperated, but Alan remained unflustered. 'I'm sure if there is a
danger, the Professor will identify it. I'm told he is the foremost
brain the police possess.'

This might have been sarcasm, Julia couldn't be sure, but if so,
it was delivered with enough finesse to ensure it went largely
unnoticed.

There was another hesitation. Then the chairs began to scrape
again and the villagers got up and filed solemnly past Julia and
Professor Malcolm. Travers, his wife and Cynthia Walker all
looked them straight in the eye as they left.

Julia realized she had misread the mood of the community.
They were afraid of Pascoe, but they were confused too, wary and
suspicious.

Professor Malcolm approached the stage. Adrian was stooping

161

to pack some papers into a leather briefcase, his bald patch facing them; Jasper was standing to the side, his hands in his pockets. As always, he wore a dull sports jacket, with a new white check shirt and a tie.

'This is Professor Malcolm.'

'Yes,' Adrian said. 'We know.'

Julia was shocked by the level of hostility all three men were displaying and could only conclude that his questioning of them in the past had been as abrasive as hers had been gentle. She felt awkward and a little embarrassed.

Professor Malcolm turned towards Alan. 'Thank you for your support.'

Alan shrugged. 'I can see why people would be worried. In that sense, your work may prove useful.'

'I should think he is beyond causing further harm.'

'How benign you make him sound,' Adrian said.

Professor Malcolm frowned. 'No,' he said. 'But it was good to see you sticking up for him.'

'Got to go,' Alan said, interrupting. He turned away towards the side entrance. 'Call me, Professor, if I can be of assistance.' The door banged shut behind him.

'Hardly sticking up for him, but there's a process of law,' Adrian said, straightening. 'I'd expect you to understand that.'

'It was said admiringly. So you believe he might be innocent?'

'No, but as I explained, there is a process.'

'Yes.'

Adrian stared at Professor Malcolm. 'Anyway, to what do we owe the pleasure of seeing you again? I'd have thought you did enough damage the first time.' There was a tightness at the corners of his mouth. 'They seemed to fare better once they'd got rid of you.'

'Did they?' Professor Malcolm said. 'Did they really?'

'Is this a formal interview, Professor?' Adrian asked.

'No. Of course not.'

'Then perhaps you could inform us, when you're ready, how and when we can be of assistance?'

'Yes. I'll do that.'

Julia and the Professor waited for Adrian and Jasper to leave so that they did not have to walk together. By the time they stepped outside, the light was fading fast. Their footsteps were noisy on

162

the gravel drive as they went up to the road, passing a series of pink posters pinned to telegraph poles advertising the village fête tomorrow.

They reached the Rose and Crown and looked towards Pascoe's house, which stood in darkness, its curtains drawn. Professor Malcolm was staring at the front door, deep in thought. Someone had painted a black cross on it, but the picture of Alice pinned there earlier had disappeared.

'Where do you think Pascoe has gone?' she asked.

'I don't know. I'd have liked to talk to him today.' He looked at her. 'This is going to be awkward for you, isn't it?'

'You mean with Adrian and . . .'

'Yes.'

Julia nodded slowly. 'It would be easier in many ways if they were my friends, but . . .'

'Your mother's?'

'Family friends. Mine, too, but of a different generation. It feels like I'm betraying them.'

She expected him to offer an explanation of why this wasn't the case, but he was staring at his feet.

'I'm sure,' she said, 'that things will ease as people come to accept that there's no threat and that going back . . . well, it's not ideal for any of us, is it? We don't like it, so why should they?'

They faced each other in silence. Then Julia gestured in the direction of Pascoe's house. 'Why does a man come back from a war to confess to a crime that he didn't commit?' she asked.

'Guilt,' he said. 'Perhaps. I don't know, but I would like to talk to him now.'

'When I saw him this morning, he said, "I could have done it." He said that twice. He said everyone wanted her, but no one could possess her and that there would be punishment.'

Professor Malcolm shook his head. 'It's hard to know what to read into the outpourings of a disturbed mind. I called the police about Pascoe while you were out and asked them to find him.'

Julia thought Professor Malcolm was no longer as confident in Pascoe's innocence as he pretended.

'I was surprised to see Alan there tonight,' he said. 'How did the three of you become friends? You were like a family unit at the passing-out parade. You, Alan, your mother. Was there any sign of that before the murders?'

163

'Alan kept his distance. It was, I think, an unspoken mutual agreement with my father.'

'They didn't get on?'

'They did, but they worked together. They wanted to get away from things at home, I'm sure.'

'So how did it happen that you became friends?'

She thought about this. 'I suppose he and Mum must have talked a lot after Sarah's death and Alice's disappearance, and then after my own father's death. I don't know. It happened gradually. I would . . . I would come home from school and he would come round for dinner. There was no big deal made of it – it seemed natural to me. My mother liked caring for someone. I don't know if he can cook. I don't imagine Sarah did much.'

'It just happened naturally?'

'Yes. My mother wasn't used to doing things in the house and the garden, so . . . You can see how it happened . . . two quite traditionally minded people.'

He waited for her to continue.

'Then, none of us really wanted to be at home for Christmas that year and Alan loves skiing, so he said he was going to a small hotel in Zermatt and asked us if we wanted to join him. And we did.' Julia thought of the sloping roofs and pine beds and fat continental duvets, of the thick snow and the lights and the chocolate cake she had consumed in the bar below each tea time. 'It was quite a magical time, actually. It was the beginning of things getting better.'

'You shared a room with your mother, Alan on his own?'

'Yes, of course.'

'And that's remained the pattern?'

'Yes. If you're asking me whether they're having a relationship, then the answer is that I don't know for certain. They maintain an old-fashioned discretion.'

He looked at her. Benignly, she thought. 'Good night,' he said.

He turned away and she watched his slow, shuffling walk. She saw now that he had a slight limp. Did he want her to invite him home again?

'Professor Malcolm.'

He stopped and turned back.

'I'd love to invite you in for something to eat, but . . .'

'I quite understand,' he said. 'You're not my nursemaid here. I

164

shall do perfectly well in the pub.' He smiled. 'I'll see you tomorrow.'

'Actually . . .' He stopped again. 'It's not that I don't want to be involved,' she said, 'but I think my mother would be upset if I didn't spend most of the weekend with her. After all, I've not seen her for three years. It would stretch her tolerance.'

He nodded. 'Understood.'

'What will you do? If you like I can drop you home, or . . .'

'Don't worry about me. I have things to be thinking about and getting on with. I have a book to review for the *Journal of Clinical Psychology*, so I can amuse myself in the sunshine. I'll see you on Monday, will I?'

'I think I saw on my mother's wall diary that she's out to-morrow night. Why don't you come round then?'

'But you can't cook.'

'No, but . . .'

'Then I shall. It will be my pleasure. I'll bring the ingredients, so don't worry about that.' He smiled at her. 'Call me if there is a change. Until tomorrow, then?'

'Until tomorrow.'

When Julia arrived home, she locked the front door as she came in, pulling across the chain. In the kitchen, she found a plate covered in Cellophane on the side, together with a note. 'Sorry, forgot to say that I was out. Hope this is okay. Won't be back late. Love, Mum.'

Julia returned to the front door to unhook the chain, before going to the back entrance to pull across the bolts. Then she walked through the house checking that all the windows were shut and screwed down.

Aristotle was not there, so she assumed he was with her mother.

Julia got herself a glass of wine and ate at the table, chicken with mango and an orange, lettuce and walnut salad. It was refreshing and light.

Afterwards, she went upstairs to her room, opening the window, but locking it with the safety bar. A gentle breeze carried the sound of laughter up from the de la Rues' garden next door. The tent for the fête was up, its pennants fluttering in the breeze against a darkening sky, the clouds shadows against the last of the red sunset.

Julia sat down on her bed, taking out the papers she had tucked away earlier. She opened them up, and read first her father's statement then her mother's.

She went to her desk and got a pen, then returned to her mother's statement. She underlined a passage: '*As I walked down Woodpecker Lane, I glanced in through the window of Alan Ford's house. I saw him crossing from one side of the kitchen to the other with a cup of coffee in his hand.*' Then she skipped a few paragraphs, before taking the pen to another section: '*I arrived home and saw my husband working in the garden. I went upstairs to change out of my church clothes. When I came down to the kitchen, he was digging the flower-bed by the hedge.*'

Julia looked at the passages again, then placed the papers on the table beside her and lay flat on the bed. She was glad Professor Malcolm had not gone over these statements with her.

The door opened below and Julia looked at her watch. It was almost ten o'clock. Her mother went into the kitchen, then climbed the stairs and walked down the landing.

The door opened and Caroline's face appeared. She was smiling as she stepped in and Julia thought she might be a little drunk.

'You found supper?'

'Yes. Thanks.' Julia sat up and swung her legs round, so that her back was to the radiator and she wasn't directly facing her mother. 'Did you have a good evening?'

'Yes. I'm sorry, I'd clean forgotten . . .'

'It's all right, Mum. Life doesn't stop just because I come home.'

Caroline hesitated. 'You were at the meeting,' she said.

'Briefly.'

Caroline was looking at her. 'I'm not sure I quite understand.'

Julia thought her mother's tongue was loosened by alcohol. 'No. I'm sorry . . . I can see why not.'

'You're a career army officer and now . . .'

Julia moved so that her back was against the head of the bed and she was facing her mother. 'It's because I can't tiptoe around it any more.'

'Around what?'

'Around the past.'

Caroline was frowning. 'I don't understand.'

'No one ever talks about it. It's like this . . . this thing that everyone is terrified of.'

166

'That's an odd way of putting it.'

'Tell me how you would describe it.'

Caroline sighed. 'Do you know what effect an event such as this has on a community . . .'

'Of course I do, Mum, I was here.'

'You were a child.'

'And that makes it worse. An adult understands. When you're a child, everything is half-hidden.'

Caroline was staring at the floor, but she was gripping her left shoulder with her right hand, unconsciously defensive.

'They say you helped Pascoe yesterday when he was brought home.'

'Only because I don't like to see a lynch mob at work.'

'He frightens people.'

'He frightens me.'

Caroline looked up slowly. 'I still don't understand.'

Julia leant forward. 'I cannot let it rest. I wish I could, more than anything I wish that, but I can't, my mind won't allow it.'

'Because he has been released?'

'Because I have not asked certain questions myself.' Julia was reaching out her hand in a gesture of supplication as she spoke. 'Because I was a child.' She could see her mother still did not understand. 'What if Pascoe was innocent? If . . . if he is guilty, then what's to be lost? If he's guilty then we'll just be more sure of it and . . . that is a good thing. It's doubt that is corrosive.' Julia looked at her hands. 'Everyone has a right to examine their past, Mum.'

There was a long silence, each of them avoiding the other's eye.

'And what if Pascoe's guilt can never be proven to your satisfaction – to the satisfaction of you and those with whom you choose to ally yourself. Are we then condemned to a cycle of perpetual revision, so that none of us can find peace? Do we not deserve that? Will no one allow that?' Caroline was looking out of the window. 'There are others here apart from you with feelings that will never settle, that can never be neatly closed off and forgotten. Can you imagine what this does to Alan?'

Julia stared at the opposite wall, chastened. 'You don't like Professor Malcolm, do you?'

'I pass no judgement on the individuals, they do what they

have to in a process that's necessary. We believed that process was complete, that's all. Now I see we were foolish to think that there would ever be a life beyond this.'

'You were civil to him at the passing-out parade, more than civil.'

Caroline sighed. 'I didn't understand why you brought him there, either.'

Julia turned to look out of the window beside her. A crescent moon bathed this part of the room in light now, but Caroline stood at the far end, her face shrouded in darkness.

'Your father didn't like him either.'

Julia recognized that this was a calculated blow. There was a long silence. 'Sometimes,' Julia said, 'I think you protect me from Dad.'

'What do you mean?'

'Protect his reputation.' She listened to the sound of a lorry trundling down the hill into the village.

'It's funny,' Caroline said, her voice quieter, 'I think the reverse. I'm so worried about him becoming an unmanageable icon for you that I feel I run him down, but I don't want you to have a one-dimensional picture. He was a complex man, but his faults were just human ones.'

Julia swung her feet off the bed. 'Can I ask you a question?'

Caroline did not answer.

'Didn't you find it odd that Sarah went to the common that day?'

'What do you mean?'

'I mean, if Pascoe is guilty, then Sarah was just "going for a walk", but you don't just go for a walk in your Sunday best, do you?'

'Our church has never been like that, Julia, you know that. It's not a "Sunday best" kind of village.'

'It still seems odd.'

'Sarah was odd.'

'Yes, but even eccentricity can be consistent and explicable, whereas this just seems . . .'

'What are you getting at?'

Julia hesitated. 'You don't think it is possible she was meeting someone?'

'Then why would she have taken Alice?'

'Right. Yes.' Julia realized that just because they had never talked about this didn't mean her mother hadn't considered it. She breathed in deeply. 'In your statement to the police, you say that you went upstairs to change and then, when you came back down, you saw Dad digging the flower-bed by the hedge?'

There was a hesitation. 'Yes.'

'But when I ran to the fence after seeing Sarah's body, Dad had just started mowing the lawn and I don't recall any sign of the flower-bed having been dug.' Julia wished she could see her mother's face.

'You're playing a dangerous game with a past you don't understand.'

'That's enigmatic.'

'No, it's not. But suspicion is a disease. You've not seen what it can do.'

Julia stood and took a step towards her mother. 'Come on, Mum, please. Support me.'

'In what? The destruction of all that is left to us?' She shook her head. 'Because that is the only thing suspicion can achieve.'

'That's . . .'

'Enough.' Caroline raised her hand. 'Please. I don't understand, but I won't try. I'll ignore what you're doing in the hope that somewhere good sense will prevail, but remember, it's not all about you.' Caroline cleared her throat. 'I actually came in here to tell you I'm going to lunch with the de la Rues tomorrow, before the fête, and they would love to see you, if . . .'

'You told me already, Mum.' Julia nodded. 'Yes, of course.'

After Caroline had gone, Julia shut and locked the window, pulled the curtains and got into bed, staring up at the dark ceiling, listening to the water-heater, which was noisy enough to shut out any other sound. When it stopped, she thought she could make out an owl in the distance, from the direction of the common.

The moonlight crept through gaps in her curtains, falling in scattered pools on the wall opposite.

Julia heard one of the floorboards on the stairs creak, then another. There was silence for a moment, then she heard the soft shuffle of her mother moving away, back to her room. If she had been seeking a softer meeting, she had changed her mind and returned to bed.

Julia realized that her mother had not even asked her about Beijing. Nor had she answered the question about the flower-bed.

CHAPTER TWELVE

so, the following morning, Julia and Caroline walked round to lunch along Woodpecker Lane, past pink posters advertising the village fête, which were pinned to the telegraph poles along the line of the hedge. Ahead, the gate into one of the de la Rues' fields was open, with a large sign saying 'CAR-PARK' directing traffic into it.

The de la Rues' home was called Bell House, because it had once been a school and the old bell still hung above the big oak front door. It was a Victorian building, not an especially attractive one, but inside Henrietta had worked hard to make it homely, sparing no expense. The hall was lighter than Julia remembered, its carpet removed and the floorboards beneath polished, an Oriental rug laid over them.

There were three steps down into the kitchen, which had been extended, with a door open on the far side leading out to a con- servatory. Julia could see Jessica de la Rue's blonde hair, but the other guests were out of view.

There was an island in the middle, with a large bowl of fruit salad, several full of crisps and an open bottle of red wine.

There was a young shout of 'No,' and a blond-haired boy charged into the room, carrying an aeroplane, followed by Jessica. '*Not* on the table,' she said to him, before catching sight of Julia

171

and moving briskly across to kiss her. 'Give me the plane, Danny. *Not* inside.'

Danny tried to duck past, but Jessica caught him and swung him underneath her arm as she mounted the steps to the door to the hall. She looked over her shoulder, mouthing an apology to Julia.

Jasper de la Rue came in and Julia was too close to the door to avoid having his arm draped over her shoulder. She was led through to the conservatory, where the table was laid. His annoyance over her presence at the meeting last night seemed to have been forgotten. There was a flagstone floor in the conservatory, the room to the right, now also with polished floorboards, transformed into a day-room, with comfortable sofas in dark, rich red and newspapers spread on large ottomans, the front page of *The Times* spilling on to the floor.

Outside, the garden was a hive of activity. The line of pennants on top of the tent still fluttered in the wind and the trestle tables that made up the stalls were up and, in most cases, already covered in produce. Julia watched Hattie Travers walk from one side of the lawn to the other carrying a pile of books.

'The boys are playing tennis,' Jasper said, and it took Julia a moment to comprehend that he was probably referring to Alan, among others.

Jasper was called back by his wife and Julia stepped out of the open doors on to the thin strip of gravel path then the lawn beyond it. She watched Hattie Travers reach the second-hand bookstall and begin to stack the books on the table, Cynthia Walker helping, her little girl sitting cross-legged on the grass below, reading. Ahead, beyond the line of trestle tables, the oldest de la Rue girl was trying to play badminton with her younger sister. They squealed with delight, then collapsed on the ground, flat out on the grass, beneath the net, staring at the sky. They were dressed for the summer, with bare legs, white plimsolls, and bands in their hair.

James Rouse was sitting on a rug on the bank watching them, wearing a red and white striped shirt, jeans that were too tight and a pair of black brogues. Julia raised a hand in greeting, but moved off in the other direction, towards the swimming-pool and the tennis court beyond it, squinting against the bright sun as it broke through a gap in the clouds.

The swimming-pool was shielded by a brick wall that had been erected for safety, and there was a large grass area beside it, where her father had manned 'Toss the Caber' all those years ago. Adrian Rouse stood there now, a drink in his hand, looking out over the wooden fence to the field that led down to the common. The sign next to him advertised 'Pony Rides'.

As she passed, Adrian seemed to sense that her eyes were upon him, for he turned and looked briefly in her direction before, once again, returning to his solitary view of the common.

The tennis court was behind a high beech hedge and as Julia walked through the gap in the middle of it, she heard Alan say, 'Bugger.'

He'd missed a shot and was resting against the fence. He was sweating, his hair hanging over his forehead. He smiled at her and pushed away. At the other end of the court, Michael Haydoch raised his racket in greeting.

'He's too fit,' Alan told her.

'He's too fat,' Michael said.

Julia squatted on the bank beside the hedge to watch. Michael was serving. He was wearing a pair of white shorts, white socks and tennis shoes, his shirt discarded by the side of the court. As he threw the ball up and prepared to strike it, she watched the muscles tensing in his arm, abdomen and legs. His hair was shorter than she remembered and the pelt that ran from his chest to the waistband of his shorts seemed denser. He was sweating, too, but not as much. His head was so much narrower than Alan's, though perhaps that had something to do with the density and length of their hair.

Julia watched the ball flying to and fro across the net. Alan was the more skilled player, with a strong top-spin on his forehand, which forced his opponent from one side of the court to the other, but he was not as fit as Michael, who never gave up on anything.

Eventually, Michael dropped a ball short, which had Alan almost falling into the net on the far side of the court. He straightened and caught his breath, putting his right hand in the small of his back.

'Persistent bastard,' he said to Julia.

'Who's winning?'

Alan gestured to the other side of the court with his racket. Michael looked at her, without expression.

They returned to their respective ends and Michael served again. He was a tall man and his serve was fast and straight. Alan looked chubbier because of the baggy shorts he was wearing, but Julia could see that he would benefit from losing weight. He had a loose-fitting tennis shirt on which seemed to emphasize rather than hide his tummy.

They fought this point ferociously and for a long time Alan seemed to control it, but once more Michael managed to drop the ball suddenly short and this time Alan fell as he tried to reach for it, careering into the net. He lay there for a second then got up, smacking his racket briefly against the ground as he stood and walking back to his end of the court without catching her eye.

Julia did not look at Michael to see his reaction. She was a little embarrassed and turned away, just as the youngest of the de la Rue girls came through the hedge to tell them that lunch was ready.

As Julia walked into the conservatory, Jessica took her arm and sat her down in the chair next to hers. A few seconds later, Michael came in, with a towel around his shoulders, the sweat glistening on his tanned upper body. Julia saw that Jessica was smiling at him.

'Are you going to put your shirt on, Michael, or are we supposed to sit here and drool?'

'Sit there and drool.'

'Come and sit on the other side of Julia,' Jessica said.

Julia found she was flushing. Jasper de la Rue, Adrian and Leslie Rouse and her mother were all opposite, looking at her. Alan had still not appeared. Michael went to get a T-shirt from a bag in the room next door and returned, fully clad, to sit next to her. She didn't know whether to greet him or not. 'It's okay,' he said. 'You don't have to kiss me.'

'You're covered in sweat.'

'Working up an appetite.'

'Did you win?'

'Result inconclusive, technically, but yes.'

Alan came in and sat down at the other side of the table,

between Leslie Rouse and Henrietta de la Rue. Adrian was staring at the table.

'How Alan hates losing,' Michael said.

'And you don't?'

'Not as much as him.'

Jasper had already carved the chickens in the kitchen and put the meat on a large, Mediterranean plate. Henrietta passed Julia a plateful.

'What are you doing at home?' Michael asked.

'Between jobs.'

'What have you just finished?'

'Nothing much.'

'Which country?'

'China.'

'Perfecting the art of the monosyllabic answer.'

'What do you want, Michael?' Henrietta asked, poised over the chicken.

'Breast for preference, Henrietta, but anything will do.'

To her annoyance, Julia felt herself going red in the face again.

'Well, what have you been doing?' she asked, when they had both received their plates.

'Left the Service.'

Julia nodded. She was hoping to get into conversation with Jessica, who had turned half to the right in an attempt to feed her little boy.

'I gather you've got yourself hooked up with that charlatan,' Michael said.

Julia frowned, trying to pretend she didn't understand what he meant.

'Professor Malcolm.'

'He's just an academic,' she said.

'That's not what he thinks, though, is it?'

Julia did not answer.

'So you're telling everyone Pascoe is innocent?' His voice was loud. Conversation around the table, which had been in a lull, suddenly died off.

Julia took a sip of the white wine Jasper had just poured. 'It must be *possible* that he is innocent surely, and that some other psychopath was responsible.'

Caroline Havilland was looking at her plate, so was Alan.

175

Adrian was staring into the middle distance. Only Leslie Rouse still looked in her direction. Julia thought her comfortable face the most hostile.

'But Pascoe confessed,' Jasper said, frowning, standing to fill other wine-glasses. 'Why would he do that if he wasn't guilty?'

'Why would he confess if he was?'

'I don't understand your logic.'

'Most people who are really guilty don't confess, do they? And if you read Robert Pascoe's statement, it's not convincing.'

'In what way?' de la Rue asked.

'Well, he doesn't mention anything . . .'

Julia caught sight of Alan looking at her. Of all the people around the table, his expression seemed the least disapproving. 'Go on,' he said, quietly.

'There was no mention of Alice at all and . . . well . . . I mean, if he was confessing, wouldn't he have said something about . . .' Julia could not progress further. Caroline was avoiding her eye. 'I mean,' Julia went on, 'what about the other man in the leather jacket – the stranger they never traced?'

'What are they talking about, Mummy?' Danny asked.

Everyone turned to look at him.

The silence was broken by the sound of Alan's chair being pushed back. On the way to the lavatory, he passed behind Julia and ruffled her hair affectionately. Then Jasper de la Rue and Leslie Rouse began talking and gradually conversation picked up again.

'Thanks,' Julia said, under her breath, to Michael.

After lunch, the de la Rues decided that coffee would be taken in the pavilion by the swimming-pool, away from preparations for the fête. Caroline had slipped away to help make sure that everything was running properly.

There was shade up by the pool and Julia preferred to sit in it rather than swim, though all the de la Rue children and James jumped in as soon as they had changed. The cloud had broken up now and it was warm again.

The sound of a trumpet drifted up from the garden below, as the band began to warm up.

Alan came through the gate, disappeared into the changing-hut, then emerged and dived into the pool, his tummy bulging over the waistband of his shorts. He and James played piggy-in-the-middle with the two girls.

Michael came up and lay flat along the edge of the pool on the spot where Sarah had been filmed in her yellow bikini. He had taken off his shirt again and she tried not to look at him.

Adrian Rouse and Henrietta walked in with the coffee. Adrian was wearing a yellow V-neck sweater, Henrietta a dowdy denim skirt. They sat in the shade.

As Henrietta poured the coffee, Julia heard them talking about the weather and how good it had been. Henrietta asked Adrian about their holiday plans and he explained that they were going to Cornwall, without the children since James would be away and Elizabeth was going off with her boyfriend. Julia could not imagine Leslie and Adrian enjoying a holiday together.

She could add little to the conversation, since she had no holiday plans.

Alan and James were still teasing the girls.

The younger of the two girls was wearing a pink bikini with white spots. She appeared to have no sense of the appropriate space and distance that should be kept between a young girl and a man who was not her father. James did not seem bothered by this and allowed her to clamber on his shoulders, but when she swam over to Alan, Julia saw clearly that he was uncomfortable with the physical intimacy. He gently but firmly put her back down into the pool, or swam away, trying to make a joke of it, but she pursued him.

James did not notice this, neither did anyone else. Michael was still lying flat out on the other side of the pool, with his eyes shut.

But to Julia, it became more pronounced and awkward until, eventually, Alan got out. James and the girl tried to persuade him to come back in, but he refused irritably.

Julia stood up and went over to Alan, who was sitting in a chair. She ruffled his hair as she passed, understanding how painful his loss was and how easily one could be reminded of it.

She turned to smile at him, then wandered out of the enclosure. As she went, the band struck up, marking the official opening of the 1997 West Welham Village Fête.

As he came over the neck of the valley to West Welham, Mac stopped by the side of the road, the car shuddering as it came to a halt.

177

He got out and climbed on to the bank, so that he could look down on the village, before taking off his sunglasses and cleaning them on his shirt, squinting and holding his hand above his head to shield his eyes from the sun.

There was some smoke rising from beyond the church and he could see a big tent in one of the gardens close to Julia's home. As he had before, he thought about how far removed this genteel valley of middle England was from his own terraced home in Leeds.

He got back into the car and drove on down, pulling slowly into the car-park at the pub. He had been here twice before to stay with Julia, shortly after they had left Sandhurst, and knew that the house owned by Pascoe's mother was in a narrow lane the other side of the Rose and Crown.

Before getting out, Mac took another look at his notebook. He had copied down the names from Richard Claverton's fishing journal.

The two separate columns reflected, in some way, he thought, two opposing sides: Ford, Haydoch and Rouse in one camp, Claverton, Pascoe, Danes and Wilkes in the other. Mac had crossed out Claverton and Danes's names, since they were dead, and this left only Pascoe and Wilkes in the right-hand column. Common sense dictated that Pascoe had to have been the author of the letters to Claverton.

Mac couldn't be certain, but he thought that the names were divided by rank. Pascoe, Claverton and Danes were soldiers, and he guessed that Wilkes was, too. He had met both Ford and Rouse and was confident that Haydoch was probably an officer as well. One side was enlisted men, the other commissioned officers.

As he put the pad in his pocket and walked round the corner, he saw that the windows in the pub were open and trade was brisk. He had been half expecting to find some form of protest, but life in the village seemed utterly normal. Everywhere there were posters advertising the village fête and he could hear a band tuning up.

He knocked on Pascoe's front door. There was no answer so he tried again.

The curtains were drawn upstairs, but, if he was in, Pascoe wasn't receiving visitors.

After knocking twice more, without success, Mac walked into

the Rose and Crown. There were two or three men leaning against the bar, deep in conversation, but it was noisy and Mac couldn't hear what they were saying. He attracted a few idly curious glances, before he removed his sunglasses.

The landlord was plump, with an unkempt moustache. He was assisted by a thin youth whose face was covered in freckles. Mac waited for one of them to finish serving.

The landlord, pulling a pint of Guinness, finally glanced in Mac's direction.

'I was looking for a Professor Malcolm,' he said.

Conversation around the bar dipped. The two men next to him stopped talking and turned round.

'David Malcolm. I believe he is staying here.'

The landlord was looking down at the Guinness he was pouring. 'Top of the stairs, left, end of the corridor. Room five.'

'Thanks,' Mac said. He smiled at the man closest to him and wove his way through to the door in the corner.

The stairwell was beyond the toilets. It was narrow, its carpet threadbare. At the top, he went through a fire door into a corridor that looked as if it had been recently refurbished. The carpet here was new and the pictures on the walls had brass lights above them.

Number five was next to the fire exit and Mac looked down through the glass panel to the car-park and his old Fiesta, tucked in at the end. He knocked.

There was no answer.

He was about to knock again when the door opened. It was gloomy inside and Professor Malcolm looked as if he had been asleep. 'Mac,' he said.

'Sorry, is this . . . ?'

'No, come in.' He yawned. 'I must have fallen asleep again.'

Professor Malcolm yawned once more and stretched. There was an open box on the desk in the window that contained a number of brown envelopes. There were some papers next to it, with a book face down on top of them, but Mac's eyes were drawn to the wall. It was hard to see who all the photographs depicted, but he could make out the Havillands and Alan Ford, and the Rouses, whom he'd met once while walking up on the ridge with Julia. And Alice, of course.

Professor Malcolm sat on the bed.

Mac saw that the woman in the centre was Sarah Ford – it was the same picture he had seen in the newspaper today, next to an inside article that had given more details of Pascoe's release. Looking at her now, she reminded him in a way of Julia. They had similar classically beautiful faces and both had lustrous dark hair, though Sarah's was longer and straighter. And they shared that sardonic, amused smile.

'Is this man Pascoe innocent?' Mac asked.

'Possibly. On the central issue, anyway.'

Mac frowned in confusion.

'He's not a particularly attractive character. I would say he was certainly watching Sarah.'

'Who is guilty?'

'We don't know.'

Mac stared at the picture of Pascoe on the wall. He looked much younger than he had in the newspaper. 'Why did he confess if he was innocent?'

Professor Malcolm stretched, pushing his arms back and rolling his neck. 'I'm not certain. I think he probably had severe post-traumatic stress disorder and, therefore, was an easy target for the police.'

'Why do you have all this?'

'I'm conducting a review of the case. Julia is helping.'

Mac frowned again.

'In her own way,' Professor Malcolm added.

'Who are the photographs of?' he said. 'And why are they in a circle?'

Professor Malcolm pointed. 'Ford, the husband, the Havillands, de la Rues, Rouses, Pascoe and Haydoch. Those closest to her here in the Welhams. Mostly concentrating on geographical proximity at the moment.'

Mac leant over to get a closer look. He saw immediately that they had been shot by a police or army surveillance unit or by someone with similar equipment.

Mac looked at a photograph of a tall and strikingly good-looking man.

'Which one is this?'

'Michael Haydoch. A friend of Sarah's. Also from the same regiment.' Professor Malcolm was looking at the picture. 'As you probably know, because of the proximity of the base, this is effectively a dormitory village for the regiment, principally for its officer class, though Pascoe and his mother lived in the cheaper housing beside the pub.'

Mac straightened. Because of the size of the two of them, the room seemed small and the atmosphere intimate. Perhaps it was the relative darkness.

'Mitchell Havilland was the commander,' Professor Malcolm went on, 'Rouse, Ford and Haydoch all junior officers.'

Mac watched Professor Malcolm's face as he talked. His hair was grey and thin, his face lined and worn with age, but what was most noticeable about him was his big, broken, bony nose. Mac wondered how much to confide in him.

'Thank you for coming,' Professor Malcolm said. 'As a matter of fact, I'd fallen asleep waiting to hear from the police who are trying to locate Pascoe. He seems to have disappeared, which is worrying.'

'I thought there were too many coincidental overlaps. It made me . . .'

'Quite.'

Mac looked at the photographs again. 'I don't understand why Julia is helping.'

Professor Malcolm didn't answer immediately. Eventually he said, 'I think it better if Julia tells you that, Mac.' He looked up. 'I know the two of you are close. But it really is a private matter for her.'

Mac took a piece of paper from his pocket, opened it out and handed it to Professor Malcolm.

' "Havilland, Lieutenant Colonel Mitchell," ' Professor Malcolm read. ' "Investigation into death. No discrepancies found, save for informant. No further action due to his psychiatric condition. Current battalion CO informed official complaint made and investigated. No action to be taken." '

Mac took out his notebook, turned it to the correct page and handed it to him. 'I think Pascoe must be the informant referred to there and this is a list of the people who were present at Mitchell Havilland's death. Both Danes and Claverton apparently shot themselves within three days of each other in August last year. I haven't yet spoken to Mrs Danes, but Claverton's wife said he would never have committed suicide.'

'Wives always say that.'

181

Mac put his hands in his pockets and leant back against the door. 'Claverton began receiving letters from Winchester Prison, where Pascoe was, warning him that it was time to "tell the truth". There were then unexplained "visitors" to his house, and after each of the letters and the visits Claverton went into a steep decline. The only person he confided in was his friend Danes.'

Professor Malcolm was looking at the list of names in front of him. 'Of those still alive, Pascoe and Wilkes are from the ranks, the others officers? Is that why the two columns?'

Mac thought this was a highly intelligent observation. 'I can't say for certain Wilkes is from the ranks, but I assume he is. I copied the columns from a fishing journal that Claverton wrote. The symbol I've written above – the H with a circle around it and a cross through – is what he drew above it.'

Professor Malcolm was frowning again. 'Forgive me if I'm being stupid, Mac, but I'm not certain I follow this.'

'Neither do I. I put Julia's name into our computer to see if there were any prior charges or investigations, which is an entirely routine procedure for any investigation. I expected nothing to come up and nothing did for her, but there was this under her father's name.' Mac pointed to the piece of paper in Professor Malcolm's hand. 'Since then, every official avenue I have pursued has proved a dead end. The main file on the computer is locked. The hard copy is absent from the registry, signed out a year ago and not returned. The basic personnel files of the men involved have been removed from the regiment where they belong by my superiors in the Military Police.'

Mac turned once more to the photographs. 'I'm telling you because the overlap in the names seems too much of a coincidence to me.'

'Discrepancies in accounts of Havilland's death. What are the discrepancies?'

'I have no idea. If I said anything ... well, it would be speculative and ...'

'Speculate.'

'It could be anything.' Mac shrugged. 'But what I think you have to ask yourself is, why is there official nervousness and secrecy? Richard Claverton told his wife in an unguarded remark years ago that Havilland would not have been seen as a hero if he'd come back from the war. She took that to mean that something would have come to light about him upon his return. Of course, Havilland's death is public property for the army in many ways. If he didn't die heroically . . .'

'Or wasn't killed by the enemy at all.'

Mac looked at Professor Malcolm, who was staring at the floor, deep in thought. He couldn't tell whether this was an informed guess or just an idle thought. 'It would suggest,' Professor Malcolm went on, 'either that his death itself did not transpire in the way commonly supposed, or that there was some other information that would have been made known had he lived long enough to come home.'

'He would have returned to face an ongoing investigation,' Mac said.

'Correct, but jumping to conclusions. It is more likely, surely, that Mr Claverton was referring to the circumstances surrounding Havilland's death?'

Mac did not answer.

Professor Malcolm stood and walked to the window, then turned round and leant on the desk. 'Claverton and Danes were eliminated because of a piece of knowledge they possessed.'

'Claverton and Danes were tough men, terminated clinically, possibly with their own weapons.'

'Pascoe is now out, of course . . .'

Mac nodded. 'Yes. But anyone who has or is pursuing the information is also at risk.'

'All the officers seem to be all right. None of them has been targeted.'

'Not yet. Not that we know of.'

'Whatever you do,' Professor Malcolm said, 'don't tell Julia.'

'I can't agree with that.'

Professor Malcolm shook his head. 'I don't understand.'

'You agreed it was possible that Claverton was referring to something that predated the war, but would have come to light had Havilland returned from it. Anyone working in this area is at risk and I won't . . .'

'You're jumping to conclusions.' Professor Malcolm shook his head again. 'You will increase the risk by pushing her to explore an area she has no reason to venture into.'

Mac got the sense that the Professor wanted time to think. He turned towards the door.

'Mac . . .'

He turned back.

'I know how . . . I know how it is between you, but please don't tell Julia. Apart from anything else, I think the simple heroism of her father's death is something she needs to cling to for the time being.'

It was still bright outside as Mac walked down Woodpecker Lane, putting his sunglasses on once more. He realized he was sweating and that it had been hot up there in that little room. A fair-haired child in a bright yellow dress walked past him clutching helium-filled balloons with one hand and her mother with the other.

Mac paid his entry fee to the fête and walked forward into the milling throng. There were two large lawns, separated by a flower-bed, the one he was standing on as flat as a bowling green, with trestle tables assembled around its edges and a tent at the end, temporarily obscuring the view of the common. He scanned the crowd for a sight of Julia's wavy dark hair.

Beyond the flower-bed there was a larger area and Mac could see a group of ponies being led in a line and the top of a tennis-court fence in the distance. He passed the tombola, then caught sight of a coconut shy on the far lawn, next to the ponies, and made his way to it through the crowd. He paid a pound for five small wooden balls and threw them hard and straight, knocking off four coconuts. He was offered a prize but, since the choice seemed mostly to consist of teddy bears, declined.

Mac caught sight of and approached Adrian Rouse, who was standing by the sign advertising pony rides. He did not see Mac until he was standing right next to him, and there was a moment's hesitation as he struggled to put a name to the face.

'Mac.'

There was still a hesitation. 'Yes. Of course.'

Rouse proffered his hand, then almost immediately turned away to talk to the children who were waiting in line for their turn on the ponies. Mac took half a pace back and watched the little girl in the yellow dress hurrying across the lawn towards them. He could see no sign of the mother for a moment, until she, too, rounded the flower-bed at a run, catching her daughter with fury in her face.

'I've told you *not* to run off.'

The child looked at her mother then burst into tears. The

woman hugged her. 'You *promised* to hold my hand.'

Smarting at Rouse's unfriendliness, Mac turned away and retraced his steps. As he rounded the flower-bed, he ran into Alan Ford.

'Mac.'

'Hello, Colonel, how—'

'Mac, please – it's Alan.'

They shook hands. The most memorable thing about Alan Ford, Mac thought, was his smile, and he found himself thinking what an easy man he must be to serve under. He wore a red rugby shirt and a pair of washed-out blue cotton trousers and was sweating.

'Sorry not to be able to help the other day.'

'Oh. No, I'm sorry to have troubled you.'

'My hands are tied.'

'Yes.'

'Looking for Julia?'

Mac hesitated. 'Yes.'

'She's at home. Got a headache.'

This might have been a joke, Mac wasn't sure. Alan was obviously helping Adrian Rouse with the pony rides and suddenly he felt like an intruder. He walked on round the flower-bed towards the exit to the road and, as he went, passed Caroline Havilland standing behind a stall loaded with cakes. 'Hello, Mac,' she said, her smile as welcoming as Alan's.

'Hi.' He thought it uncanny how much Caroline looked like Julia, or the other way round.

'Looking for Julia or wanting to buy cakes?'

'Er . . .' Mac smiled.

'She's at home. You'll find her there.'

Seeing that Caroline was busy – an old lady had just chosen and handed her three large cakes – Mac raised his hand in thanks and turned away.

'Good luck,' Caroline said.

Mac turned back. He smiled, not sure what she had meant.

Julia was not at home. Mac tried the doorbell twice, but there was no answer. He waited a long time and it was only when he got back to the car that he acknowledged his disappointment. He wound down the window and took out his mobile. The top end of the car-park was higher than Woodpecker Lane and he could make out the corner of her roof over the line of the hedge.

The call was switched to an answering-machine.

'Hello, Julia, it's Mac . . .' He did not know what to say. 'Just calling to see how you are. Give me a ring later or . . . I'll try again this evening to see if I can catch you.'

Mac started the car, turned into the lane and put his foot flat on the accelerator, causing the Fiesta to backfire loudly.

At the neck of the valley, curiosity overcame him and he stopped. He flicked through the notebook until he found the number of the regimental base and dialled it, getting out of the car and climbing the bank as he waited for the connection. Below, the band had started up again.

'Duty officer, please.'

Mac waited.

'Lieutenant Benson here.'

'Benson. Major Rigby. Thanks for your help the other day. Got one more problem that can't wait until Monday.'

'Yes, sir.'

'Another name for you. Wilkes. Same again. Up-to-date address and telephone number.' As he was talking, Mac was turning the pages to get to where he'd written down Claverton's address last night.

'Yes, sir. I'm afraid I'll have to call the Colonel.'

'I shouldn't worry about that, Benson. It's only a routine matter and it's a Saturday. I don't want to be responsible for interrupting his weekend.'

There was a pause. 'Well, sir, the thing is this. After your last call, the Colonel telephoned Major Rigby at SIB Woolwich and he denied that he'd ever called here.'

Mac took his mobile phone from his ear and pressed end.

'Shit,' he said.

The doorbell awoke Julia and, for a moment, she was disorientated. Her room was bathed in evening sunlight and her watch told her it was eight thirty.

She stood up and tried to shake the sleep from her head. In the mirror, she saw that her hair was awry and her face creased from the pillow. She could not even remember lying down.

Aristotle was in the hall and rolled over as she approached.

Julia stepped over him, rubbing his tummy briefly with her foot and wondering who could be calling at this time of night.

Professor Malcolm was standing in the doorway. His hair was still wet and had been combed back neatly across his scalp. A few tufts of grey chest hair poked out of the front of a clean but crumpled white shirt. He wore a smarter pair of green cords, the same brown brogues on his feet and was carrying a Sainsbury's shopping bag.

'I'm sorry. Am I too early?'

She looked at him and put a hand to her ear. He frowned in confusion. 'Shaving foam,' she said, 'in your ear.' He stuck in a bony finger and cleared it out.

Julia led him through to the kitchen and he put the bag on the side. Aristotle followed them and set himself uncomfortably across the step.

'I should have cooked,' Julia said, as he unpacked the contents of the bag, but he didn't respond. He got out a frying-pan, a chopping-board and a long thin knife from the rack above the Aga. 'Have you got a wooden spoon?' he asked, before noticing that the wooden implements were in a pot in the corner.

He took an onion from the bag.

'What are you doing?' she asked.

'I'm chopping onions.'

'No, I mean, what are you cooking?'

'Professor Malcolm's risotto master-class, step one: chop onions.'

Julia watched him sweep the onions into the frying-pan, with some butter, then lift up the top of the Aga and switch the pan across.

'Did you have a good day?' she asked.

'Yes, pleasant enough. I puffed my way up to the top of the ridge and read my book in the sunshine.'

'Looking down upon the village fête.'

'Yes.' He stirred the onions gently. 'I wasn't sure my presence was likely to be welcomed. But I did go to the village shop . . .'

'To get some jelly babies?'

He turned to her and smiled. 'The woman there recognized me.'

'Which one?'

He faced the Aga again and continued stirring. 'I cannot recall her name. Thick black glasses, dark, very curly hair . . .'

'Ruth.'

'Yes. That's right. There are two of them, aren't there? Sisters. Or say they are.'

Julia frowned, heavily. As a child growing up in a village, you would, of course, be unlikely to take something like that at anything other than face value.

'Ruth seemed keen to talk, so I said I would return with my assistant on Monday.'

Julia sat down on the kitchen table, wanting to think and talk about something unrelated to the murders, but finding herself instead trying to work out if her mother had deliberately lied to protect her father in her statement to the police. She didn't have enough confidence in her own memories to be certain that her mother was lying.

Had Adrian Rouse's statement implicating Pascoe also been a lie? Was he trying to protect her father, too?

Mitchell had never liked the Rouses. Adrian, in particular, had often fallen victim, in words at least, to his darker moods – 'boring as all hell,' was a description she recalled.

'You should learn to cook,' Professor Malcolm said.

'Yes. There hasn't been time.'

He was pouring in some rice now. 'Arborio?' she asked.

'Yes.'

'What's different from normal rice?'

'Short grain, but fat. Creamy texture when cooked right. Restaurants sometimes try to get round the laborious cooking process by sticking in a lot of cream, which doesn't work.'

'Right.'

Professor Malcolm had brought a bottle of white wine and he now found a corkscrew in the drawer, opened it and poured some into the pan. He turned to Julia. 'Would you like a glass?'

'I'm sorry,' she said, galvanized into action. 'We have masses in the fridge.'

'This is open.'

She got two glasses and he filled them. He took a big gulp.

'The only thing I don't have is ground ginger. Your mother is bound to have . . .' He saw the look on her face and smiled. 'Okay.

188

You try the larder, I'll have a look in the cupboards here.' Julia had just gone into the larder when he said, 'Got it.'

'Ginger?' she asked.

'Yes. Ginger risotto. Don't frown. You'll not be disappointed.'

'Who taught you to cook?'

'Books.'

Julia sat down at the table again. 'I bet you read a lot as a child.'

He hesitated. 'Yes. Yes, I did.'

The risotto was creamy and filling. Julia admired Professor Malcolm's capacity to drink and it was not long before they were on to one of the bottles in the fridge.

After they had finished eating and he had enjoyed her compliments, Professor Malcolm produced a packet of Marlboro Lights and a lighter. He offered her one, which she took and suggested they step out on to the terrace.

He looked funny smoking, though also like an *habitué*. He noticed her smiling.

'Man cannot live by bread and water alone, you know. It's the wine. I can never resist when I've had a drink.'

The night was cool and the light on the terrace attracted a moth that fluttered above their heads. Julia walked to the edge of the steps, sucking in the smoke. Mixing it with the fresh air made her light-headed.

She watched him inhale deeply, lean his head back, his Roman nose pointing upwards, and blow the smoke into the night sky.

'Your mother is proud of you,' he said.

Julia took another drag of her own cigarette. 'She's a selfless woman.'

'You feel she interferes.'

'No, not really. She's at pains not to, actually.' She looked across the hedge. One of the lights was on upstairs in the Ford house, probably in Alan's bedroom. 'But I sometimes feel that she protects me from my father, just as she did when he was alive, and it makes it worse.' Julia sucked in the smoke again, but it was less satisfying. 'I don't think you really understand.' He was about to answer, but she cut him off. 'I mean intellectually you do, but emotionally you don't.'

'Well, I never had a father. So in that sense you're right.'

'I'm sorry, I didn't mean . . .'

189

'No, come on . . .' He shrugged. 'I wasn't scoring a point. I'm just agreeing. You're right. There's a difference between under-standing and feeling. There is emotional intelligence.' He looked at her. 'You were an only child.'

'It's not so much that.'

Professor Malcolm waited for her to go on.

'When I was a teenager,' she said, 'say fourteen or fifteen, I was horrible to my mother. I mean, really horrendous. I blamed her for everything, somehow, as though she'd driven my father away.' Julia turned to him. 'I'm not saying this was logical.'

'Being a teenager isn't logical.'

'I lionized my father and hated my mother.'

'That was inevitable. If your father had been alive, you'd prob-ably have hated them both.'

'Perhaps. At some point I think you do reject parental influence, but then, later on, you realize how much you have taken from them, good and bad. You're fashioned in their image, like it or not.'

'Forgive me, but I'm not sure I follow.'

Julia took another drag of the cigarette, blowing the smoke from the side of her mouth, slowly. 'After the skiing holiday you saw on the video, we went into a shop at Edinburgh railway station and there was a small doll there in a tartan dress, which I wanted. My father wouldn't buy it for me, so I stole it.'

'I knew you were a criminal.'

She smiled. 'I don't know why I stole it, but I did. Dad didn't catch sight of it until about twenty minutes into the journey to London.'

'He was angry?'

'No, he was totally calm. He made us get off the train, wait for two hours to get another one back to Edinburgh and then he took me to the shop and forced me to say sorry. We had to stay an extra night in the city and . . . we didn't have much money.' She waited a moment. He was still frowning in confusion. 'Look,' she went on, 'we're all adrift in the adult world, yes?'

'In a manner of speaking.'

'For better or worse he's my fixed point.'

'Role model.'

'If you want, though I think it's more complicated than that. He wasn't an easy man, I'd be the first to admit, but there was

190

something about him that infected people. He . . . radiated belief. He believed in right and wrong, decency, honour – all the things no one believes in any more.'

'Integrity.'

'Yes. Integrity most of all. You know, I couldn't say this to anyone else. It would sound po-faced and naïve, but it's true. I once tried to explain it to someone at school and they teased me about it for months. Everyone did.'

'And your fears gradually invalidate not just every memory that came before his death but everything that you have done since.'

'You know, I don't really want to talk—'

'And your mother protecting his image makes it worse, because you don't know what she's really protecting you from.'

'Discussion over, please.' Julia had not intended to speak sharply.

'It's okay, Julia. I will not wrest control of this from you.'

'Please don't make it about that.'

He raised his hands. His cigarette had burned right down and he was holding it gingerly between two long fingers. He moved along the terrace. The tree-tops on the common were ghostly in the moonlight, a sea of blackness beneath them.

'The search of the common will begin on Monday.'

Julia did not respond.

'And the police cannot find Pascoe anywhere.'

She waited for him to continue, but he did not. She tried to understand whether he was attaching significance to Pascoe's disappearance, but it was hard to clear her mind of memories and concentrate on rational thought.

'What do you hope to prove by the search?'

'It's not a question of proving anything. If we can find the body, it will clear up the biggest mystery of all. It might start making sense of things.'

Julia felt the same atavistic sense of fear at the thought of being confronted with Alice's remains after all this time. 'I don't think you should go ahead with this search.'

'Why not?'

'You have people's goodwill – you heard what Alan said. I mean, won't a search alert them, put them on the defensive?'

'I don't see why. It's about evidence. Without evidence, there can be no case.'

191

'I know, but . . .'

'And it's about clearing up a mystery. Come on,' he said. He threw his cigarette out towards the hedge. 'Let's do the clearing up.'

Julia waited, momentarily reluctant to follow him in.

Mac had forgotten about his date with Susannah, the receptionist from the gym.

'You've forgotten,' she said.

'No.'

She smiled. 'You have.'

'No. Really.' Mac looked down at his jeans and T-shirt. 'I always dress like this.'

Susannah was wearing a tight-fitting pair of black trousers and a simple white top. Her short blonde hair had been newly washed and dried and she wore light makeup.

'I thought we said eight thirty?'

She shook her head, not losing her cool, apparently still amused.

'Okay, hold on, I'm there.' Mac went to get his jacket and slip on the old pair of loafers he wore to go downstairs and get the milk.

'Do I get to come in?'

'No.'

'What are you hiding?'

He was back at the door, checking that his wallet, mobile and keys were all in his jacket pocket. 'My true nature.' He pulled the door shut behind him and they walked down the first few flights of stairs in silence.

'You were working today?'

She shook her head again, still laughing at him. 'No, otherwise I wouldn't be finished yet, would I?'

Of course, she worked the evening shift.

'What have you been doing?'

Mac shrugged. 'Oh, nothing much. A lot of work. Nothing much.'

They went into the bistro downstairs and were shown to a small wooden table in the corner beside the window overlooking the pavement. A fan turned overhead and Mac looked at the black and white picture of a couple kissing on a Parisian street, which he had seen countless times. For a Saturday night, it was far from busy, but the food was unspectacular. It was simply a convenient venue for them both.

Mac's mobile phone rang and he took it out of his pocket and mouthed an apology at Susannah. It was only when he heard Rigby's rough voice that he realized he'd been hoping it was Julia.

'Could you hold on a minute?' he told Rigby. He walked outside. 'Yes, sir.'

'Macintosh, I'm sorry if I'm disturbing you on a Saturday night,' Rigby said, with uncommon civility.

Mac was on his guard.

'I need you to be in my office at nine o'clock on Monday morning with this case typed up and ready to go. Sir Robert Quemoy, the Permanent Secretary at the MoD, will be there and you will need to brief him, then you'll be straight out to Cyprus, so pack your bags with some shorts. There's something we need you on out there.'

'With respect, sir, the case won't be finished by then. I can happily brief Sir Robert but—'

'I'm sure you'll be finished by then, Mac.'

'No, sir, I won't. The girl has been ill, so I've not even got to speak to her yet.'

'Macintosh.'

'Yes.'

'Be in the office, on Monday morning, with this report finished and typed up and your bags packed.'

The phone buzzed in Mac's ear. He put it back in his pocket and returned to join Susannah.

'Work?' she asked.

'Er, yes.'

'A long face.'

Mac smiled. Susannah was looking at a menu, so he picked up the one in front of him and did the same.

'You don't give much of yourself away, Macintosh.'

'Yes. I mean . . . no. I'm sorry.'

She looked into his eyes, but he dropped his gaze to the menu again. He knew that she would be willing to sleep with him tonight and he had been looking forward to it, but he wasn't going to now and this meal was going to seem a long one. He waved the waiter over. As usual, Julia Havilland was going to spoil simpler pleasures.

*

When he got back to the flat that night, after making his excuses to a confused and probably hurt Susannah, Mac called the Rose and Crown and asked to be put through to Professor Malcolm's room. The phone was picked up on the third ring and Mac was grateful that he sounded awake. 'Professor, I'm sorry to bother you so late.'

'Mac. What is it?'

'I was just thinking. Did you say earlier that you suspected Mitchell Havilland of these murders?'

There was no reply.

'I mean if Pascoe is innocent, then . . .'

'Mac, I did not say that. I did *not* say that.'

'No, okay. I'm sorry.'

'And please don't talk like that.'

'No. I'm sorry, of course not. It's just you raised the possibility that Havilland might not have been murdered by the enemy.' Mac picked up the phone and moved to his chair by the window. There was a light breeze. 'I wondered, if it had been one of his own side, why someone might have wanted . . .'

'Please, Mac. Don't wonder. Not about that.'

'Right.'

'Goodnight, Mac.'

'Goodnight, Professor.'

Julia pulled the curtain back, ready to shut the window and lock it, but, for a moment, glancing into the de la Rues' garden, she was convinced that she saw a figure – Pascoe – watching.

But it was only a pot, in the corner of the hedge.

She fastened the window and pulled the curtain shut, then walked to the door and switched off the light. She couldn't remember if she'd locked the front door and was forced to go downstairs to check.

It was locked.

Julia moved quickly back upstairs to her room, sat on the bed, ran her hand through her hair. She lay down and closed her eyes, aware that she no longer looked forward to sleep.

Shortly after lunch on Sunday, Mac was sitting at his desk in Woolwich, head bent over Julia's file. He'd summarized most of

194

the relevant sections and thought he had done his work reasonably thoroughly. He had not interviewed the staff at the embassy, but he did have their statements and Julia didn't dispute either their accounts or those given to him by the sergeants. Mac had just finished typing up a section on the background and there seemed little doubt that the initial argument had arisen over different points of view about how the source had been treated and what might have contributed to his detection.

The gaping hole in this file was any indication as to what defence Julia's lawyers might advance in the event of a contested court-martial.

Mac had phoned Julia three or four times today, at home and on her mobile, but had been met only with answering-machines.

He tried her mobile once more, but with no luck. He leant back, gazed at Rigby's office and wondered what Sir Robert Quemoy would ask him tomorrow. Whatever it was, he was going to have to stall, because there was no way he was going to allow himself to be packed off to Cyprus.

Mac chucked his pencil on to the desk and closed the file. He got up, picked up his car keys and walked out, locking the office behind him. He went downstairs slowly, deep in thought.

Outside, in the courtyard, Mac could see Maurice sitting on the Registry steps, smoking a cigarette. He walked over. The large clock-tower left this section in shade.

'Good afternoon, Maurice.'

'Good afternoon, Macintosh.'

Maurice had almost finished his cigarette and Mac noticed how his hand shook as he put yellow fingers to his mouth. His glasses were dirty and dandruff was collecting on the shoulders of a thin blue short-sleeved shirt.

'What brings you in here on a Sunday?' Maurice asked. 'Still looking for file six six seven forty-three forward slash B?'

'Showing off your memory again, Maurice. You'll be telling me next you were once on *Mastermind*.'

'Semi-finals.'

'Yes, I know. Registry doesn't know how lucky it is.'

Maurice pointed his cigarette at Mac. 'None of you know how lucky you are.'

'No, well . . .' Mac turned to face the sun.

'You haven't answered my question,' Maurice went on.

195

'Am I still looking for the file? Yes.'

'Maybe it's gone to the shredder.'

Mac turned back. 'Is that a joke, Maurice?'

'No.'

'Why do you say that?'

'Well, what else happens to a file like that that goes out and never comes back?'

'Why put it in Registry in the first place if you're going to shred it?'

'Because you have to. But if you take it out again, you can just say you lost it.'

Maurice finished his cigarette and tossed it on to the tarmac. They both watched the last of the smoke rising from it.

'You talk about this file, Maurice, as though you were familiar with it.'

'Do I?'

'Yes.'

'Well . . . I can always recall anything that interests me. Remind me what it was about.'

'The death of Mitchell Havilland. Mad Mitch, who died in the Falklands War. Got the Victoria Cross.'

Maurice nodded. 'Oh, yes. Dashed out to save a wounded corporal.' He shook his head. 'Most unlikely.'

'So you remember the file?'

'Possibly.'

'Come on, Maurice.'

The man's expression, which had been playful, was serious now. 'It's not much of a job, Macintosh, but it's the one I have.'

There was a black wrought-iron fence next to the white stone steps and Mac propped himself against it.

'How could I persuade you to tell me?'

'You couldn't. You're a detective. If I tell you, you'll act upon the information.'

Mac took out the notebook from his pocket, opened it to the right page and handed it to Maurice. He looked at it. 'What?'

'That's a list of those present when Havilland was killed, isn't it?'

Maurice glanced at it for a few seconds more, then handed it back. 'Why are two of the names crossed out?'

'They're dead.'

'Bad for them.'

'Very bad for their wives. I suspect both of them were murdered.'

Maurice was hesitating. 'Don't get into something you don't understand, Mac.' He pointed at the book. 'Look at the names.'

Mac glanced at the page in front of him.

'Battle still raging,' Maurice went on, 'spread out all along the ridge. This group trying to assault a machine-gun post at the far end, overlooking Port Stanley. Havilland dies saving a corporal.' Maurice was looking at him. 'That's the official version, right?'

'Right.'

Maurice pointed at the book again. 'Look at the names. Havilland, Ford and the other two on the left. All officers. Havilland is the battalion commander. Only four soldiers. Four officers, four soldiers.'

Mac was still frowning.

'It's not your average military formation, is it, Macintosh? Not for a battle.'

Maurice walked up the stone steps and in through the swing door. Mac followed him but, back behind the safety of his counter, Maurice raised a hand. 'No, Mac, that's all I can do for you.'

'One more thing.'

Maurice sighed.

'Simple thing.'

'Go on.'

'I need to find one of these men. Claverton and Danes are dead and Pascoe is missing so I must get hold of Wilkes. Normally I go straight to the regiment, but this lot won't co-operate.'

'There's a surprise.'

'So how do I find him? The MoD records office will have some kind of address for him, right?'

Maurice was looking down at the register open in front of him. 'Yes, should do. Won't be open until Monday, though.'

As Mac left, he turned back and saw Maurice pointing up to the notice saying 'Sin Bin'. He shouted, 'And bring back your own bloody files!'

On Sunday night, Julia was watching television, sitting in the chair closest to it. The detective drama had just finished and she couldn't be bothered to get up. Her mother and Alan were in the kitchen, Caroline playing 'The Girl From Ipanema' on the piano.

The news came on. The first headline was, 'Welham Common case to be reopened; new search for child's body tomorrow.'

Julia switched off the television. She got up, shut the door, then switched it on again.

The report began with pictures of some police tape at the main entrance to the common. There were two cars by it, and Julia realized that these pictures had been shot tonight. A policeman stood behind the tape.

The door opened and Caroline and Alan came in. Julia could see their reflection in the window. Slowly, they sat on the sofa behind her.

The report used the grainy pictures taken of the common at the time, which she had seen often before, then the photographs of Sarah and Alice.

There was an interview with Lionel Weston. He denied that the case was being reopened, saying the police just wanted to be sure they had left no stone unturned.

Julia watched the faces in the window. She thought that both Alan and her mother looked pale and peculiarly small, like children. She did not know what to do, so did not move. Once the report was over, they both got up and went out again. The door banged lightly against its latch, until Julia got up and closed it.

Then, she switched off the television and went up to her room, where she sat down on the bed. She wanted to give Alan a hug and tell him it would be all right, but she was worried that, for all his attempts to appear unruffled and co-operative, she was hurting him deeply.

What if they found Alice's body?

How would he feel then?

CHAPTER THIRTEEN

A LOUD BANG WOKE HER.

Julia got out of bed, pulled out of a dream in which she had once again seen her father charging out from the rock in the direction of the machine-gun nest, Pascoe's pathetic wails carried on the wind to the place where she was sheltering.

It had sounded like a door banging and she could see from the trees in the de la Rue garden that a strong wind had got up. She reached for her old blue cotton dressing-gown on the back of the door and looked at her watch. It was eight thirty.

Aristotle staggered to his feet when she reached the kitchen and waved his tail. She let him out of the back door and put on the kettle, pleased to have the house to herself and assuming her mother must have already gone to work.

She made herself a big cafetière of coffee and turned on the radio. It was tuned to the Radio Four *Today* programme, but she wasn't listening. She was thinking about Alice and the prospect of a renewed search.

Julia had a picture in her mind of Alice's face sticking out of that pile of leaves. She imagined a silver cross nestling on the bare bones of a skeleton.

Eventually, she got up and went back to her room to change into her running kit.

*

As she passed Julia noticed Alan's car in his drive.

She came to the T-junction opposite the Rose and Crown and stopped opposite two large satellite vans in the car-park, one white, one blue. Both satellites were packed flat, not yet pointing at the sky, but the door to the white van was open and a young man in a blue outdoor jacket was drinking coffee or tea from a white polystyrene cup.

He stared at her, then raised his hand. Julia smiled, before breaking into a run again, turning into the lane before the Rouses' house and pushing herself hard up the hill. She stopped at the top of the ridge, looking down over the corner of the village green and the entrance to the common where two policemen stood in front of the white tape, a small crowd ahead of them. There were three large white vans parked along the far side of the green, next to the village shop.

A single dark cloud covered the sun and filled the air with a light drizzle, the wind driving it into her face. As she began running again, Julia caught sight of a figure bobbing towards her along the ridge. To begin with, it seemed almost inanimate, rising and falling like the float at the end of a fishing-line, caught by the currents, the face hidden beneath a hood, but as its owner flicked off the hood, she saw that it was Michael Haydoch.

'Well, well,' he said, as he came up to her. 'Look what the cat dragged in.'

The wind tugged at his hair. She noticed how lined and weatherbeaten his face looked, the rain dribbling down across it, hanging from the end of his nose and resting at the corners of his mouth.

'You're escaping from the search?' he asked.

Julia glared at him. 'Thanks for the other day.'

'That's my pleasure.'

'Why do you do it?'

'I saw no harm in getting you to explain yourself.'

'What do you mean?'

'We all know why you're doing it, Julia, but it's not going to help anyone.'

'What do you mean by that?'

He frowned. 'Do you need a hearing-aid?'

'What do you mean, "We all know why you're doing it"?'

He took a step closer to her. 'I mean that we all know why

200

you're doing it, and most of us probably have some sympathy, but no one, except perhaps you, sees any merit in turning it over again or in doing anything to help the absurd fat man.'

Julia looked towards the Rose and Crown. She could not tell if the curtains were still drawn over Professor Malcolm's window at the back. 'I'd like to talk to you.'

'The feeling's not mutual.'

'You were her friend. I saw you walking together.'

'That's not a crime.'

'No, but it's a reason why you might be able to help. I can't talk ... you know, with some of the others, it's difficult ...'

'Why?'

'Too personal. Come on, you can see ...'

'I'll be no help.'

'Could you stop being an arse-hole.'

'You are in danger of looking like you're losing your sense of humour.'

'You're in danger of getting a smack in the mouth.' Julia found herself smiling.

'You can come over,' he said. 'We can talk about what you got up to in China.'

'And we can talk about your work too. That's going to be a riveting conversation.'

'I told you I left the Service. I'm a businessman now.'

'Really?'

Michael was looking down over the valley, one foot pushed slightly forward. He had on a tracksuit, but it was tight and she could see his wiry, muscular legs. She watched as he wiped the drizzle from his face.

A car emerged at the end of the valley beneath them, moved slowly along and then turned into the Rose and Crown car-park. Two men got out and cut across the road to the entrance to Alan's drive.

'Tabloid reporters, that lot,' he said. 'They came to my house, looking for an angle. I told them I'd break their necks if they didn't piss off.'

'That was helpful of you. What did they want?'

'They wanted "community living in fear". I don't know. That sort of crap.'

'Michael, could you stop being like this?'

'Like what?'

Julia looked at him. 'If Sarah and Alice were alive, what do you think they would be doing now?'

'That's below the belt.'

'Pascoe didn't do it and you know he didn't.'

'I don't know anything.'

'Professor Malcolm will solve this.'

'He couldn't find his way out of a paper bag.'

'That's not true and your recollections could help . . .'

'No.'

'Please.'

He hesitated. 'I hate the way I'm susceptible to you.' He looked at her. 'I bet everyone is susceptible to you.'

'Can I come over today?'

'I won't be there. Tomorrow. Tomorrow night. And if I don't like what you say, I'll throw you out.'

When Julia ran back down the main road, she saw that a crowd had gathered on the village green. She slowed to a walk by the Rose and Crown, but kept going. There were three satellite trucks now, all with their doors open and their dishes pointing towards the sky. At the first one she passed the same man was sitting on the step with another cup of coffee or tea. He nodded at Julia again.

The search had begun.

The trucks, vans and cars blocked off two sides of the green. One had its rear door open and she could see two people inside sitting in front of two monitors. In the middle of the green, Cynthia Walker was giving an interview to one of the reporters. As she passed, Julia heard her saying, 'If Pascoe is innocent, if the person responsible for this crime is still living in this community, then we have even greater reason to fear for the safety of our children . . .'

Most of the cameras were waiting at the entrance to the path. There were five or six on tripods, their operators standing near by. Several were smoking and there was a low hum of conversation. No one took much notice of Julia as she approached then ducked under the white tape, but the two policemen, who had been looking equally at ease, approached her.

'I've come to see Professor Malcolm and DCI Weston,' she said.

'Are they down here?' The men let her through, pointing to indicate an affirmative answer.

Julia found that it was cooler as she entered the common. Despite the wind, the run had made her sweaty.

Around the first bend, she found three men talking together. One wore a denim jacket, the other two raincoats.

'Looking for Weston,' she said.

'Up ahead,' the man in the denim jacket replied, looking at her curiously. She was glad she had chosen to wear a tracksuit and not shorts.

She continued. The wind was stronger, shaking the boughs above and moving the dappled pools of light ahead.

DCI Weston stood in the middle of a group of men on the exact spot of the murder. Professor Malcolm towered above him, but had his back to her so he didn't witness her approach.

Weston nodded at her. 'Nothing yet.'

The circle around Weston widened to include her. Julia could see two men with metal detectors: one on the bank above them, another on the slope leading up to the clearing at the centre of the common. Both had the instruments strapped over their shoulders and were moving slowly, swinging them in even semi-circles.

'All right!' The one on the slope raised his hand. Two men whom Julia had not yet taken in climbed up from the path towards them. Both had shovels and they waited as the man pointed to the spot, then hesitated a moment more before beginning to dig. Julia could hear the spades striking the earth. They dug rhythmically, dumping the dirt to their left after each swing down.

'Okay,' one said.

There was a hush. Perhaps it was her imagination but she thought that, despite himself, Weston was leaning forward in anticipation. The two men were on their hands and knees, scraping away the last of the dirt.

One sat back on his haunches. The other followed, holding something above his head. 'Another tin,' he said.

Weston breathed out. Professor Malcolm did not look concerned.

'Brilliant idea,' Weston said.

'Are you using radar?' Professor Malcolm asked.

'Yes, but don't expect anything from that. I don't suppose he buried her in a lead coffin.'

'What?'

'Never mind,' Weston said.

'Come on,' Professor Malcolm said, taking Julia's arm and pulling her gently aside. 'I need a break and I said we'd go and see the sisters in the shop this morning.'

The three men by the fork in the path were laughing as they rounded the corner but fell silent as they passed. A gust of wind tugged at her hair and a strand of his fell into his face. Julia waited for him to say something, but he was deep in thought.

As Julia and Professor Malcolm ducked under the white tape and moved forward, a woman in a blue jacket tapped her male colleague on the shoulder and he reached for his camera. They approached with intent.

'Are you a resident?' the woman asked, and Julia saw immediately that she was pretty, her neat oval face shaped by auburn hair.

Julia didn't answer. She didn't know why she had been chosen – perhaps they had all spoken to Cynthia Walker already. Another crew joined in and suddenly there were many. They blocked her way.

'Excuse me,' she said.

'Do you live in the village?' the first reporter asked.

'What do you think of the new inquiry?'

'What new inquiry?' Julia shot back. This was a mistake. It encouraged them.

'The search. Are people here angry?'

'Do you want the case reopened?' the first reporter asked.

Professor Malcolm shoved himself ahead of Julia and punched his way through the middle of the throng, like a rugby forward. She was surprised by his aggression but grateful.

The crowd did not follow.

He crossed the green ahead of her, in the direction of the post office. The entrance to the shop was low, forcing them to duck. A small bell tinkled, but for a moment they stood alone in the gloom.

Julia looked around. More than anything in the village, the shop was a time warp. The post-office counter was to the right, but otherwise the place sold little, just sweets, mostly, which were laid out in their boxes and jars across the counters and tables around them. There were cola bottles and sugar snakes, and Wagon Wheels and jelly babies. Beside them were some small white paper bags. The younger of the two sisters, Ruth, had come through so quietly that neither of them had noticed her.

'Hello, Ruth,' Julia said.

'Julia.' Ruth smiled thinly. She did not seem to have aged. Her hair was still black and cut short. She wore metal-rimmed square glasses. 'It's good to see you home,' she went on, without enthusiasm, then ushered them through the gap in the counter. She hesitated, as if deciding whether or not to lock the front door, before leading them through to the back.

'Have they found her?' Ruth asked.

Professor Malcolm shook his head. 'Not yet.'

'Edna's not well,' Ruth explained, raising her eyes to the ceiling to indicate that her sister was in bed upstairs. She rounded the corner to the kitchen. They could hear her preparing something and exchanged glances. Julia had expected to continue this morning with the address book and the telephone, and this interview felt less academic and more personal.

Julia was surprised by the cramped, dated conditions in the house. The living room was small, the furniture dark. The curtains were half drawn, with additional net curtains pulled tight behind them, so that the sunlight barely penetrated. There was a glass cabinet full of pictures next to a table pushed up against the wall and covered with a white lace cloth. There were children in some of the photographs, perhaps nephews or nieces, and Julia couldn't imagine them enjoying a visit here. She wondered if these two women were really sisters: a lesbian couple moving in together in a small English village in the 1950s or thereabouts must have found it easier to say that they were.

Professor Malcolm raised his eyebrows and smiled at her. They both sat in uncomfortable, saggy chairs, with wooden arm-rests. 'Same talent for interior design as my aunt,' he whispered, as Ruth returned with a tray. He smiled at her and Julia hoped she hadn't heard. The two sisters always sat next to each other in the choir stalls at the church – two quiet, respectable members of the community.

'Edna's not well,' Ruth said again, placing the tray on the table beside Julia. She poured the tea and went to the chair next to the window, which looked the most comfortable and was directly opposite the television.

'You've lived here long?' Professor Malcolm asked.

'Almost forty years.'

'As I mentioned on Saturday, we're conducting a review.'

'I know.'

'It's only a formality.'

'I hope not.'

Professor Malcolm inclined his head. Julia got the sense that he was about to lead her like a witness.

'Did you know Sarah Ford well?' he asked.

'She sang in the choir sometimes.'

Julia was surprised to learn of Sarah doing anything as community-minded as singing in the choir. She didn't remember this.

'Originally,' Ruth went on, 'they all came.'

'All of them?' Professor Malcolm asked.

'Yes. The woman. The husband. And the girl.' She nodded between each one, as if ticking them off in her mind.

'Alan and Alice?'

'Yes. To begin with, they even came to choir practice on Tuesday nights.'

'Then what?'

'The husband stopped coming, then the girl, and eventually none of them came.'

Julia wondered why Sarah had been the last to stop coming.

'Did Sarah have a good voice?' Professor Malcolm asked.

'Yes. But I think vanity brought her to us. She didn't value it properly.'

'Did you like them, Ruth?'

Professor Malcolm shifted forward in his seat.

Ruth sighed. 'Sarah Ford was a flighty woman. Vain and arrogant.'

'And the little girl? Did you get to know her?'

'She was sweet.' Ruth almost smiled. 'She was.'

'Which other men sang in the choir?'

Ruth nodded, acknowledging she was going to have to answer this question. 'Mitchell . . . Julia's father. Adrian Rouse. Alan Ford, of course.'

'Was there any man you saw with Sarah often? Outside church and the choir, I mean.' Professor Malcolm's voice was soft. 'I'm sure you're not a gossip, Ruth, but the work you do . . . you must hear talk.'

Ruth nodded. 'I'm *not* a gossip.'

'Of course. Of course.'

'Edna likes walking.'

'Yes.'

'She used to walk on the common every day.'

'Before the murders.'

'Yes.'

'Did she see Sarah?'

'Sometimes.' Ruth breathed in deeply. 'It was just that she always seemed to be with . . .' Ruth looked at Julia and stopped.

'With Mitchell?' Professor Malcolm asked.

Julia had sensed already where this choreographed interview was leading and shame had been enveloping her like a cloak.

'Yes,' Ruth went on. 'They always seemed to be together, that was all.'

Professor Malcolm was now thinking. 'Were they on their own?' he asked eventually. 'When you or Edna saw them, were they typically alone?'

Ruth frowned.

'I mean, was Alice there?' He looked at Julia.

'Every time I saw them, it was with Alice.' Now Ruth looked at Julia. 'Sometimes with Julia, too.' Julia blushed. 'Edna saw them alone, I think.'

Professor Malcolm sipped his tea, then sat back in his chair. Julia could not see what he was getting at.

'Did you see much of Alan back then? Talk to him?'

'No. He's a charming man, but he was less happy then.'

'In what way, exactly?'

Ruth shrugged.

'How was he with Sarah?'

Ruth shrugged again, as if it was none of her business how husbands and wives were together.

'Affectionate?'

'I suppose so.'

'Did you detect any friction?'

Ruth didn't respond.

Professor Malcolm took another sip of his tea.

'Ruth,' he said, 'there's something I'd like to put to you.' He leant forward in his chair again, his elbows on his knees, fingers supporting his chin. 'Around the time the Ford family moved to the village, Alice looked like any other little girl of her age. That is to say that she was unremarkable. Scruffy, a little tomboyish on occasions, even. But as we approach the time of her death, it is clear that her appearance is changing. She is suddenly smarter. Much smarter. Her appearance, from being normal, is suddenly ... well, I would say a little inappropriate. She is being moulded, you might say, into the image of her mother. It's a striking development when you know to look out for it. Did you notice this?'

'No.'

'Does it ring any bells now?'

'She was neat. Always well dressed.'

'Uncomfortably so?'

Ruth shrugged once more. She did not understand, or did not wish to understand, the implication.

'Did you ever ... This is an uncomfortable subject, I know, Ruth, but did you ever see a man taking what you would consider an inappropriate interest in little Alice?'

Ruth was looking down, her narrow hands clasped neatly together. Julia saw that she wore no rings.

'We didn't like the way ...' Ruth's voice trailed off. Professor Malcolm waited. 'We remember Robert Pascoe as a boy, you see.' She looked at Julia, then back at him. 'We hate all this ...'

She meant the protests. Julia noticed how she always used 'we', as if there were two bodies, but only one mind. She was unsure whether it was attractive or unsettling.

'You didn't believe,' Professor Malcolm said, 'that Pascoe could have committed the ...'

Ruth was distorting her mouth in disgust, interrupting Professor Malcolm's question. Her demeanour was more than negative, it was total dismissal. 'He was a such a nice boy, shy. They said he was ... that he liked children. We ...' She looked at Julia. 'It couldn't have been true. It wasn't. It was all made up, it was a fabrication.'

'Made up by whom?'

Her mouth had hardened. Julia thought she'd waited a long

time to tell someone in authority this and was going to take her time.

'Sarah Ford was a bad woman, but the people she mixed with weren't the likes of Robert Pascoe.'

'You think the police . . .'

'We think the officers closed ranks and protected themselves. Who was Pascoe? How could he defend himself?' She looked at Julia then back at Professor Malcolm. The inference stretched beyond Pascoe, as if the officer class – among which, Julia assumed, were numbered her own family and the likes of the de la Rues – had even arranged the war. Julia had never imagined the two old women sitting here with such anger. 'By the time he came back from the war,' Ruth went on, 'he was ruined. He'd have said anything. That's what his mother told us. She went to see him in prison but she could hardly ever get a word out of him. He wouldn't agree to an appeal, nor speak to a psychologist or any-one who could help him. Mrs Pascoe – Elaine – she said he didn't want to leave prison.'

'Did you—' Julia stopped. The question had formed in her mind from nowhere. She felt the blood pounding in her head and Professor Malcolm was looking at her. 'Did you—' Julia realized that her inability to articulate the question was pathetic and unprofessional. 'Did you think,' she said, in a level voice, meeting Ruth's eye, 'that Sarah Ford was having an affair with my father? That's what you're saying. Pascoe was a scapegoat.'

Ruth did not answer. She was beginning to look worried, as though she might have said something she shouldn't. Professor Malcolm smiled reassuringly and, as if responding to an off-stage signal, they all stood up at once. He mumbled his thanks.

Outside, squinting against the sun, Professor Malcolm glanced across at the church.

'Could you tell me,' she said, 'the point of that?'

He looked at her disapprovingly, as an unemotional man does to an emotionally charged woman. 'Calm down,' he said.

'*You* should calm down,' she said. 'You heard all of that on Saturday and led the interview so I would hear it for myself.'

'Calm down.'

'No. It seemed like an attempt to humiliate me.'

'I think you're being a little irrational, Julia, and you're wrong. I didn't hear that on Saturday, though I got the impression she would tell us something along those lines. And, anyway, if I was going to hear anything, I thought it important you heard it for yourself. I was under the impression that that was what this was all about.'

Julia put her hand to her forehead to stem the headache. She realized her defensiveness was making the situation worse and she tried to force herself to relax. 'I don't think she said anything we didn't already know.' She became aware that, though they were speaking quietly, some of the journalists standing on the village green had turned their heads.

'I thought,' Professor Malcolm said, instinctively turning his back on them, 'that she said a few things I wouldn't have expected.'

'Like what?'

'She believes there has been some kind of conspiracy.'

'Yes, but not a very developed or convincing one. The whole officer class closing ranks? Why?'

He was frowning.

'Can I ask you something?' she said.

'Yes.' He was looking at the reporters now, who seemed to have lost interest.

'Why do you keep asking about, you know, this business about Alice's appearance having changed in the last year of her life? I thought you said the crime was about the woman.'

'Yes. That's right. My analysis of the crime scene suggests that. But,' he was gesturing with his arms now, 'there is a whole picture here to be assembled, and a couple of things puzzle me. My hunch is that if we pursue them they may illuminate important corners of that picture.'

'And the way Alice was dressed in a couple of photographs . . .'

'It's more than that. It's a development. When I asked you about it, I could see clearly that it had crossed your mind at some point over the years. It's not earth-shattering, perhaps it will turn out only to be a small thing, but it was a *change* that occurred that year and there's a reason behind it. Until we discern the reason, I would like you to ask people about it – all those who might have known them that last year. In the same way, Alice's body puzzles me. I cannot explain why we haven't found it yet. Perhaps we will, but if we don't then there is a mystery there, too.' He half turned. 'It seems clear that Pascoe confessed because he had lost his mind. He was just an easy target for the police by the time he

210

got back from the war and no one helped him.' He was staring into the middle distance. 'I suppose the question is: has he, despite everything, somehow managed to get it back . . . the shock of his mother's death, perhaps . . .' He turned back to face her. 'I wish we could find him.'

'Where do you think he has gone?'

'I think he's somewhere not too far away. I would say that Pascoe, by nature, is a watcher.' He pulled up the belt on his trousers. 'You'd better get on,' he said. 'I left the room open. I think I should return to the search to hold Weston's hand. I don't trust him not to give up.'

CHAPTER FOURTEEN

JULIA WENT HOME, CHANGED AND HAD A CUP OF COFFEE, THEN WALKED down to the pub, climbed the external staircase and knocked on the door of Professor Malcolm's room, just to make sure he had not come back. There was no answer.

Inside, it was neat and orderly. The bed had been made, his small grip was by its side, but there were no other personal effects.

Julia sat at the desk. In front of her was a letter signed by Weston, formally requesting her and Professor Malcolm to proceed with 'a review of the evidence' in the case of the Crown v. Pascoe. She folded it up and put it into her pocket, trying to put out of her mind the search, which seemed to hang in the air like mist.

It was lighter than yesterday, the morning sun now spilling across the desk, and Julia pulled over Sarah's address book and turned to H. The entry she sought read, 'Haydoch, Mickey'. It was in Sarah's handwriting.

Julia had never called Michael 'Mickey'. She wondered what kind of friendship Michael and Sarah had enjoyed. Could Sarah have had a friendship with a man where sex *wasn't* an issue?

She returned to the point she'd marked yesterday and continued.

The first number she dialled was dead. The second rang for a long time.

'Hello, Katherine Bowman.'

'Katherine, my name is Julia Havilland and I'm working on a review of the evidence in the Welham Common case. You may have seen in the press that the accused man has been released on appeal.'

'Yes. It's dreadful.'

'That's right. Well, the police are duty bound to review the case and that's what I'm engaged in. We're contacting all of Sarah's friends and relatives to try to ascertain if there are any avenues of inquiry worth pursuing that were overlooked at the time.'

'Right,' Katherine Bowman said. She sounded more confident than most of those Julia had reached on Friday.

'My first question is what was your relationship with Sarah?'

'I was at school with her.'

'Which school was that?' Julia had not yet spoken to anyone who had been at school with Sarah.

'Cheltenham Ladies' College.'

Julia hesitated. Somehow she'd not imagined Sarah going to such a conventional public school.

'You were friends, obviously.'

'Yes.' Katherine's voice was firm.

She was not ashamed of having been Sarah's friend and Julia warmed to her. 'A lot of Sarah's friends seem to want to qualify that description.'

'Well, Sarah isn't easy but, then, many people who are interesting are not, in my experience. I wouldn't have married her, but she is capable of being a good friend if you accept her limitations and don't expect too much.'

Katherine was not the first respondent to slip into talking about Sarah in the present tense and Julia imagined that she was talking to a tall, bulky, confident woman. Not conventionally good-looking, probably, for this was someone, she thought, who had not been challenged by, or in competition with, Sarah.

'Why did you say you wouldn't have married her?'

'Too emotionally high maintenance.'

Not for the first time, Julia wondered what Alan had seen in Sarah.

'What were her limitations as a friend?'

Katherine Bowman sighed. Julia could hear a child crying in the background now. 'Jonathan . . . *Jonathan*, stop. Sorry, yes?'

'No, my apologies. You're busy. You talked about her limitations as a friend?'

'Yes. I liked Sarah, but she was unreliable. One minute, you would benefit from her full attention. She would come and see you and be totally charming and interested in everything going on in your life, then the next she would forget something important, like turning up to a dinner or . . . I don't know, she would call two days later and act as if you'd never had a conversation at all. It's hard to explain, but my point is that she was fun, she was lively, she was interesting. If you didn't expect anything, then she was good to have as a friend.'

'Why do you think some people felt ambiguous towards her?'

'People expected too much. Men, in particular.'

'Did she know a lot of men?'

Katherine laughed. 'Did she sleep around? She liked men, that's all I'll say, except that I'm not sure she *really* did. She couldn't disentangle sex and affection. She slept with men because that was what they wanted, but didn't engage with them. You know what I mean. If I was being unfair, I would say she toyed with them. Led them on, then dropped them without explanation or apology. She couldn't really relate to men without involving sex and I wouldn't have thought she had many male friends *per se*. But . . . look, that was a long time ago. That was at school. I didn't see her for a long time before . . . well, before the end. She probably changed a lot, but at school, you know, *then* introducing Sarah into a room full of boys was like triggering a nuclear explosion.'

Julia could tell Katherine was smiling.

'You never met her husband?'

'No. We lost touch when she went to the Slade. Well, we had lunch once or twice, exchanged Christmas cards, but I felt I was making most of the effort, so contact petered out. I was surprised to learn whom she married, but I never met him.'

The boy had started crying in the background again. Julia waited to see if Katherine was going to attend to him. 'Why were you surprised?'

'Well, Sarah was really the school black sheep, you know. She was expelled for being caught with drugs, cigarettes, alcohol *and* a boy from the town in her room. It was hard to imagine her doing something as conventional as marrying an army officer, but I never met him, so I don't know ... Maybe he was an un-conventional army officer.'

Julia thought of Alan with his battered brogues and too-short trousers. He was hardly unconventional.

'Did you meet Sarah's family?'

The boy was crying louder. 'No. Sarah never talked about them.'

'Isn't that odd?'

Katherine had picked the child up. Julia could hear him whimpering. 'I don't know if it was odd. I know she was an only child and that her parents were well off. She never lacked for money, always the best of everything. More than that I can't tell you.'

Katherine was whispering to the boy now. Julia thanked her, replaced the receiver, stood and walked to the other side of the room, switching on the overhead light. She stared at the photograph in the centre of the wall.

Julia tried to contain her personal enmity, but it was hard. She recalled the way Sarah had stood next to her parents on the afternoon of the fête and touched her father's arm then his cheek in a gesture of idle sensuality, oblivious to her mother's presence.

They had been on the far side of the garden, in the rough section of grass used for tossing the caber, and when she approached, Sarah had turned to her and smiled, before returning to the conversation. She had then said to Mitchell and Caroline that she would love to provide a diet for Julia because she knew 'how tough it was to be overweight'.

Julia had always felt that children – all children – irritated Sarah as a distraction from the adult world.

She tore herself away from the sardonic smile on the wall and sat down again at the desk. She wondered how Katherine Bowman could have liked Sarah. She wondered how anyone could.

The next successful call was more straightforward. A man called Damian confessed to disliking Sarah. He'd travelled with her to India after she had been expelled from Cheltenham, one of a group of four. Damian said Sarah had gone initially as the girl-friend of his then best friend, but had soon embarked on a campaign of promiscuity. The picture he painted of Sarah was essentially the same as Katherine Bowman's, but without affection.

215

There were two more dud numbers then Julia reached Simon Crick on the Cranbrooke exchange. At the end of her explanation, he said that he was a photographer and that he had had some business with Sarah.

'What kind of business?' Julia asked.

There was a hesitation. 'Sarah was a model.'

'What kind of model?'

'Not the kind you're suggesting.'

Julia was silent. She did not know why this news was surprising. Sarah had been easily beautiful enough to have been a model.

'She gave it up when she had the baby, then came back when she wanted the little girl done.'

'What?'

His voice betrayed irritation. 'She was modelling the little girl.'

'What kind of modelling?'

'Any kind. Advertising, mostly. Kids' clothes. That sort of thing.'

Julia was staggered by this. Alice had never mentioned it. It had been kept entirely secret. Then she remembered the list of incoming sums of money in the diary.

'Why do you think Sarah told no one about this?'

He did not answer for a few moments. Then, 'I've no idea. Maybe she didn't want her husband to know. I was never to phone her at home. She insisted on calling here.'

Julia felt sure that this man, too, had slept with Sarah and felt queasy at the way Alice had been dragged into that world. Adults were so unscrupulous.

'Do you think . . . Where is your office, please?'

Something in the man's voice, a wariness, made Julia think this was worth exploring.

He hesitated. 'Cranbrooke. Gerard Street Mews.'

'Would you mind if I came round? I can be there in fifteen minutes.'

'I'm out for lunch.'

'It *is* part of a review of the Welham Common case, Mr Crick.'

He sighed. 'All right, if you're quick. I'm only here until one.'

After putting down the receiver, Julia pulled over the appointments diary and flicked through its pages once more. There was no reference at all to a Simon Crick, photographer. Why would Sarah choose not to put those appointments in when she was brazenly listing assignations with her lover – the M of the diary? Had that been, after all, an attempt to taunt someone, perhaps her husband? Julia noticed that there were a number of appointments with a Dr Simon, sometimes with the word 'hospital' written next to them. She wondered if Dr Simon was really Simon Crick the photographer and 'hospital' a code. Certainly, some of the entries had 'Alice' next to them. Julia looked all the way back to the start of the year and counted them. There were ten with Dr Simon, four with the word hospital alongside. There was another Cranbrooke number by the last entry and Julia called it to see if it was simply a different line for Simon Crick, but there turned out to be a real Dr Simon and, after a short explanation and wait, Julia was put through to him. He spoke with a slight South African accent and told her he was too busy to talk now, but was happy to see her if she wished to come by the surgery this afternoon, though she'd have to wait for a break between patients. Julia said she would be there. She walked out without leaving a note and took the stairs on the fire escape three at a time.

As she crossed the main road on her way home to pick up her car, Julia saw a small crowd and at least one reporter facing a camera. She hurried across the junction and down Woodpecker Lane, where she saw Alan bending over the flower-beds by the front of the house. He saw her and straightened up.

She thought of the search and felt guilty again at the digging into the past that she had just been engaged upon.

'Julia. What are you up to?'

This question was somehow unexpected. 'Not much. Are you not going to the base today?'

She saw the uneasy, hurt look in his eyes. 'I'm sorry,' she said.

He turned his head, looking in the direction of the common, though his house blocked any view of it. His jaw was thrust forward in a gesture of thoughtfulness. 'Impossible to be here,' he said. 'Impossible not to be.'

He turned back to her, but did not meet her eyes. He had a trowel in his hand and was looking down. It was a feminine stance. It was how her mother stood, favouring the good leg over the one injured in a childhood riding accent, and Julia wondered if this was what happened when you became close to someone: their mannerisms became yours and vice versa.

'Probably not my business to say,' he said, 'but your mother and I . . . we feel you may be being . . .' He met her eyes. He was embarrassed, she thought. He was doing her mother's bidding. 'I don't want to patronize you. Neither of us do, but we feel you may be being misled.'

'By whom?'

'By . . . outside forces.'

'UFOs?'

There was the shadow of a smile at the corners of his mouth. 'No.'

'You mean Professor Malcolm?'

He looked away again. 'Well, whoever. The point is . . .'

First Michael Haydoch, now Alan. Julia was annoyed by the attempts to dissuade her. 'It's a formality, Alan. It has to be done, this review. He's been good to me and I'm just . . .'

'*He*'s been good to you.'

It was a few seconds before Julia realized that he was drawing her attention to all that he – and by extension her mother – had done. This was a test of loyalties. She found herself resenting it, and thus him, but she could see the wariness in his eyes. This was a terribly difficult time for him, she could see that.

'I'm really sorry, Alan.' Her tone was apologetic. 'I wouldn't want in any way to—'

'The point is,' he was looking at her square on now, his eyes conciliatory, almost pleading, 'we can't go back. You must see that. We can't go back to the era of suspicion. It was too painful. You *must* see that.'

'I'm sorry, Alan.' She had heard the panic in his voice. 'I'm sorry, but it is only a formality. It's just going over the evidence as a formality.'

'I'll give you an example,' he said, raising his finger. 'Mr Ford . . .' it was an effective imitation of Professor Malcolm's East European burr '. . . when you say the girl's godfather, Adrian Rouse, was affectionate, in what way exactly? Was he *physically* affectionate? Did you ever sense that he liked to be *alone* with her?'

Julia reddened. 'I understand,' she said.

'Perhaps we should go for a walk,' he went on. 'Not today.' He gestured at the common. 'When the circus has gone.'

Julia nodded. 'Yes,' she said. 'That would be nice.'

As she walked round the corner, Julia thought of how her

mother had changed. Her father's death had made her independent, confident and, in some ways, assertive. Alan was less domineering than Mitchell and more pliable.

Mitchell Havilland would never have done her dirty work.

Julia parked in the cobbled mews off the top of the high street in Cranbrooke and knocked on the door. An old, vamped-up Mini was parked outside.

Simon Crick was a good-looking man, with closely cropped dark hair and a round face. He wore a white T-shirt, black trousers and black shoes, and smelt of aftershave and soap, as if he had only just got up. Before he had opened his mouth, she knew that he was uneasy about her presence and that he was going to lie to her.

It was a skill she had developed over the last three years: the ability to tell when a man was about to lie to you. She had never been conscious before that it *was* a skill, nor had she imagined it would be of any use to her outside the narrow, stress-filled confines of her work. But it was plain. She saw it clearly. This man was hiding something.

The order of living in the house here was reversed. Downstairs there was a large, open-plan room with a bed in the corner and a kitchen at one end. The floor was wooden, the furniture modern, the windows shielded by blinds not curtains. Crick led her up a spiral stone staircase to the photographic studio above. It was a light room, mirroring the one downstairs exactly, except that the area occupied by the kitchen was a walk-in storage cupboard. There were many custom-built drawers.

There were several lights up in the middle of the floor and a white screen had been pulled down over the red-brick wall at the far end. His camera was in the centre of the room, on top of a sturdy black tripod, and there was a tall wooden stool, which he now sat on, placing his right foot on one of the bars and leaning on his knee. There was a sofa by the window, in front of the blinds, and he motioned for her to sit, but she shook her head.

'Did the police talk to you after the murders back in 1982?' she asked.

'Yes. I'm not sure I understand,' he said. 'Are you with the police?'

'No. We're conducting an independent review.'

He waited, then looked at his watch. 'What do you want?' he asked. 'As I told you, I have to go to lunch.'

'I'd like, if possible, to see some pictures of Sarah.'

'She's been dead fifteen years. I haven't kept them.'

Julia turned and wandered slowly into the alcove. There were many drawers, listed by letter – one letter for each drawer except X, Y and Z, which shared the last. To her right, there were four shelves and she stared at the equipment stacked upon them.

'What sort of work do you do?'

'Different kinds. Portraiture, mostly. Advertising.'

Julia was still looking at the equipment on the shelves. Some of it was familiar. It was what the surveillance specialists in 14 Intelligence Company used. 'Long lens for your stills camera. Small video camera, complete with lipstick buttonhole lens. That's not for advertising work or portraiture, is it?'

'There's a small detective agency here. Very occasionally I do some work for them. Mostly errant husbands.'

'Must pay well?'

'It does.' He sighed. 'It's mucky, but it pays the rent.'

'Did anyone ever employ you in connection with Sarah?'

'No.' He looked at his watch again. 'Look, I'm sorry, but I'm getting late. If there is something specific . . .'

Julia nodded. 'I'm sorry.' She looked at him. On the phone, Julia had assumed Simon Crick had probably slept with Sarah but, seeing him in the flesh, she thought he was gay. Yet if their relationship had only been professional, she could not comprehend the source of his wariness.

'Just one question. About Alice.' She watched his face closely, but there was no reaction to the little girl's name. 'In the six months before her death,' Julia went on, 'Alice was . . . What's the best way of putting this?' Julia took a pace towards him. 'Sarah was dressing her daughter like a little princess. That's what brought me out here. I mean, if she was being formally modelled and photographed, then perhaps there is a connection. The little girl was being made to look . . . *sexy*. Did you notice that?'

'I wasn't concentrating that hard.'

Julia stared at him. He turned to look out of the window, across the roof-tops to the abbey in the distance. 'I took pictures of the little girl,' he said, 'mostly for children's clothing companies. I took sample pictures at Sarah's request first, then there were a couple of jobs. One was for a clothing company I was doing any-way. They needed young models. I suggested Alice. The other was for a toy company. That was a job Sarah found and she persuaded them to use me as the photographer. The child turned up, Sarah minded her. Quite honestly, I didn't notice her much.'

'There was nothing that struck you as odd about it?'

Simon Crick thought about this. Genuinely thought about it, Julia believed. 'No,' he said.

Julia drove out of the mews a few minutes later and waited just around the corner on the high street, keeping an eye on the rear-view mirror. The preponderance of grey stone often made the town and its quaint shops feel gloomy, but it was lifted today by the sunshine. As she waited, a group of boys from Cranbrooke School walked past, their sports jackets slung over their shoulders.

Cranbrooke was built around the boys' school at its centre. The abbey had come first, then the school, then the town. The girls' school, which she'd attended, had arrived later, further up the hill.

The boys went into the newsagent next to her.

Julia saw Simon Crick's Mini turn out. He roared past, without seeing her, his eyes focused on the road ahead, and she watched him disappear down the hill and turn right opposite Woolworth's into Staunton Street.

She got out and walked back to the mews. She reached the door, took the car keys out of her pocket, opened up the Leather-man tool on her key-ring and looked at the lock. It was a basic Yale. She glanced briefly back down the street, then opened one of the attachments, stuck it into the lock and pulled the door handle towards her. It took her less than five seconds. She waited for the tell-tale beep of an alarm, opening the scissors on the Leather-man, ready to cut the wires, but if there was an alarm, he had failed to set it.

Julia walked briskly up the stairs and into the cupboard. She flicked on the light-switch to her right. The light was dazzling.

The drawer for F was full. Each set of slide negatives was marked with a name, written on a white sticker. They seemed to be in alphabetical order, but Julia could not find one for Ford. Then she saw that there were aberrations in his filing system and that some of the photographs were not in alphabetical order. She estimated there must have been two or three hundred sets of negatives in this drawer and she flicked through all of them. Some didn't have white stickers on, so she had to take them out and hold them up to the light. They were mostly portraits.

There was nothing in F.

There was nothing in S either.

Julia walked to the stairs and listened. There was no sign of anyone, so she came back, her footsteps noisy on the floorboards.

She tried A for Alice, but there was nothing there either, and this file took the longest because it had the lowest density of white stickers.

Julia stepped back once more and looked around the cupboard. There was something in this room with which Simon Crick was not comfortable.

She noticed a tall, free-standing wooden filing cabinet in the corner with a door and a lock. Julia took out her Leather-man again to open it. The solid wooden door swung back to reveal more drawers, again listed alphabetically, though this time with more than one letter to each level.

Julia opened the drawer for F and G, which was full of white folders. She picked up the top one and saw immediately that this was what Simon Crick had to hide.

This was his dirty work.

All of these were surveillance pictures. Here, a couple sitting in a restaurant, photographed through the window.

Each file had a name written in pencil or Biro on the outside.

As Julia found the file marked 'Ford' she felt the hairs rising on the back of her neck. She hesitated, then forced herself to pull out the contents.

She placed the photographs on the table and stared at them.

It was her father fucking the woman up against a tree, her legs wrapped around him.

Julia pushed the photographs away and they spilled on to the floor. She put her head in her hands, placing her thumbs in the corner of her eyes and pressing and pressing until the pain was intense.

She lifted her head and breathed in deeply, before stooping to pick the photographs up. She placed them back on the table.

It was not her father at all, but Adrian Rouse with more hair. For a moment, she looked at her shaking hands.

She breathed in deeply, straightening, before bending over again to look at them.

In the top picture, Rouse and Sarah were talking. It was a wide view and Julia could see clearly the wizened tree stump behind them in the centre of the common. In the next shot, Adrian was closer to her. He wore a green outdoor jacket, she was in just a sweater, a skirt and some wellington boots.

Then he was kissing her, Sarah leaning back against the tree stump. Then intercourse. He was fully clothed, but somehow he had removed her skirt. She still wore a jumper and the boots, but her hips and legs were bare and wrapped around his middle.

There was a closer shot. The muscles on her thighs were tensed as she gripped him, her skin white and smooth.

There was a photograph of her face, which looked even more beautiful when distorted by pleasure. There was a shot of his face, too, which was twisted with aggression.

In the next image, Sarah's arms were above her head, her face covered by her jumper as Adrian lifted it off, his mouth over her nipple and breast, her back arching towards him. Now his trousers were around his ankles. Sarah was naked but for her boots and she was kneeling in front of him, her long dark hair hanging down, her body startlingly white in the sunshine, but lean and beautiful, her breasts full as she leant forward. Adrian's head was tipped back, his eyes closed.

In the last photograph, Adrian still had his jacket on, but he had taken off his trousers and boots and was lying on his back. Sarah was completely naked now and she was straddling him, sitting up straight, with her head bent back so that Julia could see clearly both the pleasure in her face and the tension in the muscles of her thighs.

Julia breathed in hard.

She heard a car outside. She slipped the photographs back into the folder, pushed the drawer shut and closed the door of the cupboard.

She moved into the main room.

The car door slammed.

She walked to the back and looked at the window. There was a drop of ten feet or so into someone's garden, but there was a window lock and no key evident. She took out the Leather-man once more, but small locks could be buggers.

The doorbell rang.

She turned back. At least it wasn't him.

Julia stood still.

The doorbell sounded once more.

Eventually she heard the car door being shut again and the sound of whoever it was driving off.

She went down the stairs quickly, shoved the file inside her jacket, holding it under her armpit, looked out of the window and slipped into the mews, heart pounding.

Mac had assumed that he would be first in, but when he reached his desk they were already gathered in Rigby's office. He could see Sanderson and Rigby and a taller man he assumed must be Sir Robert Quemoy, but they made no move towards him so he took Julia's file from his top drawer and began to check through it.

Five minutes later, Rigby opened his door. 'Mac,' he said.

He picked up the file and walked down to the end, closing the door behind him. Rigby sat behind the desk, Sir Robert Quemoy in a chair next to him, Sanderson leaning against the wall with his back to the window.

'Take a seat, Mac. This is Sir Robert Quemoy, Permanent Sec at the MoD.'

Mac shook his hand firmly. Sir Robert wore a blue suit and loafers and was a strikingly good-looking man, with a broad smile that revealed a set of teeth with a large gap in the middle, a sun-tan and long, curly brown hair. He looked young to be occupying such a position. No more than forty, Mac thought.

Sanderson was staring at him, his legs crossed languidly, his narrow weasel face set in its permanent scowl.

Rigby cleared his throat. 'Given the potential sensitivities of this case, Sir Robert has been anxious to be kept up to speed.'

'Yes, sir, but as I explained on Saturday night, I'm afraid I've not quite finished.'

'I thought we said the case had to be finished by today.'

'Yes, sir, but as I've indicated I need a few more days to complete my work thoroughly. I have not yet spoken to the girl.'

'What's wrong with her?'

'I believe she is ill, sir.'

'Ill in the head, or physically ill?'

'Physically ill, sir. I can give Sir Robert an account of my progress to date.'

Sir Robert leant forward. 'Captain Macintosh.' He looked at his colleagues. 'There is just one thing before we get into that. We've received a report that somebody has been impersonating Major Rigby.' Mac looked at him. 'That wouldn't be you, would it?'

'With respect, sir, why would I want to impersonate Major Rigby?'

No one smiled.

'A woman called Sandra Claverton called for you this morning, Mac,' Rigby said. 'Do you have any idea what she might want?'

Mac looked from Sir Robert to Rigby and back again, before glancing down at the number he'd written on the buff-coloured file in his hand. He could feel the tension in his back. 'Since we're on to the subject,' he said, 'I do have some questions. I'd like to know what has happened to file 66743/B, which Major Rigby signed out and never returned.'

Mac saw that they all knew exactly what he was talking about. Rigby was staring at him now, as well as Sanderson.

'Let me be plain,' Sir Robert said. 'You have an investigation to complete, for which this has no relevance whatever.'

'How do I know until I have seen the file?'

'I'm telling you it has no relevance.' Sir Robert's voice was soft. An iron fist in a velvet glove, Mac thought.

'With respect, sir, I was given the investigation—'

'For which, as I said, this has no relevance.'

'And, as *I* said, how can I know, if I can't see—'

'*Captain Macintosh.* Please.'

'I don't understand why the file has been removed.'

'Captain Macintosh,' Sir Robert put his hands in his pockets, 'could you tell me how something that transpired in the Falklands War could *possibly* have any bearing on the criminal investigation you are engaged upon?'

Mac looked at them.

'You're to hand over the case to Sanderson,' Rigby said. 'He'll brief you on the incident in Cyprus. The flight is at one o'clock.'

Mac glanced down at the file in his hand. He did not know what was driving his own stubbornness. Perhaps it was the way he could sense their fear, but not its cause.

'I had a call on Saturday,' Mac said, 'from a reporter on the *Sun*. Got wind of something. Glamour girl in trouble, all that. I tried to put him off, of course.'

'Is that . . . a threat?' Quemoy asked.

'Of course not. But I believe it's important that we are thorough in how we approach Captain Havilland's case. I don't think the newspapers should be given the impression that there is any *suppression* going on.' Mac looked at Rigby, who dropped his eyes to his lap. 'It's a sensitive case, as you say.'

There was silence.

Quemoy stood. 'All right, Macintosh. You have a day or two to complete this, but if you leave this office for any reason in the pursuit of this investigation, I want Sanderson here to accompany you. Is that clear? When you've finished, we will reconvene. Interview the girl and please confine your inquiries to matters that might possibly be relevant instead of matters that certainly are not. I'm sure I don't need to warn you that impersonating a fellow officer is a criminal offence.'

Once Quemoy had gone, Mac took his address book from his bag and walked towards the loo. Sanderson watched him go.

As soon as he was out in the corridor, Mac went straight down to the yard and across to his car. He drove out of the gate and down the road outside until he got to a lay-by at the bottom, underneath a giant poster advertising the new Mercedes estate car.

He stopped and called the Ministry of Defence switchboard. 'Records office,' he said.

They gave him another number, which rang for a long time before a man answered, 'Records.'

'Captain Macintosh of the Royal Military Police. I urgently need to get hold of a former corporal by the name of Wilkes. Falklands War veteran. I want a name and address.'

'I'm afraid I'll need written authorization for that.'

'Can I fax it to you?'

Mac was wondering if he had any headed paper at home.

'No, sir. I'm afraid you'll have to send it.'

'Look, this is a criminal invest—'

'Those are the rules. They are there to protect retired men's privacy.'

Mac breathed out heavily. 'Well, can you at least tell me that you have it?'

'Not without authorization, sir.'

Mac ended the call in frustration. He leafed through the directory he had put inside the back of his book, which listed home telephone numbers. He thought that if Maurice had been working the weekend he would be off today. Mac didn't like to think what Maurice got up to on his days off.

'Hello.' There was music in the background – a classical recording Mac didn't recognize.

'Maurice?'

'No. Hang on a minute, I'll get him.'

It had been a man's voice. There was a long wait.

'Maurice, it's Mac.'

'For Christ's sake, Mac.'

'What?'

'You were not supposed to know that Rigby had taken out the file. I've been told to stay at home indefinitely.' Maurice's voice, which had been angry, had immediately collapsed into self-pity.

Mac cursed himself inwardly. 'I need your help, Maurice.'

'Don't be so self-important.' The music seemed to have got louder. 'I can't help you, Mac, I'm sorry.'

'Maurice, I give you my word—'

'Oh, come on . . .' Maurice was angry again. 'It's not like it's the first time. It happened in Vietnam. I'm sure it happens in every war.'

It took Mac a few seconds to work out what Maurice was talking about. 'What happens?'

'Fragging. Or whatever they call it. Killing your officer.' There was another pause. 'That's all I'm saying, Mac. You've got me into enough trouble.' He put down the phone.

Mac tapped his fingers against the keys in the ignition, then took his notebook from his pocket and placed it on the steering-wheel in front of him.

Ford was not going to be co-operative, which left, of the officers, Rouse and Haydoch. He doubted Rouse was going to be any more helpful – certainly he'd been inexplicably hostile at the fête.

Pascoe was the key, but he was missing. Wilkes was the next best potential source. He had already spoken to Mrs Claverton, so

Mac thought that perhaps Danes's wife might supply him with an address for Wilkes at the very least.

After leaving Simon Crick's studio, Julia went into the newsagent, bought a copy of the *Daily Telegraph* and folded the file into it. Then she walked down the high street, turned into Cross Keys Lane and entered the Swan. The pub's interior had not changed much since the days when she had sat here illegally as a schoolgirl, its tacky décor not endearing it to the staff, thus, by convention, leaving it free for the pupils.

It was almost empty now, but for some parents having lunch with their son. The boy had red hair and freckles and was wearing the bright blue and gold blazer of the cricket colours, which did not suit him.

A shaft of sunlight lit a triangular patch of the table in front of her. Julia wasn't hungry, so she ordered coffee and, since there was a pot on a hot-plate on the side, it came immediately, with long thin ginger biscuits.

Julia did not know what to think about the pictures. She didn't know what they meant. She didn't know if she would tell Professor Malcolm about them.

They were disturbing. They stimulated an explosive cocktail of thoughts and memories. The common had been a place of childhood innocence at least until the day of the murders, but here was evidence that that had been merely an illusion, even a conceit.

Julia thought again of Alice. Of the pink dress and makeup. Somehow, that image and the pictures of Adrian Rouse and Sarah fucking – the corruption of the idyll – all seemed connected.

Julia tried to think about something else.

She flicked through the newspaper. The search of Welham Common was front page news. Inside, there was a story about the Security Forces in Ireland predicting a new ceasefire.

Julia leant back in her chair.

Her time in Ireland now seemed to have occurred in a different life altogether. Indeed, everything in her working life was like that – all parcelled off in her memory and unconnected to anything else. Sometimes it was as though she had not really lived it at all.

The army would throw her out, of that she had no doubt, and

the thought now struck her with the certainty of truth. She wondered when the crunch would come.

She thought about Mac. What in the *hell* was he doing getting himself involved? For a moment, she felt intensely annoyed with him, but it faded. It was impossible to be irritated with Mac. She wondered what he was doing now. Probably talking to the two sergeants, meticulously noting down details of her aberrant behaviour. Trying to find a way out for her when there wasn't one. She pushed the business section of the paper to the edge of the table. She had never once read one, or attended a careers fair or compiled a CV – not a proper one, anyway, with neat typing and hobbies. Opera, jazz, sport, dealing with very scared minds and looking at an execution as evidence of your own failure. What did that qualify you for? Loyalty and betrayal. Conscience and a lifetime of suspicion. Which particular piece of carpet-tile and standard-issue furniture did this qualify you to occupy?

She picked up her mobile phone and dialled Mac's number. He was on answering-machine. She put the phone down on the table in front of her.

Mac, she thought, had contentment. Lots of other things, too, but that most of all. His life had been hard, but he had it. Julia could not remember contentment, or imagine the shape, feel and weight of it. Where did it spring from?

Mac's father had abandoned the family just at the age when he had become aware of what it meant, but he had dealt with it quietly and it underscored his basic decency. Was confronting the past brave, or was forgetting it more courageous and clever?

She thought about her father and of the image that played out in her dreams, the great roaring bull of a man in full combat fatigues, soaked with the mud of battle, breaking cover and charging out to save the life of a soldier. Did circumstances make heroes or did heroes seek out circumstances?

She was playing with the corner of the white envelope and her mind kept returning to the pictures within. It ought to have been surprising, but wasn't. Nothing about Sarah was surprising. Confronting Adrian Rouse directly with them was out of the question, but she didn't want to tell Professor Malcolm, either.

Before leaving Cranbrooke, Julia went to visit Dr Simon.

His surgery was at the bottom of the high street, below the

abbey and close to the railway station, in a new building that he shared with three other doctors. It was called the Cranbrooke Practice.

While she waited, Julia watched a heavily pregnant woman playing with her two young boys on the floor. They drove the trucks and the cars around noisily, each engagingly involved in his own world as the mother shuttled between them.

They went in to see Dr Balen. A few minutes later, Julia was summoned to see Dr Simon.

He was exactly the kind of doctor that Sarah would have had. He was tall – well over six feet – with jet black hair and a large moustache. He bore more than a passing resemblance to Omar Sharif.

There were toys on the chair, so Julia perched uncomfortably on the bed, but the room was too small for him and the resultant atmosphere too intimate.

He asked for accreditation or identification and she handed him the letter and her plastic army ID card. He looked at both without comment, before handing them back to her. He did not mention the search.

Julia crossed her legs and took out her notebook. 'You remember Sarah and Alice, I presume?' she asked.

'Yes, of course.' He leant back in his chair, a stethoscope still around his neck. 'They were some of my first patients after I moved here from South Africa.'

'Where from?'

'I beg your pardon?'

'I mean, whereabouts in South Africa?'

'Cape Town.'

Julia smiled. 'Brave man to move here from there.'

He shrugged. 'Things were different then.'

Julia was embarrassed, realizing that it was possible he had not been classified as a white. 'Did you know Sarah well?'

'As much as you know any patient.'

'Was there anything about her that gave you any hint as to what happened?'

He was shaking his head vigorously. 'I was her doctor.'

'No evidence of abuse or anything like that.'

He shook his head again, but a smile had crept into the corner of his mouth. 'She was quite a feisty woman. I don't think that would have been an issue.'

Julia looked down at her notepad. 'What about Alice?' He was waiting for her to continue. 'As her doctor, did you notice anything out of the ordinary, any signs of abuse or neglect?'

'On the contrary, Alice seemed to have been in unusually excellent physical condition.'

'What do you mean, "unusually excellent"?'

He shrugged. 'Nails. Hair. Teeth. Any cuts always very clean. If anything, I would have said Sarah was an overprotective mother. She . . . every time the girl had a snuffle, she was in here. Always wanting antibiotics. I refused to prescribe them, sometimes, because if they take them like that as children, they're no use when they're really ill.'

This was again so at odds with the neglectful, disinterested mother Julia remembered that she was silent for a few moments. 'What about the relationship between mother and daughter? You probably wouldn't have been aware, but Alice was being professionally modelled towards the end of her life and . . . Sarah may have been developing what could almost be seen as, well, an unhealthy interest in her daughter's physical appearance. And one other thing, she seems to have made a lot of appointments to see you.'

'I'm not a psychologist so I'm not going to comment on the relationship between mother and daughter, except to point to what I've just told you. In general, I always found her an endearing child. Well behaved, eager to please. Quiet. As to the number of appointments, yes, Sarah Ford and her husband had had some problems conceiving and we were, at that time, working with them both to ascertain whether any genuine difficulties or obstacles had emerged. We'd established that there were none with her, so our attention was turning to her husband. However, the nature of his military duties made hospital appointments difficult to keep.'

'But they had Alice all right?'

'Yes, but that was before I was Sarah's doctor. I believe . . . I think you will find that Alice was in fact conceived before . . .'

'Before what?'

He realized he had gone too far. 'No, I'm sorry.'

'This *is* a criminal investigation, Dr Simon.'

He was waving his hand. 'Yes, I know, I know. It is no great secret. But the point is that sometimes it is easier to conceive when you are not trying than when you are.'

'So Alice was conceived before marriage?'

'Yes. That's what Sarah said. She did not give me to believe it was a secret, nor was she shy of it, but . . .'

'And they were unable to have more children?'

'It was too early to say they were unable. They had been experiencing difficulties, that's all.'

Dr Simon had been looking at the clock. He gave her a patronizing, almost admiring smile. She stood up abruptly and thanked him.

Outside, Julia leant against the wall in the sunshine, not knowing what to make of the fact that Alice had been conceived out of wedlock. It made sense of why Alan had married Sarah, of course, but didn't seem to have any other relevance.

The description of Sarah as a protective mother was more confusing. At the start of this process, she would have claimed to have known the relationship between Alice Ford and her mother well, but as she proceeded, she felt less and less sure of its dynamic.

The easiest way to get out of Cranbrooke from the surgery was to drive past the station, cross the railway line and come back on the main road that skirts the bottom of the hill, but just as Julia was about to turn left to cross the line, she saw Mac in his familiar beaten-up old white Fiesta driving past the park in the direction of the abbey. Instinctively, Julia found herself following, at a distance.

Mac turned left in front of the abbey, past the coffee-houses and sweet-shops Julia remembered so well from her schooldays here. Then, down towards the playing-fields, he turned left again. Julia could see this was a residential side-street, so she pulled over in front of the boys' school cricket pitch and waited.

She gave him about two minutes, then got out and walked round the corner. There was a cricket match in progress.

Mac's car was parked right at the far end on the other side so Julia crossed to the opposite pavement and walked slowly down towards it. There were small terraced houses, with wrought-iron fences and small yards in front of them, with well-tended flowerpots and plants. Julia guessed they were mostly occupied by elderly and retired people, of whom there were a great many in Cranbrooke. At school, they had joked bitterly that the town was full of schoolchildren and the elderly – 'those waiting to live and those waiting to die'.

In each house, there were two big windows on either side of the front door, one looking into a living room, the other into the kitchen. As she came to the end, Julia slowed still further. There was a light on in the kitchen of the last house and Mac was standing with his back to the window, his bulk filling most of it. He was turning his Akubra hat in his hand, the way he always did, and there was a woman opposite him, under the light, with her head down. She had dark hair and, as she looked up, Julia saw both that she recognized the woman and that she was crying.

Julia had to wait an hour for Mac to come out. He stopped on the step and put his hat on his head.

'Hello,' he said.

She found herself not knowing what to say. Her hands had been in her pockets, fingers scratching at her legs. She took them out and rubbed her palms together. 'What are you doing here, Mac?'

'Working.'

Julia looked at her feet. 'Who was that in the house? I recognized her.'

'Jennifer Danes.'

'As in Richard Danes, one of my father's regimental sergeants?'

'Yes.'

Julia frowned. 'Why were you seeing her?'

Mac looked at her. 'Have you got time for a coffee?'

He fell into step beside her, looking across at the boys playing cricket, squinting against the sun which was directly above the clock-tower on the pavilion.

Julia was suddenly, almost hysterically pleased to see Mac's big smiling face. He was nothing to do with it – nothing to do with West Welham, or with Sarah, or corruption and lost innocence, or with *any* of it.

They reached the main road and stopped. He looked at her. 'Come on, then. This is your place, you went to school here, make a suggestion.'

'Beneath the abbey,' she pointed, 'there are some coffee-houses.'

They walked in the direction of the junction. An elderly white Volvo belched along and a pretty young woman in a T-shirt and tight jeans pushed her pram across the road past another group of boys sauntering up the hill in the direction of the school.

'Why was Mrs Danes crying?'

Mac shrugged. 'The memory of her husband.'

'I don't understand.'

'All in good time.'

Julia had led them through a narrow alley and past the sweet-shop on the corner.

'I meant to say thank you for your letters in Beijing . . . sorry I kind of stopped replying. Is your mother okay, Mac?'

It was a few paces before he replied. 'No,' he said. 'Not really.'

'I thought it was in remission?'

'It was.'

'I'm sorry.' She touched his arm just above the elbow, but he didn't react.

'There's nothing anyone can do about it so there's no point in being sorry.'

Julia wondered whether this was something he wanted to talk about and then why she had taken so long to ask herself that question.

'The thing is,' he went on, 'people don't necessarily respond well when they know they're going to die.'

'In what way?'

'Well, it's almost as if she wants to tie everything up before she goes.'

Julia did not understand. 'To do with you?'

'She never wanted me to be in the army, doesn't like it and never has. She'd give anything to see me out and "happily" settled down . . . married.'

'Why doesn't she like . . .'

'My father was . . .' He looked at her. 'My father was a non-commissioned officer, a corporal.'

'I didn't know your father was in the army.'

'She hates anything to do with him. Whatever he did was wrong.'

Julia thought it odd that Mac's mother didn't derive pleasure from seeing her son as an officer when her husband had been in the ranks, but perhaps it was that the military gave father and son a potential link – a bond to which the mother had no access.

'How is Judith?'

'That's a good question, to which I don't know the answer.'

'What happened?'

'Well,' he said. 'Judith was . . .'

'Pretty.'

'Insecure.'

'I thought she was nice.'

'Exactly. Nice.'

He smiled, his big, broken nose pulled to the right. In this, he reminded her of her father. 'What about Paul?' he asked.

She smiled back at him. 'Well . . . Paul.' They were still walking. 'I think I wasted three years of his life.'

'I don't suppose he considers it wasted.'

'I bet he does. I hardly saw him.'

They crossed in front of the abbey and entered the first coffee-house on the left. There was a bell on the door and it was dark inside. They took a table in the corner, the room empty but for a group of three boys from Cranbrooke and three girls. The boys had draped their sports jackets over the dark-coloured chairs and faced the girls, like an interview committee. There were occasional slightly exaggerated forced laughs.

Julia had her back to the room, facing Mac. He was smiling. 'Once,' he said, pointing to the group in the corner, 'I suppose that was you.'

She turned round and looked at them.

'Not often,' she said. 'I was painfully shy.'

'But much in demand.'

'Hardly.'

'You? Bollocks. I don't believe it.' He leant back in his chair. 'Still, if you think it was bad being you, you should have tried being me.'

'And what was so traumatic about that?'

'Oversized, gawky, uncomfortable. As attractive to women as Goebbels and Giant Haystacks rolled into one.' He smiled at her. 'Haystacks was a wrestler,' he said, by way of explanation. 'A fat one.'

'I'm not that ignorant.'

There was another laugh from the other side of the room, then a young girl in a white pinny came over to take their orders. Julia asked for millionaire's shortbread and tea, Mac just a cup of coffee.

235

'Mind you,' Mac said, when she'd gone, 'we didn't really have too many tea-shops in my bit of Leeds.'

He smiled again and Julia thought how attractive he was. He had a big face – big mouth, big nose, big tuft of sandy hair – and his smile brought it to life. It was a self-conscious gesture and she liked that about him, too. He was the opposite of smug, never quite at ease with himself.

'You're going to give me another lecture on privilege.'

'Me, lecture you? Never.'

'What did the sergeants say about me? Are they back from Beijing?'

'Yes.' Mac turned over his hands on the table-top and examined his palms. 'And they said exactly what you'd expect. I got the impression they were fond of you, actually.'

Julia looked at the table, suddenly embarrassed by the way in which she had let people down. People she liked, who had trusted and admired her.

'You seem almost indifferent.'

She shook her head. 'I don't really want to talk about it.'

'I have to speak to you at some point,' Mac said, quietly. 'Officially, I mean.'

Julia was staring at her hands. 'There's nothing to say.'

'If there's nothing to say, then you've no defence.'

'I don't want a defence.'

The girl came over with a tray. They were silent while she unloaded it.

As soon as she'd gone, Mac leant forward once more. He had picked up his hat and was turning it in his hand, but he now let it fall to the floor beside him. 'We could look for mitigating circumstances . . .'

'Like pleading insanity?'

'If you try to explain, I can help. They'll be nervous about you – glamour girl, Sword of Honour, war-hero father and all of that.'

'No, absolutely not.'

'Hear me out.'

'Mac. The answer is no.' She looked at him. 'You still haven't said what you were doing seeing Mrs Danes.'

He leant back in his chair. 'You'll think it stupid.'

'Why?'

'Well, you know I studied history.'

She shrugged. 'Yes.'

'I was hoping to write a history of the Falklands War.'

Julia frowned heavily. 'I think that's been done a few times, Mac.'

Now he looked embarrassed. 'Yes, I know. I just wanted something outside of the army.'

Julia felt chastened. 'I'm sorry. It's – it's a good idea.'

Mac leant forward again and put his arms on the table. 'I wondered, actually, if . . . ages ago, you showed me some of your scrapbooks – when I came down to stay after Sandhurst, and there was a leatherbound diary that somebody called . . . Was it Rouse? A friend of your father's gave it to you.'

Julia hesitated. 'Yes.'

'Would it be possible to borrow it? Just for a day or two?'

Julia tried to think about this. 'I suppose so.'

'Thanks.'

'But I'll have to ask Adrian first. It's a private journal, he might not . . . I mean, he said it was to give me a three-dimensional picture of my father in the last weeks, I don't think it was meant for public consumption.'

'It's just for background, not quotation.'

'I'll still have to ask him.' Julia began pouring her tea. 'What did Danes have to say about the war, or have you not found him yet?'

'Er . . .' Mac cleared his throat. 'Actually, Danes is dead. Shot himself. His best friend committed suicide as well, Richard Claverton.'

Julia had a sudden, strong mental image of Danes with his balding head, stocky body and arrogant swagger. She remembered Claverton, too. They had both seemed such strong men and she was again shocked by how easily vital lives could be extinguished.

'They both committed suicide?'

Mac hesitated. 'I believe so.'

'That seems very unlikely.'

Mac seemed on the point of saying something else, but instead he shrugged. Julia frowned at him heavily.

'There was an inquest,' he said.

'Did your department look into it?'

'Yes, I believe so.'

'But they didn't find anything amiss?'

'No.'

'Was it Rigby?'

'Yes.'

'I thought you said he couldn't find his way out of a paper bag.'

Mac did not reply.

'Why are you being evasive?'

Mac sighed. 'I'm not. It's just awkward . . . I'm trying to work out whether to bring it to anyone's attention, but Rigby doesn't respond well to criticism.'

When she got home, Julia did not invite Mac in while she went upstairs to get Adrian's war diary, a little irritated that he had insisted on taking it today. 'I couldn't get hold of Adrian,' she said, when she came back. 'I'm not sure it feels right but I trust you, obviously, and if he says no quotations, you'll respect that?'

Mac nodded. 'Of course.'

Julia handed it to him and immediately regretted it. Mac leant forward, kissed her cheek, touching her upper arm easily, and got into his car. She bent down and looked at him through the open window. 'What are you doing, Mac?'

'What do you mean?'

'Aren't you supposed to be working on my case? How come you've got time to be running around writing history books?'

'Talking to you is all I've got left to do.'

'Oh . . . right.'

She looked at him. Did he look duplicitous? She couldn't tell. He seemed . . . suddenly shifty, somehow. She stepped back and watched him reverse out of the drive and, as he pulled slowly away down Woodpecker Lane, she felt a pervasive, inexplicable sense of unease and discomfort, as if an inability to trust Mac was the worst development of all. Professor Malcolm was right. Suspicion was like a disease. It ate away at you until you had nothing left.

She walked back into the house and, in the kitchen, found a note from her mother. It was bridge evening at the Rouses' and there was another salad in the fridge. She would be back around ten thirty.

The light was fading, but there was plenty of this long summer's day left and Julia decided she needed to get out and think. She found Aristotle lying in the larder, where it was cooler, and stimulated him into action, wishing, in a sudden emotional volte-face, that Mac hadn't gone. He always disappeared when she would have been happy for him to linger.

As they walked down through the village, Julia passed the detritus of the media's presence – crisp packets and a couple of white polystyrene cups – which she told herself she'd pick up on the way back.

She descended towards the common, Aristotle loping ahead. It was darker under the trees at this time of day, but the air was still warm.

Julia turned off the main path and walked up to the clearing at the top, standing on the edge of it. She thought that the photographs of Adrian fucking Sarah must have been taken from about this point, perhaps a bit further away, Simon Crick furtively hidden in the trees. Who had commissioned him? Had her own father been jealous of a new lover?

Julia sat against one of the tree stumps. She was in shadow here, but the clearing was still light, the sun spilling over the tops of the trees.

She found herself thinking of Pascoe. Surely it was not possible that he was still here, somewhere close, watching, as Professor Malcolm had suggested. It would be in his interests to get as far away from the village as possible.

When Julia looked up, she saw a figure standing in the middle of the clearing and, for a moment, her heart jumped as she thought it might have been Pascoe, but it was Alan and, as he saw her, he raised his hand and walked slowly through the long grass.

'I saw Aristotle,' he said.

'The world's most disloyal dog.'

'Independent-minded.'

She stood up and brushed the twigs from her backside. 'I guess they didn't find anything with their search,' she said. He shook his head. 'At least that's an end to it for ever.'

'That's what we said last time.' He sighed, almost inaudibly. 'It never ends. Shall we go and find Aristotle?'

She followed him out of the clearing, past the wizened tree stump, which was now out of the sun. They walked in silence, Julia slipping her arm into his and forcing his chubby cheeks into an easy, good-natured smile. Perhaps it was her imagination, but his eyebrows seemed to have grown bushier.

As they reached the main path, Alan asked whether she wanted to go the long way or the short way home and she chose the former. The next section of the path was muddy, then they reached drier ground as they began to climb a gentle incline. 'Don't you find it lonely living alone?' Julia asked, without having intended to broach so intimate a subject.

'No.' He took a few paces. 'Well, sometimes.' He thought some more. They had almost reached the furthest point on the common. 'In a way, that has been the one thing to come out of all of this. It has broken down the barriers that would normally exist in a community such as this so that I never feel alone.'

'It must have been difficult today,' she said.

'Every day is difficult.'

'I think about her every day, too.'

They walked a few more paces. 'There's always a gap,' Alan went on, 'not just for the person she was but the person she would have been.'

Julia understood exactly.

'I think lost potential is almost the worst of it,' he said. 'To begin with, all I could think about was her vulnerability and my failure to be there to protect her when she needed me, but . . .'

The only sound was that of twigs cracking beneath their feet on the firm section of the path. They had turned towards home now. The path was wider here, the trees less dense. To their right, another track led diagonally down the slope to the edge of the common and, on this side, the view through the trees was out across a broader valley, one road climbing straight up the hill opposite then descending directly into Cranbrooke, another winding its way up to a junction further along, close to the regimental base.

A large tree trunk was set back from the path on the left and Julia remembered herself and Alice running along it, seeing how far they could jump into the long grass beyond.

'As I get older,' he went on, 'I see you, others, doing so well. So pretty and bright and clever, and the worst of it is that I can't visualize Alice as a young woman at all. The memories I have are old and I find myself staring into the void that is the space my Alice would have filled.'

Julia nodded and held his arm tighter, feeling that her life here was becoming schizophrenic, half on the outside of this community, half in the place she had always been. Alan seemed least aware of the awkwardness of this, or perhaps simply the most understanding.

They walked on in companionable silence. 'I've come to feel,' Julia said, 'that we should not expect to get through life with nothing bad happening. It's not realistic. You have to factor that in and—'

'But many do.' He looked at her. 'Many sail through life with nothing amiss ever happening. So why did we get singled out? That's what causes resentment. The injustice. That's what we've both had to face.'

Julia nodded. She thought he meant this experience had been responsible for bringing them all together, but it was hard to think of anything good having come from it. Gently, she removed her arm from his.

When she got home, Julia ate the salad, drank a glass of wine and went to bed. She had not made any attempt to contact Professor Malcolm, because she needed time to think. The white folder with the pictures of Adrian and Sarah was in the drawer in her bedside table, but the images it contained were still in her head.

The curtains were drawn, but moonlight spilled across her duvet.

Her right hand rested on her stomach.

She rubbed her feet together, thinking of the muscles tensing in Sarah's thighs and buttocks and the way her face was distorted with pleasure.

Julia shut her eyes, thinking of the sardonic smile on Sarah's lips.

She created space in the duvet and rubbed her hand gently to and fro on the smooth skin of her stomach, her fingers finding the waistband of her knickers then the soft hair within, her legs held tightly together. Two of her fingers edged down towards the gap, those beside them forcing her legs apart.

Julia heard the front door open and spun over on to her side.

After that she could not get to sleep, her mind trying to put into some kind of order the things she had found out that did not make any sense.

Sarah, whom Julia had always thought a disinterested mother, taken only with adult pursuits, had turned out to be interested in her daughter to the extent of *grooming* her. Sarah had taken Alice on modelling assignments, which no one knew about, with a photographer who had also, by coincidence – or not – been employed to creep around the local beauty spot taking surveillance pictures of Sarah being fucked by one of Alan's friends and, at the time, regimental colleagues.

And yet Alan and Adrian, the husband and the lover, still appeared to be friends.

Julia could not imagine Adrian and Sarah having an affair, or guess at what on earth they would have found to talk about. If she had not seen the photographic evidence with her own eyes, she would not have believed it.

The moon was still bright and Julia sat up and pulled back the curtain to look out, feeling restless.

She got out of bed and sat at her desk, then moved out into the corridor and climbed up to the attic, itself bathed in light from the Velux window.

Julia pushed open the window and stuck her head out, the common ahead shrouded in a ghostly mist that encircled it closely, like a cap.

Alan's house stood in darkness, but, as she turned her head further, she saw that there was a light on in Pascoe's home in the lane beyond the pub.

Julia looked at her watch. It was one o'clock in the morning. She bit her lip, then descended the stairs quietly, curiosity tempered but not extinguished by fear.

She dressed in her room, then let herself out of the front door, not bothering to lock it behind her.

Outside, the village was silent, her footsteps loud as her shoes scuffed the loose gravel on the tarmac.

She reached the pub, which stood in darkness, then walked on into the lane. The light from Pascoe's house had been turned off – unless it had come from somewhere else.

She was about to turn away, when she caught a glimpse of someone – a figure flitting out of sight in the living room beyond the kitchen.

Her heart began to thump.

For a moment, she stood still and was about to knock when she

242

thought better of it and climbed up on to the wall at the end of the lane, dropping over the other side into some gorse bushes, before fumbling her way along in the shadow of the trees and climbing back up again above a garden bathed in moonlight. She was clearly visible to anyone looking out of a window inside the house, so an approach by stealth was impossible, but she slipped off the wall quietly then edged towards the back door, which she could see had been crudely forced.

Julia lifted it carefully and pulled it towards her.

She stepped inside. Moonlight spilled into the room on the left, but the corridor was dark and the smell of ingrained grease and dirt again caught in her nostrils.

'Hello,' she said. 'Pascoe?'

Her voice, like her body, was tense. She began walking down the corridor to the stairs, thinking that anyone waiting for her would be lurking here. She moved swiftly and darted through the kitchen to the front room, prepared for sudden physical confrontation, but no one was there. For a second, she thought a figure might have been hiding in the shadows and flicked on the light. The room remained just as bare and nothing seemed to have been disturbed.

Julia moved to the bottom of the stairs. 'Pascoe?' she called up.

She could see no light so she climbed carefully up into the darkness above. The curtains were drawn on the landing, so it was gloomier than the hall below and the floorboards creaked.

'Pascoe?' Julia whispered.

Her footsteps seemed impossibly loud as she walked forward into a room on her right and switched on the light, but this room, too, was empty. There was a large cupboard and one single bed, which had clearly been slept in. It had a Snoopy duvet cover, and an ancient, scruffy teddy bear lay on top of it. Julia turned and just, for a fraction of a second, out of the corner of her eye, saw the rapid motion of something solid, before it smashed into the side of her head and everything went black.

Julia awoke. She tried to sit up, but the pain was intense. She laid her head back down and closed her eyes again.

She waited, then forced herself upright. The room was still light and she put her hand to her head. There was no blood on her fingers or, so far as she could tell, on the floor.

Julia shut her eyes against the pain for a few moments more, then opened them and slowly stood up. The house was silent. She had been hit with a short wooden plank, which had been dropped on the floor. Beside it, in the doorway, was a chisel with a blue handle. She stooped and picked it up, turning it over in her hand, assuming it had been dropped in the confusion.

She moved slowly back to the landing then down the stairs. There was a breeze and the back door was banging gently against the wall. She bent to look at the area around the handle and saw clearly that the chisel had been used to force the door open.

Outside, the lane was still quiet, as if nothing had happened.

When Julia got home, she took the chisel out of her jacket pocket and put it in the drawer together with the statements given by her parents and the photographs of Sarah Ford being fucked by Adrian Rouse.

Mac sprinted up the stairs. He was out of breath when he reached the top. The door of his flat swung on its hinges. He looked at it for a moment, then walked forward, pushing gently.

The flat had been turned over. The drawers of his desk had been taken out and their contents emptied all over the coffee-table, the sofa and the floor. The kitchen cupboards had been rifled; a pot of honey lay broken on the ground.

Mac walked through to the bedroom. They had turned out the drawers here, too – his clothes were lying all over the bed. He picked up some T-shirts, then dropped them again. 'Shit,' he said, under his breath.

Mac returned to the living room, then went out, pulling the front door shut and jamming it as best he could.

Outside, he turned left, scanning the street, walking swiftly along the pavement, past the French bistro and the Hart's convenience store, before crossing the road and stopping to look into the window of the sofa shop opposite.

He moved on, crossing the road again, waiting for a break in the traffic and pretending to be idly looking back up towards his flat.

At the bottom, Mac turned left into Northcote Road and crossed to the other side, once again stopping to wait for a break in the traffic and looking back in the direction he'd just come from.

He walked all the way to the end of Northcote Road, then stepped into a coffee-shop by the crossroads, seating himself at a table by the window.

Perhaps he was just being paranoid, but if they'd searched his flat, then it was logical that they might be tailing him. What worried him was that they might have followed him during his meeting with Julia. Would they make anything of that?

He could not understand what they had been looking for in his flat.

Mac ordered a coffee from the waitress, then took out the notebook that Julia had given him earlier.

Rouse's handwriting was neat and the pages well thumbed. Originally, he had written directly into the book, but some of the later events had been recorded in a smaller notebook then pulled out and stuck in. There were some rough pencil sketches, too, good ones, Mac thought, and, in this, it was reminiscent of Claverton's fishing journal. One was of a helicopter flying over a barren ridge, entitled 'San Carlos', another was of a line of soldiers walking in full kit across a desolate hillside and was entitled 'Tabbing'. Both looked as if they had been done after the event, from memory.

He returned to the start and began to read.

Wed 7 April. It could be war. Hard to believe. After all that's happened in Welham, it seems like God's idea of a bad joke, but then maybe it's what everyone needs.

Word we're going tomorrow. Southampton, then leave on Friday. Cops came to base today to talk to Alan again. Frustration all round with their efforts. Still not found man in leather jacket the old lady saw who seems obvious culprit. Asking everyone offensive questions. Especially fat psychologist. Alan generally silent. Still not certain if he goes tomorrow, or stays. Mike H says Alan doesn't see point of staying, because Alice is dead and everyone knows it. He's being given a wide berth. None of the usual piss-taking, obviously. Mike H says good for him to get away.

Alice is on everyone's mind. Even the lads remember her and Sarah from events on the base. Sports day etc. There's gossip in the ranks, but dries up when an officer enters. Most gossip centres around S. Air of unreality all round.

War or not? Nobody knows.

More fired up in the afternoon. CO briefing on parade ground. Mitch says def off tomorrow unless w****** change their mind again. Not nec war, but should be prepared for any eventuality. Says not many soldiers get a chance like this. Quite inspiring. Made it sound like the world was going to be jealous not to be in on the action. Everyone more aggressive afterwards. At last, action, not speculation. Busy, now, much to do. Windproof smocks finally arrived. Can't believe they've had this stuff sitting around at HQ UKLF. Probably trying to hold on to it for their skiing holidays. Mitch got on and said if they didn't f****** release it, he'd go up and take it himself. As usual, emphasis on getting things done and no time for time-serving w******. He'll never make General. Or maybe he will.

I gave a briefing today in role as Battalion I/O. What a joke. We've had int from naval lieutenant who was in South Georgia and a Marine officer who surveyed the coast intending to write yachting guide. Gave best idea of terrain I could, but it's not exactly extensive. We'll just have to wait.

9 April. Going. Gone. Leslie not at docks. Glad, in the end. Some of the men were leaning against the rail, playing 'spot the war widow', debating which of the men would be 'buying' it, if it comes to a shooting war, and parcelling out their widows.

11 April. Atmosphere generally more relaxed on board. Alan seems to be moving forward, though still silent and keeping self to self. Main complaint of men is restriction to daily intake of two cans of beer, which is seen, not without reason, as arbitrary. Much grumbling about food. Standard good, but queues too long – an hour for each meal. Mitch concerned they're all going to go soggy, which doesn't seem likely. General feeling is it probably won't come to war and Argies will back down and get off our islands, but, if it does, most desperate to get on and 'kick them in the bollocks'. A lot of enthusiasm for killing some 'Gooks'. Most can't understand why the hell islands are ours anyway. Language of some of the men is all Vietnam, Gooks, zapping, etc. They all seem to think they'll be going in by Huey to the sound of 'Ride of the Valkyries' or whatever it was. Suspicion of press men on board, because Yankee press seen as stabbing boys in 'Nam in the back. Mitch thinks this is good. All men ordered not to talk about Ford case to press. Some grumbling about this, but despite impact back home, now largely forgotten in ranks. Gossip is all on-board stuff. Officers' mess different kettle of fish.

Daily O group at five with Mitch. Various matters. Theft of ship's property. Use of ladies' lavatories. Need for medical training – esp gunshot wounds. Also rumour control. Rumours get out of hand in no time.

Also rumour today, police would be flying to Ascension to interview member of regiment re Ford case. Men think it is Alan. Mitch went ballistic. Total bollocks, he said. Detailed self and Mike H to find who started it – hopeless task.

13 April. South of Gibraltar. O group dominated by int that Russian trawler is following. Men instructed not to throw rubbish over. Responded by jacking off into plastic containers and dumping them over the side. Idea is to dissuade Russians from invading by convincing them we're the master race. Said to be Danes's idea – no surprise. Mitch thought it was funny.

Also, men to be discouraged from standing naked in corridors while waiting for showers. Fears it titillates homosexuals among crew.

After group finished, Mitch took self and Mike H aside. Worried about whether Alan up to it. He doesn't speak to his platoon sergeant, Danes. Rumours now circulating about Private Pascoe – came from a letter, apparently. Mitch expressed the view that everything back home, however serious, has got to be forgotten. Always going to be rumours. Anyone caught circulating them will be removed and taken home. Mike H said he thought Alan was improving and capable of controlling Danes and halting the bullying of Pascoe (seen in tears yesterday). Too much time to dwell on the ship. Mike H said they'd pull together in time. Better if news from home that they've found the man in the leather jacket and put him inside. Otherwise vacuum filled by rumour. Mitch thinks possible to stop it, but it's not. Can't control what people think and say below decks.

Sat 17th. Freetown. Sierra Leone. Not allowed ashore. Local

Brits gathered to cheer us from the jetty. Men making masturbation hand signals to the women and chucked one of the leftover plastic vials ashore – 'closest we're going to get to a shag'. Locals rowed out in small boats to try to sell artefacts. The men dropped various objects over the side, shouting, 'Remember Rorke's Drift.' Danes the ringleader. CO said he wasn't going to try and stop it. Danes has taken to going everywhere without a shirt and a steward got the wrong message last night and tried to make a pass at him in one of the out of bounds crew bars. Claverton prevented Danes from pushing the man out of a porthole.

Mon 19th. Crossed equator. Perhaps it is improved weather, but no one has talked about Welham for two or three days. Alan seems more back to normal jovial self. He patted me on the back today. Seems to have platoon more under control. Mike H says he had a set-to with Danes which appears to have cleared the air.

Mon 19th. It really is war. Helicopter containing members of D squadron SAS got an albatross stuck in its engine and crashed into sea: 22 dead. Sobering.

Sense of nervous readiness. Only problem is Alan and Danes again. Mitch too busy and preoccupied to notice any more – 'Time for them to b***** get on with it', but hope it will not be a problem. Actually, Alan and Mitch hardly ever communicate directly. Mike H spoke to Danes and was told that Alan was an uptight w***** who knows nothing about tactics and couldn't lead his men out of a paper bag. Trouble is Mike H and Danes and Mitch are all of a type – gung-ho, no bullshit, break the door down, etc. Alan is competitive enough, just a bit more reserved. Less in-your-face. The men say he's taciturn, but not surprising, given the circumstances. Think Danes may feel Alan should have stayed at home.

Sense of relief we're behind Mitch. Was talking to Wilkes today who said he'd not thought about it before but was f****** grateful he had a commander he could respect and not some w***** out to make his career. The men feel Mitch is looking out for them.

However, feel there is danger of falling victim to a 'cult of personality'. Mitch doesn't stand bullshitters or arse-lickers, but equally doesn't really listen to a word anyone says. Any criticism is 'negativity'. Sucks people in like a vortex. Personality so strong it can be overpowering. It's 'Mad' Mitch all right, but sometimes a little less force might produce more considered results. Still, rather him at this point than anyone else. He doesn't leave you much room for doubt.

From now on, the pages were pasted in.

Landing. In the landing craft. Can't believe this happening. Strong sense of complete madness of my life and incomprehension as to how came to this point. Mitch steadied everyone. Again, good to have no time to think or room for doubt. Pushed off in blackness and landed without incident, though all a bit amateurish. Argies should have responded, but didn't. Water freezing.

Little contact, but retreating troops above San Carlos shot down a Gazelle. Air crew escaped and bloody bastards started shooting at them in the water. Mitch says that tells us all we need to know about the f******.

Then we were into air attacks. Got to hand it to the Argie pilots – flying so low we could see into their cockpits. Brave. *25 May. Atlantic Conveyor* sunk, with helicopters on board. Three Chinooks, six Wessex, a Lynx. We're going to have to bloody walk. We got out the maps. Sixty miles, difficult terrain. Making this up as we go along.

26 May. Tired. Endless walking across totally featureless terrain. Feels like a Boy Scout outing gone wrong. Thank God for mountain-climbing experience – sod all use, but did bring fleece and gaiters. Kept warm and kept out most of the wet. *29 May.* Goose Green taken, with loss of 'H' Jones and others. Mitch briefed us and said his action f****** brave. Indicated Argies had shot some of our boys while they were waving a white flag. No more info as yet.

3 June. Mitch gave advance-to-contact orders, then brass flew in and all reined back in. 'As you were.' Danes said he'd shoot Mitch if he tried that again – consensus was that we need more rest and planning. It's been bloody cold. My guess fifty/fifty decision. Boss's argument was that we'd made good time and element of surprise might allow us to split apart their defences, whereas if we wait for air support and the whole cavalcade, they'll know we're coming. Maybe right, maybe wrong. Ballsy as always. Same thing, though. Cult of personality. Forceful. Only Mike H dared say he might be wrong.

When he had finished reading, Mac stared out of the window. The last of the evening sun fell fully on his face and he closed his eyes for a moment. He could see more clearly now why Mitch had exerted such a hold over his daughter, even in death.

He sipped his coffee, which had arrived while he'd been immersed in the notebook.

The remark about Danes threatening to shoot Mitch appeared only to have been made in jest. He couldn't read anything serious into it but he did wonder why the diary had given no details of the battle. It was not extensive as a record of a war, but it seemed odd to have gone to the trouble of writing it without bothering to fill in the punch-line.

Perhaps Rouse just hadn't felt like it, after the trauma of battle. He could understand that but, then, why not junk the whole thing? The line drawings and the stuck-in pages suggested he had gone back to it at a later stage.

Mac stood and looked at his watch. It was getting late, but he wanted to try to track down Wilkes, whose address, but not telephone number, had been supplied by a tearful Mrs Danes. Like Sandra Claverton, she seemed to have been kept in the dark about her husband's past, but at least Wilkes's name appeared in his address book.

Mac turned out on to the street, his eyes moving in an arc from one side to the other. He did not think he was being tailed.

Half an hour later, Mac walked up a dull, decaying concrete staircase, before stepping on to a long balcony, a series of yellowing doors to his right, the skyline to his left. It was dark here. There was a strong smell of stale urine – the acrid odour of London's concrete underpasses and corridors.

Mac realized he was on the wrong floor, retraced his steps to the central stairwell and climbed up another flight. It smelt of urine up here, too, more strongly if anything, or perhaps it had simply lodged in his nostrils.

The flats looked appallingly run-down. The yellow paint on the doors had faded to a dirty green and one or two of the frosted windows were broken. He found number forty-nine and his heart sank. The two panes on either side of the front door had holes punched in them and the window above had been completely knocked out. He tapped once, waited, then tried again. There were no lights on inside.

The flat to the right seemed more likely to be occupied, so he knocked once there and heard a dog bark loudly. A light came on in the hall. He took a step back.

The door opened and a short, dark, intense young man stood before him. He was wearing a white vest and black jeans, and Mac wouldn't have put him at much more than twenty. He was stooping slightly, holding the bull terrier's collar.

'I'm sorry to bother you,' Mac said, 'but I was just looking for Mr Wilkes.' There was no obvious sign of recognition in the boy's eyes, so he went on, 'Lives next door.'

The boy shook his head, without breaking his stare. 'No idea.'

'But he still lives here?'

'No idea.'

'But somebody lives next door?'

'Haven't seen him for days.'

'So Mr Wilkes does still live next door?' Mac looked up at the broken windows.

'Don't know his name. Short man with a moustache.'

'Right. But you've not seen him for some days?'

The young man shrugged again.

'Do you have any idea where he might be?'

'No.'

'Do you know where he works?'

He shook his head.

'Do you know anything at all about him . . . where he drinks?'

The dog, which had been staring at Mac, now wanted to get out of the flat. 'Back, back,' the boy said. 'Most drink in the Rat and Parrot across the road. Back. Back.' He yanked the dog by the collar and straightened again. 'What's he done anyway?'

'Nothing. Why?'

'There was another lot earlier. Looked like coppers as well.'

Mac looked at him. 'Two men . . . one balding, another thin face, like a weasel?'

'Something like that.'

'What did they want?'

'Same as you. Wanted to know where he was.'

'He's not done anything,' Mac said. As he turned away, the door was slammed shut behind him.

Mac walked down the stairs with his hands in his pockets and across the courtyard below. The light was fading now.

The Rat and Parrot was just about what he would have expected, a grubby establishment dedicated to serious alcohol consumption, full of Formica tables and chairs with black plastic covers. There was a pinball machine and pool table in one corner, next to a juke-box, and a large, rectangular bar in the centre. It smelt heavily of beer. A young blond man with two earrings and short, spiked hair nodded at him.

'I'm looking for someone called Mr Wilkes.' Mac pointed over his shoulder. 'Lives in the tower block opposite. Short man with a moustache.'

The youth shrugged. 'Darren!' he shouted.

An older man sauntered over. Like his assistant, he had a tea-towel over his shoulder. Mac repeated his question.

'Description rings a bell. Not seen him for a while, though.'

'Days? Weeks?'

'Not since last week, anyway. Never says much. Buys his pint and sits in the corner with his roll-ups. What's he done?'

'Nothing.' Mac stepped back. 'Nothing at all.'

Later, Mac went to the office. He had checked the car-park thoroughly for Rigby and Sanderson's cars, but it was nearly midnight and only the night staff were around.

The office was empty.

Mac noticed the top of his desk had been cleaned. He found the small key on the key-ring and opened the drawer of his desk. He took out the Browning 9 mm pistol and checked the magazine was full before loading it into the handle. He took a spare clip, then shoved the pistol into his waistband, did up the buttons on his jacket and walked towards the door.

Down below, he emerged cautiously, once more scanning the car-park ahead of him, determined to make sure he was not caught off guard.

CHAPTER FIFTEEN

JULIA'S HEAD WAS STILL SORE THE NEXT MORNING. SHE SAT UP STRAIGHT, pushed her hair gently off her forehead, rather than combing it, got dressed and brushed her teeth. The house was silent. She opened the bedside drawer and put the chisel carefully to one side, before taking out the white envelope containing the photographs of Adrian and Sarah.

Outside, it was still warm, the sky above clear, but there was a strong breeze again. At the Rose and Crown, Professor Malcolm opened the door. He was red in the face from standing out in the sun the day before.

'Hello, Rudolph,' she said.

He stepped back.

Julia handed him the envelope, then sat on the bed and waited while he pulled out the pictures and leafed slowly through them. 'A photographer from Cranbrooke took them. He doesn't know I've got them, by the way. Technically, they're stolen property.'

Professor Malcolm looked at her, then at the photographs again. He put them back in the envelope, holding it by his side and looking out of the window.

'Alice Ford was conceived before marriage,' Julia said. He looked at her. 'Sarah's doctor told me. It explains why Alan married her.'

Professor Malcolm raised an eyebrow. 'Perhaps it does.'

253

'Why only perhaps?'

'Well, it's more likely to explain why she married him.'

Julia frowned. 'I've worked out,' she said, 'why you are interested in the way Alice was being made to look like a smaller version of her mother.'

'Why?'

'Because it could tie them together in the mind of the killer.'

He nodded. 'That's true. It's not the only reason, but it's true.'

'I mean, that's the irony. We've agreed that the scene of the crime suggests that this is really all about the woman, but that in itself could be misleading. Sarah stimulated strong emotions, we know that, particularly in men. On that basis, lots of people could have killed her. But how many could have looked into the eyes of a little girl and done the same? In other words, many people had the capacity to murder Sarah, but very few to murder Alice.'

'Yes.' He was still looking out of the window.

'You don't seem to agree.'

He looked at her. 'No, I do. But my original point was just that it was a *development* that needed explaining. I agree that it might tie them together in the mind of the killer, but of course that is a *result* rather than an explanation for why it happened in the first place.'

Julia turned towards the window. She could see the trees swaying in the wind on the top of the hill. 'Sarah was using Alice as a professional model. The photographer told me. Even the doctor noted how well turned-out she was.'

Professor Malcolm did not respond. He did not seem impressed.

'Why was Sarah suddenly so interested in grooming her daughter?'

'I don't know. A sign of frustration. With her marriage, possibly. With life. Living vicariously through her daughter, seeking fulfilment while satisfying some preconceived notion of being a mother . . .'

'But she just didn't seem to me to be interested . . .'

'That's what you thought. Perhaps she was trying to show that Alice was wholly her own. It might have been about possession. It is possible to be interested *and* neglectful, because the wrong kind of interest can be worse than none at all.' He was tapping the envelope against his leg. 'Or this may have nothing at all to do with Sarah. It may be more complex. It's just . . . odd. Perhaps I'm old-fashioned, but I don't think five-year-olds should be wearing makeup.'

He stared out of the window.

'They didn't find the body?' Julia asked, changing the subject.

'No. That's another riddle that troubles me.' He turned to her. 'Why Rouse? Why was she fucking Rouse?' He leant against the desk. 'What is he like?'

'He's a family friend, but I wouldn't say I knew him well.' Julia tried to think about Rouse. 'He takes things seriously, responsibilities and so on. Maybe a bit pompous, dull, even. He did my will three years ago and his office is very orderly – he is very orderly and thorough. What you'd expect from a country-practice solicitor. He's a thoughtful man, though. He was the first to write to me after I won the Sword of Honour from Sandhurst.'

'Saying how proud your father would have been.'

'Yes. He gave me his war diary years ago, too. Said he wanted me to have a proper three-dimensional picture of Dad. He said he was a great man.' She wished again that she had not given the diary to Mac.

'What about his wife, Leslie?'

Julia didn't answer immediately. 'She's more easy-going when he's not around. A bit uptight when they're together. I never thought much of it before this. I assumed she just felt stultified by village life, but on the evidence of the photographs, I may have misread them. I feel she might have given up on life a bit. She wears dowdy clothes. Sometimes there's just a look, if you catch her at the right moment, of real *ennui* with life. Boredom. Dissatisfaction.'

'They have two children?'

'Yes, James, and Elizabeth, who is at Edinburgh University studying medicine.'

Professor Malcolm held up the white file. 'I must go and see Rouse. Do you wish to come?'

Julia was looking at her hands. 'I almost didn't give you those.'

'I'm glad you did.' His voice was soft. 'You don't have to come.'

She looked up at him.

They went to Rouse's office at the bottom of the high street in Cranbrooke. There was a car-park next to it, and as they walked round via the street, Julia looked across at the newsagent opposite, where the headline on the *Southern Echo*, pasted to a billboard was, 'Welham Search: No Body Found'.

Adrian Rouse's office was on the first floor of a tall sandstone building. The brass plaque outside read 'Rouse, Dunkin, Brane, solicitors'. Julia and Professor Malcolm climbed the newly carpeted red stairs to the small reception area at the top, but the elderly receptionist told them Mr Rouse had a touch of the flu and was at home today. Julia felt relieved.

In the car on the way out of Cranbrooke, Professor Malcolm turned towards her, his face sombre. 'There is some bad news,' he said.

She waited for him to go on. 'It would probably help if you could stop looking like an undertaker.'

'I'm persuading Weston,' he went on, 'to widen the search for the body.'

'I don't think that's going to achieve much, but I don't see why that is bad news.'

'I want all the gardens that back on to the common to be turned over and checked through. Yours, the de la Rues', the Fords'.'

Julia stared at him, then accelerated as they cleared the last traffic light and came up the hill. 'How do you – how do you expect me to react?'

He was staring out of the windscreen now. 'I'm not sure I can predict that.'

'Well, then, I've achieved something.'

'What's that?'

'Becoming something you can't predict.'

Neither of them smiled.

'You're joking, right?' she asked.

'No.'

'You *are* joking.'

'No, of course I'm not.'

Julia was frowning so hard her head was beginning to hurt. 'You can't do that.'

'I know it will be difficult.'

'You can't *do* that.'

'I'm sorry, Julia.'

'Did you know you were going to propose this from the start?'

'No, of course—'

'You did, didn't you?' She could see the flush of annoyance in his cheeks. 'I'm not going to let you get away with this.'

'I'm sorry, Julia, but—'

'There's no way—'

'There is.'

The ferocity of his voice shocked her. There was a lay-by ahead and she pulled into it, lowering her head slowly on to the steering-wheel while he stared out of the window.

'The point is,' he said, 'I just don't *understand* what happened to Alice. We cannot find the body on the common and I don't believe a murderer is going to start carrying her around like a sack of potatoes on a Sunday when you could easily run into anyone, anywhere.'

Julia sighed. 'So he carries her across an open field? Surely that is even less likely.'

'No.' His voice was firm. 'I was thinking more along the lines that she might have *run* in that direction. In the direction of home. Perhaps she never got there.'

They were silent. Julia pulled out again and drove on. When she parked the Golf in the thick gravel drive of the Rouses' house and got out, she realized that her hands were shaking. She hid them in her pockets.

They walked slowly across the gravel. The Rouses' home was about the same size as her mother's, but was built of stone, with a steep red-tile roof and a large chimney above a small, white attic window. The front door was in an arch. They knocked once and waited.

The door opened. Professor Malcolm smiled. 'Hello.'

Adrian looked at them coldly, then stepped back and ushered them through the door and the dining room to the kitchen at the back. He ignored Julia, as if she didn't exist. Leslie was sitting on a stool pushed up against the island in the middle of the room, sewing. 'Hello, Julia,' she said.

They betrayed no reaction to her presence, save for an uncharacteristic coldness of manner.

Adrian sat down at the kitchen table and Julia noticed how podgy his hands were. It was hard to imagine him as a military man.

'I'm sorry to trouble you again, Adrian,' Julia said.

'No, you're not,' Leslie retorted. She was glowering at them and Julia could see the tension and resentment in her face.

Professor Malcolm approached the table, pulled back a chair and sat down between Leslie and her husband, facing the latter.

He took the photographs out of the folder and spread them out on the table, carefully, so that no one picture obscured another. Adrian put his head in his hands. Leslie betrayed no reaction at all.

'Well,' Professor Malcolm said, 'here we are.'

There was silence.

Adrian looked at Professor Malcolm. He had an air of weary resignation. 'She already knows about it.'

Professor Malcolm turned to face Leslie. 'A smutty little photographer. Someone hired him. I never found out who. After the trial, the photographer tried to blackmail Adrian with the prints. But he told me and I dealt with it.'

Professor Malcolm now seemed confused. 'So,' he said, 'someone hired the photographer, or the agency, to follow Sarah, find out what is going on . . . if it was Alan, then he discovers that his wife has been having sexual intercourse – finds out in the most graphic possible way – with one of his best friends and the godfather of his only daughter.' He looked intently at Adrian. 'But you're still *friends*.'

'No, they're not,' Leslie said.

'But you're part of the village set.'

'We go a long way to keep Caroline and Julia happy. Were it not for them, we would not speak to Alan.'

Leslie had spoken about Julia as if she wasn't there and she flushed, feeling instinctively protective of Alan.

'Why?'

Leslie seemed to be weighing up how much she should say. 'Sarah was lost and misguided and selfish.'

'But Alan was worse?'

'Alan has always had his limitations. He's a social climber. Grammar-school boy. He *loved* the big house and the money and the beautiful wife. He hated that he couldn't control it.'

Professor Malcolm was looking at the photographs. Julia wondered how she could have missed Leslie's inner ugliness.

'You know what I think?' Professor Malcolm said.

Adrian was looking down at his hands.

258

'I think it *might* have been Adrian. I can see how a man could become obsessed with Sarah . . . with her beauty, with her sexual availability and the liberties she allowed you.' He turned to Adrian. 'I mean look at the *liberation* in these photographs, the facial expressions.'

Leslie was sewing now.

'Perhaps you hated the little girl for being in the way, but the real anger was building up in you because you couldn't *control* this woman. You could *fuck* her, but she was never going to be yours.'

'That's enough!'

Professor Malcolm turned to face Leslie. Her face was pulled tight with tension, and flushed. 'Of course he bloody wanted her,' she said. 'They all did, but look at him!'

There was silence for a moment.

'She was playing with him. She loved *corrupting*, that was what she was about, but she corrupted better men than him. *Look* at him, he's not *capable* of murder.'

Professor Malcolm was staring at Leslie. 'Which men are you referring to?'

Leslie glanced in Julia's direction.

Professor Malcolm turned to Adrian. 'Did you believe you were the only one, Adrian?'

He shook his head.

'It would help your position,' Professor Malcolm said softly, 'under the circumstances, if you were to be a little more forthcoming.'

Adrian sighed. 'It began because I took her to task one day.' Now it was his turn to look at Julia. 'It was generally assumed . . .' He was looking at his hands again. 'There was gossip about Mitchell. They were seen together so often. We all saw them. People talked. I thought it was bad for the village. Bad for the regiment.'

'She confirmed it?'

'She said she could corrupt anyone.'

'And you told her it wasn't true.'

'Yes.'

'But she corrupted you?'

Adrian did not respond.

'Say it,' Leslie hissed.

259

'Yes. She – she had this . . . She made you feel you were reaching something special – a place she had never let anyone else and then, too late, you saw that it was just a trick, a game.'

'And you hated her for it?'

Adrian did not answer.

'When were these photographs taken?'

He looked up at the pictures, without catching their eye. 'About a month before the deaths. It was the only time we . . .'

'And what did Alan say?'

Adrian cleared his throat. 'Alan has never mentioned it.'

There was silence again. Julia wanted Professor Malcolm to put away the photographs now.

'He knew,' Leslie said. 'Everyone knew what she was doing.'

'Did you go on wanting Sarah, Adrian?'

There was another hesitation, Leslie staring at her husband. 'Yes,' he said, his voice barely audible.

'Did you pester her? Did you follow her?'

'He hasn't got the balls,' Leslie said. 'He longed for her from a distance and suffered her contempt.'

'You were angry with her?'

'He's not a murderer, Professor.'

'Did you see her in those last few days, Adrian? I mean alone. Did you meet her, did you run into her walking?'

Adrian shook his head, face down.

'Hoped he would run into her,' Leslie said, 'but she was too busy elsewhere.'

'You didn't go looking for her that morning?'

'He has an alibi.'

Professor Malcolm turned to Leslie, his face betraying his irritation, but Adrian was looking up now. 'No.'

'But you'd seen her going off towards the common and you set off to walk your dogs, hoping you would "bump" into her?'

Julia could see immediately from Adrian's face that this was true.

'But,' Professor Malcolm said, heavily, 'you were too late.' He leant forward, towards Adrian. 'Do you know whom she was meeting there, whom she might have run into?'

He shook his head. Professor Malcolm turned to Leslie, but she also shook her head, neither of them convincing in their ignorance.

260

'What about Pascoe?' Professor Malcolm asked.

They both looked confused.

'Was *he* having an affair with her?'

'Of course not,' Leslie said.

'Why, of course not?'

Leslie looked confused, then realized Professor Malcolm's question had been barbed and dropped her eyes to her sewing.

'So, Adrian, how was it that you didn't manage to remember that you had seen Pascoe entering his house in an agitated state until after the war?'

Julia watched Adrian's Adam's apple move as he swallowed. 'The evidence I gave was true,' he said.

'I didn't say it wasn't. I just wanted to know why you didn't mention it until after the war.'

'Nobody asked me.'

'Really? How convenient.'

'They asked me questions, just not the right ones. Pascoe was a member of my platoon. I didn't want to implicate him unnecessarily.'

Professor Malcolm thought about this. 'So you didn't believe Pascoe was guilty. You thought he was innocent.'

'Yes. But by the time I returned from the war I was less sure of his innocence. The speculation was intense, even out there.'

'Was Pascoe shunned by the other men? Bullied, needled?'

Adrian nodded. 'Yes. I did my best to stop it, but my belief in his innocence started to fade.'

'A useful scapegoat for you all. I shan't ask how you managed to encourage his confession,' Professor Malcolm remarked.

Adrian looked at them. Julia thought his eyes betrayed a mixture of resignation and continuing fear. 'I've tried to help you.'

Leslie moved towards them. 'Please go now.'

Professor Malcolm did not ask Julia if she wanted to accompany him to see Alan, or tell her that this was where he wished to go. He didn't need to. They got into the car and Julia drove slowly out of the Rouses' gravel drive. As they climbed the hill, she pulled down the visor to shield her eyes from the sun.

'Adrian didn't kill them, did he?'

Professor Malcolm shook his head. 'No.'

They crested the hill and Julia coasted down towards the

T-junction. There was a honk behind her and she looked in her rear-view mirror to see the de la Rues' Volvo, Henrietta waving at her out of the window. Julia raised her hand.

They turned left, towards Cranbrooke and the base, Henrietta honking again as she drove off in the other direction.

Julia was concentrating on the road ahead, the hedgerows thick here with summer foliage. 'Where's Pascoe?' she asked.

'I called the police last night again. They still can't trace him. Weston is worried, actually,' the Professor replied.

'You reassured him?'

'Yes, but he'll turn up again soon. I – I'm not sure what is going through Pascoe's mind, but from the slender evidence available to me, I would say he had unfinished business.'

'In what way?'

He made no reply.

Julia slowed as they got to the top of another hill then turned right along the ridge towards the camp. There were fields on both sides, those on the left sloping gently down towards Cranbrooke. It was more exposed here and the trees along some of the hedgerows were being buffeted by the wind.

They reached the wire fence around the base, turned right and stopped in front of the barrier. With its long, low, prefabricated blocks, the camp looked desolate this morning, despite the sunshine.

Professor Malcolm got out to talk to the guard. It seemed quiet, for a working day.

He walked slowly back to the car and got in, then, as she watched the gatehouse, waiting for someone to come and give them a pass, reached over and flattened his hand against hers, to prevent her fingers from drumming the steering-wheel. He smiled at her.

They had to wait for ten minutes until a young corporal came down in a blue Cavalier to fetch them. He arranged for Julia to get a car pass and they followed him in.

The journey was familiar – all the way up the central road, past the canteen, then right before the paradeground. Lieutenant Colonel Alan Ford occupied the same office her father once had, in a grey block with large windows and, inside, the big leather chair was the same one he had had, but the desk was new. There was a silver cup on top of a tall metal filing cabinet, the curtains were a dirty yellow, the desk neat and ordered. There was an in tray and an out, the latter full, the former empty, an American flag, with a plaque at the bottom, and a picture of Alice Ford in a small silver frame.

Alan was in uniform. He was still talking to his secretary as he came in and smiled. 'Professor. Julia.'

Like the Rouses, he showed no surprise at her presence. He bade them sit on the sofa, then pulled the leather chair from behind his desk, so that he was facing them.

'I'm sorry,' Professor Malcolm said. 'I'm sure you understand. Just a formality.'

Alan was still smiling. He glanced at Julia then back to the Professor. 'Sure.'

Professor Malcolm looked at Julia too now, as if preparing to offer an explanation, then turned to the window as a lorry drove past. 'Not much activity on the base today.'

'Most of the men are on leave before going to Ulster.'

'When do you leave?'

'Friday.'

'Look, Colonel Ford,' Professor Malcolm leant forward, 'I am sorry for this. I know . . . I can *understand* . . .'

'It's all right, Professor. What can I help you with?'

Professor Malcolm pulled the photographs from the file and placed them on the desk. 'I'm sorry to do this.'

Julia looked up. There was no shock on Alan's face, or surprise.

'You commissioned these?' Professor Malcolm asked. 'You suspected your wife of having an affair?'

'I suspected my wife of having numerous affairs, Professor. I got to the point where suspicion was not enough. I needed to know.'

'I can imagine your anger when you got these.'

'Actually, it was a relief. I had told her before her death that I wanted a divorce. I've never really held it against Adrian, because she . . . well, it's complicated.'

'Is it?'

'Yes, Professor. Affairs of the heart often are. I'm sure you appreciate that.'

Professor Malcolm was looking at the photographs. He picked them up swiftly and put them back into the folder. 'I'm sorry,' he said again.

'I understand. You have a job to do.'

'Could you . . .' Professor Malcolm was pushing his hand forward, 'could you tell us a little more?'

'What do you want to know?'

'Well, you say you weren't angry with her but you commissioned the pictures. When I spoke to you at the . . . in those terrible days after it happened, you never . . . I don't recall you acknowledging there had been affairs.'

'I was angry with her.' Alan was staring out of the window now. 'Of course I was. It's not true to say that I wasn't.' There was a long silence. 'Sarah is a hard woman to describe.'

'In what way?'

'You never knew her, Professor, but we did.' Alan was looking at Julia and she was forced to smile. 'There was something about her, something extraordinarily *vital*.'

'Desirable.'

'Yes.'

'You thought you could co-exist with her, but it wasn't possible.'

'Yes, that too.' He tilted his head now. 'It's hard, looking back on it, to work out whether, at the time of our marriage, she had already begun . . .'

'She was pregnant.'

Julia saw that there was a brief look of surprise in Alan's eyes. 'Yes.' He looked at his hands. 'But I'd have married her anyway.'

'The child . . . I'm sorry to ask this, but Alice *was* yours?'

Alan looked up, annoyed for the first time. 'Of course. That's going a bit . . .'

'I'm sorry.' Professor Malcolm inclined his head. 'I'm sorry. Questions don't mean to imply or infer.'

Alan was mollified. 'All right. I understand.'

'But you realized soon after your marriage that she was – that she slept with other men.'

'I realized, or perhaps always knew.'

'You consciously made that compromise?'

Julia was frowning.

'Not consciously, no.'

'Did you suspect Sarah of sleeping with men in the village?'

Julia could tell Alan was hesitating now. She thought he was trying to spare her. 'I wasn't sure.'

264

'Were you surprised that it was Adrian?'

'By then, Professor, nothing surprised me.'

'You were reluctant to divorce because of Alice?'

Alan nodded. 'Yes, of course. I tried to find . . .'

'A way to live with it?'

'Yes.'

'But you couldn't?'

Alan was staring at the floor again now. Julia wanted to get up and comfort him.

'It must have been terrible for you.' Professor Malcolm's voice was soft and sympathetic. 'I cannot imagine living with someone under those . . . well, knowing . . .'

Alan looked up. 'Anyway, Professor, is there anything else?'

'No.' Professor Malcolm was about to stand up. 'It must be hard for you, Colonel, and I'm sure the search has made it worse.' He looked up at Alan. 'I'm sure, if it had been me, the image of my girl would never leave me, night or day.'

Alan nodded. Julia could not tell if he was warming to Professor Malcolm, or simply embarrassed.

Professor Malcolm stood. 'Just one other thing and I know I asked you this before. Was there anything – anything at all – that struck you as odd in the few days before that Sunday? Sarah behaving oddly, phone calls – anything?'

'No.'

'What had you been doing the week before?'

'Well, we discussed this, I remember. The battalion had just finished its turn as the spearhead unit, which meant we were theoretically on twenty-four hours' notice to go anywhere in the world, but the routine on the camp had been much the same as normal. I'd been getting home a bit later than usual.'

'Working late?'

'Yes. We were to go on a sniping course run by the battalion's training wing on Salisbury Plain the following week. I was looking forward to the weekend.'

'How was Sarah that week? Did she cook for you, by the way?'

Alan clearly did not see the purpose of this question. 'She did, though she had no fondness for it.'

Professor Malcolm nodded, as though this was the answer he had expected. 'Did she seem happy?'

'Not particularly. She wasn't very communicative, but then that was not unusual. As I've indicated, we weren't terribly happy and she had always been moody.'

'But you didn't talk about it?'

'About what?'

'About the fact that you weren't talking.'

Alan tilted his head to the right and ran his fingers along his lips. 'I'm afraid my response, probably not a good one, was to be taciturn myself. But this had grown into something of a habit over a period of time. There was nothing unusual about that week.'

'And Saturday and Sunday morning?'

Alan sighed. 'Saturday. Not much of a day. Raining. Stayed in. I wrote some letters, Alice watched a lot of television – I remember feeling guilty that we weren't playing with her more.'

Julia remembered the rain and her father pacing up and down during the morning of that Saturday before going out for a walk.

'And Sarah?'

'She went out for a walk in the morning. Alice went over to . . .' Alan looked at her again. 'She went over to Julia's house in the afternoon for about an hour.'

'What did Sarah do then?'

'I don't recall. In the kitchen, I think. Then Alice came back and we ended the day playing Monopoly.'

'You didn't go out in the evening?'

'No. We had lamb chops and watched some television. Same story on the communication front.'

'And Sunday morning?'

'Nothing to tell. Got up late, had breakfast, read the papers, then went to church.'

'No phone calls?'

'A few.'

'None for you?'

Alan seemed uncertain about this. 'There may have been. I honestly don't remember that kind of detail.'

'No,' Professor Malcolm said. 'Sure.' He had his hands in his pockets now and looked as if he might sit down again. 'Were Adrian Rouse, Michael Haydoch and Robert Pascoe all in the camp that week?'

'Yes, so far as I remember. Pascoe was in my platoon, so he was there. Adrian had just returned from the Junior Division of the Staff College at Warminster.'

'It must have been so . . . difficult.'

'What?'

Professor Malcolm looked at him as if he should have understood. 'The war. Pascoe.'

Alan shook his head. 'It wasn't an issue until the war was over.'

'But you must have heard rumours?'

'On the way down. But there were many rumours. That was just one.' Alan looked at his watch. 'Is there anything else? It's just . . .'

'No. I'm sorry again. I just wanted to . . .' He held up the folder. 'You can see, having got these, why I felt I had to talk to you, but that's it. That should be it. And I'm sorry, again, for the search.'

Alan did not know what to make of this.

'That must have been difficult for you, too.'

Alan looked as if he would not answer, then he sighed. 'It's all difficult.'

Professor Malcolm nodded, as if satisfied. 'Thank you for your time, Colonel.'

While Professor Malcolm had been talking, Julia had realized that she did not want to leave without making some gesture to acknowledge the depth of feeling between herself and Alan.

Professor Malcolm was in the doorway, Alan in front of his desk. She walked forward and touched his forearm. He mistakenly thought she was leaning forward to kiss his cheek and they clutched each other in an awkward embrace.

As she went out, Julia turned. Alan smiled at her reassuringly.

Outside, they walked to the car, drove round to the gate and handed in the pass. Julia thought about the way Professor Malcolm had been labouring his apologies and was certain that he had had some purpose in that interview that she could not divine.

She sensed that, somehow, he had moved far ahead of her.

'Where to now?' she asked.

'Welham,' he said.

They drove in silence for the first few minutes.

'It must have been agony,' Professor Malcolm said.

When he didn't explain, Julia said, 'What?'

He turned to her. 'Living with a woman so alluring, knowing that she was making herself freely available to others.' There was a long pause. 'I don't know many men who could do that.'

'Absolute love of a child. Don't they say that's the most powerful force in the world?'

He was looking out of the side window now. 'Yes, I suppose you're right,' he said.

Mac was waiting for Wilkes, leaning against the wall by the lift on the fourteenth floor, looking out over the A3.

The Browning was uncomfortable in his waistband, so he switched it to the inside pocket of his jacket, took a pace to his right and looked down. It was a long drop from here.

Mac heard Rigby's loud, truculent voice just before he came into view and it gave him enough time to slide up the stairs out of sight, but peering round the wall he saw Rigby's bald dome first, followed by Sanderson and another man he did not recognize. They knocked on Wilkes's door and waited. Despite his proximity, Mac could not hear what they were saying.

They thumped louder.

Then Mac heard a loud bang as they kicked and broke down Wilkes's door. He put his head round the edge of the concrete pillar, but they had gone inside.

After about ten minutes, he heard typically foul-mouthed voices emerging and echoing in the stairwell.

Mac found that he was breathing hard and clutching the Browning, which he had removed from his jacket. He waited another few minutes, then put the pistol back into his pocket, walked down the last few steps and into Wilkes's flat. It had been turned over as comprehensively as his own, but had probably been dirty and squalid in the first place. It had a seedy, run-down, unlived-in feel. Mac noted the picture of Wilkes's mother on the mantelpiece, but otherwise it was devoid of personality.

He moved among the debris, picking through it carefully. He did not know what Rigby had been looking for, but there was certainly nothing of interest here. Just clothes, some records. Not much, by any standard.

After a few minutes, Mac came back out on to the balcony.

He took out his notebook and looked at the names again, thinking of the way the 'Mike H' of Rouse's diary had come across as a strong character. Was that Haydoch? Would he be worth going to see?

He leant against the wall. What had Rigby been looking for here and in his own flat?

Julia was in the attic. She had retreated to her refuge. She took a pace forward and looked out of the Velux window, her eyes straying to the dividing hedge and the gap in the middle of it, then to the shed and the wooden plank on the side that should be nailed up properly. She wondered why no one had done it.

It was a good spot here. A vantage-point.

Julia narrowed her eyes, knowing she could not delay indefinitely, then turned and walked to her father's workbench at the end. All the tools were neatly on their hooks, waiting to be used. The screwdrivers were in a wooden rack and it took her a moment or two to accept that there was a gap in the middle of it. She took a step closer. The rack had holes all along it and the tools were pushed into them so that only the plastic handle was above the line, the metal shaft hanging below.

It was not only for screwdrivers. At one end, there were chisels then spikes, but in the middle one of the implements was missing.

Julia took the chisel from her pocket.

It fitted perfectly into the hole her father had made for it.

Julia stared at it. She took the chisel out again, then put it back to be sure the fit was as neat as she thought it was. Her father, who had been so precise in the way he did things, had made a hole exactly the right size.

This meant that somebody had come in here and stolen the chisel. She wished that her mother didn't so often leave the house open.

She walked to the window, then back again.

Thinking of the shed and the plank that had fallen from its place, she took the hammer down from its hook above the rack and turned it over in her hand. It was in as good condition as the day it had been bought. She opened a couple of the plastic drawers until she located one with the right size nails, then walked down through the empty house, stepped over Aristotle and went out to the garden and the shed in the corner. The bright sunshine made her squint.

Julia looked at the broken plank, which had rotted, then opened the door of the shed and entered. There was a black tarpaulin on the floor, which she did not remember. The mower was in the way, so she moved it, catching it on her foot and nearly falling over. She had to take down the Strimmer, a rake, a spade and a hoe, all of which hung on hooks on the wall. She tried to put the plank into place, but it was difficult because of the way it had rotted. Finally, she hammered hard.

It was impossible to get it in. She hit her thumb. The shed was too flimsy and really she needed someone to push it in on the other side. She tried again and eventually more or less got the nail in. It was a botch job, but it would do for now. Perhaps she would tell Alan and he would do it properly.

Julia walked back into the house, up to the attic. She replaced the hammer, then ran her hand along the wooden surface top.

She climbed down the steps and sat on her bed. After a few minutes, her mind returned to its earlier train of thought and she took her mother's statement from the drawer and read through it again.

As I walked down Woodpecker Lane, I glanced in through the window of Alan Ford's house. I saw him crossing from one side of the kitchen to the other with a cup of coffee in his hand.

I arrived home and saw my husband working in the garden. I went upstairs to change out of my church clothes. When I came down to the kitchen, he was digging the flower-bed by the hedge.

Julia walked down to the kitchen. She looked out of the window, then went out of the back door, across the patio, over the lawn to the gravel drive. At the end of Woodpecker Lane, she stopped, turned and came back.

She slowed as she passed Alan's house, looking in to her left.

Julia reached her own gate, then retraced her steps, walked into Alan's drive and up to his kitchen window. She looked in, then, facing the window, she retreated slowly, her feet sinking into the thick gravel until she reached the road.

'What are you doing?'

Julia turned, shocked at the introduction of a human voice into her thoughts. Professor Malcolm was smiling at her. 'They'll want to lock you up if you go on like that.'

She exhaled. 'I'll probably want to lock me up.'

'They've found Pascoe,' Professor Malcolm said. 'He's made himself a makeshift camp up on the hill.'

Julia followed him as he led the way back down Woodpecker Lane. 'A couple of lads from East Welham told their mother they'd been frightened by a man in the woods.'

'Did he do anything?' she asked.

'No.'

They had reached the pathway up to the ridge and Professor Malcolm was already slowing down. 'Are you all right?' he asked.

'About what?'

'In general.'

'I'm fine.'

Halfway up, he stopped, one leg forward against the hill, his hand on his knee as he tried to catch his breath. 'You wouldn't have expected it of Rouse.'

She thought of the photographs. 'No.'

'I suppose someone like Sarah shouldn't be allowed to come and live somewhere like this.'

'No.'

Julia walked ahead, waiting for Professor Malcolm at the top, looking down over East Welham and Michael Haydoch's house, which dominated the foreground. She remembered that she'd said she would go round there tonight. A thin bank of cloud hung over the valley, a light drizzle carried on the breeze like confetti.

Professor Malcolm climbed over the stile and walked down the path for a few yards, before crossing into the long grass and moving at right angles to the hill, into the wood.

Julia saw and smelt the smoke of a fire before she saw the two uniformed policemen next to a tarpaulin erected under an oak tree. In front of the crude shelter, Pascoe squatted by the fire, warming his hands, though it wasn't cold. He was wearing a pair of tracksuit bottoms and a dirty blue sweatshirt, its zip open to the middle of his hairless chest and the arms pulled up above the elbow. She could see that he had maintained his strength inside prison. He looked up at them, his eyes hollow and lifeless, as though he were on drugs. He ran his hand slowly over his shaven head.

'Where's Baker?' Professor Malcolm asked the uniformed officers.

They both shrugged. 'She said she'd be back,' one said.

Professor Malcolm tried to squat down, but found it impossible, so he took a step back and sat on the ground. 'Do you remember me?'

Pascoe looked up. 'I've never seen you before in my life.' He turned towards Julia. 'What's she doing here?'

'She's assisting me.'

'But I've killed her.'

'No, this is . . .'

'I don't want to have to kill her twice . . .'

Julia found herself smiling involuntarily. Pascoe's expression turned instantly.

'She's laughing at me.' He was on his feet, his body and face suffused with aggression. 'Don't you laugh at me, bitch, I could have had you . . . I . . . I could have let you live. It was my choice.'

Neither Julia or Professor Malcolm had moved or reacted physically. 'This is Mitchell Havilland's daughter,' the Professor said evenly.

Julia felt her heart beating as she watched Pascoe sit back down. 'I'll fuck her. Spunk all over her face.'

'Do you remember Mitchell Havilland, Pascoe?'

He shook his head, sober again. 'I don't remember anyone.'

'Do you remember some of your colleagues from the war? Richard Claverton? Clive Danes?'

Pascoe shook his head.

'Did you know that they had both been murdered, shot with their own Browning 9 mm pistols?'

Julia looked at him, frowning, but he ignored her.

'I don't know anything about that.' Pascoe turned to Julia again. 'Will you leave Sarah with me? I can look after her now.'

'Pascoe, you wrote to Claverton and Danes from prison telling them it was "time for the truth". The truth about what? About Sarah's death, or about something else?'

'I killed Sarah.'

'You didn't.'

'I did.'

'You didn't and it's convenient for someone else that you have spent all these years in prison . . .'

'I wanted to do it.'

'No you didn't, Pascoe. She was just out of your reach. Don't confuse that with a real instinct for murder.'

Pascoe had his head down again now. He was staring into the fire and pushing the embers with a long, bent stick.

'Pascoe, Claverton and Danes were murdered for a reason and I'm afraid you are at risk. When you told them it was "time for the truth", what did you mean – the truth about what?'

'I don't know what you're talking about.'

'Pascoe . . .'

'I like her.'

'This is not Sarah.'

'It is.'

'Who do you think might have killed Claverton and Danes? Was there . . .'

'I like her.'

'Pascoe, this is not Sarah.'

'It is. She's beautiful.'

Professor Malcolm exhaled noisily, staring down at the leaves beneath his feet for a moment, before standing. 'Be careful, Pascoe,' he said.

'What do you want us to do with him?' one of the uniformed officers asked – a tall man, with a narrow face.

'Nothing. You can leave him.'

'Leave him?'

'He's committed no crime. Leave him.'

Julia followed Professor Malcolm out of the wood, noticing that he moved faster when he was angry. 'What was all that about?' she asked.

'What?'

'Danes. Claverton. "Time for the truth"?'

'I don't know,' he said grumpily. 'I don't know.'

CHAPTER SIXTEEN

THAT NIGHT THE WEATHER CHANGED: DARK CLOUDS, HEAVY WITH RAIN, racing in from the west. Julia stood in front of her mother at the kitchen table and listened to the thunder.

'You'll need an umbrella,' Caroline said.

'No, I'll be okay.' Julia hesitated. 'I'll see you later, then.'

'I'll leave something on the side, just in case you're back.'

'I will be back. And I said, I'll make something myself.'

Caroline tried to smile. Neither of them could forget her previous attempts to dissuade Julia from seeing Michael Haydoch and, since Julia had not explained why she was going to visit him tonight, this particular aspect of the past, like so many others, now hung between them. Caroline had always claimed that it was the age gap, but Julia thought her mother was wary of Michael for reasons she could not comprehend.

Since her mother had got home tonight, Julia had stayed up in her bedroom, trying to read a John le Carré novel, without success. Her mother had played 'Song For Guy' on the piano, followed by a series of hymns such as 'I Vow To Thee My Country' and 'Jerusalem'. Each had been a curious and deliberate choice.

Julia wondered if her mother was trying to exercise a spell over her – the spell of seductive, secure childhood memories.

'Did you have a productive day?' Caroline asked, sitting at the table, but Julia had her coat on and didn't want to stay and talk.

'Sort of,' she said. 'Is Alan coming round?'

'No, I think he's trying to get everything finished this week before they go off.'

'They go on Friday?'

'I think so.'

'What's today, then?'

'Tuesday, Julia.'

'Right.'

Caroline crossed her legs. She was wearing a thin V-neck sweater, but the sleeves were rolled up, and she was resting one long, thin forearm on the edge of the kitchen table. 'How long will you be home for?'

'Er . . . I don't know.'

'Has the army . . . I mean, you said you were in trouble. Alan – Alan says it may be quite serious. I wondered . . .'

'They'll get in touch when they're ready.'

'Shouldn't you get a lawyer? Is it that serious?'

'I don't want a lawyer.'

Caroline was frowning at her now. 'Julia, are you all right? You seem—'

'I'm fine, Mum.' She straightened. 'I'm fine,' she said, more forcefully. 'I guess I'd better . . .'

'I'm sorry, I'm not sure I've been as welcoming as perhaps I might have been to your Professor. If you want to bring him home for lunch or dinner before he goes . . .'

Julia did not find her mother's attempt to appear resigned to Professor Malcolm, and the process they were engaged in, convincing, but she smiled at the way she had made Professor Malcolm sound like a boyfriend. 'I think he's okay, Mum. He doesn't want to upset anyone. It's just a job.'

Caroline looked down. She was picking some dirt from the garden off her jeans with her fingernails. 'Well, I'm sorry. I should have been more hospitable, but it's just that . . .'

'He understands. He's been doing it all his life.'

Caroline was rubbing her neck. 'I suppose that's what's so unnerving about him.'

'He's all right.' Julia moved to the door. 'He's a good man. I'll . . .' She stopped and turned back, leaning against the wall. 'Does anyone ever help around the house?'

Caroline did not understand.

'I mean with maintenance.'

Caroline tilted her head to one side. 'That's another odd question.'

'Well, Alan obviously helps.'

'Lots of people do from time to time. I'm sorry, perhaps I should be more self-sufficient, but . . .'

'No, that's not the point. I mean, it's nice the way people help each other here, isn't it? A real community.'

Caroline looked at her. 'Are you all right, Julia? You're behaving very strangely.'

'I'm fine. I just want to know who else helps around the house.'

'Alan, Adrian sometimes. Jasper, even. Leslie helped paint the spare room. Henrietta helps with the garden from time to time, just as I help with hers.'

Tension had crept into both their voices.

'All of them have helped in the last month?'

'Probably. Adrian fixed the radiator just before you came back. I still don't understand—'

'Don't worry, Mum, it's nothing.' Julia turned away. 'I won't be long.'

She let herself out and began walking down Woodpecker Lane. Alan's car was not in his drive, the house in darkness.

The heavens opened as Julia walked up the ridge and it rained with the force of a tropical storm. At the top, she stopped and looked up, letting the rain hammer down upon her for a second.

The black clouds were rolling across the valley, smothering the last of the daylight, which was now just a pencil-thin line across the top of the common.

There were lights on in the Rose and Crown, but she could not see one in Professor Malcolm's window, or in Pascoe's house.

She climbed on to the stile. This was the symbolic boundary between East and West Welham; her father had once told her that the villages had been on opposing sides during the English Civil War.

She stepped over and hurried down the zigzagging path, the wood to her right dark in the dying light as the square Georgian house rose up before her. She was looking at the edge of the wood out of the corner of her eye, but she could discern no light or smoke, or movement.

The path came right to the back of the house and there were

two gates in the wall ahead. She passed through the right-hand one then walked across a wet lawn, watching the smoke drifting out of one of the chimneys.

A powerful spotlight came on as she crossed the thick gravel. Everything about the house already reeked of comfort and ease. Of wealth.

The front door was big and looked newly painted. She pressed the bell. The door swung open.

He tilted his head to one side. 'You're soaking wet.'

It was true. Her jeans were clinging to her. He took her jacket and walked down the hall, ushering her towards a room on the left. The house's interior was as magnificent as its fine external proportions promised. She stood on a rich dark Afghan or Pakistani rug, over a flagstone floor, beneath a giant gilt-edged mirror above a mahogany dresser. At the bottom of the stairs there was a life-size sculpture of a naked woman in white stone.

He returned with an armful of towels and she took one to dry her hair. He held up a pair of tracksuit bottoms and a sweatshirt. 'Not *exactly* glamorous.'

'I'm fine.'

'No, you're soaking wet and therefore not fine.'

'No, my jacket was soaking.'

'So are your trousers.'

'They'll dry.'

He put the clothes on the dresser. 'I'll leave them on the side here. Go into the study – I lit a fire just now. Let me get you a drink. What would you like?'

'Wine.'

The study looked like where he lived. Behind the door was a fine roll-top desk, open and piled high with paper. To the right of it, the bookshelves were filled from floor to ceiling, and his computer was pressed up to the wall. The room was too well decorated to have been planned by him, since she had not yet met the male army officer who cared about décor. Julia turned round, crossing in front of the fire, which was roaring unseasonably on the hearth. There were more bookshelves on the other side of the room, too, though some were filled with CDs stacked in a neat, home-made rack. She remembered this from the terraced cottage.

'Pick one,' he said, holding up some different clothes.

'You can't expect me to wear any of those.'

277

'Well, if you think it more appropriate, I've a double-breasted suit.'

'You must have some women's clothes here.'

He looked offended.

'I don't believe you,' she said.

He was wearing a pair of khaki trousers and a white turtle-neck sweater and she couldn't ignore how handsome he still looked. Clean-cut and good-looking. The things that had not immediately appealed before the summer in which they'd made love – his thinness and the narrowness of his face – now seemed like virtues. She turned back and chose a Louis Armstrong selection.

After putting it on, she looked across at the shelves to her left. One section seemed to be history, another contemporary fiction, all organized and neat. 'Okay,' she said, 'wall-to-wall history and then, next shelf, *Bridget Jones's Diary*. What does that say about a man?'

'Pretentious. Slave to literary fashion.'

It was impossible to imagine him reading, let alone enjoying, *Bridget Jones*.

'I forgot the wine,' he said, and went to get it. For a man who had served in the SAS and then British Intelligence – MI6 – he seemed curiously vague sometimes.

Julia put on the tracksuit and glanced around the room again. There were few photographs and pictures – none on the mantelpiece or above his desk. On the wall ahead, there was a beautiful watercolour of a young girl, a bucket and spade in her hand, and an expanse of empty beach and sea beyond. He had obviously been to London because there was an *Evening Standard* on the ottoman and when she turned it over, she saw that it was today's. The front page carried a picture of a group of office workers in Ohio running from their building, the accompanying story detailing another shooting rampage. Inside, there was a photograph of the man responsible, pictured with his wife and two young children. He had killed his wife first, then the children – the latter to spare them, he had written in a note, 'a lifetime of pain'. The girl could not have been more than five and both she and her elder brother looked happy sitting on their father's knee. All four were smiling.

Julia looked closely at the faces of the children who had not deserved to pay the price for an adult's inadequacies and who

278

had lost their one chance of life to the man they had had most reason to trust.

The second story on the front page had an 'exclusive' tag and was speculation about another new search for a body on Welham Common. She wondered how they had got hold of that and imagined, for a moment, the media circus that would accompany an announcement.

Michael placed a glass of wine in front of her.

'How come you're suddenly so rich?' she asked.

'Theft.'

'No, come on. Seriously.'

He leant forward, spreading his legs and resting his elbows on them. 'I told you. I'm in business now.'

'What sort of business?'

Michael tossed a log on to the fire, sending sparks flying up the chimney, then picked up a packet of cigarettes from the table beside him and leant forward. She took one and he lit it for her.

'Since we last saw each other,' he said, staring into the fire, 'which must have been at least three years ago, if not longer, I decided that the Service and I were never going to get along in a permanent sense and so, with one or two former colleagues, I set up a business called Assured Security. Should you ever be wishing to set up an office in Moscow or Azerbaijan, or anywhere like it, you can come to me and I will make sure that your premises don't get raided and you don't get kidnapped by the Chechen Mafia, or whomever it happens to be. In fact, if you're looking for a job . . .'

'And it's profitable?' she asked, looking at her surroundings.

He nodded. 'It's very profitable, but . . . an aunt died as well.'

Michael took a long drag of his cigarette, letting the smoke drift out of his mouth, not concentrating on its expulsion. He had his sleeves rolled up and she could see the contours of the muscles on his forearms. His hands were broad. Julia wondered, again, if he had fucked Sarah, but this wasn't the first time she had asked herself the question.

'How was Northern Ireland?' he asked.

She looked down at her glass. 'Fine. I left there eight months ago.' She looked at him. 'I think you enjoy taunting me in front of everyone. You know they're all still looking at us, wondering . . .'

'Don't be paranoid. Our relationship was pleasant, if brief, but it's long over and everyone knows it.'

'And you're still punishing me.'

'Why would I be punishing you?'

'Because I cut you dead.'

'I'm a big boy.'

Julia shrugged. 'Well, I'm sorry, I suppose.'

Michael smiled at her. 'That is the most insincere apology I've ever heard, but I wouldn't worry about it.'

He leant back, resting the ankle of his right leg on the knee of his left and running his hand through his hair. 'What's your friend doing back here?'

Julia didn't think this question was as casual as it sounded. 'I think Professor Malcolm, if that is who you mean, is here because he believes he made a mistake in his diagnosis of the crime and—'

'Academics don't diagnose crimes. Doctors *diagnose* illnesses.'

'Well, these days, that's not strictly—'

'Anyway . . .' He waved his hand irritably, then threw the cigarette into the fire. Julia had not yet taken a drag of her own. 'I still don't understand what you're doing.'

'I'm helping.'

'Helping. How come a high-flying army officer has time to do that?'

'I'm on leave.'

'Voluntary or forced?'

'I don't understand.'

'Voluntary or forced leave?'

Julia hesitated. Word had probably got round already. 'Forced.'

'What did you do?'

'I don't – that's – I'd rather not talk about it.' She looked at him. 'Why did you say the other day that you had some sympathy for me and for what I was doing?'

He looked confused.

'You said you could see what I was doing and "most people" would have some sympathy.'

'I don't understand.'

'It's a simple question.' She had moved to the edge of the sofa. She put the cigarette to her lips and inhaled for the first time. It had already burnt almost to the filter and she noticed her hands were shaking again. 'Come on,' she said. 'I'm helping the Professor review a criminal investigation. Of course it makes people uncomfortable, and it's worse because I'm not an outsider like everyone else. They don't like it, they *shouldn't* like it, so why do I get the impression that everyone is trying to . . . *protect* me? Even if they have their own secrets, when they are confronted with them, it's like . . . I mean, they look at me and it's like, you know, there's only so much we can say, don't want to hurt *Julia*.'

'What secrets?'

She threw her cigarette into the fire. 'Never mind.'

'Perhaps,' he said, 'they are wise to protect you.'

He got up, walked to the sideboard then returned. He took her empty glass and gave her a huge tumbler, with plenty of ice and an enormous dose of malt whisky. Julia helped herself to another of his cigarettes and lit it. This time, she inhaled deeply.

'You know,' he said. 'Is this really doing you, or anyone else, any good? Why don't you call it quits?'

'What do you mean?'

'It's common gossip that your father was close to Sarah. Nobody knows what really did and didn't go on, it's a long time ago, so just leave it at that. Adult relationships are difficult to fathom, especially when you're a child, so give your father the benefit of the doubt, if you want, and then just forget it. Move on.'

Julia could feel the heat of the fire on her face. She took another large gulp of the whisky, inhaled deeply on the cigarette, then closed her eyes as she blew out the smoke. 'So that's what people are protecting me from?'

'No.'

Julia felt her stomach turning over.

'No,' he went on. 'That was common gossip. I don't think they're protecting you from that.'

Julia stared into the fire. The new log was resting on the red embers of two old ones, but it was catching now, the flame climbing higher up the blackened wall of the chimney behind. Louis was still singing in the background, but his sonorous tones did nothing to calm her nerves.

'I thought you liked my father.'

'I did.'

'Why did you like him?'

'I told you that, Julia, that's why you were interested in me.'

'That is not . . .'

'Don't be defensive.' Haydoch sighed. 'I liked him because he was a character, because I thought he was the original no-bullshit officer; straightforward, honest, reliable, with a lot of integrity. If he said something, you thought you could rely on it. In the war, he made sure that we had the best kit, and if he thought somebody was withholding something he'd go down and get it himself. If he didn't like the orders, he'd more or less refuse to carry them out. He hated arse-lickers and career crawlers and was never afraid to say what he thought. If he was briefing you and you thought he was wrong, you could say so and he would listen. That's why I thought I liked him.'

'That's the most loaded eulogy I've ever heard.'

'Suspicion can erode almost anything. You have read *Othello*?'

Julia did not reply.

'Is Mitchell Havilland Desdemona or Iago?'

Julia stared at the floor.

'If he was the man I have just described, then why was he so often seen with Sarah, even though she never talked about him? We were friends, but she never said a word about him and yet I saw them walking together . . . The wife of one of his junior officers.'

Michael was staring at her. 'How could he have been just helping her? Does that seem likely to you? And yet does it fit with everything I've just said? Does it? The question for you is: are you certain truth is better than suspicion?'

She looked at him. 'How can the truth be a bad thing?'

'It could be in a relationship you cannot escape from.'

'What do you mean?'

'You can escape from a wife or a husband. The wife who thinks her husband is cheating can perhaps afford to have her life destroyed by knowledge of his infidelity, so that she can begin again, but a parent and child . . . You can never escape from that relationship, can you, even if you want to? You can't choose another set of parents.'

His eyes rested intently on her. 'What do you . . . suspect your father *of*, exactly, Julia?'

She looked at him, sharply, before glancing at the fire. 'Don't get inappropriately intimate.'

'Intimacy,' he responded, 'is what you're afraid of.'

'I was intimate with you.'

'Physical, but not intimate.'

She exhaled heavily.

'You can't trust anyone, that's what it boils down to. You feel betrayed by your father's memory, because you trusted him and—'

'What happened here was evil,' she said. 'Beyond evil. How can anyone forget? Don't you see it here? Don't you look for it *every day*?'

'There was a culprit.'

'*No, there wasn't.*'

'What do you want me to do? Look under the bed at night? Sure it was evil, but evil doesn't advertise itself in *The Times*. It can be mundane. It is selfishness, insecurity, insensitivity, self-justification. It's about what you can get away with. It's about not understanding the consequences of cruelty – or not caring or even acknowledging a moral framework. *Acts* of evil can be committed easily. Not being aware of the world in which you live – or at least caring about it only in so far as it relates directly to you.'

She did not understand what he was saying. His sudden exposition had a relevance she could not discern.

He stood up. 'I'll get you another drink.'

She watched as he poured the whisky into the glass. She felt light-headed.

Julia was drunk. She was sitting on the sofa, her head spinning violently. The room was warm, so warm she wanted to take off her jumper and perhaps her shirt too. Her inhibitions had gone. 'He loved me,' she said.

'Of course. But you were jealous of the little girl. You believe he betrayed you, but you don't know how.'

Julia had closed her eyes. She could hear the sound of her own breathing.

'He was affectionate to the little girl, too, wasn't he? Very close.'

Julia did not respond.

'What did you really fear, Julia? What *do* you fear? Did you fear that love was being taken away from you?'

The room was silent, but for the crackle of the fire.

'Did you fear that the love that should have been yours was

being taken away and given to someone else, to the little girl next door? And to her mother?'

Julia wanted to speak, but couldn't.

'Given to Sarah? Given to Alice? But the truth is, that wasn't your real fear, was it? You actually feared the *type* of love he may have had for the little girl next door.'

Julia bent her head, gritted her teeth. 'Shit,' she whispered, under her breath.

'Your man, your professor, thinks it's about the woman, about Sarah. Nobody believes that. Nobody. Adults kill each other all the time, no one cares. Adult passions, adult folly, adult retribution, adult consequences . . . but *here*, the filth and the suspicion and the *hatred*, that's about what a *man* wanted to do to a *little girl*, isn't it?

'It's about the way little Alice was coveted by a man she had reason to trust. That's what people here are protecting you from. It's not just about screwing Sarah, is it? Why did he have to muscle in as a surrogate father to Alice? She had a father, didn't she?'

He was staring at her and she was trying to avoid meeting his eye.

'To paraphrase a great fictional criminal: what do we covet, Julia? We covet what we see every day.'

The machine-gun fell silent, leaving just the whistle of the wind as it whipped across the ridge and around the rocks, slicing through to their skin. The man started crying again, the sorrowful, agonized whimper of the dying.

Julia watched Mitch's blackened face, almost invisible in the darkness.

'Fuck,' she heard him say.

He was sitting behind the ridge, leaning against a rock, without a helmet, wearing the dark brown woollen hat she'd given him, his face blacked up. There was fear in the faces around him – of failure, of cowardice, of death – but she could see the strength in him and knew it was what sustained them.

The man cried out again.

Julia watched him make the decision, the certainty and determination in the set of his chin. A grunt and then he was up, another shell bursting overhead, crawling through the mud and

284

the wet, feeling the rocks tearing at him, hearing the clatter of guns, the bullets passing him by, seeking contact, but disappearing miraculously into the blackness beyond.

Despite the noise all around him, she could hear his ragged breathing and see the concentration in his face.

Progress was so slow. Another shell exploded, death tickling the air around him.

Time had stopped.

She felt a rush of fear at the blast of a closer shell. She heard the angry panic of the machine-gun ahead.

He was still on his feet, taking the last steps, with the world slowing and fate quickly closing the odds.

He tripped, almost falling, fighting for balance, sliding in the mud and the wet, boots slipping back. The boy was whimpering, his strength gone.

And now he was running downhill, the boy in his arms, clutching his stomach.

He slipped, wobbled and ran on. She felt the tears in her eyes as he came so close to them, saw the passion in his muddy face and finally felt the bullet squarely in the middle of her own back.

Like a great tree, he tumbled.

Julia saw that the body he had carried was Alice. It was her face and now, resting beside him, her eyes shut, she looked peaceful.

For a moment, there was only the sound of the wind and the shock in his face and the silent sound of a life disintegrating halfway across the world.

Then, panic.

Sudden shouting, activity, anger. They were on their feet, over the ledge, the spur to end this battle and take the last section of the ridge. Julia heard the furious screams of the men and the rattle of their gunfire as they tried to expunge their cowardice.

She saw someone kneeling in the mud beside him.

Someone else was screaming into the radio. 'CO hit, repeat CO hit, request urgent evacuation!'

Someone was tearing at his uniform, ripping the buttons open, pumping his chest, stemming the blood.

'Jesus fucking Christ!'

'Come on, Mitch, come on.'

'It's all right,' he'd have said, teeth gritted, knowing it wasn't.

Issuing last orders.

'Tell the buggers . . .'

A moment of peace, staring up at the sky, thinking of them so far away, crying inside perhaps, but too tired to let it show. Gripping the hand of the man beside him, still strong, even now. The thud, thud, thud of the rotor-blades in the distance.

And then, for him, the silence beyond human endeavour.

She looked up from his body, and a group of men stood there. They had guns in their hands and they were smiling. Michael was smiling. Alan was smiling. Adrian Rouse was smiling.

And then Mitch was sitting in front of a birthday cake in full camouflage kit, his face still blackened, Alice on his knee, the pink dress falling from her shoulders.

'This is the way the lady rides . . .'

He was bouncing her.

'This is the way the soldier rides . . .'

Alice was not laughing, or enjoying this.

'This is the way that Alice rides . . . Wheeeeeeee!'

Julia woke up. She stood up, immediately. She had been lying face down on the bed. Her throat was raw, her head pounding. She flailed her hand, as if trying to beat the air that surrounded her.

'Christ,' she muttered. 'Christ.'

The room was quiet, light spilling through the gap in the curtains. She went across to pull back the one on the right. The gravel drive was flooded in arc-light, the trees and lawn beyond still hidden by the darkness of the night. Her head was spinning. She turned back to the room. The bed had been comfortable, but she was almost naked. Had she undressed herself?

She looked at her watch. It was five o'clock. She wanted to go home, but it wasn't practical and her head hurt.

Lying down again, she wondered what her mother would think. Would Caroline think she'd let Michael fuck her? Just like that?

Julia recalled the last part of the conversation downstairs. Then she found herself thinking of the class tutorial with Professor Malcolm at Sussex University where they had discussed the phenomenon of men who entered into relationships with women so as to get at their children.

Had it really been Sarah who had wanted Alice turned into a little adult?

CHAPTER SEVENTEEN

MAC TURNED INTO MICHAEL HAYDOCH'S DRIVE, DROVE SLOWLY UP
under the big beech trees, then stopped and glanced at his watch.
It was eight o'clock in the morning. He had come because there
was still no sign of Wilkes in London and he had been hoping to
catch Haydoch before he went to work.

He stared at the house. Everything seemed quiet until his gaze
was distracted by someone drawing a curtain in an upstairs window. It took a moment for him to realize it was Julia. Then he got
out of the car, under a cedar tree. He felt like being sick. He
straightened. 'You fucking prat,' he told himself. 'You stupid prat.'

He got back into the car and, after a moment's hesitation,
looked over his shoulder and reversed up the drive.

Julia had found sleep again, but not peace. This time, she was
trapped under the bush, looking into the clearing, watching.

She saw her father and Alice emerge from the path by the wizened
tree stump and then stop. He stooped. Mitchell placed his hand
on her head and then put it to her cheek. It was a . . . fatherly gesture.

Julia almost leapt out of bed, breathing fast.

The figure had looked like her father from a distance, but it had
not been him, his face a blank, save for the familiar hair.

She looked around. Her clothes, including her jacket, had been
dried and folded on the chair beside her.

She dressed, then emerged hesitantly, but found the house was empty. Michael had gone, without leaving a note, so she crept out of the house and began walking back over the hill, breaking into a run as she tried to recall an image of her father's face, finding herself unable to do so.

By the time she reached the ridge, her head was pounding like a tractor engine as the effects of the hangover filtered through. She stopped and thought she might throw up.

It was disgusting.

The dreams were disgusting. How could her mind have become so twisted?

The weather was grey and overcast and a thick bank of black cloud still hung over the valley. She could see a light on in Professor Malcolm's window at the far end of the top floor of the Rose and Crown.

She heard the honk of a horn from somewhere in the distance and it began to drizzle, the rain drifting into her face. Despite the rain last night, the ground was firm underfoot. The wind had dropped and the temperature risen.

When she got home, Julia ran upstairs and pulled her notebook from her bag, picking up the pencil from the desk.

'Suspicion knows no boundaries,' she wrote. 'It has no shame, it knows no restraint, or pity. It is more fundamental than desire, more powerful than love, and guilt and shame are its progeny, settling on the psyche like the dawn mist after a cold night.'

Julia leant back, sighing and breathing more easily.

She wanted to take out a photograph of her father and offer some form of apology, but could not bring herself to do so. 'I'm sorry,' she whispered, instead, to him, perhaps even to herself.

How could a man with so much life and humour have left such darkness? It was like a vacuum. It was a vacuum.

Julia imagined a bath would make her feel better. First, she got three paracetamol from the cupboard and drank five glasses of water, then climbed in, lay back and placed a cool flannel on her forehead.

Julia lay in the bath for a long time. Then, after drying herself and dressing, she walked downstairs to the sitting room. She searched in the drawer for the video-tape she had shown to Professor Malcolm and put it into the machine, before looking out of the window to check that her mother was not about to reappear.

She hesitated, torn between fear and guilt, then picked up the remote control and immediately began to rewind to the beginning of the sequence by the de la Rues' swimming-pool.

Julia slowed the tape to a normal speed and watched.

Alice was on Mitchell Havilland's shoulders. He swung her round and threw her off, but she climbed on him again, scrambling up, before standing and jumping with a shriek of delight.

She swam after him, climbed up, jumped.

Julia was in the pool, swimming on her own.

Her father was holding Alice above his head, laughing. Then he half dropped her and she clung to his face, her legs wrapped around his neck. He was still laughing. He looked like he was enjoying himself. He made no attempt to move away from the little girl. Alice dropped further. She had her arms around his neck and her legs around his waist.

The camera panned. Both Alan Ford and her own mother were now in the shot. Julia stopped the tape and went closer to the television. She rewound slowly. It was only a couple of frames, but when she froze it again she was more sure of what she had seen. Both her mother and Alan Ford had been caught unawares, looking at the activity in front of them. And on each face was a look of implacable hostility.

Julia took out the tape and threw it hard against the wall beneath the window. She stood, walked quickly to the big picture of her father on the side and smashed it with her fist. The frame flew back into the radiator. She was on her knees, bent double. Her body convulsed as she groaned with fury.

The doorbell rang.

Julia stood up, caught her foot on a wire from the lamp and fell flat on the floor. 'Shit,' she said, pulling herself up again. She scrabbled around the floor, picking up the frame, trying to put the bits of glass in the front of it, looking at his creased smile now, feeling the same onset of guilt and remorse, before leaving the photograph face down at the bottom of the radiator.

She stood, wiped her eyes with the back of her hand, trying to gather herself.

Her finger was bleeding, so she put it into her mouth, before walking slowly to the front door.

It was Professor Malcolm. 'Are you all right, Julia?'

'What?'

289

'Are you all right?'

'Yes. Why?'

'You look terrible.'

'I'm fine.'

'Your finger's bleeding.'

'Is it?' She looked at it. 'Oh yes. Just cut myself.'

'Are you sure you're all right?'

He looked down at his feet, then up at her again. 'I'm sorry, but I'm late. Can you give me a lift to headquarters? Weston wants me to see the Commissioner, Breckenridge.'

Mac had got halfway back to London before he had changed his mind and returned to Cranbrooke. Adrian Rouse's office number and address had been easy to acquire and he parked next to the building.

He walked past the brass plaque at the entrance and up the stairs, stopping to adjust the Browning inside his coat. He turned round, so that he was shielded from anyone coming out of the office above and cocked the weapon, before replacing it.

The woman at Reception had hair that looked as if it housed a menagerie, but Rouse's office door was open. As Mac explained who he was, Rouse came through and beckoned him in, his face unwelcoming. He was dressed in a tweed jacket that was too small and emphasized his portliness.

'What is it with you people?' Rouse retreated behind his desk, but did not sit down. He was agitated. 'I only got rid of Rigby a few minutes ago. Don't you talk to each other?' Then he looked at Mac, as if recalling suddenly that he was not a faceless official, but a friend of Julia's. 'What do you want, Mac?'

Mac hesitated. Where was Rigby now?

'You said the matter had been closed,' Rouse said, 'so I don't see what's changed. No one is going to believe Pascoe, so what does it matter where he is?'

'Well, yes, I agree.'

'It's all bullshit.'

Mac hesitated. 'Yes.'

Rouse seemed to relax a bit. 'I mean, if you accepted that his version of events was a fantastic lie before, why does it matter now where he is or what he's got to say? No one will pay any attention to it – he's still *seen* as the Welham murderer. Certainly in the press.' He had his hands in his pockets. He was avoiding Mac's eye.

'I suppose,' Mac said, 'that if people began to accept he might be innocent, that might change.'

Rouse looked at him. 'They won't. Why should they?'

'He's been freed by a court of law.'

'It's a technicality. Everyone knows it.' Rouse turned to the window. It had started to drizzle outside and passing cars had their headlights on.

'For people looking at it,' Mac said. 'If it wasn't Pascoe, then it was someone else.'

'Of course. Of bloody course.' Rouse sighed, pacing to one side of the room, before turning. 'I've had enough of this. I can't stand any more of it. That woman . . . God, it was fifteen years ago and look where we all still are. She was bloody evil. She was wicked . . .'

'And that's why she died.'

Rouse looked at him, his face distorted by fear and aggression. 'You people said you would deal with Pascoe, but you haven't, have you? You couldn't organize a fucking piss-up in a brewery.'

'I can't speak for my superiors,' Mac said quietly, 'but I suppose it is the high-profile nature of Havilland's death that makes them nervous.'

Rouse turned, agitated again. 'I don't see what the problem is. No one will *believe* Pascoe, so all you have is one deranged lunatic making fantastic allegations.'

'Yes.'

'I don't see why Rigby's suddenly got so bloody nervous.'

'Perhaps it's to do with Wilkes.'

Rouse frowned. 'Wilkes,' he said, with contempt. 'Rigby just told me you couldn't find him either.' He sighed. He walked to the bookshelves on the other side of the room, then faced Mac again. 'Wilkes is fine.' He was silent for a moment. 'I'm sure Wilkes is fine.'

'Perhaps it's just the deaths of Danes and Claverton.'

'For Christ's sake.' Rouse stepped forward. 'They never changed their evidence. It's . . .' He moved back again and leant against the bookshelves. 'A tragedy, of course.'

Mac had been watching Rouse as he talked and was finding it hard to believe that this man had ever fought in a war. With his

291

round figure, balding head and short grey sideburns, he appeared, in this fusty, quiet office, the antithesis of a man of action.

'You people said you would deal with everything.' He looked at Mac. 'You said you would deal with it.'

Mac felt the tension in his neck and back.

The receptionist put her head around the door. 'There's a Major Rigby on the phone for you.'

'I'd better be going,' Mac said.

'Hang on a second . . .'

Rouse picked up the telephone, but Mac did not wait to hear what he had to say. He took the stairs in three leaps, ran around the corner and into the car-park, fumbling for his keys, then got into the car, pulling his Browning from his jacket pocket and reaching across to try and start the car with his left hand.

The traffic was bad as Julia and Professor Malcolm wound past the cathedral and along the river. County Police Headquarters was situated on the far side, over a bridge, in a dull sixties building surrounded by a pretty, landscaped garden.

They were taken straight up to Breckenridge's office. He nodded at Professor Malcolm and shook Julia's hand. Weston, who was in the chair next to Breckenridge's desk, leaning on his elbow, did not get up.

Breckenridge was a bull of a man, with the face of a boxer and the body of a wrestler. The neatness of his dark hair betrayed his vanity, but there were deep lines on his brow. The office was small and, on his desk, there was a small silver photograph frame, a large ink blotter and a telephone. It was neat, like Alan Ford's, as though it had just been tidied.

'This is a ludicrous idea,' Breckenridge said, leaning forward and placing his elbows on the desk. He was interrupted by his secretary, who asked if they wanted tea. They all declined.

'No. It's not,' Professor Malcolm said. Julia could see these two had sparred before and sensed an affection absent in his relationship with Weston.

Breckenridge sat back in his chair. 'Can you imagine how the media is going to react to this? You want to start digging up gardens. It's the bloody West case all over again!'

'Well, perhaps. Depends how it's handled.'

'Like hell it does.' Breckenridge waved his pen at Professor Malcolm. 'Come on, then, let's hear it – and it had better be good.'

Professor Malcolm spread out the map of the common and the village on Breckenridge's desk. He was standing to the side so as not to block Julia's view. She had not even noticed he had been carrying it.

He was very rude about the police sometimes, but she felt he belonged here – more than he had ever seemed to at the university.

Professor Malcolm pointed at the cross already marked on the map. 'Sarah's body is here.' He took a pen from his pocket and drew a circle around it. 'This is the area we've searched.'

He looked up. Breckenridge and Weston were waiting.

'Where *is* Alice's body?' Professor Malcolm straightened. 'I'll tell you where it is. It's close to where she was killed because, as we've discussed before, no one is going to risk moving it in that kind of environment.'

They waited. '*And?*' Breckenridge asked.

'Look.' He moved away from the desk. 'Someone meets Sarah?'

'*Yes.*'

'Then there are two possibilities. One, he has come to kill her straight away. Two, there is an argument and then he kills her, but either way, I don't think the little girl runs away until the knife goes in.' He looked from Breckenridge to Weston and back again, waiting for a response.

'Professor,' Breckenridge said, 'do you think we could bear in mind that we're not in a tutorial now?'

Julia was trying to suppress the image of a man who looked, from a distance, like her father, pushing the knife into Sarah, Alice standing, watching.

'My point is this. Time. *Time.* I don't think that Alice had much of a head start. A hundred yards, at most. Everything that happened, happened swiftly.' He turned back to the map. 'We've searched on the common and we have to conclude now that he did not bury her there, not least because he did not have the means to do it. He didn't bury Sarah, so why bother about Alice?'

Julia had been watching Professor Malcolm's face closely. They had discussed this before and, in terms of evidence, he was offering nothing new, but she sensed again that somehow, intellectually or in evidential terms, he had moved ahead of her.

'He kidnapped her,' Breckenridge said. 'He kidnapped the little girl and took her away.'

'No.'

'You seem to rule things out with such certainty, without having a better explanation.'

Professor Malcolm pointed at the map. 'When you think about it, these three homes aren't very far away, are they? The Fords', the Havillands', the de la Rues'. So, it comes down to this. Where does a frightened little girl run when she sees her mother being murdered?'

Breckenridge shook his head.

'She runs *home*.' Professor Malcolm slammed his finger down on the table. '*Home*. Or in that direction. This terrified little girl ran towards the place that would be safe. Home. She runs to receive help . . . from who? From her father . . . from someone she trusts. She is running, putting every last inch of strength into running away . . . perhaps from someone she knows, possibly someone she knows well . . .'

Professor Malcolm was being careful not to look at Julia, but the effect was the same. She shut her eyes.

'The little girl has panic in her eyes. She knows if she can reach the people she trusts, then she will be safe . . .'

Julia wanted to shout at him to stop, biting her lip to control herself.

'But she never reaches them. The killer stops her, but he does not move her body . . . somehow he finds a place to bury her close to where she was killed.'

Julia breathed out and opened her eyes. She realized that both Breckenridge and Weston were staring at her.

Breckenridge agreed to the search in principle but insisted he needed a day or two to work out how to handle it and didn't rule out the possibility that he would need a clearer evidential explanation for why it had come to the point where this was inevitable.

Julia wasn't certain he had made up his mind.

Professor Malcolm did not answer him on the question of evidence. Julia felt that it was something the two men had tacitly recognized was best discussed without her.

They emerged into the corridor and Julia found herself following Professor Malcolm down to a small glass cubicle at the far end. Beyond it was an open-plan office with a huge map of the county on the wall.

Julia's head throbbed with the pain of rampaging emotions.

The cubicle had a desk and a phone and, behind an uncomfortable-looking red plastic chair, there was a large cork board with a collection of newspaper cuttings pinned to it. The top one said, 'Police Bungle: Monster Goes Free', and, like all the others, reflected the public perception that the police had been incompetent, if not corrupt, in their handling of the original case.

'Julia, this is DC Baker.'

Julia looked at a short woman with poor skin and greasy hair pulled back off her forehead. She shook her hand, trying to calm her nerves. 'We spoke on the phone,' Baker explained. She was wearing a cream blouse and blue jeans. She had a quiet, easy manner and was now bending over a pad on her desk. 'I'm sorry for the delay,' she said. 'The bank records should be ready to collect today – I'll give them a call in a minute and we can go down together.' Baker looked at her. 'You asked for the Ford bank records.'

'Yes,' Julia said.

'We should be able to get them today. I'll have to chase the phone records you asked for.'

'Any sign of Pascoe today?' Professor Malcolm asked. He was smiling at Baker, and Julia felt momentarily and confusingly jealous.

Baker gave a wry smile. 'No, he's left his makeshift camp up, but he's not there today. We checked this morning.'

Julia had a strong mental image, again, of Pascoe's aggressive, distorted face.

Breckenridge hurried along the corridor, glancing in as he passed. Baker looked at Professor Malcolm and raised her eyes to the ceiling. 'He's like a cat on a hot tin roof.' She looked at the board on the wall behind her desk. 'I've got the poisoned chalice, the ultimate thankless task. Can you imagine if anything happens, or even if Pascoe's caught hanging around a school?'

Professor Malcolm had had his hands in his pockets and he now took them out and clapped them together, as if excited. 'If anything happens, it won't be what you think, so don't worry.'

Baker shrugged. 'Everyone's looking for him. Had the Military Police on today.'

Now it was Professor Malcolm's turn to frown. 'What did they want?'

'Wouldn't say. Just that they needed to get hold of him urgently.' Baker moved towards her desk and pulled back the chair. 'If you want to get a coffee or something, I'll be done and we can go down and pick up the bank records.'

They walked into the corridor outside and into the stairwell. 'Good woman, Baker,' Professor Malcolm said, once they were out of earshot.

'Yes.'

'Intelligent. Thorough.'

Julia didn't respond.

The canteen was at the far end of the ground-floor corridor. It felt depressingly reminiscent of the many military dining halls in which Julia had spent so much time. Professor Malcolm went to get her a cup of coffee and she sat at a table in the far corner, overlooking the garden. The windows were wet from some light rain, the grass glistening in the isolated rays of sunshine.

'Are you all right?' he asked, as he came to join her.

She looked up at him. 'I'm fine.' She put some milk into her coffee and two packets of sugar, stirring it and sipping before leaning back and looking out at the gardens once more. He'd bought her a small packet of biscuits, which she opened. 'Custard creams provide one of the most vivid memories of school,' she said. He leant forward, elbows on the table. 'Where *did* you go to school?'

'A comprehensive in Sheffield,' he replied.

'Did you enjoy it?'

He was looking out of the window, holding the cup in two hands in front of his face. 'No.'

'Not an academic school?'

'Hardly a school at all.'

Julia stared at the biscuit in her hand, feeling the weight of the privileges she had been offered in life. She could imagine all too easily what a comprehensive in Sheffield must have been like for a lonely boy with a brilliant brain but an ugly face and body.

She had been going to ask him about the conversation with Breckenridge upstairs, but instead, she sighed quietly and turned her head towards the garden again. She tried to force herself to relax. It was the case that a man was innocent until proven guilty and nothing had been proven.

Nothing had been proven at all.

When they got back upstairs, Julia saw a familiarly large figure occupying the doorway of Baker's office. As he turned and caught sight of her, she thought he looked uncomfortable, as if he had been caught doing something wrong. 'Mac,' she said.

He smiled at her and stepped back to allow the two of them to enter. Baker was standing behind her desk, the chair pushed up against the wall.

'What are you doing here?' Julia asked him.

'Looking for Pascoe,' Baker said.

'Why?'

Julia could see that Professor Malcolm knew exactly why Mac was here. 'Detailed off to find Pascoe,' he said.

'Second visit from the RMP today,' Baker added.

Julia was beginning to dislike her. 'Why do you want to know about him?'

Mac hesitated. 'Honestly not sure,' he said. 'Orders.' Julia could see that he was lying and he wasn't good at it. He appeared edgy and it heightened her nerves again. She found herself wanting to hold him – for everyone else to go, to disappear, and for her to forget everything and place her head on his chest.

Mac was her friend. He could be relied upon.

'I'm ready for you now,' Baker said, putting on a raincoat and following them down the corridor, alongside Mac. Outside, Julia watched him walk over to the old Fiesta and, as they got into her Golf, he turned once and raised his hand. She didn't respond.

It took for ever to get the bank records. They drove to the branch in Cranbrooke, only to be told they hadn't arrived yet. In the end, it took three hours for them to come and by then Baker had long since ordered a taxi and left Julia to it, taking Professor Malcolm back for another meeting with Breckenridge.

The box was sealed, and when she got home, Julia took it upstairs to her room to open.

Inside, there was a thick pile of paper, covering three years and finishing a month after Sarah's death. The account was registered in the names Ford, A.G. J.F., and Mrs S. The overdraft limit was listed on each sheet as ten thousand pounds, which struck Julia as high.

The first thing she noticed was the contrast between the month before Sarah's death and the month after, where spending dropped almost to zero, presumably because she was dead and Alan, by then, on his way to war.

There were many entries for the month before Sarah's death. Looking back, Julia could see that there were always two main entries in the receipts column, one of which looked like Alan's salary. The other was for five times the amount and came as a transfer on the first of each month from 'Bowring Asset Management'.

Julia swapped columns and tried to see patterns in the payments column. There were a couple of direct debits to what looked like insurance firms, there was the mortgage and, finally, after careful examination, she saw that there were repeated payments of a thousand pounds, which went out on a different day every month to the same account number and were simply listed as transfers.

On closer inspection, Julia saw that this stretched back a year, but had stopped in the month before Sarah's death.

By checking to the back of the pile, Julia discovered another thing: almost all the sheets were for one account, but at the back there were a couple that related to a different one, listed solely to Ford, Mrs S. It had been opened the week before Sarah died with a transfer of a hundred pounds. There had been no other transactions.

Julia was most interested in the large transfers from the joint account. She went to use the phone in her mother's room, got the number from Directory Enquiries, then called Lloyds Bank in Cranbrooke.

She had to produce another fax, which she sent downstairs from the hall, along with a copy of the police authorization. She gave a number at Cranbrooke CID for them to call for verification.

While she waited for the woman to phone back, Julia wondered why Sarah Ford had set up a new bank account only the week before she died. Julia imagined her going in to do it, a glamorous presence in Cranbrooke's drab bank, Alice waiting patiently beside her.

Every memory of the two of them resonated because of the way it showed how much they had looked to life beyond the day of their death.

The woman called her back and said that the account to which the sums of money had been transferred was held at the same branch, was still current, and was now listed to a Mr Michael Haydoch of the Old Rectory, East Welham, formerly of Derby Cottage, East Welham.

After putting down the telephone, Julia didn't move for some time. She heard her mother call up to her, but didn't respond. There was noise and activity below – the kettle being put on perhaps.

When she did come downstairs, Caroline was arranging flowers in a vase by the sink.

'Hi,' Julia said.

'Alan called me at the gallery.' Caroline Havilland turned. Her face was like ice. Her brow was creased, her stance defensive. A strand of hair had fallen down, but no attempt was being made to replace it. 'He said Commissioner Breckenridge asked for permission to dig up all of our gardens.'

'And what did he say?'

'Julia.'

Julia dropped her head. 'I hadn't heard about this.' She watched her mother arranging the flowers with studied concentration.

'They seem determined to humiliate us.'

Julia sat in one of the chairs by the kitchen table. 'It is beginning to look like that.'

'Are you still . . .'

'No. I've stopped.'

Perhaps it was Julia's imagination, but she thought her mother's posture seemed to relax a little.

'I think they may have been using you.'

'Yes.'

'I . . .' Caroline stopped what she was doing. She came over to Julia, took her head gently and placed it against her stomach, her hand stroking Julia's hair.

Julia closed her eyes. The light scent of her mother was familiar and she tried to suppress the unease that threatened to nullify the pleasure and comfort afforded by this simple gesture.

Julia sheltered in her room. She tried phoning Michael Haydoch, but he didn't answer and she wasn't going to leave a message. She kept on trying until it was beginning to get dark and her mother was calling her.

Finally, he answered, but she cut the line, got up, took her jacket off the back of the chair and ran out of the front door to her car.

When she got to his house, Michael opened the door. 'You lying bastard,' she said. 'You lying, lying . . .'

He looked back into the hall. Two men appeared, carrying themselves just as Michael did. One wore a dusky yellow canvas jacket, both were in jeans and trainers. They smiled at her, but he didn't bother to introduce them.

Julia stepped aside to let them pass. She hadn't noticed a black Peugeot parked in the corner, underneath the big oak at the edge of the lawn.

'Bull,' he said. 'China shop.'

Inside the hall, she followed Michael into the study where, once again, a fire was burning. 'Colleagues?' she asked.

'Business partners.'

'SAS?'

He ignored the question.

'Business meeting?'

'Trouble with Russian partner.'

'You found a solution?'

'Yes. Terminate Russian partner.' He smiled thinly. 'I was expecting you to avoid me.'

She stared into the fire, then she looked at him. 'Did I undress myself last night?'

'No.' He stood up. 'I'll get you a drink.'

'No. Not tonight.'

'So . . . what? More recollections?'

She reached across, took a cigarette from his packet and lit it. 'We've received Sarah Ford's bank records,' she said. 'We've discovered that there was a major transfer every month to your account, which ceased in the month before her death.'

He didn't flinch. 'And?'

'What do you mean, "and"? Isn't that enough?'

'You think I killed her?'

'I came over here last night to ask about this and you never mentioned anything about it. You made a lot of insinuations about people who are close to me and—'

'And it's your right to know?'

'Well, as *you* said, *someone* killed Alice.'

'And you think it was me?' His face was going a livid red. 'You've asked a few fucking questions around the village and suddenly you think I killed your friend?'

'Alice was everyone's friend.'

'And Miss Marple thinks that *I* killed her?'

'Don't trivialize this. I was here asking you as a friend, and you never mentioned—'

'And why should I?'

'Because *someone* killed her. Them. *You* said it.'

He reached for the cigarettes and lit one for himself. Every aspect of the movement betrayed his anger.

'A thousand pounds a month into your bank account,' she said, 'ceasing just before the deaths. You cannot deny—'

'That it is none of your business.'

'It's a matter of public record.'

'But the reasons are not.' He sat in the armchair again, but forward, legs splayed, in as aggressive a posture as sitting allowed. 'Let's be clear. You think that because I once had the pleasure of deflowering you, you've suddenly got the right to muck around in a past that is none of your business.'

'As I said, it's a matter of public record, the past is everyone's business in this instance, and thank you for the nasty reminder. I'm sorry it was such a joke for you.'

He blew out smoke angrily and sat back. 'You think I was having an affair with Sarah, after all, is that it?'

'I can't think of any other way to explain it.'

'Well, there is, and it's the truth. Sarah and I were friends. I had debts to pay off at the time and . . . We were discussing it one day and she said the money meant nothing to her and I was welcome to it. We had an argument about it. She said she'd be insulted if I didn't take it. I told you already, Sarah was very generous about money.'

'Not with Alan.'

'How do you know that?'

'There are enough records.'

He threw the rest of the cigarette into the fire. He had hardly smoked it.

'Look,' he said, 'I ran into debt. The reasons are none of your business. I told Sarah, in passing, and she said she'd help. I refused, but she insisted. She said she had masses of money and didn't care. We agreed that she would pay off the debt in a certain number of instalments. If you go back, I think you'll find there were about ten. Then the debt was finished so the payments ceased.'

'But your affair continued.'

The anger returned to his face. 'And if she hadn't died, I'd have repaid her the money. I've told you several times, there *was* no affair.'

'And you'd admit it if there had been?' Her face was still flushed. It was hot in here. She took off her jacket and placed it over the side of the sofa. 'Did the police ask you about this?'

'Don't be ridiculous,' he said, dismissing their efforts with a wave of his hand.

'The police did find some diary extracts which detail, explicitly, an affair, either fantasized or real, with an M.'

'M for Michael, you suddenly think.'

She looked at him. 'Yes.'

'I've told you. Sarah and I were friends.'

'Then who was M?'

'I don't know. You're the expert.'

'That's not a good enough answer.'

'M for Mitchell. Which is what you really think.' He leant back in his chair again. 'You're hoping I'm going to relieve you of that burden, but I can't.'

She pushed herself forward. 'What happened, Michael? Were you late for the meeting with Sarah that day? Did you get delayed? Did you find the body before me? Did you arrive after the police?'

He looked at her with contempt.

'Or were you on time? Were you early for this rushed meeting, waiting for her? Why were you in such a hurry to see her that day? What was *so* important that couldn't wait?'

'Look at yourself, Julia.' His voice was soft. 'Just look at yourself. You're a grown woman now.'

'Just *answer* the *question*.'

'I've told you. I want to help you, but I can't tell you what you want to hear. I cannot relieve you of your suspicion. You're killing yourself for nothing. You've got to let go. You'll never prove anything.'

'I *will*. I'll go through every bank record and phone record, every scrap of paper and every memory until I *know*.' Julia sat forward. 'Get me a drink.'

Without asking what she wanted, he filled a tumbler with whisky and ice. Julia looked down at the brown liquid. She swirled it around the ice, then drank it all.

He sat again, resting his elbows on his knees. 'There was only one man I saw with Sarah that year with any frequency. M for Mitchell. And I've tried to protect you, like everyone else has, but you won't *listen*. You go on and on and on and *on*. You want to hear the truth that everyone knows? Yes, Mitchell was fucking Sarah, and Christ knows how sordid it was all getting. They used to waltz around together like a family. Sarah, Mitchell, the little girl on *his* shoulders. Like his own daughter. It was the talk of the village and the whole bloody battalion. The boss is shagging his next-door neighbour, and that wasn't even the half of it, not to those of us in the know. It was . . .' He looked at her. 'Is this it, Julia? Is this what you want to hear?'

Julia got up and walked over to the CD player, then turned to face him, her movements hesitant, as if slowed by the amount of energy being consumed in the process of thought. She thought of Alice's pink dress.

A sexy five-year-old . . .

Fear snaked around her stomach and clutched at her throat. She could feel her heart beating fast, her head pounding with blood. It was hard to think.

He stood up and took her glass, brushing his hand on her cheek, before going to the drinks cabinet, filling the glass with ice and whisky and coming back.

He sat.

She looked down into the glass, then drank from it, waiting for the burning sensation in her stomach, wondering what she sought here. Did she really suspect this man, or was he her escape? Was he the only one she actually trusted? Her hand was shaking. She took another large sip. Her breath was rasping. Nervousness, or unease, quickened her pulse.

She stood up. 'I'm going to go home now,' she said.

CHAPTER EIGHTEEN

OUTSIDE, JULIA LEANT AGAINST HER CAR, HER HEAD IN HER HAND, attempting to steady herself. She had the same sensation as in Beijing, of losing control.

Suspicion, rather than being a response to facts, seemed to be causing her to teeter into lunacy from which it was impossible to make an objective judgement.

She exhaled heavily, looking up towards the darkness of the hill above. At that moment, the beam of a torch spun in a rapid semi-circle, as if being dropped, then extinguished, the darkness once again complete.

Julia straightened, still staring into the blackness beyond Michael's house, drawn by an image straight from the night after Alice's disappearance, feeling again that sense of pervasive discomfort at what they would find, at what a body would look like – at what had been done to her . . .

And then, suddenly, the hill was ablaze with colour and light – like a bomb she had seen in Armagh, like petrol poured on open flames. Without hesitating, or thinking, Julia ran, around the side of the house, fighting with the gate and failing to open it, before climbing over the wall and the stony path into the wood, guided by the ball of light ahead.

The trees were shadows, her breathing ragged, her vision blurring.

She ran forty paces, perhaps fifty, then stopped, sensing danger.

She ran again, seeing the flames flickering through the trees.

'Pascoe!' she shouted. Why did she think it was him?

The flames were lighting the way now and she began to feel the warmth of the air as the smell of petrol hit her. What was he doing? Trying to burn the forest? Or just out of patience and lighting a fire . . .

No, the smell was more ominous than that. It was in her mouth and throat: the sweet scent of a pig roasting on a spit.

'Pascoe,' she said, moving slowly, unwilling to go closer.

She stopped. '*Pascoe.*' She took another step. For a second or two she could not comprehend the evidence of her eyes.

'Christ,' she said, running to the burning effigy. He hung from the tree. She could see his teeth, the blackened flesh retreating around his mouth . . .

'Fuck,' she said. A blanket, she thought, then water. She took off her sweater, trying to tie it around his feet, but the flames were hot and she was repulsed.

She circled, trying to think clearly, calmly, but failing. The flames seemed to have lessened around his head, so she ripped off her shirt, knelt down a yard or so away, then lunged towards him, throwing it around his body.

She turned, ran. '*Help!*' she yelled, tearing through the trees, to the path, the hole in the hedge, the lawn and the gravel, before bursting in through the front door, into light and warmth and Michael standing, looking curious, then alarmed.

'Burning!' she shouted. 'Pascoe's burning! He's on fire.' She was out of breath. 'Ambulance! Fire!'

He reacted instantly, turning and running for the kitchen and the phone, following her out, only seconds later it seemed, into the walled garden at the back, before slamming the door against the wall, yanking the hose and dragging it towards the gate. 'We'll get the hose as close as we can,' he shouted. 'It's locked,' he said, as they reached the gate. 'I'll climb over the wall, you get back to the tap and turn it on full.'

She ran.

'There are some tin buckets there,' he shouted.

Julia turned on the tap, picked up the buckets, got to the wall, threw them over, lifted herself up on the gate, reached the top, jumped, saw the hose moving ahead of her and followed, catching him by the entrance to the wood.

'Here.' He put the hose in the bucket, let it fill. 'Go.'

Julia ran, the flickering image the only point of reference in the dark.

They passed each other, silently, shadows in the wood.

He got back first and shoved the hose in his bucket, not looking at her, cursing under his breath. It seemed to take an age to fill, then he thrust it into hers and took off, grunting almost inaudibly.

They passed each other twice more, grim anger in his face as they crossed and then, as she got back to Pascoe, the flames seemed to be dying and her bucket killed the fire around his head.

Another two staggering journeys and then the flames were out. They were standing together in the darkness, she naked from the waist up but for her bra, in front of the blackened corpse. She could make out little but the teeth.

The body was twisting in the wind.

The smell choked her again.

She turned, bent double.

He had his hand on her back, helped her straighten.

'Do you think . . .' She faltered.

'He's dead,' he said, his voice flat with defeat. She wondered if he thought Pascoe could have been saved, or if he had simply been driven by the horror of what they had seen.

Neither of them moved until they caught sight of the flashing blue light on the other side of the valley. 'I think we'd better go and help them locate us,' he said. He took her arm, put it into his shirt, which she had not noticed him remove. 'Rather they see me naked, I think,' he said.

Later, Julia stood on the landing of Michael's house, watching activity on the hill. It was all the same: the flickering tape, the men in uniform and the lights of the television cameras. She wondered who in the village would know by now, and who would sleep on, unaware.

Michael came back in, his face sombre. 'The police will talk to you in the morning.'

She nodded, staring out of the window.

'I'll take you home in your car and walk back.'

She turned slowly to him and nodded again.

They walked down the stairs and out of the front door into the drive. The cloud had cleared and it was bright now from an almost full moon.

They could hear the sound of the power generators on the hill behind.

Michael started the engine and turned the car round. They didn't talk on the way and when they reached her home, he put the keys into her hand and she got out and walked towards the house, without looking at him.

Inside, she shut the door, locked it and pulled across the chain.

Julia found her mother and Alan sitting at the kitchen table. She stood in the hallway and looked at them.

Caroline stood up immediately, came forward and hugged her. After a moment, Alan did the same, so that the three of them clung together, Julia's hands around their backs.

It took her a second to realize that her eyes were wet with tears. Her mother gripped her tighter.

Her shoulders shaking, Julia said, 'When is this going to stop frightening me?'

Alan was staring at the floor. Her mother's hand cupped the back of her head. Neither of them answered. 'We must make sure the door is locked,' Alan said. 'We must make sure all the windows are shut.'

Mac's heart sank as he reached the fourteenth floor of Wilkes's tower block and once again confronted the empty darkness of flat 4B.

He pushed open the door and switched on the light. There were no curtains, so he could see out of the dirty windows to a similar tower block opposite.

The flat was bare. There was a green sofa, a chair and a coffee-table. The newest item in the room was the television in the corner. There was a sideboard, which had been searched, its drawers sitting on top. Mac looked through them, finding an old camera, some beer mats, pens, blank paper, paperclips, some glue and a couple of postcards from Australia, depicting women with large breasts. They were both signed 'Danny' and contained no useful information.

Mac retreated to the middle of the room. He ought to have searched the flat more thoroughly on his last visit.

In the bedroom, the bed had been stripped and the mattress pushed on to the floor. Again, all the drawers were out on their sides and appeared to have been searched. Mac looked through their contents, but could find nothing personal in them – no bank statements, letters from the council or an employer. There were some tapes, an undeveloped film, a book token, with no message inside, a ten-pound note, five American dollars, a selection of porn videos and about twenty copies of *Penthouse*.

That was it.

Mac stepped back. He thought the flat had been systematically stripped.

He looked under the bed and behind the chest of drawers. When he shifted the cupboard in the corner, he found an old cheque book, crumpled up into a ball.

Mac turned towards the door. It wasn't much, but it was better than nothing. At least he knew now that Wilkes banked at Lloyds on Wandsworth High Street. It was the smaller version of a cheque book, without stubs, and Wilkes had not bothered to detail to whom he'd written cheques in the section at the front.

Mac walked to the next-door flat and knocked. Eventually the young man came to the door, this time without the dog. He was still wearing a white T-shirt.

'You again,' he said. 'He's not been back.'

'Do you have any idea where he is?'

'No, but you've done his flat over. Why did you do that?'

'Not me,' Mac said. 'You must know something about him. Where he works, who he sees, family, friends – anything.'

The boy stepped forward. 'Look it's not my fault. He never talks or nothing. Never even says good morning.'

Mac sighed. 'Have you ever seen him with a bag, or clothes, or a car with any company name on – anything to indicate where he works?'

He shook his head.

Mac looked at him for a moment more. 'All right, thanks.' He turned away, then thought better of it. 'Hold on a second.' He took out his pad and wrote down his mobile number on it. 'Look, I need to get hold of this man. It's for his own good. If he comes back, will you call me?'

'What's it worth?'

Mac sighed, inaudibly. 'What do you want?'

'A hundred.'

'Fifty.'

'A hundred.'

'All right,' Mac said. 'But you'd better call or you'll be getting something else.'

For a moment, the young man returned his stare, then dropped his eyes.

CHAPTER NINETEEN

JULIA SLEPT FITFULLY AND AWOKE TO FIND HER MOTHER SITTING ON HER bed. In this sense, and in others, she had a sense of history repeating itself. It was like the day after she had discovered Sarah's body on the common. She saw on the old clock above her that it was eight o'clock in the morning.

Caroline stroked her forehead. 'The police are here to see you. Alan has already talked to them. They've promised to be brief.'

Julia sat up, frowning, as her mother left. She pushed back the bedclothes. Caroline had brought her a cup of hot, sweet tea, which she sipped.

Julia took her time, just as she had on the morning after Sarah's death, but the feelings and emotions were different. This time, there was fear, not just emotional but physical.

Who had killed Pascoe?

Uncertainty and unease seemed to slow her down, as if they were physical, rather than emotional, entities.

Downstairs in the living room, Professor Malcolm, Mac and DC Baker stood in a semi-circle, the morning sunlight behind them, casting their faces in shadow.

Julia could see her mother through the window, working on the flower-bed at the far side of the drive.

'I suppose I should offer you some coffee?' she said.

Professor Malcolm shook his head, so did Mac. He was

310

embarrassed when Julia looked at him. Baker declined, too. Her manner was businesslike and she had a small notebook open in front of her. 'We need to ask a couple of questions.'

'Yes.' Julia sat in the armchair in the corner. Baker and Professor Malcolm took the sofa, and Mac the chair by Caroline's desk.

'You were with Michael Haydoch?' Baker asked. Professor Malcolm was staring at the floor. 'He told us you had just left.'

Julia turned to face Mac. She saw into his eyes before he had had time to look away.

She nodded. 'Yes, that's right.'

'You were just leaving when you saw . . . what?'

She sighed. 'First a torchlight, then what seemed like an explosion, though there was no sound, just a blaze of light, tearing into the night sky. Then I ran.'

'A torch?'

'Yes.'

'Unmistakably a torch-beam?'

She nodded, remembering how it had reminded her of the night of Alice's death and the torchlight search parties. 'Why is that significant?' Julia asked.

'No torch has been found at the scene.'

'Well, I certainly didn't remove it.'

Baker raised her hand. 'No. It's not a question of that.'

Baker was sitting with her knees close together and Julia thought she was the sort to have once been a school prefect, if not head girl. 'When you arrived at the scene, Miss Havilland, was there anything to suggest . . . well, anything to suggest a struggle?'

Julia shook her head.

'You found nothing else there – just the body, twisting from that branch, burning?'

Julia tried to think back and recall the scene. 'There was a petrol can, leaning against the tree trunk, but you must have found that. That was obviously what he had been doused with before being set alight. But . . . I'm sorry, I wasn't really thinking straight. There may well have been other things that I missed.'

Baker was writing in her book. 'You saw Pascoe,' she said, 'a few days ago. You called some of my colleagues out to the house.'

Julia nodded. 'Yes, he was being harassed by people from the village.'

'You just . . . came across this, or you were visiting him at the time?'

'I just came across it, but I didn't think it fair, so I bundled him back into the house and called the police station in Cranbrooke. When some of your officers arrived I left.'

'How did he seem?'

She sighed. 'He was . . . It was as if he was mentally retarded. I don't remember him saying much. He seemed a pathetic, sad figure, to begin with, but he later became aggressive.'

'Have you known him a long time?'

'I knew him before he went to prison, when I was a child.'

'But he didn't say anything to you on the day you saw him?'

'Only what I told Professor Malcolm.'

Mac's mobile phone rang. He took it out and walked into the next-door room to answer it. Julia heard him say, 'Right.' Then, 'No, I said a hundred,' and finally, 'But he's there?'

Mac came back in and raised his hand to both Baker and Professor Malcolm. Julia got the impression that they knew exactly where he was going and what he was doing. Baker told him to wait and she followed him out, thanking Julia for her time and warning her to stay inside after nightfall, if possible.

Professor Malcolm was still sitting opposite her. They were silent.

'My head cannot think clearly,' she said, quietly. 'My heart feels betrayed.'

He shook his head. 'I don't understand.'

'You, Mac. Together.'

'I could tell you we had your interests at heart, but you would recoil from that.'

'Why?'

'Look, it's all right, Julia.'

She sighed, looking at her hands in her lap. 'Why is it that I feel you have already reached a conclusion?'

He shook his head. 'No.'

She looked up at him. 'You're lying to me.'

'No. The road from suspicion to certainty is a slow one.'

'I didn't know you had suspicions.'

'Everyone here has suspicions.'

She stared at her hands again. 'Why are you going to dig up our gardens?'

312

'Because, at the end of the day, as I've said, to bring a criminal prosecution, a police investigation needs evidence.'

Julia waited for him to continue. 'There is something,' she said, 'missing from this conversation.'

Julia watched her mother straighten and wipe her brow outside. It was hot again today.

'What is it?' he asked.

'What is missing is how you have got to the point at which you are prepared to contemplate something so . . . You know what I mean. You have reached conclusions that you've kept from me. You and Breckenridge have, for example, I'm certain, had conversations behind my back that go considerably further than those I've been a party to.'

Professor Malcolm had moved forward to the edge of his seat. 'Look, it is just . . .' There was a long pause. Julia heard the sound of a mower being started in the garden. 'It's just, over time, the inexplicable elements of a case settle into a pattern where the only *potential* rational explanations begin to point in one direction.'

Julia frowned.

'You mentioned Mrs Simpson. Do you recall? The head teacher at East Welham Primary. You said she would be worth talking to. I think I'd like you to go and see her.'

'About what?'

'About Alice.'

'And you've been to see her already?'

'Yes. I came to look for you, but you were out. It was something you said actually . . . Anyway, see what she has to say.'

'I get the constant impression this is a lesson,' Julia said. Professor Malcolm did not respond. 'Like a tutorial, except that the subject matter is no longer academic.' He was staring at the floor. 'Did you ever need me . . . I mean, what's this really about? For you, I mean. I can't say that I understand.'

'It's about you.'

'I still don't get it.'

'It's not just about your father, or about justice. It's about you.'

'In what way?'

'It's about everything that you've put on the shelf. The relationships and friendships that have been curtailed or failed to reach their potential. It's about trust. It's about intimacy. It's about what happened in Beijing and why.'

313

'I don't see how my private life has any bearing—'

'No? What about relationships that are severed because you cannot bear the possibility that someone else will leave your life against your will? You make sure the power to decide remains in your hands.' He was looking at her. 'Sound familiar? What about a chronic inability to trust anyone because of the corrosive suspicion that your father, the man you *most* trusted and admired in the world, could have been guilty of – of *this*? What about the memories of him? Do they mean *anything*? Can anything be good or worthy or reliable if he was always capable of this, if it was *within* him? Intimacy is about trust, you know, and this is about giving you back your life.'

He stood up. 'Julia, don't allow suspicion to lead you to believe everyone is ranged against you, because it isn't so.' He walked to the door and stopped. 'If you make your *modus vivendi*, or should I say *operandi*, self-reliance, then one day, you will discover that all you have is the lonely embrace of old age.' He looked at her. 'Will you promise to come and seek me out after you've seen Mrs Simpson?'

She nodded.

'I mean *promise*?'

Julia frowned at him.

'It's very important.'

She shrugged.

And then he was gone, leaving Julia sitting in her father's armchair staring into the middle distance. She realized she'd not asked him about Pascoe, but then she knew, without having to be told, that it was murder and not suicide.

Julia walked out on to the terrace. Her mother was still stooped over the flower-bed on the other side of the drive. Alan was cutting the grass with the old petrol-engine mower, leaving alternating stripes as he moved from one end of the lawn to the other. He was wearing a pair of faded red cotton trousers and the leather boots he always used for gardening, with a white checked shirt – too hot for today, really. Julia could see the hairs poking out of the top of it and, as she watched him, he raised his hand to her.

There was no sign of the tension she had sometimes seen over the past week.

As he came to the middle of the lawn, he let the engine on the mower die, wiped his forehead with the back of his hand and came towards her.

'Everything all right?'

'Yes,' she said. 'Fine.'

He nodded, turning half away from her, towards the common. 'Garden's in good shape.'

'Yes.'

'Nice to have a good spell of weather at last.'

'Yes, it's hot, isn't it?'

Alan pushed his hair off his forehead again and returned to the mower. He took hold of the lead and pulled hard, restarting the engine. It jumped forward, almost out of his hands, but he brought it under control and walked on behind it. When he got to the end of each row, he swirled it around, rather than slowing down.

Julia watched. He was near the garden shed now and he had already mowed a horizontal strip around it, allowing him to use that area to complete his turn. He finished the last strip and stopped. He took off the plastic back of the mower and emptied the grass cuttings in the compost heap beyond the shed. Then he pushed the mower round to the front, opened the door and shoved it in. The plank that Julia had nailed up the other day dropped down again.

Julia walked down the steps and across the lawn in the direction of Woodpecker Lane. As she reached the gate, her mother straightened again and smiled. 'Are you okay?' she asked.

'Fine. Just off for a walk. You're not going to work?'

Caroline shook her head and rubbed her nose with the back of her hand, the trowel pointing upwards towards the sky. 'No, not today.'

Julia reached the stile at the top of the ridge, hot from the climb, and began to descend towards East Welham, moving quickly and shivering involuntarily as she passed the now unguarded flickering white tape to her right.

She turned left on to the main road and, as she did so, glimpsed the village hall beyond the shop. Its door was open and there were two police cars parked outside.

East Welham Primary was at the opposite end of the village and was itself a converted church hall, with an ugly extension approved by a planner who had been either blind or a passionate believer in the virtue of functional architecture. Julia entered through the side, via the playground, walking slowly across the tarmac yard. There were some plastic cars and bikes parked in the corner and a new set of swings between a slide and a giant noughts-and-crosses board. There had been nothing like this in her time. The door of the new extension slammed shut behind her and she walked down past the classrooms. At the end, she turned right and looked down the main corridor in the old building. All along both sides there were pegs at about waist height, full of coats and bags. At this end there were cubby-holes with the names of the children written on them.

There was a gale of laughter from one of the rooms at the far end of the corridor and Julia walked towards it, stopping at the first door on her right and looking in through the glass window. The children were painting, wearing aprons. They were concentrating hard, in front of their young, dark-haired teacher.

At the end of the corridor, Julia hesitated a moment before opening the door to Mrs Simpson's outer office. Inside, the desk was temporarily vacant, its occupant away, though the computer was on and a sweater draped over the chair.

The door in front of her had 'Head' written on it, an old sign that needed repainting. It had perhaps been nailed to the door at the beginning of Mrs Simpson's tenure, an era no one could recall except Mrs Simpson. Julia knocked and heard a soft 'Come in.'

Mrs Simpson did not appear to have changed at all. Her long grey hair was curled into a bun at the back of her head, her kindly face carefully made up. Julia realized now that she must once have been pretty.

'Julia!'

Julia smiled and they shook hands. 'Hello, Mrs Simpson.'

'I think you're old enough to call me Veronica.'

Julia found her eyes drawn to the beautiful lawn outside, which ran down to the stream. There was a class out there now, sitting in a circle around the teacher.

'Summer lessons.'

Mrs Simpson smiled. 'Yes.' She turned back to her. 'You're still in the army, I assume.'

Julia hesitated. 'Yes.'

Mrs Simpson nodded and smiled again.

There was silence.

'It's so awful about that man . . .'

Julia looked at the concern on Mrs Simpson's face for several seconds before she realized that this was a reference to Pascoe.

'Yes,' she said.

Mrs Simpson leant forward. 'I'm sorry.'

Julia did not meet her eyes. 'It's all right. I've . . . seen worse.'

'Yes . . . of course. Still . . .' Mrs Simpson stopped. 'What can I do for you?' She motioned for Julia to sit.

Julia watched the children outside. 'I was under the impression that you were expecting me.'

'Well, the Professor said you might come.' Mrs Simpson shifted her chair slightly so that she, too, was looking out of the window at the children on the grass. Julia wondered if she was recalling Alice's face.

'What did Professor Malcolm want?' Julia asked.

'He wanted me to recall Alice and . . . he had a theory he said he wanted to put to me.'

'How did you recall Alice?'

Mrs Simpson shrugged. 'As a sweet and endearing little girl, but you know that.'

'And what was his theory?'

Mrs Simpson hesitated. 'He said that he didn't think Alice was Alan Ford's child.'

Julia felt a tightness in her throat. The nervous uncertainty was in her belly and the small of her back. She recalled the dream in which her father had reached forward to place a . . . paternal hand on Alice's head.

'And what did you say?'

'I said that it was very possible that that was correct.'

'Why did you say that?'

'Well, Alice was a pretty girl, but I found the behaviour of both her parents odd.'

'In what way?'

Mrs Simpson sat forward. 'Her mother, Sarah, was very . . . concerned for the little girl. It was not something I reached a conclusion about at the time, but after talking to the Professor . . . well, it was *too* much, I think. Too much concerned for her appearance. One day, when Alice fell and grazed her knee quite badly in the yard and sustained a small cut to her face,' Mrs Simpson had

317

raised her hand, 'she was very upset. Not Alice, of course, she was brave. But the mother treated her daughter as if she were a porcelain doll. That's not healthy for any child.'

Julia waited.

'But with Sarah, no attempt was made to conceal anything. That was just the way she was. I didn't like it, but nor did it hide anything.'

Julia felt her stomach turn over again.

'And Alan?'

Mrs Simpson was uncomfortable now. 'It's just that one sees so many parents here, how they are with their children, and he was – the professor asked me and I had to agree – Alan was different in some way. When he was affectionate, it seemed . . . How can I put this politely? Exaggerated and put on. As if he was doing it for whoever happened to be standing in front of him, to prove that he was a normal father.'

Julia looked at her. 'To prove that he was a normal father?'

'Yes.'

'To prove that he had the feelings a father would normally have for a daughter?'

'Yes, but I—'

'The little girl was a battleground.' There was a long silence as Julia thought this through. 'Sarah was rubbing it in with her grooming . . . This girl is *mine*, she is *nothing to do with you*.'

'That's exactly what the Professor said.'

Julia stood up – she couldn't sit any longer.

'I'm sorry,' Mrs Simpson said. 'Have I upset you?'

Julia paced to the other side of the room, creating some distance. Mrs Simpson was frowning, as if worried that she had done something wrong.

CHAPTER TWENTY

MAC WAS IN SUCH A HURRY BY THE TIME HE REACHED WILKES'S FLAT
that he was reluctant to wait for the lift and ran up the stairs
instead. The sudden exercise relieved some of the tension that had
been building up within him.

The door had not been mended and Mac felt foolish as he
knocked on what remained of it. There was no answer so he went
in, only to discover that an area had been cleared around the
mattress on the floor, suggesting Wilkes himself had returned.

Mac went back to the landing outside, tried the swarthy neighbour and was again directed to the nearby Rat and Parrot pub.

He took the stairs at speed, ran through the courtyard below
and across the road to the pub on the corner, forcing himself to
slow down and breathe in deeply as he reached the door. Inside,
the pub was almost empty and he found Wilkes next to the
cigarette machine, away from the bar, sitting with his legs crossed,
smoking a roll-up. He seemed unnaturally thin, his face pinched
and worn. 'Who are you?'

'Captain Macintosh. Mac.'

There was a rapid twitch in Wilkes's cheek. 'You people think
you can do anything. Well, you're not forcing me away.'

Mac looked over his shoulder, pulled up a stool and sat opposite him. 'Please keep your voice down, Mr Wilkes, I'm not here
to harass you.'

'You think you can chuck some money around and make me disappear.'

'Look.' Mac placed his hands together. 'I'm not with Rigby, but you should know that last night someone caught up with Robert Pascoe, murdered him, hung him from a tree in a feeble attempt to make it look like suicide and then set him alight to destroy the clues.'

Mac could see the fear in Wilkes's eyes.

'From the evidence I've seen, I would suggest that you are next.'

'No I'm not.'

Mac leant forward. 'Someone put a Browning into Claverton's mouth and blew the back of his head off, then tried to make it look like suicide. Then he did the same to Danes. Now he's killed Pascoe. I would say, Wilkes, that you know who that someone is and unless you start to do something about it very soon, you will be next.'

Wilkes was shaking his head. 'No.'

'Whoever it is no longer trusts in your silence. He thinks you're going to talk, and whether you do or not, you're going to be terminated, just as the others have been.'

'No. No.' He picked up his Rizlas and shoved them into his jacket pocket.

'Stay where you are, Wilkes.'

'Get away from me.'

'Calm down.'

Mac took his arm, but Wilkes shook it off and walked towards the door. Mac waited, looking harshly at the surly youth behind the bar, before slipping the Browning back into his coat and following Wilkes out into the street, walking purposefully after him.

Mac caught Wilkes just as he walked through the broken door to his flat.

He knew his own strength and had Wilkes's feet off the ground inside, pushing him back against the wall. 'Talk.'

'I'll call the police.'

Mac held Wilkes with one hand, took his Browning out with the other and held it against his forehead. 'Believe it or not, I'm your last chance.'

'You're with Rigby.' Wilkes looked as if he would shit himself, his mouth quivering as he bit the edge of his nicotine-stained moustache.

'What happened to Havilland, Wilkes?'

Mac tightened his grip, until Wilkes was wheezing. 'Havilland's daughter happens to be a very good friend of mine.'

'It wasn't me.'

Mac relaxed, lowered him to the floor, still with his hands to the man's collar. He could smell the Guinness and tobacco on his captive's breath.

Wilkes collapsed and Mac let him go, watching as he bent double, his body convulsed with sobs. 'It wasn't me,' he said. 'It wasn't me. I never suggested shooting them.'

'Shooting them?'

'The prisoners. It wasn't me. It wasn't my idea and then Havilland just came along . . . shouting. It wasn't my fault.'

There was a long silence. 'He said it was an accident.'

'What was an accident?'

'The gun going off.'

'Whose gun?'

There was no reply. Wilkes had curled himself into a tight ball on the ground, so that he looked like a snail.

CHAPTER TWENTY-ONE

WHEN JULIA GOT HOME, A BOX HAD BEEN LEFT FOR HER INSIDE THE HALL.
She carried it up to her room.

The telephone records for her parents' home were at the bottom
and it took her a few moments to locate the day of the murders.

For the period before church, there were eight calls from her
home to the Ford house. Plus the two she had seen earlier from
the Ford home to here.

Julia stood up again, went to the drawer by her bed and took
out the statements given to the police by her mother and father.
Then, she went into the hall and climbed up to the attic, looking
out of the Velux before retreating to her father's desk and sitting
in the captain's chair.

Julia sat still and thought.

After a time, she heard her mother come upstairs and knock on
the door of her room. Then Caroline called up to the attic. 'Julia?'
She did not respond. 'Julia? Are you up there? I was wondering
what you wanted for supper tonight.'

When she didn't answer, Caroline went downstairs again.

Julia looked at the statement in her hand and the passages she
had underlined.

> As I walked down Woodpecker Lane, I glanced in through
> the window of Alan Ford's house. I saw him crossing from

one side of the kitchen to the other with a cup of coffee in his hand.

I arrived home and saw my husband working in the garden. I went upstairs to change out of my church clothes. When I came down to the kitchen, he was digging the flower-bed by the hedge.

With the sheet of paper clutched between thumb and forefinger, Julia jumped down from the attic, ran along the corridor and came down the stairs, only stopping when she reached the entrance to Alan Ford's drive. She checked the statement in her hand again and took in the evidence of her eyes, once more walking to the end of Woodpecker Lane, before turning as she had done before and coming back, glancing over towards Alan's kitchen window.

She repeated the exercise, this time keeping to the left side of Woodpecker Lane and stopping opposite Alan's drive. It was an incline you would hardly notice unless you were looking out for it, but it was a *fact* that all the houses on Woodpecker Lane were built above the level of the road.

From here, through the kitchen window, the angle was such that you could only see the cupboards.

Julia retreated and returned to the attic. She picked up the phone records and walked downstairs. In the kitchen, Aristotle had finished supper and was lying against the Aga, beside her mother's feet. Caroline was sitting at the table.

Julia threw the witness statement and the phone records down in front of her.

Caroline Havilland looked up and frowned.

'Your witness statement on the day of the murder. You were lying.'

Her mother's frown turned to a look of defiance.

'Alan Ford's house is higher than the road. You could not have seen him with a cup of coffee unless he had been carrying it on his head. I've paced it out. I'm *sure* that's true.'

'I'm pleased for you.'

'On the morning of the murders, Alan Ford or his wife called here twice between 9.03 and 10.14. There were *eight* calls the other way. Dad and Sarah, or you and Alan?'

Julia waited.

'Were you having an affair with Alan Ford before—'

'Don't be disgusting.'

'Well, it happened soon enough after.'

'What happened?' Caroline's eyes flashed. 'You think Alan and I . . .'

Julia was stunned.

'No,' Caroline said. 'No . . . Julia, your mind has become so polluted. I said nothing good could come of this.'

'And now we know why.'

Caroline Havilland shook her head. 'A little knowledge is a dangerous thing.'

'Don't patronize me.'

'I'm not.'

'*Yes, you are.*'

'Don't shout at me.'

'*Don't shout? Don't shout?* Don't you bloody tell me what to do, don't tell me a single thing ever again. Not ever. Not *ever*. You have lied. Everyone has lied and I was a child and I believed – *look what I have believed.*'

Julia smacked the vase in the middle of the table, sending it careering into the Aga. The bits of china and flowers scattered in every direction. Some of the water inside hit the wall, the rest dripped over the edge of the Aga.

She turned to face her mother. '*Now* you *stop* lying to me.'

'No one is lying to you.'

'*Everyone* has been lying to me.'

'All right.' Caroline leant forward. 'All right. You want to know the truth? I thought your father was having an affair with Sarah Ford. I thought that. I did. I'm ashamed to admit it, but that's what I thought. So did Alan. We were both . . . upset. We did communicate about it. I . . . I don't remember how the communication began. I could see that he was being destroyed by what she was doing. It wasn't just your father. Alan told me there had been . . . others. Your father was the last in a long line.'

'He wanted your sympathy.'

'And perhaps I his. It had come to a pitch that weekend. We had tried so hard to keep it from you. I had tried and similarly Alan with Alice. But it was no longer possible. Alan told me he believed that Sarah was going to leave him. He said he believed it was for your father.'

'So why where there so many calls that morning?'

'He said she was getting ever more brazen and open about it.

324

He said she no longer bothered to hide the telephone calls – that he'd heard her arranging to meet him on the common. I – I was trying to calm him. I . . .'

Julia stared at her.

'But it's not what you think. Your father was not the one. He was looking out for Sarah, he was concerned for her, he was . . . It's hard to explain, but he was *like* that, he liked taking on responsibility for people, he liked helping them. It made him feel valued and needed, and the more I thought about it afterwards, the more I believed he had not been having an affair with her. He was prone to a flirtation with a pretty girl, but an affair wasn't in his life plan and I've never met anyone so determined to conform to a prearranged *plan* for life.'

Caroline Havilland took a step closer, Julia one back. 'I wanted to protect you from all the innuendo, the accusations.'

'So you did it for me?'

'Not just for . . .'

'You think you've been helping me?'

Caroline stared at her, sensing the cold anger in her voice.

'Do you have any idea what this has done to me? Do you?' She took a pace forward, her mother one back, as if no longer certain how this would end. 'Do you know what I've lived with? Do you know what you've made me live with?'

'Stop shouting at me, Julia.'

'I'll stop shouting when you stop lying.' Caroline was staring at the floor. 'Did you know Alice was not Alan's daughter?'

Now Caroline was shocked.

'Who told you that? How do you know that?'

'How I know it hardly matters now.'

Julia was next to the glass door out to the tiny conservatory off the kitchen. She felt like punching her fist through it. 'You lied for Alan Ford.'

Caroline sighed, her body sagging. 'What choice did I have?'

'What choice? What *choice*?' Julia took a step closer. 'You knew that Alan was aware a meeting was due to take place in the wood. He comes to you after the murders have actually taken place and asks you for an alibi, says he *needs* an alibi, and you *provide* it? You lie for him and then you tell *me* that you had no choice?'

'He said he wasn't there, that he didn't go.'

'Oh, really? How *believable*. You have increasingly frantic phone calls all morning. You know he's aware of a rendezvous. You're both desperate to stop a divorce and a messy scene, you're terrified of the humiliation that is going to be heaped on you – oh, the terror of it, the end of your reputation in the village, the shame of being a spurned woman, rejected in favour of your next-door neighbour, the scandal—'

'It wasn't like that.'

'Wasn't it? Really? You know what's going on, you're talking to and fro, call, call, call, and then Alan opts not to go to church – highly unusual – and you come home and you don't see him and the next thing you know is that they're dead and he's asking for an alibi.'

'It wasn't like that,' Caroline repeated.

'I bet. Did he bother to come round, or did he just call again? Good means of communication. Hello, Caroline, just washing the blood off my hands, would you be so kind, if the police come round, tell them you saw me—'

'It wasn't *like* that.'

'What *was* it like?'

Caroline put her head in her hand momentarily. She seemed suddenly terribly old. 'Alan loved Alice. I couldn't, didn't . . . *don't* believe he could have harmed her. He called me. He said it looked bad, he knew that, especially if the substance of our phone calls came to light, and that he knew about the meeting. I believed him. I still do.'

'Alice wasn't his daughter.'

Caroline Havilland shook her head in confusion.

'You're having a relationship with him, so no wonder—'

'Oh, for God's sake, Julia.' Caroline half turned, then thought better of it and faced her again. 'Don't make everything about sex. There's affection. There's friendship.'

'But there's not much warmth, have you noticed that?'

'What do you mean?'

'I mean what I said.'

'He's always been fond of you.'

'Yes. The inference is that I'm the surrogate for the daughter he lost, but that's easy.'

'I don't see that.'

'There's no intimacy. There's no need for intimacy. We're not family, we're not a threat, we don't need to *conform*.'

'That sounds like—'

'Psychobabble. Think about it. Alan and Sarah were at war over Alice. Look at the pictures of Alice, remember how she was. Think about the way she was being made into a mini Sarah. It was obscene. She was a sexy little five-year-old, being groomed for some specific purpose and I thought it was perverted – I thought it was something to do with Dad, that he was having a relation-ship with Sarah and the little girl was in some perverted way part of it, but it wasn't that at all. It wasn't *any* of it. It was a fight. Sarah was taunting Alan. This little girl is *mine*. She's *nothing* to do with *you.*'

'I still don't understand.'

'It was about possession. It was Sarah saying this girl is mine, *mine*, she's nothing to do with *you* and she *never will be.*'

'I can't . . .' Caroline had raised her hand. 'I'm sorry, I can't listen to this any more.'

She walked out, up to her bedroom.

Julia waited for a few minutes, then returned to the attic, her hands shaking. She heard the front door slam, the sound of foot-steps on gravel, then the car being started up and driven off.

Julia had not moved for several hours. The house was silent. The first shadows of the evening were creeping across the garden below and the valley was quiet. The common would soon be lost in the dwindling light.

Julia looked at the garden. Her eyes followed the line of the fence to the corner where it met the hedge and the shed that stood in darkness.

She closed her eyes again and brought to mind an exact image of the day of the first search, when her father had stood with some of the men and she had watched them and felt her eyes straying to the shed and the small line of discoloured grass that told her, but apparently no one else, that the shed had been *moved* during the night while everyone in the village – everyone – had been out scouring the wood, searching for the body of Alice Ford.

Everyone but Alan.

No one, of course, had expected a father to help in the search for his daughter.

Julia thought of Professor Malcolm's confusion over the body and where it had gone. Had he worked it out yet?

It seemed so obvious. The scared, confused little girl had run across the field not to her own home, but to the one man she thought might save her. She had run away from Alan, towards Mitchell.

But she'd never made it. Somewhere, she'd been caught – perhaps by the fence at the bottom of her own back garden and she'd been murdered, in cold blood, her body hidden beneath Mitchell's shed in the dead of night to implicate him.

Julia *had* believed that her father had hidden the body there.

A new wave of doubt overtook her. What did her mother know? What did Caroline . . .

Julia turned, descended three steps, then jumped to the landing, thumping against the wall on the turn of the stairs and ducking under the low entrance to the living room.

Outside, her footsteps were loud on the gravel.

In the garage, she flicked on the light, took the big spade from the wall beside her and returned to the drive and the gathering darkness of the garden.

She pushed herself between the hedge and the shed and then shoved. It was stuck. She pushed back, the hedge scratching at her neck, then got the shovel into the ground and tried to lever up the bottom, moving along until there was some sign of movement.

There was a pop as the shed came out of the mud. It seemed light.

Julia bent down, got her hands under it and heaved. It toppled over with a loud bang.

It was light because the floor had rotted away, so the contents of the shed were left in front of her, the lawn-mower along with pots and trays full of seeds, a hoe and garden implements. She scattered them around her, lifting the lawn-mower last and throwing it on top of the shed, before moving round to the side and dragging the remnants of the structure clear.

Julia began to dig. She was sweating, imagining a man emerging from the darkness with a bundle in his arms, Alice's face hidden by a cloth. She thought of him moving the shed and then beginning to dig. He would have been sweating, too, despite the cold she recalled from that night.

All the time that everyone had been out looking with dogs and torches and dwindling hope, he had been here, burying her beneath this shed.

Julia asked herself if her mother had been here watching and helping. She remembered her mother being involved in the search, but perhaps she had slipped back to the house. No one would have remarked on anyone's absence in the dark.

There was something solid beneath the edge of her spade.

Julia turned over the earth beside her. It was a stone. She bent and picked it up. It was a long, flat stone.

The spade went in easily again. She turned more earth, waiting once again to strike bones.

The sweat was in her eyes. Her shoulders began to shake. The spade struck something hard again.

Would there be a belt, or a buckle? Had Alice been buried in her clothes? The moon had been bright that night, as it was tonight. The darkness would have provided inadequate cover, heightening the nerves.

Bright as it was, Julia thought she would still need a torch. She turned and saw the rush of something. There was a split second of terrible pain from the side of her head and then nothing.

Black.

CHAPTER TWENTY-TWO

SHE THOUGHT SHE HEARD AN OWL HOOT.

For a moment, Julia was not certain if she was alive or dead. She tried to turn, the pain in her head blinding, and caught sight of a figure close to her. She could see he was digging and hear the sound of a spade striking wet earth.

She tried to sit up, but couldn't. She closed her eyes as it occurred to her that the figure was digging her grave.

He was hooded, not more than ten feet away, his body rising and falling as he drove the spade into the earth and, as she listened to the sound, Julia found her right hand was instinctively grasping in the dirt beside her, closing around a stone.

If she moved, he would sense it instantly.

She tried to control the torrent of thought. She could see the clearing in the distance, through the trees, the wizened tree stump visible in the moonlight, but he'd chosen well – the bank on which she lay led down into a ditch, where it would be easier to conceal a grave. She closed her eyes again and steeled herself, biting her lip so hard she could taste her own blood.

She rolled, using the momentum of the slope to get on to her feet, swinging her right hand down towards the hood as he sensed her and tried, too late, to duck. Julia felt the stone impacting and heard a low grunt and then she was on her feet, running, tearing down through the trees, ducking, weaving . . .

He grabbed at her and she pulled to the left, underneath a low branch, and was free. She heard the sound of him falling, a sudden curse then a groan of agony, and she was running still, the terror not subsiding, her mind not wanting to grant her the relief of knowing that he was seriously hurt.

She hurtled down towards the path.

She stopped, not knowing which way to turn. The first rule of escape was that hesitation could be fatal, but he could too easily put himself between her and home, so she ran away from the entrance to the common, towards the old well, thinking she must hide and stay still to survive.

Julia gathered speed and then jumped off the path, clearing the bank with one leap, crashing into the undergrowth beyond and rolling away, lying stock still when she came to rest at the edge of the clearing that surrounded the well. She was breathing heavily.

An owl hooted in the distance again.

The air was alive with the sound of crickets, as if they were shouting a warning. Julia twisted one way, then the other, but the clearing was empty. It looked as if it was being lit directly by God.

She thought of the lies, of the obscenity of his public, fake grief, of the sympathy so many had felt and the comfort they'd given, of the years of neighbourly deceit.

What had he done to the little girl?

Julia stood, looking for and finding a sturdy branch, anger consuming her.

If Alan had not lied, she'd still have something of her father, because the deceit had led her to destroy his reputation, to doubt his love, drowning it in a well of suspicion, stripping her of everything he could have left behind.

She tried to recall Mitchell's big, smiling, open, frank face, but could visualize only Alan's, a leering image stoking her fury, which she fought to control, thinking of the hunting and stalking games she had played here, remembering that darkness shielded her and movement gave her away.

The seconds dragged slowly out. She heard something down to her right and snapped her head round, instinct almost forcing her into a run.

It was a footstep, she was certain – and then she saw him, breaking cover on the other side of the path, twenty yards ahead, clearly visible in the moonlight.

She crouched down, hiding behind the bracken, but keeping her eyes on him. He walked a few paces and then stopped, listening. For a second, he edged towards the trees on the other side.

He was listening for the sound of someone fleeing.

She had a chilling vision of history repeating itself, of a young girl running, petrified, the world closing in on her.

Julia closed her hands around the branch. Was it strong enough to kill him with?

He was walking towards her, up the path, slowly – ambling almost, his head on one side.

He stopped again, close to her, looking down for her footprints. Time seemed to have stopped as he walked slowly away, not turning round. Julia moved forward to the edge of the path and crouched down, ready to lunge forward. She tried to concentrate on getting a sense of the time passing.

Five minutes? Ten? Twenty? An hour?

Surely he would come back this way.

She felt cramp building in her legs and knew that she needed to straighten.

Just as she was about to do so, she saw that he was right beside her.

'Hello, Julia,' he said.

She turned to him.

She found it difficult to speak. 'You've dug my grave, Alan,' she said, eventually.

'Yes.'

His face was strange and distracted, a patchwork of moonlight and shadow.

'Alice must have run away.'

'Yes.'

'She saw you ... stabbing Sarah and ... she must have been terrified ... She did not know what to do so she ran ... across the field. She almost made it, but you got to her ... you *killed* her. You hid the body and buried it in our garden at night while everyone was on the common searching.' Julia had been talking quickly.

'Yes. You're clever. Like your father.'

Julia could hear the sound of her breathing. 'Did he suspect you, Alan?'

'Oh, yes, of course.' His voice was the more chilling for being almost casual, as if nothing had changed. 'He knew everything, you see. So *solicitous* he was. So *solicitous* for the well-being of my wife and little girl.' He sighed. 'I would have enjoyed watching him mow the lawn.'

Julia felt her whole body shake. 'He was a million times the man you are . . .'

'Revenge is sweet, Julia.'

'What did you do to my father?'

'He was a self-righteous prig.'

'What did you *do* to him?' Her voice was shrill.

'War is a beautiful thing. So much confusion and hate.'

Julia saw the knife in Alan's hand.

'You murdered him.'

'I don't like the term murdered. It's pejorative. There were some Argentinian prisoners, we were dealing with them and he came along and started shouting. Guns sometimes go off by accident, you know, fog of war . . . And the others, they shouldn't have been murdering prisoners anyway, so they had enough to hide, didn't they? But, you know, people just have to talk.'

'You'll pay for it,' Julia said quietly. 'You will pay.'

He looked at her. 'You don't normally like to talk. I like that. Sarah should have been like that. It would have been better. Sarah . . . she thought she could get away with it, you know that?' He grunted in disgust. 'She really thought she could just treat me . . .' He grunted again.

Julia tried to think back to the training exercise that had dealt with being held captive. It belonged to a different world.

She breathed in deeply, trying to suppress her fury. 'Where did you kill Alice, Alan?'

'Where did I kill Alice?'

'What did you feel, Alan?'

'What did I feel?' There was bitter humour in his voice. 'Is that what the training manual tells you?'

'Alice ran away in fear. Where did you find her?'

There was a moment's hesitation. His face was in shadow now because he had turned so that his back was to the moon, but Julia thought that he had lowered his head. 'She almost made it, Julia, do you know that? She almost made it to your daddy. If she hadn't been so out of breath, she might have been able to cry out, but . . .' He sighed. 'It was close.

There was luck. She ran along the fence and that helped.'

'You took her into your house?'

'Yes, that's right.'

'Where did you take her?'

'Well, she ran when I put her down again inside and . . . you know, I thought she might scream or . . . after all, Daddy Mitchell was just next door.'

'Where did she run to?'

'I found her in the bedroom, Julia.'

'Was she lying on the bed?'

'No, she was curled up in a ball in the corner of the room.'

'Did you feel aroused by her fear?'

'Aroused? No. I'm not a pervert.'

'What happened?'

He didn't answer.

She wanted to distract him, to strike with the branch she still held before he could react. 'Did she scream, Alan?'

He moved – just a shifting of his weight from one leg to the other.

'Did she die quietly? Did she yield gently? Did she trust you even in death?'

'Yes . . . she . . . did.'

'Did she cry?'

'No . . . I don't . . . I don't . . . I don't recall.'

'Did she fight?'

'That's enough.'

'What did you see in her eyes, Alan, as the knife went in?'

'That's enough.'

'Did you see terror? Did she know she was going to die? Do you think—'

'That's *enough*.'

'Did you watch the knife penetrating her flesh? Was her blood red? It was a knife, wasn't it, Alan? *Another* kitchen knife, a different one, you put the tip against—'

'That's *enough*.' He took a step closer. 'That's *enough*. *Enough*. *Enough*. *Enough*. ENOUGH!' He was breathing heavily. 'It's time,' he said. 'It's time.'

'She didn't know you weren't her father, did she?'

He didn't reply.

'You knew, because Sarah loved to taunt you with that by the end, but little Alice didn't know, did she? She loved you like a father still.'

'I said, that's enough.'

'She trusted you.'

'Julia!'

The call had been as clear as a bell. It was Mac's voice.

'*Mac!*' she shouted.

Alan lunged at her and she glimpsed the flash of moonlight on metal, as she ducked to one side, trying to strike down with the branch, but missing.

'*Mac!*' she shouted again.

She dared not run. To turn her back was suicide. He lunged again and this time he was standing in the light, so she saw the action clearly and struck down, once again darting away from him as she heard him groan with pain.

She had not dislodged the knife. 'Training,' he said.

'It's easier with five-year-old girls, isn't it, Alan?'

He was wheezing, like an asthmatic. He lunged again and once more she struck down with all the angry might of years of frustrated misery, thinking of her father and the bravery she believed he would always have displayed in any situation and the shame of doubting him.

'Five-year-old girls can't fight back, can they? You're a fucking coward, Alan, that's what you are. The other men, they were brave, but you're just a coward. Maybe that's why Sarah . . .'

He came again, but he was still bathed in moonlight and she deflected the blow and took hold of his arm. She gripped tight, stepped in, turned and slung him over her back, then followed through, stamping on his wrist, so that he squealed in pain and began to roll away, the knife released.

She came down, trying to pin him, but her eye had lost sight of the other fist and it hit her square in the face, knocking her sideways, the pain blinding. She was on her back and she fought to right herself, but he was fast, so fast . . .

He was on to her.

He had her.

His knees were pinning her . . .

Julia could see, suddenly, the image of her father's face, charging out from the cover of the rock and her anger at the lies and the suspicion and guilt exploded into rage as she scrabbled at his face, trying to reach his eyes, to gouge, but he was too strong. She bucked with her waist, kicked with her feet, tried to roll free, but she couldn't shift him.

Too late, she realized, he had lunged for the knife. He was off her, then on again before she could move, his hand over her face, the knife to her neck.

She had reached his eyes, trying to push her fingers into the corners of the sockets, straining every sinew to punish him. 'You'll pay,' she gasped. 'I . . . will . . . make you pay . . .'

'Julia!' she heard.

Mac was closer.

Her cry was muffled by his palm. He moved the knife from her neck and she took hold of his wrist. He was going to kill her the same way as Alice, a thrust gently into the stomach. Another hand was on her neck, both hers trying to stop the knife . . .

He was squeezing. She felt the pain and fought to push away the knife, but the tip of it was against her shirt. It entered. She felt it, but was not aware of any pain. It went further. The world was darkening, her strength going. There was a blinding pain in her stomach.

Were her eyes shut, or open? It was so dark. The weight on her disappeared, the hand was gone from her throat. But the pain did not lessen. She had vision. Blurred, dizzy.

'Julia,' she heard. 'Julia. Julia. Julia. Julia. Julia.'

She could not find her voice.

The vision cleared. Mac was kneeling over her.

Her vision blurred again.

'Julia.'

The pain seemed to be lessening.

'Julia! Fight, Julia.'

But she couldn't fight. The pain was fading. She felt almost peaceful. She wondered if this was how her father had died.

She heard a siren in the distance.

'Fight, Julia,' Mac said again.

The siren was getting louder quickly.

'Please, Julia,' Mac said, and she caught sight of his face. It was no longer blurred. She wondered if this was the last moment of clarity.

He was gripping her hand and she tried to grip back, but there was no response.

'Please,' he said.

She tried to say, 'It's all right, Mac,' but no words came out.

Her vision began to blur again.

Darkness fell.

EPILOGUE

THERE WAS A KNOCK ON THE DOOR. JULIA PUSHED HERSELF STIFFLY UP IN bed, putting her fingers beneath her shirt to feel the wound on her stomach once more. 'Come in,' she said.

Professor Malcolm had brushed his grey hair and put on a clean shirt. He had a large bouquet of flowers and a bunch of grapes. His movements were hesitant, his manner uncertain.

'A royal visit,' she said.

He smiled. 'I wasn't certain I'd be welcomed.'

'Self-doubt doesn't become you.'

He was clasping his hands in front of him like a schoolboy confronted by an austere aunt.

'I'm told you and my mother have been thick as thieves.'

'Well . . .'

'She says you've been helping her.'

'No, but . . .'

'I told her to watch out.'

They were silent. Julia looked at the morning sun streaming through the windows and spilling on to the pink blanket on the end of her bed.

'I've spoken to the university. They say that if you do not wish to remain in the army, they might be able to find you a post there.' He shrugged. 'I've no idea if you would be interested, but . . .'

'The protégé's lesson complete?'

'No.' He cleared his throat, shrugging.

She smiled at him, pushing herself up still more. 'What have you been up to?'

'Oh, you know . . . not much. Loose ends.'

'Tell me what happened.'

He looked confused. 'About what?'

'How did my father die?'

He looked down. 'Well, perhaps you'd better ask Mac. But . . . I think you'll find that the occupants of the machine-gun post they were supposed to be attacking had, in fact, surrendered. I believe the battle was over and dawn rising. Michael Haydoch had come over from his platoon . . .' He looked at her. 'Correct term?'

Julia nodded.

'They decided to "deal with" the prisoners, but at that point your father came upon them.'

Julia swallowed.

'There was an argument, he began shouting, there was a shot. I believe it passed through your father and wounded Pascoe.' He sighed.

'Alan fired the shot.'

'Yes. You would have to ask Mac. I think Alan then convinced the others it had been an accident. They were all implicated because of their part in shooting the prisoners of war, especially once the lie had begun. I think, with Rouse, it was probably also the pictures of him and Sarah.' He sighed again. 'I doubt, somehow, that there will be prosecutions, though Michael has put his house on the market and is, I believe, leaving East Welham.'

'What about the Rouses?'

'I don't know. I think they may stay. They've been through so much in the village. I would think Adrian will be forgiven. That seems to be the prevailing mood.'

Julia stared out of the window at the blue sky beyond. 'Was . . .' She hesitated. 'Was my father having an affair with Sarah?'

Professor Malcolm shook his head. He had lost his bashfulness now. 'No. Michael Haydoch was the M of the diary and I think probably Alice's father, too, though he denies it and it is possible Sarah didn't even know the answer to that particular riddle.' He

339

ran his hand through his hair, then put it over hers. 'Your father didn't need an escape, Julia. He was happy where he was.'

'I thought . . .'

'Yes?'

She pushed herself up again. 'I think that . . . I've had so much time to think.'

'Too much, over the years.'

'Yes, but I think I worked out that what I feared was that I had lost him before he died, that I'd done something wrong and he had turned away from me and from us during those last months . . . do you understand what I'm saying? It was the extra burden of having lost him twice – in that last year and then for good. And that let in the suspicion and from there . . .'

'And you were wrong.'

'Yes.'

Professor Malcolm put his hands in his pockets. 'I rather wish I'd met him, actually.'

'Yes. I would have liked that.'

Professor Malcolm shook his head. 'There aren't many reliable people in the world.'

He stepped back and looked at her. 'I must go,' he said.

'Will you come again?'

He smiled once more. 'Perhaps.'

He turned and moved to the doorway, before hesitating and turning back to face her. 'Good luck, Julia.'

'I'll see you soon.'

'Yes.' He was looking out of the window. 'Yes, of course.'

He walked out.

The door was jammed half open and Julia leant forward so that she could see down the corridor. She watched him as he shuffled slowly along, his limp evident. He ran his right hand over his head then put it in his pocket and, as he reached the swing doors at the end, she thought he would pause and look back, but he didn't and they banged shut hard behind him.

She looked at them for a moment.

She wondered if he would come back through, smile once more and wave goodbye.

The doors opened again and a younger, slightly taller figure came through.

His walk was funny, too – somehow ungainly – and he was holding a large bunch of flowers.

As Mac caught sight of her, he smiled. Julia hesitated, then raised her hand, and waved a greeting. She realized she was smiling, too.